To Please a Lady

To *Please* a *Lady*

LORI BRIGHTON

 Montlake
Romance

Published by Montlake Romance
PO Box 400818
Las Vegas, NV 89140

ISBN-13: 9781477848333
ISBN-10: 1477848339
Library of Congress Control Number: 2013909620

For my mother,
Your courage, compassion, and imagination
are a constant source of inspiration.

Prologue

LONDON, 1856

James McKinnon had struck it rich. It wasn't a bucket of money, nor a chest full of pirate treasure, which would be odd anyway, considering he was in the heart of London. No, it was a basket of potatoes that tumbled from the back of a wagon as it turned a corner too sharply. But it was a treasure indeed to someone whose belly was cramped with hunger.

He huddled against the rock wall of the Deer Isle Pub, watching as the potatoes dropped and bounced, falling from the crate like golden coins gleaming under the dreary sunlight that managed to pierce London's morning clouds.

Not just potatoes . . . turnips as well!

Wearily, he glanced around the square. Nary a soul could be seen, the morn too bitterly cold for most. He huddled deep within his woolen jacket, attempting to ignore the sting of snow as it whipped around him, pelting his face like bullets. Still, he knew others like him were out there, hiding in the shadows, waiting within the alleys for the right moment to pounce. Despite the chill wind piercing the holes in his jacket, James grinned. Aye, there were others waiting, but none as fast as he. He might be thin for his age, but he was as tough as any street rat.

He'd known, hadn't he? This morning when his mum had been crying into her apron over their measly breakfast, worried that they'd have to find work in the factories, he'd told her something good would happen. He'd felt it in his gut. This late in winter it was a bloody miracle. He didn't even like potatoes and turnips, but he still knew it was a gift from heaven, as his da used to say.

He waited until the driver was good and well around the corner and then jumped from his hiding place and scurried across the road, splashing through the sludge of snow, mud, and other things he was better off not identifying. At one time, when he was a young lad, they'd eaten the finest meat and best potatoes. He should have been training to be a footman by now, but that had been when his da still lived. Now they were lucky if they had one decent meal a day.

His foot hit a particularly deep puddle. James cringed, stumbling. Aye, he might be able to ignore the snow, but he couldn't ignore the water that seeped through the holes in his boots, soaking his stockings and numbing his toes. He gritted his teeth, crossing his arms over his chest in an attempt to stay as warm as possible. It would be worth the discomfort when he saw the look upon his mum's face.

Close . . . he was so very close to the treasure. He kicked off the ground, racing as fast as he could. He had to reach the food before the other street rats staked their claims. It wasn't exactly stealing; after all, he couldn't catch the driver to let him know. Besides, if he didn't take the food, someone else would. He smiled. Almost there.

"Watch out!" a man cried out.

James spun around, just missing a drunken sailor weaving his way down the footpath. As James turned, regaining his balance, he noticed the three boys headed his way, darting from the alley across the lane. No! He couldn't lose the treasure now. Frantic, he dove toward the pile, his patched trousers providing little protection as he slid on his knees toward the basket. When his numb fingers gripped the smooth wooden handle, he almost cried out in relief. But he couldn't rest. If he didn't get the basket and leave immediately, he'd have a fight on his hands. Aye, he was good, but against three he wouldn't have a chance. He lifted the basket, clutching it to his chest, and turned, preparing to flee. His glee was short-lived, as he ran directly into a hard chest that smelled of unwashed body and ale.

Before he had time to react, firm fingers pinched his left ear . . . hard. "Caught ye, ye thief!"

James cried out, stumbling to his knees. The basket fell from his hands, the potatoes and turnips bouncing across the lane, splashing through snowy puddles. He could save them, if only he could scoop them up before another coach rounded the corner and smashed them to bits.

"No, sir! I swear I wasn't stealing. I found the basket in the lane! Was just left there, it was!"

"Up with ye!" The man pulled hard, forcing James to his feet.

He bit his lower lip, refusing to cry out, although it felt as if his ear was being torn clean away. The food was gone, but he had more important things to worry about now. James stumbled after the burly constable toward an enclosed wagon. Already the other children were streaming over the basket of food. James could only watch them, his hope fading as he was shoved into a coach, the door slammed shut. He gripped the bars of the single tiny window and peered out onto the road. Gone . . . all of it. Picked over by hungry rats.

With a cry of anger and frustration, he slammed his fist against the bars.

"Won't do ye any good," a man chuckled behind him. "Why don't ye come over here, let me have a look at ye."

James spun around, spotting the beast standing in the corner. "Sod off!"

The man laughed, stumbling as the wagon took a sharp corner. "Young lad, ye won't last long where we're going. But maybe I can protect ye, for the right price."

A shiver of unease raced over his skin, but he refused to show his fear. Where he was from, a man who couldn't control his emotions was as good as dead. "Where is he taking us?"

"To visit the queen, of course!" He cackled, laughing so hard he stumbled off balance and fell into the dirty straw in the corner of the wagon and merely lay there. His laughter drifted away, and after a few moments the sound of snoring erupted from between his crusty lips. Disgusted, James looked out the window once more.

The pale faces of London rushed by as the wagon bumped along a cobbled road. Not one person looked his way; they were too busy with their own desperate lives to worry about an inconsequential, poor lad. His panic grew. He'd heard stories of children being taken to prison, whipped, and hanged, never to be seen again, and for silly little crimes, like stealing a bun. But no one cared.

"No," he whispered. This couldn't be happening. If he was in the gaols, who would feed his mum? His sister? "Please!" he cried out, shaking the bars. "Help me!"

But the wagon continued on, twisting and turning its way through the narrow streets of London until James's legs gave out and he slumped to the ground. What would his mum think when he didn't appear for dinner? James drew his knees close, trying to get warm, attempting to form a plan, something, *anything*. Yet when the wagon finally stopped, his mind remained blank. It was over. He'd end up in Newgate; perhaps he'd hang. His family would starve.

The door wretched open, squeaking in protest. The constable stood there, his chin covered with dirty gray whiskers, his dark eyes soulless. There was not an ounce of compassion on his bullish face. James would not beg, for the man would not care. "Come on, out with ye."

Large, dirty hands reached into the wagon, latched onto his jacket, and pulled James outside. "I didn't do nothing, I swear."

"Shut your mouth." The constable released James only to land a beefy fist against his mouth.

Pain exploded behind his eyes, followed by the metallic taste of blood seeping across his tongue. Dazed, he was barely aware when the man dragged him toward a massive stone structure. He didn't have time to mull over his options before the guard pulled him into a long, dark corridor.

"Getting a pretty pence fer ye," the man growled, pulling the door shut and locking it. Trapped. He was trapped inside a hell that smelled of waste and decay. He tried to ignore his fear and think of a way to get out of the utter disaster he'd suddenly found himself in.

Money for him? It must be a mistake! "Ye have the wrong lad, sir!"

The constable didn't respond. James tried to twist away, but his grip was too strong. The man jerked him down the dark hall, past rows of cells where beady eyes peered at him through barred windows. The sickening scent of hopelessness hovered around each prisoner. His future looked bleak indeed. At the last door, the constable paused.

"Sir, I promise, you've got the wrong lad! No one wants to pay money for me!"

"She does."

She?

With a thick, heavy key he unlocked the cell and tossed James inside. He stumbled across the slick floor as the door slammed shut, trapping him. James fell into the wall, pressing his hands to the stone, his harsh breath echoing through the small room. It was dark. So dark he couldn't see a bleedin' thing, only a square patch of gray where the door stood. This was to be his life, then?

He bit his lower lip and looked heavenward, refusing to cry. A soft scratch whispered across the floor. James froze. For a second he thought it was a rat, but no, it was too loud, too big.

James shoved away from the wall, his hands fisted at his sides. "Who are you? Who's there?"

"Who are *you*?" a voice growled through the darkness. Not quite a man's voice, but a lad probably the same age as he was. James's curiosity grew, and despite himself he couldn't deny the relief he felt. At least he wasn't alone.

"I don't know why I'm here," James admitted, hating the way his voice caught.

"We don't either." Another voice, another lad.

"We?" Startled, James moved closer. Sure enough, as his eyes adjusted to the lack of light, he could make out two forms seated on a wooden bench. "You don't?"

The lad shook his head. He was the smaller of the two, although still large, and apparently more talkative than his friend. "Was walking with my mates one moment, and the next, hauled into the wagon."

Similar to what had happened to him. "And you?" James glanced at the giant. He was a good head taller than they were. But the giant didn't say a word. James had a feeling he didn't speak often. "How long have you been here?"

"A day," the smaller gent said. Aye, he was a gent, James could tell from his refined voice. But a gent in a prison made even less sense. "And he arrived this morning. I'm Alex. He's Gideon, but he doesn't like to talk."

A day? Despondent, James sank to the ground, leaning against the damp wall. No reasoning, no answers. Would he be stuck here forever? Rot and die? Trapped in this hell that smelled very much like death?

"I'm James," he said softly.

"Will they hang us?" Alex whispered.

James didn't respond, fear of the unknown keeping him silent.

"Most likely," Gideon said.

James felt his entire body go still. He didn't want to die. A cold knot of fear and sadness formed in the middle of his chest. "Blast it! I didn't do anything!" His voice echoed around the small room. James stumbled to his feet. "Do you hear me?" he cried out. "I didn't do anything!"

The soft fall of footsteps echoed down the hall, answering him. James stiffened, and the other two lads did the same. There was more than one . . . two? Three?

"Guards," Alex whispered. "Damn you, why'd you have to say anything?"

The steps grew in volume, thick and heavy, but underneath the sound of thumping was something else . . . the light tap of a smaller shoe. The sudden sound of whistles and cheers from the other prisoners startled James. He stumbled back toward the other two boys, who had also stood.

"Why are they so excited?" James asked.

"Don't know," Alex whispered. "Maybe it's something good. Someone important. Someone who can get us out of this mess."

"We're in the gaols," Gideon growled. "How good can it be?"

"Anything is better than rotting in here," Alex snapped back. "No matter what happens, I say we fight together."

He didn't trust these lads, but James nodded quickly, knowing it was always better in numbers.

The footsteps paused. James's heart leapt into his throat. When the door screeched open they fell silent, still. A tense moment passed when suddenly a lantern burst to life, momentarily blinding them. James raised his arm, blocking the light.

"To yer feet," the constable growled, having no idea they were already standing. The big bull stepped into the room, lantern held high. James glanced briefly at Alex and Gideon. He'd been right: they were all around the same age, at least within a year or two.

Alex was dressed in fine clothes, his dark hair combed neatly into place. Gideon wore rags much like James, his dark hair overly long, hanging in front of eyes that glared at the door.

"Look lively, you street brats," the constable growled.

"Now, Constable," a woman said softly from the shadows, "is that any way to speak to such fine gentlemen?"

James went cold. A bleedin' woman? The constable snorted in disbelief. But the woman didn't seem to mind. She moved into the cell, her skirts rustling over the stone floor, two large brutes following her. Over the scent of rot and refuse, James could smell something sweet and utterly feminine. Heaven.

It was too bloody good to be true. When she stepped into the light James went speechless. She was small, not much taller than he. Her pale face was pure perfection, and for a moment he wondered if they had died and were being greeted by an angel. He heard Alex and Gideon gasp and knew they were just as stunned. She wore a light lavender gown that shoved her breasts up toward her face, and a bonnet that covered her hair. He couldn't see her eye color, and he so desperately wanted to know the shade.

"Oh dear," she whispered in a voice that held the slightest accent. Her pretty little mouth formed a pout and she shook her head in despair. "Wavers, do give them the baskets."

One of the beasts guarding her stepped forward and handed first Gideon, then Alex, and lastly James a basket. He could smell roast chicken wafting from the container and he had to force himself not to tear it open. All three boys merely stood there, waiting.

"Can you tell us why we're here?" Alex finally asked.

"Well," she sighed, clasping her hands together. She wasn't as old as his mum, but she was much older than they were. "You were all unfortunately caught doing something criminal, according to the constable."

James glanced at the two lads, wondering what they had done, but neither spoke. She paced the small cell, the erotic scent of sweet flowers floating around them. James breathed deeply . . . lavender! He suddenly recognized the smell. His mum had grown the flowers in pots around the house.

"And unfortunately even young criminals are harshly punished here."

James swallowed hard, his fear returning. "I didn't," he blurted out. "I didn't do anything!"

She stepped toward him and rested her gloved hand on the side of his face. James froze, shocked. "I understand, but the constable is the law." She released her hold and strolled toward the door. "Still, there might be a way to gain your release."

They hesitated, looking at each other in wariness. Not one of them trusted the situation. His da had taught him to use his brain, but it was so very muddled at the moment.

"What?" Alex finally asked, a pleading note to his voice that they all felt. "What can we do?"

"You'll come with me." She stepped into the hall and glanced back. "Unless you'd rather stay here?"

She disappeared around the corner. The three of them merely stood there, staring at the empty door with mouths gaping wide in surprise. Finally, James managed to glance at Alex and Gideon. "What does she mean?"

"Come on," a guard growled from the hall. "Ye got a chance out, I'd take it."

That did it. Alex was the first to move toward the door, clasping his basket to his chest as he raced after the woman. James hesitated only a moment, then followed with his basket in hand. Gideon was the last in line. They trailed after her small, dark form, ignoring the growls, curse words, and whistles of the other prisoners. James didn't know where they were headed, but surely this angelic being was offering them something much better than their prison cell. The guard unlocked the door and moved aside. Hesitantly, they stepped into the courtyard, the brilliant light of the rising sun startling.

But it wasn't the dingy boys beside him who caught his attention. No, it was the woman leading them toward a purple carriage . . . a woman with hair that glowed like pale gold. A veritable angel she was, of such startling beauty that James found he could not speak. He'd thought her pretty, but he'd been wrong . . . she was perfect. The man named Wavers helped her across the cobbled courtyard and into her gaudy carriage. When the three boys continued to stand there, shocked speechless, she peeked outside.

"James," she purred, fastening her gaze on him. "Do enter and sit, please."

Lord almighty, she had lavender eyes a shade darker than her dress. He'd never seen eyes such a color. She had untied her bonnet and it was resting on the bench next to her. He swallowed hard, unnerved by her beauty, but more so by the fact that she knew his name. She waved a delicate gloved hand toward the bench seat opposite her. He glanced warily at the other lads. Gideon was glaring daggers at him as he ripped chunks of meat from a chicken leg. Alex merely looked confused, nervous.

"Please, James."

And because she looked so bloody kind and beautiful, but mostly because he didn't want to return to that prison, he climbed into the stunning carriage and settled his boney arse upon the velvet cushion, reveling in the softness. What was she thinking by having him here? His fear wavered, replaced by deep curiosity. Was she someone his da used to work for? He rubbed his aching brow, unsure, confused.

"Please." She smiled. "Do eat."

With trembling hands he lifted a chicken leg from the basket and sank his teeth into the soft meat. It slid silkily smooth down his throat. He felt bloody guilty eating such lovely fare while his family starved. Dare he slip some potatoes into his pockets in hopes of returning to them?

"I know you're confused," she said, glancing first at him, then the other two who waited outside.

She had a lovely, fine accent that sounded like birds singing. A voice that sent a thrill through his body and heated his blood in an embarrassing way. He wasn't sure which was more appealing, the food or the woman.

"I only wish to help you."

Her heavenly scent made him only too aware of his unwashed body. Aye, he knew he wasn't bad to look upon. His mother had warned him more than once to stay away from the factory girls, who giggled whenever he came near. But he was also smart enough to know he paled in comparison to the woman across from him. Besides, she was at least ten years older. So what did she want from him? He set the chicken down, swiping his greasy fingers across his trouser legs, not hungry anymore. Something was wrong, so very wrong.

She was tiny, a fairy maiden who almost didn't seem real. Almost as if she'd stepped from the Irish fairy tales his mum used to repeat when they were a happy family . . . when his da still lived. "What do you want with us?"

"Want?" He stiffened as she leaned toward him. He could see, from the corner of his eye, that the other lads were also watching her . . . waiting. There was something about the way she smiled that worried him, like she had won a game he hadn't realized they were playing. She moved across the carriage, settling uncomfortably close and resting a gloved hand on his knee. Heat shot to his groin and cheeks. He almost groaned in embarrassment. Who the hell was she?

"I've an offer for you, James." The words whispered warmly across his ear.

A sinful image popped to mind. An image of his lips touching hers. The world around him faded as she moved closer, her soft body pressing to his side. His gaze focused on the low neckline of her gown, slowly traveling up her pale, delicate neck to her red, red lips.

"I'd like for you to work for me."

His gaze jerked to her beautiful lavender eyes. They were like a world unto themselves. He blinked in stunned surprise. "Work?" His voice squeaked.

Those beautiful eyes grew serious, almost desperate. "Indeed. I need you, James."

In that moment he knew he would have done anything for her. He would have sold his soul. Given his right arm. Hell, given his life. He felt like a man for the first time in his life. "Yes, my lady."

She rested back against the seat and he wondered how old she was. Not too old for him, he hoped. "I'm in desperate need of help." Her beautiful lavender gaze went to the boys standing quietly outside. "Alex, Gideon, please join us."

They glanced warily at each other.

She pressed her gloved hand to her chest. "Please, I do need your assistance."

That settled it. A damsel in distress always won out. Alex squared his shoulders and marched around Wavers. Gideon reluctantly followed. The carriage bounced as they settled into the seat across from James and the woman. It suddenly felt too crowded in the small interior. It was obvious they were all confused, troubled, caught between wanting to agree to anything the woman asked and wanting to bolt for the door.

Although she had pulled him under with her beautiful face and words of need, life had taught him to be leery of anything too good to be true. "Doing what, exactly?"

She leaned forward, the bodice of her gown gaping again. Sweat broke out across James's forehead and he wished desperately he was alone with her. "Have you ever known pleasure, James?" She rested her hand on his knee. His cock flared to life and he practically jumped out of his skin. "Have you known the pleasure of a woman?"

He swallowed hard, not daring to answer such a sinful question. Just last week Sarah Ellen had allowed him to slide his hands up her skirt, but that was as far as he'd ever gotten. But Sarah

Ellen didn't compare to this woman. This woman who wanted him—*him*—to save her for some reason.

She slid Alex and Gideon a sly glance. "There are so very many women who wish to find pleasure from handsome young lads such as you."

Her words struck him through the heart. Reality made him ill. Aghast, he jumped back, away from her touch and her evil offer. His attraction fled as quickly as it had arrived. "Whore myself?"

Alex had gone pale, while Gideon merely glared at her as if he'd expected nothing less. She leaned back in her chair looking highly amused. She behaved as if it was completely natural for a lad to whore himself, and completely natural for a women of such beauty to offer.

"I've seen you, James. I've seen the way the girls watch when you walk by. They like you. They want you. You could find great pleasure in the arms of a woman."

He flushed, partly in pleasure, partly in embarrassment, but mostly in confusion. Where had she seen him? "But . . . but 'tis a sin," he muttered.

The woman was daft if she thought he'd whore himself. He glanced at the door, wondering if he should excuse himself now and if she'd allow him to take the rest of his meal. Or would they toss him back in the gaols if he dared to decline?

"And stealing isn't?"

He swallowed hard and glanced her way. She knew, did she? What else did she know?

"Money, James." She whispered the words, but he heard them all the same. "I will make sure your mother and sister never starve again. They shall live in a warm, lovely cottage with all the food they could ever want. Think of it. Imagine it. They will never go hungry again."

A picture of his mother and sister in all their boney gory flashed to mind. Plenty of food? They wouldn't have to work in the factories and lose a finger, or worse. But how would he ever face his mum again? He couldn't, could he?

"How do you know so much about me?" He lifted his gaze, interested despite himself.

She pressed ever closer, her lips on his ear so the other two lads couldn't hear. "Save your mother and sister from the factories . . . or worse. Be the man your father wanted you to be."

What did she know about his father? Still, her comment hit him hard. Alex and Gideon watched him quietly, wariness and nervousness in their eyes because they knew they were next. She would offer them the same, but would they agree?

"My life would be over," he said, his voice cracking. His mum would kill him if she found out. "I'd have no family."

"I'll be your family. I'm not taking your life. The very opposite. I'm offering you splendor. Passion. But most importantly, I'm offering you a way to save your mother and sister."

"I don't . . ." Heated embarrassment shot to his cheeks. "I don't know how to pleasure a woman."

She smiled, trailing her hand down his arm. "Dear boy, don't worry. You won't work immediately." She shrugged as if unconcerned. "We'll wait a couple of years until you're more secure in your abilities."

"What will we do in the meantime?" Alex demanded.

She nodded to Wavers, who shut the carriage door, trapping them in the gilded cell. "Help in the stables, be footmen. Rather easy work, much easier than the work they would make you do here, in the factories or on the docks."

Two years and he'd be almost sixteen. James took his lower lip between his teeth. In two years he'd be man enough. "You promise we won't have to whore ourselves until we're ready?"

She released a trilling laugh as she knocked on the roof of the carriage. "Of course! And if you decide it's not to your liking, you may remain a footman. What say you, James?"

The carriage jerked to life. He shivered and glanced once more at the other lads. A picture of his mother and sister in the finest of silken gowns, feasting on goose, flashed to mind. He'd never have to worry about them again. Never have to steal. He would be the man his father had wanted.

He might be selling his soul. He might not ever see his family again, but he had this chance . . . this one chance to save them. James swallowed hard and tilted his chin high. He owed his father this much. "Aye, I agree."

She took his hand in hers and smiled warmly at him. "Oh, James, I'm so pleased. We're friends, we're all going to be great friends."

Chapter 1

She was bloody mad.

Completely and utterly insane.

She wouldn't at all be surprised if they locked her away in Bedlam because no normal person would ever even think of visiting a brothel. And certainly the cold, perfect Lady Beckett would never, ever do something so sinful. Yet here she was sitting before the infamous brothel owner herself, Lady Lavender.

Yes, indeed, Eleanor had lost her senses.

"Someone gentle you say, Mrs. Richards?" Lady Lavender flipped through a small leather book, those equally infamous lavender eyes darting from page to page. She treated the transaction as if it was business, and perhaps it was to her. If only Eleanor could think of it that way.

"Romantic?" Lady Lavender added, glancing up through thick, dark lashes.

Eleanor gave a quick nod. The netting over her face tickled her nose, but she didn't dare brush it aside. She'd even covered her coveted blonde locks with the same netting to make sure no one could identify her. She looked like a bloody beekeeper but no one seemed to mind. No, because in a brothel that catered to women, discretion was a normalcy. She'd been both bemused and relieved when not one person had glanced her way upon her arrival in an unmarked hired hack. Even when she'd given an obviously pretense name to the large man who answered the door, he hadn't blinked.

She had to admit that she was rather intrigued by the brothel owner, who had always seemed more myth than true heroine. Lady Lavender . . . a woman spoken about in only whispers. Although Eleanor had always considered herself trim and elegant, she felt a giant sitting across from the delicate brothel owner. Pure perfection. Her pale skin and equally pale hair practically glowed, like she was a veritable angel, if one didn't notice the cold, calculating look in her beautiful eyes.

"Gentle," she whispered, her golden brows drawing together as she concentrated.

Eleanor had seen the woman once while shopping along Regent Street. A flash of lavender skirts, for she always wore the color. For a moment she'd thought she'd imagined her. But no . . . the elder Lady Beckett had paused to look in a shop window and Eleanor, waiting for her mother-in-law, had gotten her first true sighting. It was only a brief glance before her future mother-in-law tried to urge her forward. But she'd been so shocked to see the woman she couldn't seem to move.

"Do not stare; you will be ruined for even acknowledging the woman," her mother-in-law had reprimanded. *"In our world she does not exist."*

Oh, but she did exist, and young women from all stations in life, from all countries in the world, loved to discuss the madam. As a debutante she'd first heard rumored whispers of a brothel for women. Years later, all of England knew, and the current sweep of innocents and their inane conversation about the sinful place. Only last week she'd heard a group of them talking.

"Melissa Turner dared to say good day to the woman in public! Was sent to a nunnery and no one has heard from her since."

"I hear she imprisons the men . . . forces them—"

"Oh bother it, Jenny; do you really think any man must be forced to do that?"

But they would break off, as always, the moment they caught sight of Eleanor. With flushed faces, they would mumble good day, drop into curtseys, and rush off, praying she would not alert their mothers to their gossiping ways. And she never had, because despite her initial disgust at the thought of a brothel for women . . . she had, deep down, been curious. Always curious. Something her mother had warned her about too many times to count.

"No woman with a curious mind, who questions everything, will ever land a husband!"

"I have the perfect person." The infamous Lady Lavender snapped her book shut, jerking Eleanor from her memories.

Perfect person. Oh dear Lord.

Before Eleanor could properly prepare, the woman pulled on the silken bell cord that hung near her massive desk. Eleanor's heart leapt into her throat, although she knew if one looked at her they would see nothing amiss. No, she'd had years of practice masking her feelings. She was the very definition of control. At one time mothers had forced their daughters to emulate her, and young men had used her as an example when searching for a wife. Eleanor bit her lower lip to keep from laughing. How would the *ton* feel about her should they uncover her location?

"He will arrive at any moment."

A warning shiver raced over her spine. If she was going to put a stop to this nonsense, it best be done now. Eleanor took in a deep, trembling breath. She was not nervous. No, she was never nervous. So why was she twisting her gloved hands together? Gritting her teeth, she forced her fingers to uncurl and lie still upon her lap. Her green taffeta gown suddenly felt too stifling, the neckline too high. Blast it, she couldn't seem to breathe properly.

"Yes. He'll be utterly perfect." Lady Lavender pushed away from her desk and stood. "I'll be only a moment. Shall I get you something to drink?"

"Sherry, please."

Determined to calm her racing heart, Eleanor studied the office as the woman strolled to the sideboard. She had to admit she was a bit underwhelmed by the entire place. The rumors were so very much gaudier than reality. In reality it was a beautiful English estate surrounded by sweet-smelling lavender. She wasn't sure if she should be disappointed or amused.

Marble flooring, golden sconces, French wallpaper . . . the place reeked of sophistication and elegance when she'd been expecting the gaudiness of a true brothel. Lord, it felt as if she was sitting in her mother's parlor. Well, if her mother collected French paintings of naked couples indecently embracing. The risqué artwork hanging above a cold hearth was the only thing so very bold about the place.

The door opened. Eleanor jerked her head toward the foyer, but it was only the tall mountain of a man who had greeted her upon her arrival. At least she'd taken his grunt as a greeting. She didn't like the look of him . . . a man who used his fists instead of reasoning.

"Wavers," Lady Lavender said, handing the sherry to Eleanor. "Please send for James. If you'll wait a moment, Mrs. Richards?"

She'd given a false name, of course, too nervous to give her true identity although it was said that the queen herself would have to pry the client list from Lady Lavender's cold, dead hands, she was that adept at keeping secrets. But the rumors didn't ease her worry. Whether society believed it or not, Lady Lavender was human, and humans made mistakes.

The brothel owner started toward the door when fear got the better of Eleanor. "Wait!"

Lady Lavender turned quite calmly and quirked a blonde brow. "Yes, my dear?"

Eleanor tugged off her gloves, needing something to do. The heated blush that rushed to her cheeks was a combination of embarrassment, shame, and the intense heat of the room. Why didn't the woman open a blasted window, for God's sake?

"Yes?" Lady Lavender prompted impatiently.

"I'm not . . . sure."

Lady Lavender sighed and nodded toward Wavers, who stepped back into the hall, giving them some privacy. "What is your purpose, my lady?"

"Pardon?" Eleanor stood, too nervous to sit. She'd saved her pin money for weeks in order to afford this place. Not that she didn't have the funds. She had plenty, but it would be missed. And so she'd taken a coin here and there that wouldn't be noticed. And now . . . now she was thinking of leaving when she'd already paid? Giving up when she'd spent months concocting her escape?

"Why are you here?" Lady Lavender seemed annoyed, which made Eleanor feel all the more guilty for wasting the woman's time. She was a businesswoman; she didn't have time for silly misses, and Eleanor was most certainly being a silly miss.

Heat crawled torturously slowly up her neck. "I . . . I want to find pleasure, of course."

"Why?" There was no empathy upon Lady Lavender's face. She was quite serious as she crossed her arms over her full bosom.

The heat shot to Eleanor's cheeks. Dear Lord, she never, ever blushed. "I . . . I . . . want to know passion."

Lady Lavender gave a nod. "You want someone warm and gentle, and James is perfect."

James. She liked the sound of his name. "James," she whispered out loud.

"Just try him." As if he was a new French pastry. It was a dare. She shoved the glass of sherry into Eleanor's hand. "What have you to lose?"

In other words, Eleanor had already placed her reputation in jeopardy by coming here, she had already paid, why not partake in the pleasure the visit might bring? Besides, she never ever backed down from a dare. "Very well."

She settled in her chair and drank her sherry, the liquid burning a fiery path of courage down her throat. Lady Lavender didn't bother to hide her grin of amusement, as if she had won a battle of some sort. Without another word, the woman moved into the foyer, closing the door behind her. The room went utterly silent. The only sounds were the soft patter of rain against the windows and the tick of the porcelain clock on the mantel.

With a sigh, Eleanor set her glass upon a side table and surged to her feet, pacing the room. It was like a bloody museum. Pure perfection, not a thing out of place. She picked up a porcelain dog from the fireplace mantel. There was no warmth . . . no . . . love . . . no family. It reminded her only too much of her own home. She didn't want to be reminded of home . . . not here and especially not now.

Yet the sickening feeling that she was going to get caught wouldn't go away. Perhaps Graham, her ever-knowing butler, would appear at the door and shout "ah-ha!" The thought was disconcerting, to say the least. The urge to run overwhelmed her. No one need ever know that she had visited. Yes, she could leave. Return home and forget this madness.

The door opened. Too late. Eleanor spun around, her heart leaping into her throat. The small porcelain dog fell from her hands, bouncing across the carpet, but she was barely aware. The man who stood in the doorway wasn't exactly what she'd been expecting. But then she wasn't sure what, exactly, she'd been expecting.

"My lady." He smiled kindly and bowed low.

A gentleman, then? Why did that thought only add to her unease? Eleanor backed up a step, thankful the fire was not burning, for her skirts would have been singed black. He shut the door behind him. She felt utterly trapped.

Yes, she'd wanted someone gentle, but she hadn't expected a man who spoke with a refined accent and dressed like a lord. It was sacrilegious in some way. When he started toward her, she dropped to the ground, scooping up the porcelain pup merely to have something to do. Tall, sinewy, with broad shoulders and a narrow waist enhanced by his black jacket and silver waistcoat, he had a lovely form, she could admit. In fact, years ago as an innocent she would have found his wavy light brown hair and brilliant eyes quite handsome. Eleanor surged to her feet, dog in hand.

A few steps away he paused, as if not to overwhelm her. A rush of heat fluttered in her chest. She clutched the porcelain dog to her bosom. This was James. *The* James who would kiss her . . . touch her . . . a stranger. She could admit he had kind eyes, warm eyes of a rich green much like the moss that used to grow in the forest near her aunt's country home. Moss she'd pretended was a bed for the fairies that lived amongst the trees. A time long, long ago when she'd still been innocent.

He reached out and took her hand, carefully uncurling her fingers and taking the dog from her grip. And she allowed him, allowed him to touch her because she was too stunned to stop him. He replaced the piece, then slowly brought her hand forward. The entire world slowed as he bowed low, pressing his warm lips to the back of her bare hand. A shiver of awareness washed over her, a tingle that swept from her hand all the way up her arm. She jerked away, determined to retain control of her emotions.

Although he obviously practiced like one, he did not in the least look like a whore. Just like that, nervousness gave way to curiosity. There was no predatory gleam in his green eyes. No . . . no animalistic desire in his smile. No wicked curl in his soft brown hair. He looked . . . kind. Almost . . . boyish. Yes, she had wanted kind, but not a *lad*!

"How old are you, exactly?" she blurted out.

He smiled, a charming smile that produced a shallow dimple on either side of his mouth. "Almost twenty-seven years of age, my lady."

Lord, she was older than him by a good six years. She flushed, feeling highly uncomfortable. What was she doing here? It was mad. Disastrous, and it was becoming more insane with every moment she remained. She needed to leave before this went any further, before she completely ruined her reputation. She started toward the chair where she'd left her gloves. The room tilted. She felt odd. Slightly dizzy, as if the world spun.

Helpless, she lifted her head and met his gaze. For one brief moment everything fell away, crumbling into nothingness, and it was just the two of them. No worries. No rules. No fear. As if her body was no longer her own, she took a step closer to the man, drawn by his very essence.

"Are you ready?" he asked, his voice smooth and calm.

"I should . . ." She wanted to say yes, she realized with a start. She wanted to slip her hand into his and follow him to his bed-chamber, to let him touch her, kiss her, and that frightened her more than she wanted to admit. She gave a quick jerk of her head. "No, I'm not . . . sure."

"Let me make you sure." He gave her a kind smile as he took her bare hand and led her toward the chair where she'd been sitting earlier. The feel of his skin on hers sent her heart hammering. Fingers wrapped around fingers, palm to palm, it was much too intimate.

"If I decide to partake, I . . . I should not like to run into anyone in the halls," she said as she settled on the chair.

"Don't worry," he said. "We do not partake in the halls."

She flushed; he smiled.

"I apologize. I understand that you're a tad nervous." He settled in the chair next to hers. "But Lady Lavender provides the highest of discretion. She staggers the appointments so that you will not run into any other client."

"I see." For one long moment they merely stared at each other. Her heart hammered madly in her chest, so hard she thought for sure it would break free, run out the front door, and race back to London without her. Ridiculous. She was a grown woman; he was practically a child. Why was she so bloody nervous near him? The heat that had come on so quickly earlier returned. She couldn't breathe.

"Are you well?" Suddenly he was beside her, kneeling by her chair, his palm pressed to her thigh as if he was truly concerned.

When she didn't respond, just stared at his bold touch, he reached forward and undid the strings of her bonnet. She was too weak to care. What was wrong with her? She thrived on controlling her emotions. She never showed weakness. Ever! Yet here she was acting like a virginal debutante.

James lifted her bonnet, setting it on the side table. No longer hidden, she waited for his reaction. His warm gaze ran over her face, taking in every detail from her slim nose to her full lips and large blue eyes. He did not change his expression, did not wax poetically about her beauty, nor did he gasp in wonder as men had done in the past. "Would you like a drink?"

She nodded, thankful he did not spout any romantic nonsense; she wouldn't be able to stand the falseness of it all. As a young girl, she'd been flattered by the attention men had given her. Now it merely annoyed. James stood and moved to the sidebar. Eleanor released the air she hadn't realized she held. Lord, they were in Lady Lavender's study; anyone could come in at any moment. So why didn't she leave while she could?

He moved back toward her and held out the glass. When she didn't reach for it, he leaned forward and settled the drink against her palm, their fingertips brushing. Heat shimmered through her body. Yes, he was attractive, but she knew it was the suspense of his touch that was truly making her nervous.

"Drink," he demanded kindly.

Eleanor swallowed an unladylike gulp of the brandy. The liquid lit fire to her throat. She gasped, shoving the drink back into this hand. Fortunately he didn't laugh, merely set the drink on Lady Lavender's desk.

"Are you sure, my lady?" He looked so bloody sincere she wanted to laugh, or perhaps she wanted to cry. "Are you sure you want this?"

She took in a deep breath. She'd come here; her reputation was most likely already ruined. She was tired of being a coward, damn it all. "Yes, I'm sure."

He smiled, a kind smile that for some reason set her at ease, and she suddenly found herself smiling back. Her smile fell as he took her hands and pulled her to her feet. She tried not to stiffen, yet her body now had a mind of its own. And so she stared at his neck, at the pulse thumping in a steady beat. For a brief, insane moment she wondered what it would be like to kiss that spot. Slowly her gaze traveled over his chin to his lips. She wanted to taste his mouth. Wanted to breathe deeply his musky scent. She wanted honesty, no pretense. She wanted . . . him.

He reached forward, resting his hand near the crown of her hair. "May I?"

She gave a quick nod, wondering if she would have agreed to anything at the moment. Gently, he pulled the pins from her locks and let the strands tumble down around her shoulders, whispering across her back.

"Beautiful," he said softly, placing the pins in her hat.

She flushed, oddly uncomfortable under his sincere gaze. She didn't take compliments well. Never had, for she had heard too many insincere words of love to take them seriously. He didn't seem to mind her lack of response, merely drew a lock of hair through his fingers. She hated the color. Hated that the golden blonde had drawn the attention of more than one man. Hated that when she was young, the bucks would stammer over her, trip over themselves to give her a compliment. The difference was they'd never looked at her as sincerely as James.

She shifted, unsure what to do, looking everywhere but at him. It was a ruse, and he was a fine actor, for she had to remind herself that she was paying him for his kindness. For all she knew, he beat puppies when he was not whoring. And she was alone with him. Utterly alone with a man not related, a stranger.

He moved back, leaning against Lady Lavender's desk. "You still seem unsure."

"I am." She flushed. "I've never done something like this, of course. Am I to merely sit here while you wax poetically about my hair?"

The corners of his lips twitched. "Has no one ever given you compliments?"

She crossed her arms over her chest, feeling oddly vulnerable. "Actually, many times." *Long, long ago.* "And I found it as annoying then as I do now."

He did not seem offended, as she had hoped. Instead, he reached out and drew his finger down the side of her face. Her pulse raced. When he stepped closer, looming over her, Eleanor's gut tightened in a way she'd never experienced, wasn't sure she appreciated. Yes, she'd felt the thrill of attraction, but never this heated, this intense. He wore a spicy aftershave that reminded her of the woods in summer. Of stables and the countryside. It was not the exotic scent of India that most men of the *ton* wore. No, this was more . . . natural, and damn it all, she liked it. She liked him.

"Might I kiss you?" he asked.

Startled by the bold question, she met his gaze. It was the moment that would change her entire life, if she so dared. If she was smart, she'd leave. If she was smart, she'd push him away. If she was smart, she'd remind herself of what she had to lose. Apparently she was far, far from smart. "Yes."

He didn't hesitate, but cupped the back of her head, his warm fingers sliding into her hair. His body didn't touch hers, but his lips did. They brushed softly against hers. A gentle kiss, a pleasant kiss that she rather liked. Yes, she could live with this kiss. She wouldn't mind this kiss.

"Yes?" he whispered, his mouth warm against hers.

"Yes."

His fingers tightened in her hair and he pulled gently until her head tilted back, and then he was kissing her again. He kissed her with the greatest of care . . . the gentlest pressure, the softest flick of his velvet tongue. A shiver of unease and desire whispered over her. A feeling she'd never experienced before. His firm lips molded to hers again and again. For fear of falling, she wrapped her arms around his neck.

Her breasts felt heavy, her nipples hardening in an embarrassing way as her breasts crushed to his chest, yet she didn't care. He caught her groan with his mouth. When his tongue delved between her lips, the ache in her belly spread lower. He didn't crush her to him, demanding more. No, he merely kissed her, yet she knew he wasn't entirely immune for she could feel the hard swell of his cock pressed to her skirt.

His warm hands slid around her hips, spanning her narrow waist. But as his grip moved toward her arse, reality came crashing down. Her eyes opened. Dear God, what was she thinking? She shoved her hands into his chest and pushed back, stumbling away from him. Her breath came out in harsh pants she did not recognize as her own, the sound of lust.

"I'm sorry." Tears burned her eyes as she smoothed down her skirts, finding fascination with the fern pattern upon her gown. What had she done? Her body no longer felt her own, her soul tarnished. She had the oddest feeling the world would know what she had done the moment she stepped foot into London. She'd be branded a sinner, a cheat, a liar.

"What is it?" He started to reach for her, obviously concerned. He seemed genuinely startled by her unease.

She stepped back, shaking her head. He couldn't touch her because it was wrong, but mostly because she feared if he brought her close, she wouldn't want him to let go. "I just . . . I can't. I'm sorry."

"Why?" James asked, grabbing her hand. His fingers were warm, strong, as they wrapped around her cold palm. So very much larger than she, he could prevent her from leaving if he wished. She jerked away and snatched up her bonnet and gloves.

"Because." She started toward the door. "If my husband ever uncovers the truth, he will not only kill me, but you as well."

Without another word, without further explanation, Eleanor tore open the door and fled, vowing never to return to Lady Lavender's den of sin again.

Chapter 2

"She left without partaking?"

"Yes." James relaxed into the chair across from Ophelia's desk. The very chair where Mrs. Richards had sat only hours ago. He scratched his jaw thoughtfully, wondering over her true name. She was a beautiful woman, there was no doubt, and he'd been stunned for a brief moment when he'd taken off her bonnet and gotten a good look at her features. But her beauty was forgotten when he'd looked into her eyes . . . brilliant blue eyes full of fear and sadness and a resolute determination he knew only too well.

"Do you agree?" Ophelia said.

James jerked his gaze to her. "I'm sorry?"

She sighed impatiently, realizing he hadn't been paying attention. James grinned sheepishly, but she didn't return his smile. She'd changed in the years since Alex had left. Changed, even in the past few months, and not for the better. He worried about her, although he knew she'd merely brush aside his concern if he spoke aloud. But she couldn't hide the fact that she'd gotten thinner, didn't smile as often, and rarely slept. She seemed desperate for something he didn't understand, and he was no longer sure what she wanted.

He didn't blame Alex in the least for leaving, yet he did think the man could have done it in a more compassionate manner. He had no doubt Ophelia felt betrayed by their parting, for it had been far from pleasant. As cold and calculating as she was, women always tended to take things personally. Still, he'd understood Alex's frustration with the woman.

Yes, Lady Lavender was a tyrant at times. Yes, she was manipulative, even demanding. But James owed her his life. He owed her the life of his sister and mother. If she hadn't found him in that prison, he would have hanged, his family would have starved. For those reasons he would be forever loyal to the brothel owner, even if Alex hadn't been.

She stood and paced to the windows that overlooked those rolling fields of lavender. She'd paced a lot in the last few months. "It happens often . . . women lose their nerve." She turned, the pale lavender day dress she wore swirling around her trim ankles. "It doesn't matter that men are intimate with whomever they wish, often betraying their marriage vows and wives. For some reason women think they must take the moral high road."

He didn't miss the bitterness in her voice, a bitterness that hardened her tone much more often lately. He wasn't sure how to react to this new Ophelia. He'd always thought of her as more of a male friend than female. Cold, calculating, a veritable law unto herself.

She never asked how he fared, didn't care to know what was in his heart, which was fine by him. No, he escorted her to the occasional gaming hell, escorted her when she went riding, and even when she'd gone hunting last summer. Often, she had him take dinner in her chambers, where they'd make pleasant enough conversation. But they were friendly up to a point, never discussing anything personal. Honestly, he'd never really cared what she thought. Now he regretted treating her like a man. He had a feeling she was succumbing to her demons, whatever they might be, and he hadn't a clue how to help her.

"How fares Gideon?" he asked, mostly to change the subject.

She waved her hand through the air in a dismissive manner. "You know what he's like . . . the man is as unbendable as steel." She released a harsh laugh. "Refuses to submit."

Submit? He had to bite his tongue. *Submit?* The word irritated him for some reason. She'd never implied before that she owned them. But her words made it seem as if they were almost . . . slaves. He shifted, suddenly uneasy as a handful of memories came rushing back. Memories he'd brushed aside all too often in the past.

"I understand," Alex had said over two years ago. *"I understand why you feel loyalty toward the woman, but James, think on it. You, Gideon, and I, brought here together by blackmail."*

James had bristled at the comment, always loyal to Ophelia. *"Not blackmail."*

Alex released a harsh laugh. *"She told you if you didn't do as she said, your family would starve to death."*

"And she was right, we would have. No one gets anything for free, Alex. She expected me to work." He smiled, a smile that he hadn't quite felt. *"There are worse ways to make a living, you know."*

"Indeed," Alex had whispered, but James knew he hadn't agreed.

Alex had grown up in luxury, while James had spent most of his time in the rookeries, where loyalty was the only bloody thing a person had to his name. If you were disloyal to your mates, you might as well slit your own throat, for you were as good as dead.

"Perhaps I'll send Wavers to escort him home," Ophelia said thoughtfully.

He doubted Gideon would appreciate an escort. He despised commands of any kind. Alex and Gideon had never accepted or trusted their new lot in life. They had continually watched Ophelia with a mixture of distrust and hatred that James hadn't exactly understood.

Yes, the intimacy had been awkward at first, but he knew there were certainly worse ways to make money for his family. She fed and clothed his mother and sister, and for that he would be eternally grateful. It had been a business transaction between them that had blossomed into some sort of friendship.

"He will apparently be gone longer than I'd expected. I never should have loaned him out." She moved toward James, the heady scent of lavender following. He stiffened when she settled on his lap and rested her palm against his cheek. "But you . . . you're the only one who listens. The only one who obeys."

He gave her a forced smile. Submit? Obey? They were words she'd never used around him before, words he wasn't sure he appreciated. But she was so bloody childlike in the rare moments like these that he didn't dare hurt her feelings. "Of course."

She sighed and stood. "I do worry about Gideon."

He did not stop her when she moved away, heading toward the hearth where a low fire burned. She was silent for some time, staring moodily into the flames, and he was thoughtful whereas he was very rarely anything but content. Perhaps it was Ophelia and her sudden melancholy.

Or perhaps it was the memory of the many tedious conversations with Alex and Gideon over whether Ophelia could be trusted. Or maybe, just maybe, it was Mrs. Richards, who had left so quickly only an hour or so ago. A woman who had portrayed herself as cold and confident, yet whose sad eyes had given away the truth. But suddenly James found himself discontent. His skin itched, his body tensed as if he wanted to move, run . . . but where?

"You have an appointment with Mrs. Trillium in an hour." Ophelia was all business now, her voice hard and uncompromising. The childlike woman was gone as quickly as she had appeared. "Prepare yourself."

He nodded and stood, knowing a dismissal when he heard one.

"And James, this time actually go through with the deed." There was that hint of a smile once more, reminding him of the woman he'd come to know and respect.

He returned her smile. "Of course."

But he didn't feel any better when he moved into the hall, his mind still on Gideon and Alex. He didn't feel any better because he couldn't ignore the fact that Ophelia had changed. *He* had changed. James paused at the stairs and rubbed the back of his neck. Perhaps he missed Alex and Gideon. Even if they thought he was an idiot for remaining loyal to Ophelia, he still thought of them as friends. Aye, he was merely a tad lonely.

He rested his hand on the baluster, preparing to push Ophelia, Alex, and Gideon from his mind when he heard his name whispered from down the hall. "Mr. McKinnon."

He paused, frowning. Maids were forbidden to speak with the men, as Ophelia didn't want anyone falling in love, or worse, filling the house with bastard children.

"Sir." One of the housemaids peeked around the corner. Sarah, or Sally, or . . . Millie. Yes, her name was Millie. A young, freckle-faced thing who looked as nervous as a bird trapped by a hungry cat.

Curious, he stepped down from the stairs and started toward her. "Yes, Millie, what is it?"

"A . . . letter." She held out the note, her brown gaze darting from corner to corner, as if expecting someone to lunge for her at any moment. How very odd. He glanced from her pale face to the missive she held. There was no writing on the envelope, and he wondered how she knew it was for him, unless . . . someone had handed it to her directly. Her hand trembled so hard the paper actually rattled, an indication of her guilt.

He took the envelope. "Where did it come from?"

"A . . . a man gave it to me while I was at the market. Handed me coins to make sure you got it."

"You're positive it's for me?"

She wrung her hands together, her slippered feet shifting across the floor as if eager to run. "Yes. Been waiting three days to catch you alone."

"Very well. You may go."

She looked more than relieved when she scampered off. Who in the bleedin' hell would be sending him a secret note? Most likely some enamored client. He sighed, settling on a chair in the hall and opening the letter. It had happened more than once that a client had fallen in love. Ophelia would make quick work of letting the woman go. But no, this was not the flowery writing of a female, nor did it smell like perfume. He instantly recognized Alex's scrawl.

James,

I hope to find you in good health and happiness. I once more offer my sincerest invitation for you to visit any time you wish. Grace also welcomes you. I'm writing yet again because I have not heard from you in months . . .

James stiffened, surprised. He'd sent at least three letters in the past two months and had wondered why he hadn't heard from Alex. He'd assumed the man had started a new life and had no room for his past. He certainly hadn't begrudged him his need to move on.

I fear someone is intentionally keeping my letters from you. I'm sending this missive once more in hopes that you will receive this dire message. I ran into some surprising information before I left. I have wavered over whether to tell you or not, knowing your thoughts on Ophelia, but feel I must.

Gideon's father and mine were friends. You know that I've always thought there was a connection between the three of us . . . a reason as to why Lady Lavender chose me, you, and Gideon. Do you think you might be connected as well?

35

"James?" Ophelia suddenly appeared in the foyer, startling him. "You're still here?"

"Just going." He surged to his feet, forcing his lips up as he tucked the note into his waistcoat pocket.

He hadn't a clue why he had the urge to hide the letter from her. Perhaps, he thought, he merely wanted to spare her feelings. Or maybe he thought to protect the maid who had delivered it. But no, he knew deep down there was another reason, a more sinister reason. Hell, Alex and Gideon were getting to him after all. He was starting to wonder about Ophelia's true intentions.

"Good day." He nodded toward her and stated toward the stairs. He could feel Ophelia watching him with such intensity he was surprised his back didn't catch fire. Slowly, James climbed the stairs. He had no doubt she would uncover his secret eventually. Nothing happened in this estate that she did not know about.

His fingers curled into fists as he resisted the urge to pull the note out and read it again. Of course they weren't connected. How could his father be connected to Alex's or Gideon's? It was mere coincidence. James stepped into his room and closed the door. So why then did he not show Ophelia the letter? Bemused, James pulled the note from his pocket and reread it.

Do you think you might be connected as well?

"Impossible," he muttered.

He would not let Alex and Gideon fill his head with nonsense. He'd always been his own man, made up his own mind, and he wasn't about to start believing such foolishness now merely because they suggested it. Smashing the note within his fist, he tossed it into the fire, watching the flames burn the paper until nothing but ash remained.

* * *

One couldn't *sneak* into her husband's town home. No, because her husband's ever-faithful butler was always there, always waiting, always watching. Eleanor despised the man. Had from the very first moment she'd stepped into the house as Lady Beckett, wife of the esteemed Lord Beckett. She'd been an innocent, eager to please, and the butler had corrected her French, embarrassing her in front of her new husband. Her relationship with the staff had been fractured ever since. They mocked her, held no respect for her, and she knew the servants told her husband every little detail of every little thing she did. It was a house full of lies and mistrust. Unfortunately she'd been sucked into their dark world.

And now . . . now she had even more reason to be leery of the butler. She felt as if she had bathed in shame. As if the emotion hovered around her, crawled across her face proclaiming to all that she was a sinful, sinful woman. She had visited a whorehouse. She had kissed a man who was not her husband. And worst of all . . . she had liked it.

"Good day, Graham." She untied the ribbon of her bonnet, standing in the cold marble foyer. If Lavender Hills felt like a museum, this place felt more like a mausoleum.

"My lady." He stepped aside, allowing her access, albeit reluctantly, always reluctantly. He had large eyes set in a wide face with an enormous nose smashed against his skull, as if he'd been hit one too many times. He looked like a toad. An odious toad. "Did you have a pleasant time shopping?"

"Yes." She realized only too late that she held no packages. She should have known that his attempt at conversion had been a trap. "My dresses should be arriving at the end of the week."

"I shall alert the staff," he replied dryly. He thought her a silly fool who did nothing but spend her husband's money. It didn't matter that most of her husband's money came from marriage and her family fortune.

Eleanor tilted her chin high and dared not defend herself for fear that it would reek of guilt. After all, she had no need. She was the lady of the house, or so she had to remind herself. Of course the reminder hadn't helped before, and it didn't now. Not when the old gargoyle was staring down his bulbous nose at her. Truly the man would give children nightmares . . . if she had any. Thank God she didn't.

She lifted the bonnet from her head, hoping she'd done an adequate job of repining her hair, and handed the hat and her wrap to the maid who came rushing around the corner. "Is Lord Beckett in his study?"

"Yes, my lady," Graham intoned. "Although he has a visitor."

She thought nothing of his comment, and started toward the steps. Her husband often had visitors, and she certainly didn't mind the company, for it meant he was otherwise occupied. She was merely grateful she would not have to see him, afraid he'd read the guilt upon her face and know she had kissed another man. Just thinking about James sent heat to her cheeks, bringing on a profound blush that she knew was most telling.

She rested her hand on the baluster, preparing to retire when the sound of feminine laughter rang through the house. Eleanor froze. She recognized that throaty giggle. Anger and humiliation raged through her body. The guilt she felt at visiting Lady Lavender's all but disappeared.

Overcome, she spun on her heel and swept toward the study. She didn't bother to knock, but threw the door wide, letting it bounce against the wall and startle the woman seated indecently close to her husband. Christopher did not jump, of course, but merely glanced back at her with mild interest, pulling at his perfectly trimmed mustache. At least Mrs. Handler had the decency to flush and lean discreetly away from Eleanor's husband.

"I wasn't expecting you to return so quickly." He lifted his glass of scotch and drank, his gaze sweeping over her with ill-disguised annoyance. How charming he'd been when he'd courted her. Charming still upon the rare occasion when their friends and family visited. They didn't know the real man. No, only she was privy to the monster within.

She forced her lips to lift. "Obviously not."

His gaze narrowed ever so slightly. *Tread carefully*, her mother had said when she'd complained about his temper. But she'd quickly tired of tiptoeing around the man. This was her house too, her marriage, her life. Despite what the entire of England seemed to think, the world did not live to serve her husband's every need.

Mrs. Handler gave a shrill, nervous laugh and stood, brushing down the brown velvet skirts of a gown cut much too low for day wear. "I was in the area, and thought to stop for a visit."

"Of course you were." Eleanor stared daggers at the plump woman, hating the fact that five years ago she been reduced to begging Mrs. Handler to stay away from Lord Beckett. It hadn't worked, and she'd sworn she would never humiliate herself again.

Her husband leaned back and casually crossed his long legs with all the ease of a man who had no conscience. She could admit his dark hair and eyes were attractive, but if one looked below the surface, they would see the truth. "Mrs. Handler is moving in next door. She's leasing the town home."

It was the final blow. He'd stuck the dagger in her back, and that was the twist. Cold humiliation crystalized throughout her veins, her body, freezing her soul in a way that made her feel brittle. "Really?"

Mrs. Handler looked away, her round cheeks red. "Yes. As you know, my let was up, and I needed a place for me and my children."

"Of course, and there were no other homes in all of London." She threw them both a smirk. He would not crush her spirit, no matter what her punishment. He'd been able to control the young, innocent Eleanor because she cared so desperately what he thought of her. She was older, wiser, and she no longer cared.

"If you'll excuse me."

She didn't bother to curtsey. Ignoring her husband's glare, she spun around and swept from the room, determined to keep her head high. She'd been married only a short time when she'd started to hear the rumors . . . her husband had not been faithful during courtship, nor after marriage. The truth had been bad enough to swallow then, but now his mistresses were moving in next door? She'd be the humiliation of the *ton*. People would whisper behind painted fans even more than they did already. How much was she to endure? Thank God Graham wasn't in the hall; she couldn't stand to see the man now, of all times.

"My lady," Mrs. Handler called out.

Eleanor froze at the foot of the stairs, gritting her teeth. How much was she to endure indeed? Apparently a lot. Should she ignore the woman, continue up the steps? No, because then they would think she cared, and she was past caring if her husband slept with all of London. Slowly, she turned. When she spotted Graham hovering near the parlor her skin crawled.

"Graham, leave us," she demanded.

The man turned slowly and left, but she had no doubt he was listening from around the corner. The house was full of her husband's spies. She'd found that out when she'd allowed a friend to visit without his permission a week after they had married.

"What is it?" There was no need to pretend friendship with the woman. Amusingly enough when they'd first met some six years ago, Eleanor had actually thought they could be friends. Mrs. Handler had seemed genuinely kind. Maybe in another life, the woman had been. Perhaps she had merely been seduced by Lord Beckett, as Eleanor had. But her compassion for the woman had long since died.

"I want . . ." Mrs. Handler stepped closer and lowered her voice. She was pretty with her round features and full figure, yet she was the complete opposite of Eleanor. There were many nights when Eleanor lay awake wondering if her husband had ever truly been attracted to her, or if he preferred someone with a more curvy form. "I need you to know how much I care about you both."

Eleanor blinked at her, bemused. Surely she had misheard. "Care? About us both?"

"Indeed." She nodded so hard that the topknot of dark hair slipped, a silky-straight strand falling down around her chin. "I know you do not believe me, but there is nothing worse than an unhappy marriage; I should know. But I'm content now, and I only wish you the happiness that I have found."

"Yes, but you were fortunate, for your husband died."

Mrs. Handler gasped, startled by her blunt words. Eleanor didn't care. She barely cared about anything anymore, and that was the worst of it. Worse than the pain and heartache . . . the numbness.

The woman wrung her hands together, obviously nervous, as she should be. "When a man and woman are forced into a union in which they don't enjoy each other, it is not surprising that there may not be love between the two."

"That's where you're wrong, my dear." Eleanor smiled. "We were not forced. I had every intention of loving my husband. Unfortunately, he didn't love me. No, instead he loved the maid, the cook, my best friend, and that was only within the first week of our marriage."

Lady Handler flushed, tucking the loose lock behind her ear. "I'm sorry. I did not mean for him to fall in love with me."

Eleanor released a harsh laugh. "You think he's in love? Then it is I who feel sorry for you. As you will soon uncover, Lord Beckett is incapable of love." Eleanor was determined to waste no more time on the woman. She turned and started up the steps. "Have him as often as you like. If it will keep him from my bed, I bless your union."

She knew her voice carried to Graham and didn't care. She knew that Mrs. Handler would most likely tell her husband what she had said, yet she didn't bloody well mind in the least. No, because in that moment as she made her way up the steps she was determined. Determined that she would make another appointment with Lady Lavender. She was determined, just once, to know passion. Two could play his game.

She pushed open her bedchamber door, startling her lady's maid, who sat sewing by the fireplace. "Fanny, you know the Rutherfords' sinful masked ball?"

"Aye, I do." Fanny watched her warily. "Everyone does."

"Wonderful. See if you can get me an invitation. It's time I started enjoying life once more."

Her lady's maid smiled as she stood. "About bloody time."

Eleanor crossed her arms over her chest and moved to the fireplace, enjoying the warmth of the flames. She'd heard the rumors. She knew Lady Lavender often attended the ball, escorted by her male whores. If her husband was going to kill her, she might as well die happy.

Chapter 3

There was only one ball in polite society where Lady Lavender was invited every year: the Rutherfords' masked dance. It was a scandalous affair that was hardly appropriate for young bucks looking for wives and virginal debutantes, but for the more adventurous members of the *ton* it was a night they would not soon forget. James knew for a fact Lady Rutherford was no client, but merely loved to be the talk of the *ton*, and inviting Lady Lavender certainly created talk.

For the past six years, Lady Lavender had been invited, and for the past six years, James had been her escort, trusted and loyal lapdog that he was. Which made the fact that he had been suspicious of her for the last few days only add to his guilt.

He considered her a friend. They considered him her pet. He tried not to let it bother him; most of the time it didn't. But then he spotted *her* . . . Mrs. Richards, the woman who had been so aghast at his youthful age . . . the beautiful if cold-looking blonde who had left him, rejected him, really, for some reason. Aye, when he spotted her he didn't want to be seen as Lady Lavender's little toy. He merely wanted her to see him as he was . . . a man.

He shifted from behind the marble column to get a better view and watched her float across the room like a bleedin' dove amongst foxes. She wore a pink silk gown trimmed with lace and roses, the bust so low her creamy breasts were on proud display. The familiar rush of heated lust swept through his body. She belonged here, a queen amongst subjects who paled in comparison. She belonged more than any of them. It wasn't merely her beauty that set her apart from the rest, no, it was her confidence, her very being. Although she wore a mask the same rose color as her gown, he was sure the woman was Mrs. Richards. Yes, she belonged here, at balls with the wealthiest London had to offer. So why the bleedin' hell had she risked it all by visiting a brothel?

"Because if my husband ever uncovers the truth, he will kill me."

Her words had haunted him in the days since he'd seen her last. Of course any husband would be irate if he found he'd been humiliated. In fact, they'd had to deal with more than one angry spouse, which was why Ophelia kept only the most brutal of guards on staff. But there was something about the woman's words that disturbed him. Almost as if . . . as if she truly believed her husband would kill her.

He scanned the crowds and found Lady Lavender easily in her rich purple gown. Sure enough two hulking guards stood behind her. She was in deep conversation with a young, handsome dandy who had most likely been dared to speak with her. She would not notice if he slipped away.

James briefly touched his black mask, making sure it was in place, then moved along the outskirts of the ballroom, avoiding the crush of visitors, and headed toward Mrs. Richards. He did not intend to speak to her, of course. He'd destroy her reputation. But he couldn't deny that he was curious about the woman and at the very least wanted to know her real name. Was she titled? Did she have children? A million questions flooded his mind when he'd rarely been curious about any of his clients before. What was it about her that had him so enthralled?

He paused beside a potted palm, half-hidden by the plant, and took a glass of wine as a servant went by. Mrs. Richards chatted with a few patrons, but for the most part she strolled casually through the ballroom, her face unsmiling, her gaze only mildly curious, as if she'd merely stopped by on her way to something more important. Hell, what was wrong with him? He'd never cared about a client before. Caring interfered with business.

"No, it can't be," a young woman in a brilliant yellow gown whispered furiously, drawing James's attention. She stood only a few feet away, huddled close to another woman, both twitching their painted fans excitedly. "It is! That blonde hair . . . that cold demeanor . . . dear Lord, it's Lady Beckett!"

"Indeed! I never!" the older woman exclaimed.

"Neither I! The epitome of elegance and grace, here?" They both giggled behind their fans, but spotting James they broke off, flushing. They had the courage to attend the ball, the gall to gossip about others, yet they would not look him in the eyes.

"Ladies," he murmured with a slight incline of his head, intent on teasing them.

Their flushes spread and they clutched onto each other, scampering away as if he'd threatened to steal their virtue. James sighed, downing his wine, and found her again. *Lady Beckett.* A lady then. He wasn't in the least bit surprised. Her elegance and the large jewels she wore gave her away. He started to turn away, his curiosity sated, when she inclined her head ever so slightly. Their gazes met. For the briefest of moments something warm and surprising flashed in her cold, blue eyes. Shock, a little nervousness, and something else he couldn't quite identify. She jerked her attention away from him, and the moment was gone before it had barely had time to begin. But James was sure of one thing . . . she had recognized him.

Aye, she'd recognized him, and he'd been thoroughly dismissed. He watched her walk away with a small group of other elegantly dressed women. Women who would never risk their reputation by visiting Lady Lavender's, yet she had visited, hadn't she? James frowned, annoyed for some reason. He had a feeling he would never, ever see her again. Why that bothered him, he wasn't sure. He turned away from her, determined to forget the woman with the sad eyes, a woman much too good for the likes of him.

He had other clients to dwell upon and she was merely a fleeting star in a night sky full of brilliance. He glanced around the room, looking for someone who might be interested. There were plenty who whispered seductive words, who had grabbed his arse a time or two, but none of them appealed at the moment. Still, there was always a surge of interest when they made an appearance. And so he would smile mysteriously, wink at a woman or two, and come Monday there would be a few new clients added to the list.

It was the same thing every year, over and over again. Most guests at the ball were either young and curious or old and bored with life. He should be grateful for his position, he'd reminded himself repeatedly in the last few days. After all, he'd never in his life tasted champagne before he'd met Lady Lavender. Never slept on silken sheets or worn the finest of French fashion. And never would he have been able to support his family.

She'd promised him riches, and she'd come through. So he didn't mind the lewd glances and occasional wandering hand from women . . . and men. At least he had never minded before. But tonight . . . tonight was different. Tonight he felt the odd desire to crawl out of his own skin, to be free of it all, to know something different.

He shook off the unsettling feeling. He was here to do business for Ophelia, the woman he owed. More business meant more money for his family. And so he smiled charmingly at the ladies he passed, although he wanted to frown. He smiled, even when they looked him over like he was nothing more than prime horseflesh. Smiled although he knew he did not belong here and never would.

"Sir." A servant paused next to James, tray in hand.

"Thank you." James set his flute upon the tray and started to turn away, intent on capturing at least one new client that night.

"No," the man whispered furiously.

James paused, glancing back. The man's face was utterly red with embarrassment. He didn't speak, merely slid a folded note toward James. Frowning, James took the missive and moved away. Another mysterious letter. Surely Alex wasn't contacting him here, of all places. He slipped behind a column, hidden from view, and opened the note.

Head through the kitchen and meet me in the back garden.

Dare he hope that Lady Beckett had written the note? No, he wasn't that lucky. But it was obviously from a woman, if the feathery handwriting and floral scent were any indication. It must be a client, one who frequented the estate, for they were the only ones who would be so bold. He glanced toward Lady Lavender, and as she met his gaze, she understood. He needed no permission, as long as he was working.

He placed the note into his jacket pocket and followed the corridor toward the back of the house. The dancing, laughing guests did not notice, for he'd learned early in life to become one with the shadows. The farther into the house he traveled, the quieter it became. He followed the dimly lit corridor past many wealthy paintings of landscapes and dour-looking relatives. Past maids and footmen scurrying to get drinks to spoiled guests. Even past a few couples kissing in the shadowed corners. It was a ball that was not for the innocent. Nothing surprised him anymore.

At the end of the corridor he could see the serving maids rushing around the kitchen, various meals in midpreparation. He breathed deeply the scent of bread, roasted duck, and other delicious servings. It was one of many benefits of his station in life . . . the meals. Meals he never could have imagined, let alone tasted, as a lad. He turned left and headed out the back door. He knew the layout well, for he had entertained more than one tryst in Lady Rutherford's gardens.

The night air was cool and crisp. Only a few stars were visible, for they were not far enough away from London to escape the gray cloud of smoke produced by the factories. He shifted his gaze west to the stone wall and beyond. There was the countryside. Just beyond those hills. And out there, hours away, his mum and sister breathed in the clean air. Perhaps tonight they were eating his mother's famous beef stew and wondering where he was, what adventures he was on. The thought made him uneasy, melancholy.

He smoothed down his jacket and glanced around the garden, looking for signs of a gown, the giggle of feminine laughter. No one. He moved down the shallow steps and followed the gravel path around the corner to the rose gardens, the air heavy with the sweet scent of roses. A scent that reminded him all to clearly of Lady Beckett. He paused near a fountain of a naked baby spewing water from his mouth.

Not a soul, which was odd. Usually there was at least a couple or two kissing in the privacy of the gardens. He started to turn when he was greeted by the crunch of feet over gravel. Not the soft whisper of feminine slippers. No, these were heavy, hurried. A shiver of unease raised the fine hairs on the back of his neck. James spun around.

The two hulking forms that suddenly appeared from the shadows didn't exactly make him feel better. "Can I help you gentlemen?"

Gentlemen, for they were dressed in evening attire. But they were young, pocked-faced lads who were barely out of the schoolroom; spoiled brutes who were all too common in the *ton*. They were looking to prove their worth, and unless he could talk his way out of the situation, he had a feeling this wasn't going to end well.

"Yes, you can help us by leaving," the shorter man said, heading left as his friend went right. "You don't belong here."

Contempt hovered heavily around them. James knew society thought of him as the scum of the earth, the worst of all sinners. Yet Lady Lavender kept them so isolated he'd rarely dealt with such men.

"I'm sorry to report that we were actually invited. In fact, Lady Rutherford practically begs us to join her gathering every year."

"Blasphemous," the shorter man hissed. "Your kind are only welcome in hell!"

His surprise gave way to anger. "Certainly you can respect a man who is merely trying to make a living," James said, spreading his arms wide in mock innocence. He could feel the cold press of the dagger he had strapped to the inside of his jacket sleeve, and he itched to take it out and show them just who he was. One didn't grow up where he had without leaving home prepared. But he knew very well that he'd hang if he cut a gent.

"You're sinning, and you're destroying our women by seducing them. You think society won't see you in the gaols? It's coming, whore."

James's worry flared. It wasn't the first time he'd heard rumors about the government closing Lavender Hills. Is that why Ophelia had been acting so odd lately? Was she worried about her business? "Oh no, they come quite willingly, I promise. Perhaps if you spent less time harassing innocent men and more time learning to please your women, we wouldn't be having this conversation."

The taller man growled, his hands curling into fists. James felt a grim sense of satisfaction. They thought to toy with him? He was itching to hit someone, and these men would do quite well. To hell with them all.

"Demon spawn," the shorter man hissed.

"Let he who cast the first stone and all that," James said, shrugging off his jacket and tossing it atop a box hedge. He wouldn't use the knife. No, he would hang, and as discontent as he felt with life at the moment, he didn't want to bloody hang. But he sure as hell wasn't going to give in without showing them exactly who they taunted. Perhaps next time they'd think twice.

"We aren't sinners. There's a difference between gambling and drinking and becoming a whore," the taller man said, tossing his own jacket aside. They were getting down to business, and frankly, James looked forward to thinking about something other than Ophelia and Lady Beckett.

"Ah, but doesn't the Bible say that all sins are the same in the eyes of the Lord?" James rolled his sleeves to his elbows, unveiling the dagger strapped to his forearm. A little warning they took to heart, if their nervous gazes were any indication.

"It also says to smite your enemies," the man hissed. "You are destroying good people and good families because of your sinful ways."

"A bit dramatic, aren't you?" James released a wry laugh. "And which good people do you speak of . . . *you*?" His mocking laughter sent them over the edge.

"Better than you, rat."

James expected the first punch and ducked easily, jumping to the side and avoiding the shorter man's reach. What he couldn't avoid was the third man who snuck up behind him. He heard the thump of feet only too late. Suddenly James's arms were pinned behind him.

"Bastard!" James cried out, trying to twist away. "Cowards!"

The shorter man swung his arm forward, his fist connecting with James's stomach. The air burst from his lungs and stars flared to life. He would have sunk to the ground if the third man hadn't been holding him. Another fist connected with his chin, jerking his head back. Pain shot across his jaw, down his spine. He would not cry out. No, he welcomed the pain because it meant he would feel again, feel something, *anything*.

"Teach him," the man holding him said, "that no one touches our women."

Another fist hit him in the gut. His stomach cramped, and he had to swallow the bile that surged up into his throat. He didn't have time to recuperate before someone punched him in the cheek, snapping his head to the side. The animalistic need that he'd buried deep within years ago raged to the surface. The urge to rip them to pieces surged to the forefront.

With a roar, James jerked free, spinning out of reach. He hit the short man first, propelling him back into a rosebush. The anger within him would not be sated; it pushed, pulsed, becoming a thing unto itself. He swung his fist toward the taller man at the same time the coward who had held his arms kicked him in the stomach. James stumbled back, doubled over.

"Who's out there?" someone called from the back stoop, the voice echoing across the garden.

Just as suddenly as his attackers had arrived, they were gone, fleeing the scene, even leaving behind their jackets. James fell to his knees, and then onto his back, staring up at the dark sky. Weak, spent, he lay there gasping for air as music from the orchestra drifted out the ballroom windows.

He heard the rustle of a silk skirt, just barely audible over the roar of blood to his ears. The scent of roses whispered around him, and for a moment he thought he dreamt, or perhaps they'd knocked his knob too many times.

"Is he well, my lady?" A footman hovered over James, his concerned face fading in and out of focus.

"I'm not sure. Go find Lady Lavender."

Yes, it was her voice. Lady Beckett. He couldn't quite believe she was there. Stunned, he remained silent, afraid of scaring her off. A silken dress caressed his hand as she leaned down near him. He had to resist the urge to reach out and grasp onto her ankle and beg her to stay.

"What have you done?" she whispered, shaking her head. The golden curls, silver in the moonlight, swayed hypnotically over her shoulders. She pushed her mask to her forehead and scanned his face with concern.

"You shouldn't be out here," he muttered through his swollen jaw. He wanted her, but he didn't want her bloody sympathy.

"Nonsense," she whispered, sliding her arm around his waist. "Now come, sit up. You'll feel better."

He doubted that very much, but allowed her to slip her warm arm around his waist and help him to his feet. Taking advantage of the situation, he leaned into her slight frame, breathing in her rose scent. She was stronger than she looked, and he was impressed when she helped him to a crate outside the back door. The lanterns hanging from the eves spun, the merry sounds of the ball fading and pulsing in and out of focus. Aye, he'd been hit a few too many times, drunk a little too much brandy.

"Speak to me, James," she whispered, standing in front of him with her gloved hands clasped tightly against her bosom, almost as if . . . as if she cared.

"I'm well enough," he said gruffly. He would not mistake her worry for affection. No, she was merely sympathetic. He curled his hands against his hard thighs, resisting the urge to reach out to her, to bring her close and crush his mouth to hers. He merely wanted that hollow, empty feeling inside his chest to be gone. Damn it all, he wanted the peace he'd had before she arrived.

"You're not well." She settled beside him and gripped his chin, turning his face toward her. The gasp of shock and dismay that separated her lips warmed his unwilling heart. "What happened?"

"Just having a bit of fun."

She tsked. When she took out her handkerchief and started to reach toward the cut near his mouth, he leaned back. Too much. Hell, it was too much. He'd lived over ten years on his own, and this woman, with her sad eyes and kind touch, was making him crave things he couldn't have.

Her brows drew together. "Perhaps they were having fun, but I doubt you were."

"On the contrary." He took her handkerchief. Hell, he didn't even remember getting hit in the mouth. "You should leave, go back to your ball before you're missed. There is no need to risk your reputation for me."

She crossed her arms over her chest, sending her bosom so high it threatened to spill from the low neckline of her gown. Her arms were bare and the air chill, but she didn't complain. "I'm the eldest of five. Helping others comes rather naturally to me."

"I see." But he didn't see. He didn't understand how this woman who had been so cold, who had fled Lady Lavender's so quickly, could be here now, attending to his wounds. Bold as you please. He pressed the handkerchief to his lip. It smelled of rose-water, refinement, cleanliness, wealth, *her*.

"Does this happen often?" she asked, her voice softening.

There was that blasted sympathy back in her blue eyes. "No, not often. We don't go out into polite society enough for it to happen often."

"I see."

And yes, of course she saw. She saw that he was shunned. She saw that he was belittled. She saw that he was someone she should not be in association with. He shoved the handkerchief toward her. For some reason he no longer wanted her here.

"Why did you follow me?" he asked, despite himself.

Even under the dim light of the lanterns he could see her flush. "I . . . I . . ."

Slowly, James stood. "You could very well have ruined your reputation. In fact, you still could."

"I know." She stood, tucking the bloodied handkerchief into her cleavage, right where her heart beat. James swallowed hard, his chest feeling suddenly tight. She did not cringe over the dirty linen, she did not toss it aside, but pressed it there . . . close to her delicate breastbone. "It was stupid."

"Indeed."

She frowned, peeking up at him through her lashes. "I just . . . couldn't let them beat you to a pulp, you know."

She still hadn't answered his question. He worked his jaw, rolling it around and around, attempting to ease the ache, attempting to understand the confusing and tumultuous emotions that swirled within. "Yes, but why are you here?"

He didn't know why he asked, and perhaps he would regret the question, but the words slipped from his split lips before he could take them back. She looked away, gazing toward the windows alight with lanterns from the party. Guests danced and flirted, completely unaware that they were being watched. Once again he was on the outside, but she was there with him this time.

"I merely wanted a chance to talk to you."

The sudden murmur of kitchen maids caught them both off guard. Lady Beckett glanced toward the kitchen. He could sense her unease. Part of him wished she would just go and leave him be already; part of him wanted her to stay forever. Although she could be caught at any moment . . . she remained.

"What is it?" he asked warily.

She boldly met his gaze. "I've changed my mind. I'd like a meeting with you."

His heart slammed wildly in his chest as sinful images flashed to mind. This woman's long, pale limbs wrapped around him, her naked body writhing underneath, her gentle moans tickling his ear. A heated flush of desire pierced his groin.

"I see." He was surprised and, yes, bloody well interested in the prospect. The night was suddenly looking much brighter, the world a better place. "When?"

She rubbed her forehead. "Thursday next. Three o'clock."

It was all so formal. Yes, it had always been formal, a basic business transaction. But for some reason he didn't want to do business with her. He merely wanted . . . *her*. He wanted to see the coldness melt from her eyes, wanted to hear her moan his name.

"Well?" she asked, her voice a breathless, husky whisper of excitement and nerves.

"I'll pencil you in," he said dryly.

She tilted her chin high, that ice goddess back. His mockery had not gone unnoticed. "Good."

James was suddenly tired. So very tired of it all. He sank back onto the crate. He didn't want to think over his troubling emotions. He didn't want to contemplate Lady Beckett's interest. Perhaps he should start drinking to numb it all, as Gideon was prone to do. "You best return now."

"Of course." But she remained. There, in that back garden between the kitchen plants and the roses, she paused, her cool façade slipping away and worry taking its place. "You'll be all right?"

"Fine," he snapped a little too harshly.

She nodded. Biting her lower lip, she turned and fled toward the back balcony, the swishing of her skirts the only sound in the quiet night. For one long moment he merely stood there, staring at the doors where she'd disappeared inside. Had her entire presence been a dream? No, he could still smell her rose perfume surrounding him, or maybe that was merely the garden.

He followed her path as quickly as his aching body would allow, moving up the shallow staircase even though every step hurt. Through the windows he watched the wealthiest of London. Inside, the crowds had swelled but he found her moving elegantly along the outskirts of the ballroom. She belonged there, with them. Wealthy, titled, acceptable.

"James?"

Startled, he turned to face Lady Lavender. And he belonged with Ophelia, hidden away from polite society.

She lifted the hem of her skirts and started up the staircase. "Are you all right?"

He met her halfway, eager to be done with the night. "I'll heal."

Catching sight of him, she gasped. "Oh dear." She gently gripped his chin, tilting his head toward the lantern light much like Lady Beckett had done only moments ago. But whereas her touch had been one of sympathy, Ophelia was merely making sure her property was not ruined.

"What have they done to your beautiful face? Bastards."

He smiled, although it hurt. Aye, he might not trust her, but he belonged with Ophelia; he sure as hell didn't belong here. "Indeed."

She sighed, releasing her hold and slipping her arm through his. "Best if we left."

"Very well." He led her down the steps and toward the front of the house. It was over. His brief jaunt into cultured society had not been met with success. It was only a harsh reminder that he fit in nowhere, and never would.

Chapter 4

Eleanor waited impatiently in a small parlor, staring unblinkingly at the pretty French wallpaper with the little birds. Expensive, hand painted, and it was lost on her. She'd been sitting there a good ten minutes, if the porcelain clock on the mantel kept accurate time. But she did not think about the wallpaper, she did not think about her husband or family, nor did she think about her reputation. She thought only of James.

When she closed her eyes at night, she saw only James's bloody face. She smoothed her gloved hands over the dark green dress she wore, a color that matched James's eyes. A simple day gown with a jaunty black bow at her neckline and piping around the sleeves. A dress that would not identify her as the fashionable Lady Beckett.

They had beaten him, and if she hadn't noticed when he'd left the ballroom, if she hadn't followed, if she hadn't sent the footman outside when she had . . . they could have greatly injured him, or worse. And if London uncovered the fact that she had been there, in the garden with him, her life would be destroyed. Yet it didn't seem to matter to her.

Here she sat . . . waiting. Waiting for a man she couldn't stop thinking about, and all because of his kind, warm eyes and his bold and gentle touch. The door creaked open. Her entire body came alert, but she didn't dare turn. She knew who stood there. Somehow, in some way, she could sense him.

"You've returned?" He sounded only mildly surprised.

Did he care? Was he attracted to her as she was to him? Or was she merely another woman within a long line of many? She wouldn't even think about the others he'd satisfied. Besides, surely her husband had slept with just as many, yet ladies found him utterly rakish and charming.

"Yes," she said breathlessly. "I have."

"To check on my welfare?"

She stood and turned to face him fully. No hiding. No silly games. "No."

He paused halfway across the room. His black trousers, white shirtsleeves, and brown waistcoat fit his trim body to perfection. He could have been a lord; he could have been a country gent. He was neither, but for this moment, this next hour, he was hers. She studied the faded bruises that marred his otherwise perfect face, hoping to see some sort of happiness. His gaze remained stubbornly guarded.

"I see," was his only response.

How she wished she knew what he was thinking. "Are you well?"

He gave her a brief smile. "I'm fine."

For a long moment neither of them spoke. He was waiting for her explanation; she was waiting for the nerve to speak. "There are conditions . . . that is, if we are to further this relationship."

He took a step closer. "Yes?"

She licked her suddenly dry lips and paced in front of the fireplace. He made her nervous. For years, she'd wished only for the truth, honesty. Now she had it with James. There was no pretense between them, only mutual understanding, mutual need. She craved his honesty, yet it frightened her. "I wish to go slow."

"Courtly love? Candlelight? Chocolates?"

She frowned, wondering briefly if he mocked her but deciding she didn't care. Before she could continue with her list of demands, he stepped in front of her, blocking her path. She drew up short, staring first at the fine linen of his waistcoat, and then farther to his square jaw. The dark scruff that covered his lower face was most likely there to hide the bruises, but it only added to his appeal. No longer did he look the lad. Her gaze fluttered to his lips, up farther to his green eyes. No, he was no lad. He was a man, a beautiful, healthy male who knew how to please her in more ways than most.

He held out his hand. "Come with me."

It was a command. She hesitated only a moment, then slid her fingers around his. It did not matter that she wore gloves, she could feel the heat of his skin even through the leather. With a gentle tug, he started toward the door, leading her slowly into the foyer. She didn't bother to lower the netting on her bonnet.

Her heart thumped heavily against her ribs. Her knees practically buckled when her foot hit the first step. Would the guilt keep her up at night? Come morning, would she regret her decision? Up the stairs he led her, to where she knew her life would change forever. The entire world seemed to stand still; even her breath paused. She could hear the soft murmur of words and moans from behind closed doors, almost like an erotic dream. Instead of being embarrassed, the heated flush that swept through her body was something entirely different.

Desire.

She pressed her hand to her lower belly, attempting to calm the flutter of nerves. As if sensing her unease, James slid his arm around her waist, drawing her closer. Did he keep her there for support or to prevent her from fleeing as she had last time? Side by side, they fit perfectly together. She could know the same passion that was being experienced in those rooms. She *would*.

He paused outside a door and glanced down at her. "You're sure?"

"Yes."

He opened the door, revealing a room of rich green hues that matched his eyes. A pleasant room. The sort of bedchamber that a titled gent might own. But she knew what that perfectly elegant room represented . . . a den of sin, lust, carnal need. James watched her with an intensity that frightened her as much as it stirred her longing. He wanted her, but he was waiting for her to proceed.

Sinful.

The word whispered through her mind over and over, with each step into his room she took. She tore her gaze from James. She ignored the voice, ignored the feelings of guilt that swirled low, churning within her gut. Done. She was done being the scorned wife. Done watching her husband entertain mistress after mistress while she stood helplessly by.

She tilted her chin and moved elegantly around the room, surveying what would be her quarters for the next hour. "'Tis lovely."

A warm fire burned in the hearth of a marble fireplace. A four-poster bed with a dark green coverlet stood against the far wall. Red roses were in a vase upon a bedside table. It was beautiful, warm, seductive, and inviting. It was everything she had expected when she was a young innocent searching for romance, a romance that had been a myth until now. But she supposed in its own way this was not real, considering she was paying for everything. She felt James come up behind her.

Oh dear Lord. She was *paying* him. She was paying a whore. What those men had done to James in the Rutherford's courtyard would be nothing compared to what would happen to her if anyone uncovered her secret.

Sinner.

No! Damn it all, she was tired of the numbness, tired of the lack of love and passion. Tired of waiting day after day to die. This was the moment . . . the moment she would change her life . . . the moment she would stop living for others and live for herself.

She didn't care. Did *not* bloody care.

Determined, she spun around, threw her arms around his neck, and kissed James. She felt him lean back, shutting his door, heard the gentle click of the lock, but she didn't break her hold. He rested his hands on her hips and drew her up closer to his hard body. She wanted to forget, merely wanted to feel. Eleanor shoved her tongue into his mouth in a kiss of sheer determination. But James, the man she was paying to love her, pushed her back.

"Wait," he said breathlessly. "Slow down."

A fiery path of humiliation raced to her cheeks. She'd been rejected by a whore. Why not? Her own husband hadn't wanted her, not really. He'd only wanted her family's fortune and a beautiful, docile wife to get with child, a woman to control.

"Don't look at me like that." He clenched his jaw hard. She'd never quite seen him so angry. Not even while fighting the men in the garden. No, in the garden he'd seemed resigned, almost welcomed the pain they caused. "I want you."

He took her hand and pressed it boldly to the front of his trousers. The hard length of his erection met her palm. Shocked, Eleanor didn't dare move. Her breath caught in her throat as desperate need raced through her body.

"Then take me," she said harshly.

He released his hold. "Not yet. You asked for passion. You asked for romance."

"And women always get what they pay for?"

He slid her a wry glance, making her wish she'd kept her mouth shut.

"Very well." She turned away from him, staring moodily into the fireplace. Why did she always have to turn sarcastic and shrewish when confronted? Confused, unsure, she crossed her arms over her chest, feeling very much alone. "Shall you feed me chocolates?"

Warm fingers brushed the back of her neck. She hadn't even heard him approach. Eleanor trembled, closing her eyes. She'd noticed that about him . . . that he moved as silently and stealthily as a cat. A thief in the night. Unable to stop herself, she sank into his hard body, his chest warm and strong against her back. For one brief moment she savored the feel of being held, supported.

"Romance, yes?" he whispered against her ear.

She gave a jerky nod of her head. Why not? She hadn't had romance in years. It might prove entertaining. His fingers trailed down her neck, over her shoulders, brushing the area above her clavicles and undoing the jaunty bow of her bonnet. He tugged the hat free, the weight gone, and although she wore a gown and undergarments, she felt oddly naked.

"'Tis a lovely room," she said, her voice husky. Lord, had she already given the compliment? It was hard to remember, hard to think when his fingers were lightly massaging her shoulders and neck, pulling her into a deep and seductive haze.

"Thank you." Suddenly he stepped away, leaving her feeling off-balance. She didn't dare glance back to see where he went. Looking back would show she cared. Caring made one vulnerable, and she'd learned very early on in her marriage that showing vulnerability made one weak. Hell, James made her weak.

"Sherry? Wine?"

"Brandy."

From the corner of her eye she saw his smile as he moved to the sideboard, a small table with a marble top covered with shimmering crystalline decanters. He was all ease and elegance as he poured the drink, then started back toward her.

It was only as she turned to take the offering that she realized he'd rid himself of his waistcoat and wore only his shirtsleeves and trousers. Dear Lord, it was truly happening. Her pulse flickered an unsteady beat. She snatched the drink from his hand and took a gulp. The fiery spirit caught her by surprise, tearing the air from her body and making her cough.

"Careful," he said, no mockery, only concern in his eyes.

The room spun. Perhaps she should have asked for wine. "Th . . . thank you."

He took the glass and set it on the side table. "There is nothing to be nervous about."

She nodded. Why were there two of him? "I'm not nervous." It was a lie and they both knew it. What had happened to her perfectly controlled façade? She shook her head, clearing her thoughts. Perhaps she shouldn't have drunk that sherry Lady Lavender had offered when she'd first arrived.

"I do what you wish." He settled his hands on her shoulders and turned her to face him. "I stop when you wish. All you need to do is say so."

Sinful.

She ignored the voice, determined to see this through. "Well then, shall we get started?"

He smiled softly at her, the sort of smile one would give an innocent who didn't quite understand something important. Then again she supposed she was an innocent where the bedchamber was concerned. Oh, she'd heard women wax on about the passion one could find in the arms of a practiced man, but she'd assumed they were merely exaggerated stories.

James reached out and took her hand, his fingers slipping gently through hers. Palm to palm, he led her toward one of the two chairs in front of the fireplace. "Sit, please."

The instinct to decline parted her lips. It was a fight deep within her that had been born when she'd married her husband. The only way to protect herself, to keep her dignity, had been to fight back when her husband demanded anything of her. But James was not Lord Beckett. No, James had kind, warm green eyes instead of black.

And so she settled upon the chair and watched him warily as he picked up a book from the fireplace mantel. She frowned. If he thought to read to her from the Marquis de Sade, she would throw her brandy in his face. She'd unfortunately found a volume by the author amongst other disgusting readings in her husband's study when they'd been married only a year. The words and drawings had terrified her. He'd laughed at her unease, telling her that all men read the books.

Horrified, she'd fled to her parents' home, but her mother had slapped her across the face for leaving and sent her back to her husband. She'd learned her lesson then . . . the golden girl who had been her parents' shining star only shone if she did exactly what they expected of her. It wasn't about what she wanted; it wasn't about romance or love. It was about what the world expected of her.

He settled in the chair next to hers. "Shall I read?"

She didn't bother to respond.

Or maybe he'd read Byron, like most of the young bucks she'd met when she'd been a debutante. Although her husband hadn't read poetry. No, he hadn't spewed romantic nonsense, he'd been blunt and demanding and she'd thought he was a refreshing change. She'd been so very wrong. Still, she'd thought James above such nonsense.

"I count the dismal time by months and years," James started, drawing her attention to him. "Since last I felt the green sward under foot, and the great breath of all things summer-mute met mine upon my lips. Now earth appears as strange to me as dreams of distant spheres or thoughts of Heaven we weep at."

She was gone with his words, floating back to summer days as a child when she would visit her aunt Jeanie. Warm days wading in the river, stormy nights listening to the rain against the window of her bedchamber. There she was never afraid. Never. They were the days when she had felt most free.

"Nature's lute sounds on," James continued, his voice husky and enchanting, "behind this door so closely shut, a strange wild music to the prisoner's ears, dilated by the distance, till the brain grows dim with fancies which it feels too fine, while ever, with a visionary pain, past the precluded senses, sweep and shine streams, forests, glades, and many a golden train of sunlit hills transfigured to Divine."

The silence startled her back into the present. He watched her curiously, as if attempting to understand, to know her secrets. She felt as if she would drown in his gaze. She looked away, disconcerted.

"Who wrote it?" she asked, mostly to make conversation.

"A woman, actually." He gave her a brief smile. "Rather famous, Elizabeth Barrett Browning."

"What's it called?"

He settled the book upon the table, his movements slow and unhurried. "The Prisoner."

Eleanor felt dazed. Was he trying to tell her something by reading the poem? Was she so obviously the clichéd wealthy, married woman unhappy with her philandering husband?

"I don't care for poetry. I find it silly." It was a lie, or had been. At one time she had adored the sweet words of a lyrical note. But now they only made her want to weep. Poems taught one to dream. She'd had dreams at one time, long, long ago. Dreams of a knight in shining armor. Dreams of a romantic marriage.

"Is it not to your liking?" He clasped his hands together, resting them on his flat belly. He had long fingers, artistic hands. "Perhaps something else . . ."

She had no time for dreams, only for survival. Eleanor reached out, resting her hand on his sleeve. "No more."

He looked at her hand; she looked at him, mesmerized by the way his lashes lowered, throwing shadows over his cheeks. Mesmerized by the way his hair glistened almost golden under the firelight. The way that pulse beat in the side of his neck.

He was beautiful. An Adonis, and she suddenly, desperately wanted him. "Kiss me."

He lifted his gaze. "Tell me your name. Your true name."

She swallowed her fear. "Eleanor."

Heat traveled up her neck and into her cheeks, but she didn't care. Guilt be damned. She leaned closer to him, closed her eyes, and waited . . . waited. When she heard him shift, moving nearer, a jolt of anticipation swept through her. She didn't dare open her eyes, afraid she would bolt. Instead, she breathed in his musky scent as he drew closer, felt the heat from his body as he drew nearer. And then there was the slightest brush of his hand on the side of her face when he cupped her cheek. A soft caress, a gentle touch.

In her entire life she had kissed no one but her husband. She'd had no idea that kissing could be soft, gentle. No idea that she could find pleasure with a man. No, she would not think about Lord Beckett. Not now. She would merely enjoy James's mouth on hers. When his tongue slid across her bottom lip, she swore she felt a shock of lightning. Eleanor jumped, startled, and pulled back.

He did not laugh, nor sigh. He did not whisper words of compliments or love, but she could see the lust in his gaze and it fueled her own need. She didn't respond, merely closed her eyes and leaned forward. This time when her lips met his she was prepared. It was a soft press of his mouth, his lips molding carefully, gently to her own. A warm tremor raced down her spine.

Bemused, she started to pull away when his had slid from her cheek to the back of her head, his fingers in her hair. She barely had time to realize what was happening when she suddenly found herself lifted and settled upon his lap. The realization that she was sitting on his thighs was all but forgotten when his tongue delved between her parted lips. Her heart hammered in her chest, warmth flooding her body.

His kiss was not cold and slobbery, but warm and wonderful. Eleanor parted her lips, pressing her hands to his stomach, feeling the muscle and ribs and she moved up his chest to his broad shoulders. She was highly aware of his hard thighs beneath her bottom, of the rub of his tongue on hers. Highly aware of the heat spreading down her body to that aching place between her legs. A feeling she hadn't felt in years. She didn't have time to think, time to be embarrassed, for as he kissed her all rational thought disappeared. Eleanor was completely and utterly lost.

He tore his mouth from hers, his breathing harsh as he pressed his lips to her jawline. The scruff along his face scratched erotically against her sensitive neck. There was no doubt, James knew how to kiss a woman. Eleanor groaned, a completely wanton moan that tore from her throat in an animalistic way, shocking even her.

"You taste lovely," he muttered.

The hard pulse of his erection throbbed against her bottom. The urge to shift, to rock against him overtook any control. And then his teeth nipped at her earlobe, and the shivers that raced up and down her spine were almost too much to bear. Her eyes rolled back, the air suddenly heavy, her corset too tight. An aching need to have more, *know more*, trembled through her body.

He tasted like brandy, like passion, like safety. Timidly, her hands slid around his shoulders, her fingers tiptoeing over his linen shirt, sliding around his neck. Bemusement, pleasure, and need crashed through her. She'd been married for over ten years, yet her husband had never made her feel this way. She marveled over the warmth of James's body. She wanted to memorize every detail of their moment together. His hands moved from her shoulders down her arms to her waist, leaving behind a wake of heat as if he touched her everywhere at once.

She focused on that desire. There were no worries, no thoughts, only pure pleasure. His hands slid from her waist upward . . . suddenly his palms were cupping her breasts. His lips pressed to her neck as his thumbs brushed across her hardened nipples. Lost. Gone. She didn't mind a bit. Would never stop. Never wanted him to cease.

"You're beautiful." His voice had grown deeper, raspy. Although she'd heard pretty words before, they felt utterly new. He left her breasts and slid his hands down her back, around her bustle.

"Th . . . thank you," she stammered.

He gripped her arse and pulled up against his hard erection. His fingers found her skirts and bunched the material toward her thighs. She took nothing for granted, but savored it all. His musky scent, the warmth and strength of his body, the touch of his fingers as they slid underneath her skirts, brushing against the sensitive skin of her upper thighs. He was so kind, so very kind, but the feel of his steely muscles made her only too aware that like her husband, he could control her if he wished.

She wore no bloomers, and as his fingers brushed the silky nest of curls shielding her femininity, she wasn't sure who was more surprised, she or James. He pulled back, his gaze meeting hers. But there was no shock in his green eyes, only a desire that made her blush.

"Do you want me to touch you, Eleanor?" he whispered.

"Yes, please."

His finger slid between her damp folds. Eleanor's head fell to his shoulder as a groan tore from her lips. She'd been drugged, utterly seduced by the pleasure of his touch. "So very soft."

His lips nuzzled her check as his finger slid into her aching sheath. The invasion sent a sudden and unwelcome image of her wedding night flashing to mind. An image she'd thought long dead, buried.

"Spread your legs," her husband had demanded.

"But . . ."

"Shut your mouth and do as I say."

She flinched, remembering the pain as he slammed into her tight body. Eleanor squeezed her eyes shut, tried to forget her husband, that night, and her life after. Damn it all, it would never go away. Sudden tears stung her eyes, humiliating in their weakness.

The memories were there, always there, and she had her husband to remind her. He owned her body and mind.

"Stop," she demanded.

James drew back, his hand still on her bare thigh. "What is it?"

The concern upon his face overwhelmed her. No one looked at her that way anymore. No one cared. Not even her family. She felt herself softening, weakening, and she didn't like it one bit. How would she ever survive?

"Nothing." She shoved his hand away and her skirts down as far as they would go. "Perhaps this was a mistake. I'm married. This is wrong."

She started to stand but he latched onto her arm, stopping her. His grip pressed against her bruises. Eleanor sucked in a sharp breath, her heart hammering with fear. She looked away, embarrassed, confused by her own emotions.

"I will not hurt you," he whispered.

"I know that." She said the words with a fierce determination. She wasn't sure if she was trying to make him believe, or make herself.

"Eleanor, what is it?"

"Nothing, you merely startled me."

"Nonsense," he snapped.

Before she could protest, he gripped her wrist and shoved her sleeve up her arm. He went utterly still. Blast it, she had hoped he wouldn't notice, or at least wouldn't care. She didn't look; she didn't need to. When she'd received her first bruise those years ago she'd inspected it carefully, trying to understand how her husband and body could betray her. She'd hidden it away like a bastard child. But now . . . now she barely noticed them.

"My God," he whispered. "What happened?"

"Nothing." She jerked her arm away and pushed her sleeve down. Perhaps she'd wanted him to see. Perhaps she'd wanted sympathy from someone, anyone, just once. And perhaps, just perhaps, she didn't want to hide her shame any longer. But she was alone in this hellish world. No one could help her.

"I have to go." She stood, her legs weak and trembling. But she'd been weak before. With hands that shook, she scooped up her bonnet. "Thank you, James."

He stood as well. "My lady . . . Eleanor . . ."

She held up her hands, warding him off. "No, you don't understand. I've spent years hardening my heart. Your kindness will only make me weak. And weakness will get me killed." She backed up a step, two. "Please, just let me go."

Thank God, he didn't respond, merely stood there stoically and watched her turn to leave. Eleanor replaced her bonnet and opened the door. James might be concerned, but he would forget her. He had plenty of women to take her place. Sadly, she feared she would never, ever forget him.

Chapter 5

James had slept with many women in his long career. Some were still clients and friends, others had come and gone, drifting away upon the breeze of time. Some he thought of fondly, others . . . not very much at all. But never had a woman troubled him as much as Eleanor.

Five days. It had been five days since he'd last seen her. Five days since he'd uncovered the unsettling realization that her husband was a monster who abused her. He shifted, uneasy, wishing to pace away his thoughts, but that was difficult to do when one was in a carriage.

A few days ago Lady Lavender had proclaimed that they were going to London for a brief visit. London only made him think of Eleanor, everything he'd lost and couldn't have. Hell, everything reminded him of Eleanor. The scent of roses in the garden of the hotel. The taste of brandy. The husky laugh of a woman standing on the street as the carriage swept by. He'd even suggested shopping in popular districts in hopes of seeing her. Desperate, disgusting.

He'd known from the very first meeting that Eleanor was in an unhappy marriage. After all, why would she be visiting

Lavender Hills if not? But he hadn't known . . . never could have guessed . . .

He sighed, brushing aside the curtain just enough to look out onto the dusty, crowded streets of London. It was not his place to question the women or their husbands. Besides, what could any of them do? Women had very little say in their lives. And he . . . he had even less. He rubbed his brow, hoping that perhaps her husband had merely had a momentary transgression. Aye, he could hope, even if he knew it to be a lie.

Lady Lavender shuffled through her correspondences, mulling over her own problems, while the wheels rumbled over cobblestone. As the day was warm, they were headed to the gardens at Hyde Park. Ophelia enjoyed nothing more than shocking the gentry by appearing in public from time to time. Putting them in their place, as she called it. But he knew they were in London for another reason. She was investigating something or someone.

A small crease formed between her golden brows as she scanned a missive. Something important indeed was troubling her. James studied her pale face, the dark smudges under her eyes confirming that she hadn't been sleeping. Her narrow waist seemed even smaller, if possible. Despite his troubling suspicions toward the woman, he couldn't help but be concerned.

"Is all well?" he asked.

She glanced up, and in that unguarded moment, he saw her for what she truly was . . . merely a woman worried. A beautiful and wealthy woman, but still merely a woman. A human being, if one would. Nothing to fear, nothing to admire. Something inside him eased, as if a knot had come loose. She smiled at him, and in that moment it felt like they were friends again.

She waved the missive aside, dropping it to the seat. "Not at all. Merely from Gideon. He will be staying longer than we'd agreed."

In other words, the man hadn't asked for her permission. Typical Gideon. It was no secret that he and Ophelia despised each other. "I'm surprised you let him leave at all."

She flushed, her eyes growing hard, and he remembered only too late that she didn't like to be questioned. "'Twas good business."

He'd overstepped his bounds. At times it was so bloody hard to tell when he could speak freely and when he couldn't, even after all these years together. He was her favorite because he respected and appreciated what she had given him . . . a chance at life. The entire staff knew she preferred him, yet he couldn't deny that he often wondered how much he truly knew about the real Ophelia. James resisted the urge to sigh as they rolled down Regent Street.

"Of course, my apologies for interfering."

Uneasy once more, he glanced out the window. He'd never enjoyed London, although he wouldn't voice any complaints. It reminded him too much of childhood. The stench of the Thames, the unruly crowds, the dust that hovered in the air from the coal and factories. He much preferred the countryside where one could breathe. But he supposed that was the Irish in him.

"I don't trust her," Ophelia admitted.

James slid her a glance. "Her?"

"The woman who hired Gideon, I don't trust her." She was handing him an olive branch by admitting as much. "We're in London so that I might have Wavers uncover what he can about the family."

"I see." He knew better than to question her further, although he could admit to himself that his mind was spinning with curiosity. What the hell was Gideon up to? One never quite knew. In all honesty, James didn't understand why Gideon still worked at Lavender Hills. Perhaps Alex was right and there was something holding him there. They all had secrets.

"James, do stop the carriage. I'd like to shop at the antiquities store near the corner. The one where I picked up that lovely Chinese vase last summer?"

"Of course." She always shopped when something was bothering her. It was a way to forget, he supposed.

He knocked on the roof. The carriage pulled to the side of the lane because Ophelia demanded immediate obedience in her staff. The door opened and James stepped outside, quickly scanning the streets, making sure there were no threats, no angry husbands out for revenge. In a way he wasn't only whore and friend, but also guard. He turned to help Ophelia down.

She stepped gingerly from the carriage, ignoring the gasp of shock from her fellow shoppers. Protective mothers took hold of their daughters' hands and rushed them away. Husbands glared. Some visitors had not yet noticed them and stood peering into windows, chatting with friends and family. But they would turn and stare soon enough. Another reason he hated London, for everyone knew precisely who they were and where they went at all times. The gossip rags would be full of information come tomorrow morning, most of it exaggerated half-truths.

He started to turn toward the antique shop when he spotted a group of four women standing near a dressmaker's window. For a brief moment he merely stood there, wondering what had drawn him to their party. They were a pretty lot of varying ages, a wealthy group if one were to go by the fit and cut of their clothing. He started to turn away when one woman stepped back, separating herself from the others, and suddenly he knew the reason for his interest. His breath caught in his throat.

"I'll only be a moment," Ophelia said to the footman and driver, but James was barely aware.

He was too fascinated by the tallest woman in the group, the one who stood to the side as if she didn't belong . . . Eleanor. The veil covering her face hid her from prying eyes, but he knew the gentle roundness of her jaw, the golden sparkle of her coifed hair, the fullness of those lips.

"Do you mind if I stroll?" James asked Ophelia, tearing his gaze from Eleanor. "My legs are cramped."

"Of course." She moved toward the shop, flanked by her two bodyguards, without concern or suspicion. She trusted him, and that thought made him feel guilty, but not enough to stop him. As she disappeared inside, he returned his attention to Eleanor.

Although she stood tall and serene, a veritable goddess, there was something about her stillness that reeked of loneliness. Slowly, he started toward her, drawn by some invisible connection he didn't understand. He only knew that he desperately wanted to protect her.

"I'd say emerald is my color, don't you agree?" one woman asked the other, but Eleanor remained quiet, so still, so lost that she didn't even notice him until he was directly behind her.

"Tell your friends you are taking a hack home," he whispered near her ear. "You don't feel well."

She stiffened, but thank God, didn't glance back. For a moment he thought perhaps she didn't recognize his voice. He could not speak louder, he could not grab her hand and tear her away, as much as he wished. Desperate, he curled his fingers in silent frustration, unsure how to get her to agree, short of abducting her.

"Why?" she finally whispered.

The joy he felt at her response was maddening. Even though he knew it was uncouth to have feelings for his clients, it didn't seem to matter. "I'm saving you. Now, tell them, head down the footpath, and then turn right."

Whistling a tune under his breath, he strolled down the footpath as if he hadn't a care in the world, merely a man out for a leisurely stroll. He paused where the street intersected with another, feigning interest in the passing carriages, but all the while he watched her from the corner of his eye.

Instead of ignoring his demand like a good lass, she actually took a few steps back from her friends. "I feel a slight headache," he heard her say. "I really ought to return home."

"Are you sure?" an elder woman asked.

James didn't wait to hear more but turned on his heel and headed right, the euphoria of being with Eleanor again superseding his common sense. Ophelia would notice his absence, of course. He wasn't sure where he was going or how long he would be gone, and he would most likely have to lie upon his return, something he rarely, if ever, did. None of it mattered. No, because the only thing that mattered was being with Eleanor once more, even if for a moment. A shiver of awareness caressed his spine, a tingling awareness that said she followed behind him. Spotting a cab, he lifted his arm and waited near the edge of the street.

"What are we doing?" Eleanor whispered behind him.

He latched onto her hand without even looking at her. "Come, hurry." He gripped her waist and tossed her inside the hack before someone noticed. "Toward Westminster, please," he said to the driver.

"Aye, governor."

He jumped into the cab and closed the door so they were hidden from prying eyes, praying they had not been spotted. How stupid he was to put her in danger. Selfish, greedy, for he could admit he wanted desperately to see her, talk to her, touch her again. He was doing this for himself, as much as for her. Sadly, he didn't feel the least bit of guilt.

"Where are we going?" she asked breathlessly, half-hidden in the shadows.

"Somewhere we can . . . talk." He leaned forward and lifted her veil. The unwashed reek of the cab was slowly being invaded by the light scent of roses. "There. Much better."

She flushed but didn't look away, her gaze bold and daring. Obviously she wanted to be here as much as he wanted her with him. The realization was tantalizing indeed. Neither spoke about their mutual attraction. Neither admitted how reckless they were being.

"There is a little tea shop not far. It's highly unlikely you'll be recognized there."

"If I am?"

She did not seem worried. The air practically vibrated with an odd mixture of tension, attraction, hope . . . but not worry. He shrugged, leaning back, feeling oddly relaxed. "I'd be happy to drop you off near your home. 'Tis your decision to make."

For a long moment, as the carriage rattled through London, she didn't speak. They were both tempting fate, and they both had so much to lose if caught. Neither seemed to care.

Finally, her shoulders sank and she fell back into the cushions, grinning. "No. I rather feel like some tea."

James grinned in kind. He'd never seen her smile, he realized. Yes, a mocking smile, a cold, demure smirk, but never this . . . purity. Innocence. He could almost imagine her as a debutante, before her husband had ruined her. Yes, he'd known the moment he met her that her marriage was not a happy one; he'd also guessed that deep down she craved adventure, happiness, excitement. But didn't everyone? "Are you sure?"

She leaned forward and nodded. "Positive. Now, tell me what you are doing here."

Although the scoop of her neckline was demure by most standards, he couldn't help but notice the creamy curve of her breasts. He clenched his jaw and forced his gaze upward. She wore a gown the color of the summer sky when a storm was approaching . . . a blue-gray that made her eyes sparkle.

"Lady Lavender has business in London."

"I see." She was quiet as she played with the tassel that hung from her reticule. "And do you always escort her wherever she goes?"

He shrugged, knowing there was an underlying question there. He might not be an expert in love, but he'd catered to enough women to know when there was something amiss. "Usually."

"I see."

And so did he, he saw very well indeed. He smiled as he moved across the coach and settled beside her. Much to his pleasure she didn't move away. "What, exactly, do you see?"

She glanced up at him through her thick lashes. "You are her favorite."

He shrugged. "Perhaps."

She stared at his thigh where it pressed intimately against hers. Even through the layers of her skirts he felt her heat. Craved her heat. Her touch. Her kiss. His gaze dropped to her lush mouth, then lower to her elegant neck where a pulse fluttered like a butterfly.

"And will she not be angry when she finds you are missing? Or did she give you permission?"

He leaned closer to her, breathing in the clean scent of woman and rose soap. "Can I trust you with the truth?"

"Of course."

He pressed his lips to the shell of her delicate ear. She shivered beneath him. "I snuck away."

"Oh." She was quiet for a moment and he wondered what she was thinking. When he'd never cared much before about his clients and their thoughts, he found he wanted to know everything about Eleanor.

"Why?" she asked, looking up at him. "Why did you sneak away?"

He drew back, noting her flushed cheeks with satisfaction. She liked him, perhaps as much as he liked her. Perhaps more. The realization sent his pulse pounding. He could have her . . . so easily here and now. She was ready and willing to be seduced, and he was an expert. Damn it all, she deserved better than a tickle in a carriage. "Because I noticed a woman who seemed utterly miserable. And I can't abide it when a woman looks ready to cry."

She clenched her jaw, that resolute look of determination hardening her gaze once more. "No need to worry. I never cry."

He wasn't sure whether to be amused or saddened over her admittance. "Never?"

"Not any longer."

"Because your life is so wonderful?"

"No games," she said, shaking her head. "We both know that I would not have visited you if my life was wonderful. I do not cry because . . . because he enjoys it too much."

James stiffened, his amusement fading. Pure rage rushed through his body like nothing he'd ever experienced before. Hot one moment, cold the next . . . he no longer felt in control of his emotions. What the bleedin' hell had happened to him?

He didn't dare react, but remained calm, relaxed against the seat. "Your husband?"

"I do not wish to speak of him. You have possibly ruined my reputation and my life. If this should be my last day, then I demand you make the deed worth it."

He reached out, sliding his fingers down her smooth cheek and tucking a silky lock of hair behind her ear. "Very well." He leaned close, so close his lips brushed hers. "Prepare, my lady Eleanor, for the most pleasant day of your life."

He slid his fingers under her chin, tilting her head back and intending to thoroughly kiss the woman when the carriage slowed. "Blast it," he muttered a mere breath away from her mouth.

Eleanor giggled. James drew back, surprised and delighted by such an innocent laugh. Her eyes shone with the light of a woman who had no idea about the wicked ways of the world. She looked . . . happy. He had made her that way. As much as it thrilled him, the thought also terrified him, for he knew their relationship was only temporary. What if she came to rely upon him? Hell, what if he couldn't get her out of his mind?

When the carriage stopped, James was actually relieved. He pushed open the door, tossed some coins to the driver, and turned, reaching for Eleanor.

"'Tis raining," she said, as she peeked outside. Her veil was back in place, her identity a mystery once more. He glanced up at the gray clouds. He hadn't even noticed the drizzle.

He held out his hand and took her small palm in his, rethinking his rash decision to steal her away, rethinking his entire life. He wasn't even sure what had induced him to bring her here, of all places. "Yes, but rain is good."

She tilted her head to the side in a thoughtful manner. "Why?"

"Well, for instance, rain makes the flowers grow." He nodded toward the foxglove growing in patches on the grounds of the church. A church he'd visited often as a child. Suddenly the memories came flooding back, churning through his body, tearing at his soul. He took in a deep, trembling breath and forced his attention to Eleanor.

Even though her face was covered, he could tell she smiled. "That is all you have to offer?"

"Rain will keep people inside." He forced himself to speak although his heart was thumping madly. He looked around the area at the many unfamiliar faces, expecting to see his sister, even himself, in the eyes of the children who strolled by. "Which means it is less likely that we will be noticed."

"I will grudgingly give you that."

"Truly kind of you." He tightened his hold on her hand.

She kept him grounded, he realized quite suddenly. When he'd gone through life in a numb, albeit content, existence . . . she'd forced him into the world. He wasn't sure how to feel about that realization. "And you might be able to use the rain to your advantage. For instance, if someone asks where you were . . . you might say the carriage was stuck in the mud."

She slid her arm through his, and although her body merely brushed his side, he felt her heat all the way to his soul. They started through the gardens of Westminster. "Do you always look on the bright side?"

"Why not? The alternative is to be bleak and miserable."

"It's very hard to be happy when those around you are determined to see you aren't."

"I'm sure it is," he said, squeezing her hand gently. He didn't like the look she wore; it was all too common where he had come from. Hopelessness, defeat. He wanted her smiling again. "Cremorne Gardens, have you been? We are going tomorrow evening."

She stiffened, that proper missus still there, deep down. "Of course not. It's not exactly a place for someone like . . ."

He quirked a brow, amused. "You?"

She looked away. "No, someone like my husband. As we are married, what I do affects him." She gave him a forced smile. "Now, where are we? How do you know this area? I am not quite sure I won't run into anyone I know."

"I used to live only a few streets away a long, long time ago when my father was a driver for a wealthy lord."

She jerked her head toward him, obviously surprised. "I see. And after?"

"This way." He led her underneath a yew. "We eventually moved to a . . . cheaper spot."

"I see."

And it was obvious by the gentling of her voice she did see. When his father had lost his job they'd thought he'd easily find another. He hadn't. Their money had dwindled, until . . . he drew her closer as a group of young factory working bucks came strolling by, their eyes a bit too greedy when they gazed upon Eleanor's fine figure. Eleanor didn't judge him, although she had every right. She did not look down upon him although she could have. He realized, with a start, that he was glad she was here. He wanted to share his memories with her.

"You are holding me rather close," she whispered. "It's rather presumptuous of you."

"We have kissed."

"That does not give you the right to handle me like I'm a doll, or child."

"I would never presume as much." He knew her game. She wanted to retain that façade of control, as if she had some say in her life, because in reality she had so very little. "I merely did not want to draw attention. Two well-dressed people walking as friends would draw attention. But like this . . . as a couple we don't."

It was a lie, of course. Eleanor would draw attention no matter where she went and with whom. Her bearing, her beauty . . . she was like no other.

They left the gardens and started down the lane. "We'll pretend to be married then?"

He nodded. "It would be for the best." She didn't respond but he could tell that brilliant mind of hers was spinning. He wondered what she thought, desperately wanted to know. He tore his attention from her and gazed across the road.

"There it is." He smiled, feeling an odd mixture of emotions. "Still here after all these years."

It was a small corner shop that sold sweets and tea. He and his sister had visited the shop often for a treat when his father had worked nearby. But he realized quite sadly the memories were bitter and better left in the past. The rain thickened. Perhaps it was better not to dredge up a lost cause. Yet something pulled him to that building on the corner.

"Hurry." He latched onto her hand and started running across the street, fearing that the tea shop would fade away into the approaching mist and he'd lose all chance to know who he had been. It was an odd mixture of longing and desperation that made him move.

"James!" Eleanor laughed as her feet slipped over the cobbled streets. But he held her tight; he would not let her fall. They paused at the door, catching their breaths.

"Are you well?" he asked.

She straightened her bonnet, making sure the netting was in place. "I suppose."

They glanced at the windows, both wishing to step into the warmth but neither wanting to be recognized. Only two women were inside drinking tea and chatting near the counter. It had changed, he realized with a start. The shop might still be here, but it was different in some way. The area was more crowded with buildings and people. The shop itself had been a red brick that was now painted white. Everything and everyone had moved on without him.

"Shall we go in?" Eleanor asked softly, as if sensing the turmoil within.

He nodded and pulled open the door, a bell overhead jingling merrily. As he stepped inside, following Eleanor, the world became entirely too real. His past and his present did not belong together, yet here they were, clashing within that very moment.

"James?" Eleanor whispered, watching him curiously.

He forced his lips to turn upward. He was so bloody good at acting as if everything was well, it came naturally even when he wanted to scream, to hit something. He pulled out a chair from a small table near the window where they could watch others run from the rain, their umbrellas doing little under the fierce wind. "I'm sorry. Is this all right?"

"Yes, quite well."

He nodded and headed toward the counter. His body was not his own. He couldn't seem to feel his heart beat inside his chest. His skin tingled, his lips numb. He headed toward the old man who was busy placing cakes underneath a glass stand. "Tea please, and a pair of those petits fours."

The old man behind the counter straightened and nodded. It wasn't until he stood that James recognized him. Shock and dismay chilled his very being. Deep wrinkles marked the area around his eyes and mouth. What hair he had left had turned gray. "Of course. Will bring it to you."

Mr. Swift. The man who had always given them an extra peppermint, winking and whispering not to tell his wife. Mr. Swift, who had seemed old then, even older now. So much older. The world had changed, there was no going back.

From the kitchens he could hear Mrs. Swift singing, the sound so familiar that for a moment he almost felt six again. Rationally he hadn't expected to see them here after all these years. If they recognized him, how would he explain his sudden appearance?

How would he explain Eleanor? Unsettled, he turned and headed back to the table.

"They're all so busy," she said, watching the people race down the footpath, off to work or perhaps to the shelter of their homes. Except for them. They were here because neither of them truly had a home. Not anywhere safe and warm and comforting. And for the moment they belonged here in this tea shop as much as they belonged anywhere else.

"Most people are, aren't they?" he replied softly. "Always in a hurry."

"No." She lifted her netting yet kept her back to the shop so the few patrons would not see her face. "Not my acquaintances. They lie around in bed half the day."

He didn't miss the fact that she called them acquaintances and not friends. Did she have any friends, anyone loyal to her? Anyone she could go to for assistance? He was prevented from asking when Mr. Swift appeared, tray in hand.

"Thank you," James muttered, somewhat relieved when the man merely nodded and left them in peace. "Do you not have friends to chat with and visit?"

She lifted her cup and sipped, taking her tea plain. "Perhaps. But they don't truly know me. My dreams and hopes." She released a wry laugh. "I sound like an utter ninny."

"You don't." In other words, they didn't know her husband abused her. They didn't know she lived a life of pain and suffering. No, because she did a damn good job of hiding it behind a façade of a woman of elegant perfection. The perfect life. He suddenly understood why he was so drawn to this woman . . . they were both playing a part. Both trapped and trying to make the best of it.

"What happened?" she asked, leaning over the table, closer to him. "Why did you move away from here?"

He had a feeling she was trying to change the subject. He dropped his gaze to the brooch at her neck, a colorful French painting of a couple embracing. It looked like an antique, something his mother had owned once . . . before she'd started selling her jewelry for food. "My father lost his position and then his life."

"Oh James, I'm so sorry." The kindness in her eyes was almost his undoing. If only someone had shown such compassion back then. She wrapped her gloved hands around her teacup. "Did you move in with relatives?"

"No. My mother tried to work in the factories, until it nearly killed her. Fortunately, Lady Lavender found me just in time." He drank his tea, letting the warm liquid soothe him. "If it weren't for her, my mother and sister would never have made it out of the slums. I probably wouldn't have lived."

"You send the money to your mother and sister?"

He nodded. Her eyes softened, and he was lightly sickened by her obvious concern. She dropped her gaze to the little cakes with white-and-pink frosting, as if embarrassed to show she cared. "It's very kind of you."

"Believe me, I'm not martyr." He didn't particularly want to discuss his past, and he certainly didn't want to discuss his position at Lady Lavender's, at least not with Eleanor. "The brooch . . . where did you get it?"

She lifted her hand to her chest, smoothing her fingers over the piece, a painted brooch of lovers embracing. "It's nothing really. A cheap trinket. It was my aunt Jeanie's. The only thing of hers that I own."

Obviously the woman was important to her, but he didn't push the subject. He noticed the hint when she quickly grabbed a little cake and stuffed it in her mouth.

Her eyes widened in surprised delight. "Oh my."

He grinned. "Still good?"

She covered her mouth with her hand as she chewed and spoke at the same time. "Not good, delicious."

"They were my sister's favorites." He immediately regretted the remark, having no desire to discuss his past or family. But the words had slipped unguarded past his lips. She didn't push him. It was yet another thing he respected about this woman, this stranger, really. Both of them had pasts, both of them had secrets, but neither of them pushed the other to give more than they could.

She glanced back at the counter where Mr. Swift was clearing away dishes. "How have they not been discovered?"

"They have, but they won't move."

"They'd be quite the thing at my next gathering . . ."

He rested his hand atop her gloved one. "Eleanor, darling, you can't hire them; they would realize your true identity."

"And who am I?" She frowned and pulled away. It was a harsh reminder that they were merely playing house. Pretending to be a happy couple. "A wife? A sinner? And don't call me darling."

"Why not?"

"It's what my husband used to call me, before we married."

So, Lord Beckett had charmed her until the marriage papers were signed and sealed, and then the true monster had appeared. Perhaps they'd both been tricked into a life neither wanted. "Fine. I'll call you Ellie, then."

She looked up, startled.

"Yes, I shall call you Ellie."

"It's what my aunt used to call me." Her face grew soft, her eyes hazy. He knew in that brief moment she was back there, with her aunt, a woman who was obviously special to her. A memory that she cherished. She sighed, shaking her head, and the fog of the memory cleared. "I really don't know why you must call me anything. After today we shall most assuredly never see each other again."

The truth, yet it didn't sit well with him. Damn it all, he liked being with her. At Lady Lavender's he felt trapped in an endless future. In London he felt trapped in the past. But here, with Ellie, there was only the present.

"Blessed be!" a familiar feminine voice cried out. "I'd know ye anywhere, James McKinnon!"

James flinched. It was too late to run. "Blast it."

Eleanor seemed more amused than worried. "James *McKinnon*, is it?"

"My dear boy!"

Mrs. Swift raced toward them, a whirlwind of activity. Age could not change that about her. The woman came to a stumbling halt before their table, her large bosom bouncing as she clapped her hands in front of her, releasing a puff of white flour into the air.

"I never in my life thought to see you again. How are you?" She reached out, flapping her arms as if she wasn't quite sure what to do with them. James had the horrifying feeling she wanted to hug him.

"Good, very good indeed." James stood as the woman's husband shuffled toward them, grinning a toothless grin. He had the good decency to look somewhat embarrassed by his wife's burst of energy.

"Thought I recognized ye," he said. "Told Mrs. Swift, I did, to catch sight of the young man out front."

James gave them a tight smile and rubbed the back of his neck. Wonderful, he could thank Mr. Swift for this reunion. The other patrons had turned and were glancing toward them with a curiosity that didn't put him at ease.

"It's been ages!" Mrs. Swift said. "Where do ye call home? Please, ye must tell us everything!"

"There isn't much," he muttered, raking his hand through his hair. The fact that both Mr. and Mrs. Swift looked so very excited to see him made James ill. If they only knew what he truly did to survive, he doubted they'd be so happy to see him.

"Do you have children?"

He didn't miss the hopeful plea in Mrs. Swift's voice, as if all anyone lived for was having children. He glanced Ellie to share her amusement, but she had grown sullen and was staring at the tabletop. Something had changed. Perhaps she was worried about being recognized, or tired of the deceit.

"Two children," he said softly. "Two girls."

Ellie glanced up at him. This was not the dominating, cold woman who ruled the *ton*. This woman was sad, lost, alone. Something was wrong, very wrong.

"We have a lovely town home in Chester," he added. "But are merely visiting London."

"Oh, I'm so happy fer ye." Mrs. Swift rested her hand on his shoulder. "After yer da passed on, I wasn't sure what became of ye. Then ye left without word. When yer poor Mum died, I wasn't sure if we'd ever see ye or yer sister again."

Suddenly the world came sharply into focus. James stiffened, his heart hammering wildly in his chest. *"When yer poor Mum died, I wasn't sure what had become of ye or yer sister."*

Mum, dead? No, he'd misheard, or . . . or she was wrong. "My mum?" They were the only words he could seem to get past his suddenly cold lips.

"Aye." She shook her head, sighing. "Her death was a shock to us all. Hard to believe it's been five years. How we missed your little round faces visiting the shop."

But he was barely aware of what she said. Barely aware of the people around him. The floor suddenly felt very, very far away. The room spun, his body growing numb. No. It couldn't be. The thought that his mother was dead, had been for some time, seemed incomprehensible.

"We must go," Eleanor said gently, slipping her hand into his. Her touch brought him back into a harsh reality he didn't want to explore. "But it has been lovely meeting you, truly."

He didn't hear their words of farewell. Was barely aware as Eleanor led him from the shop. The world had gone muted, gray. His mum . . . *dead*. Five years. How? He shook his head and jerked his hand from Eleanor's kind grip. No, it couldn't be. He wouldn't believe it.

"You didn't know," Eleanor said.

They paused there on the footpath while the rain fell heavy around them, soaking their clothing. She didn't have her veil down. For some reason that bothered him. He didn't respond as he reached for the gauzy material and tugged it over her face. It was a lie, or a misunderstanding. She couldn't be dead. He would have heard.

"Oh James, I'm so sorry."

He was briefly aware that she felt compassion for him, true sorrow. How very odd. He felt nothing in return. No anger. No pain. Not even shock any longer. He lifted his arm and hailed a cab. It wasn't true; it couldn't be. "Are you well enough getting home on your own?"

She nodded. "Of course."

He helped her into the carriage.

"James," Eleanor whispered, her voice catching. "I'm so sorry."

He didn't respond, merely nodded to the driver. The carriage took off with a jerk, the curtain fell into place, and he could no longer see Ellie. Still he stood on the footpath while the rain soaked his clothing, trailed down his face in rivulets.

His mother was dead? But that would mean Lady Lavender hadn't told him the truth. James watched the carriage disappear around the corner. It would mean, dear God, that Alex and Gideon had been right about the woman all along.

Chapter 6

The rain had tapered off, but it didn't matter much as Eleanor was a sodding mess by the time she reached home. As always the door opened before she even reached the stoop. Eleanor handed her dripping bonnet to Graham, not bothering to say a word to the man. Instead, with her chin high, she swept up the stairs and through the house, leaving behind a trail of rainwater and not feeling the least bit guilty about the mess.

Graham didn't matter. Her husband didn't matter. Even her own problems didn't matter. The only one who seemed to matter was James. James and the shock he'd experienced when he'd found out his mother had died. James and the hollow look in his gaze as he stood on the footpath in the rain, watching her leave.

Nothing made sense anymore. Not her feelings for this man, not his loyalty to a brothel owner whom Eleanor knew didn't give two figs about him, and not the death of his mother. If Lady Lavender had been sending money to his family, wouldn't she have known about his mother's death? Life had made her a cynic, but she could admit, grudgingly, that perhaps Lady Lavender had not told him out of kindness.

She managed to make it to her chamber without running into her husband. Fanny was waiting for her in the attached dressing room, the older woman napping in a chair. At the sound of Eleanor's approach she jumped. The nervousness upon her face would have been amusing if Eleanor hadn't known whom the woman feared. Everyone was ill at ease in this house thanks to her husband. It was a dark and dreary place indeed.

"Dear God." Fanny stumbled to her feet. "What a sight you are."

"Help me out of this dress? It's become quite chill and heavy."

When she'd first married, she'd had a young, vivacious lady's maid who had become quite dear to her. After the first few months of marriage, her husband had fired the girl while Eleanor had been at church. She had her suspicions that her husband had flirted with the maid and been rebuffed. Or perhaps her husband had merely wanted to get rid of anyone she might care for.

"Of course, my dear." Fanny helped her undo the bodice. "Poor child."

When she'd hired Fanny three years ago she'd been truthful with the woman . . . she would be let go if they became too close. Instead of keeping her distance, they'd merely decided to remain reserved toward each other in her husband's presence. She didn't know what she'd do without Fanny, the only person who knew the truth about her life, the only person who cared.

No, that wasn't true. She paused, glancing out the small round window to the gray skies above. James knew, and he seemed to care. Perhaps it was an act, or merely typical human compassion. She sighed as she stepped out of her sodden skirts. Yes, James was a stranger, yet he knew she despised her life. He knew she craved the pleasure between a man and woman. He knew her deepest, darkest secret, and he could destroy her if he wanted. The realization struck her hard. She'd handed her power over to another, something she'd sworn never to do again. She'd turned into a fool and all because of a man with moss-colored eyes.

"Where have you been?" Fanny whispered.

"Merely . . . out. I came home early because of a headache."

She tsked. "Best come up with a better excuse. Your mother-in-law returned to check on you an hour ago."

A cold chill washed over her that had nothing to do with her damp clothing. Her mother-in-law knew. Her husband knew. Frantically she clawed through her mind imagining and discarding excuse after excuse.

"When she found you were not here, she grew oddly silent, suspicious-looking witch." Fanny took her robe from the hook. "I don't know what you're up to, and I don't want to know. But remember to feign normalcy when you lie, hold their gazes, and for God's sake, don't blush."

Eleanor nodded, nerves getting the better of her. She felt ill, her stomach roiling with a familiar tension. Always tension; she was bloody sick of the worry. "No, not the wrap, a dress. The plain brown with the satin trim."

Fanny quirked a brow but returned the robe. "You know he'll kill you if he finds out you're doing something he doesn't approve of."

Blunt words, but the truth. She realized Fanny was merely trying to warn her. "I know," Eleanor whispered. But truth was he would probably end up killing her anyway. Why should she not enjoy herself before it happened? She released a harsh laugh. Yes, she was mad indeed.

"Did anyone see you?" Fanny asked kindly.

"No. I don't think so."

"Well." She pulled the dry dress from a hook. "All will be well then. Let's not worry when nothing has happened and might not."

The woman pulled the gown over Eleanor's head. Fanny might put on a brave face, but she was just as frightened of Lord Beckett as the rest of the staff. Eleanor could see the woman's hands trembling as the smoothed her skirts over her crinoline.

Eleanor grasped Fanny's shoulders and pulled her to her feet. "It was worth it. Not just what I did, but—" She paused, trying to find the right words. "Just being myself for once. The freedom of it all. It was worth it, no matter what happens."

Fanny's lower lip trembled, the fear in her brown eyes genuine and disturbing. "Will it be worth it if he kills you?"

Eleanor sighed and pulled the woman close, hugging her. She suddenly missed her family. Her younger sisters and brothers, the loving kisses and companionable touches. Affection. She missed affection. "That moment of freedom will last me for years."

"Or it will give you the itch to have more."

Fanny knew her too well. "No," she lied, pulling back. "Of course not."

As Fanny parted her lips to argue, they heard the door to her bedroom squeak open. A noise that sent a chill down her spine. They both stiffened, remaining eerily silent. She refused to allow the servants to oil the hinges, for she'd wanted a warning when her husband arrived.

"It's him," Fanny whispered. "I can feel the wave of evilness."

Eleanor felt the manic urge to laugh. Truth be told, Fanny was right. She swore she could sense the man and his darkness. She'd learned early on to control her features, to always retain a calm façade so as not to incite her husband. But even now, after years, inside she cried out in fear. Would this be the day, she wondered as she always did, that he killed her?

"Shhh." She turned, giving Fanny her back. "Button my gown. Hurry."

"Darling," her husband called out in an overly jovial voice that crawled across her skin. The nicer he was, the more she had to fear. Dear Lord, did he know already? Terror clawed at her gut. She knew he'd had spies follow her in the past, but usually when she went out with his mother he let her be, trusting his mum, if not her.

"Coming," she called back.

"Go," Fanny whispered, pushing her forward. The servant knew the longer they kept him waiting, the angrier he'd become. It was all about power with her husband. He liked to control his surroundings, his life, and the people within it. Unfortunately, he had enough money and position in society that he could.

She pushed open the dressing room door and stepped into her bedchamber. "What is it?" There was no point in being polite. He would most certainly think something was wrong if she didn't act her normal cold self.

His icy blue gaze roamed over her face. "Mother said you left early because of an aching head."

Do not blush, do not blush.

She nodded, moving to her dressing table and pulling the pins from her hair, her back to him. "Yes. You know how trying shopping can be." At one time she'd loved to shop. Had been thrilled when her husband had been generous with his spending money. It was the one thing he lavished upon her . . . clothing, shoes, bonnets. But she realized soon enough that it was merely another way to control. He would not have a wife who was not wearing the highest of fashion; what would it say about him? And so her love of shopping had faded, much like her love for most things.

He strolled toward her, his reflection visible in her mirror. He wore a suit as black as his heart and eyes. "You shouldn't travel alone."

She told herself to keep breathing, to smile prettily, to act as if nothing out of the ordinary had happened. "I was quite safe."

He took the brush from her table and began to stroke her long locks. She stiffened, resisting the urge to shove him away. How she hated when he touched her, hated it even more when he pretended to care.

"Then think of your reputation," he said.

His reputation.

"If anyone would have seen you traveling alone, your name, and *mine*, would be tarnished." He pulled the brush through her hair. To anyone else it would have looked like a loving touch, but she knew better. She felt the slightest tightening of his hand in her hair.

He sighed. "First the Rutherford ball, and now this? What is becoming of you?"

She gritted her teeth, refusing to answer.

"Do be more careful."

"Of course," she said. "It was stupid of me."

"Indeed." He continued to brush her hair and she waited uncomfortably for him to finish. The minutes ticked by, and still he stood there. Just when she thought she might scream for him to leave, he paused.

"By the by." He smiled. "Mother returned before you."

"Did she?" She shrugged. "The hack got stuck in the rain, took a moment for the driver to escape."

He clucked his tongue. "A hired hack? Really, what shall I do with you?" He pulled back so that her neck bent at an uncomfortable angle. The spicy scent of his sandalwood aftershave hovered around her. "See that you don't mention your lapse in good judgment to anyone."

He set her brush upon the table and tightened his hold on her hair. Turning her head, he placed a chaste kiss upon her check, his mustache tickling her skin. Her stomach clenched, bile rising to her throat. How she hated his touch.

"For if word got out, well . . ." He released his hold and started toward the door. "It could be quite disastrous for both of us."

Her fingers curled in her lap, her heart thumping angrily in her chest. "Of course."

"I'll be at the club tonight; don't wait up."

She lifted her hand, grasping the brush tightly. Her pulse pounded with a heated anger she could barely control. It was only when the door shut behind him that she was able to breathe with some normalcy. But the hatred was still there, still burning brightly, bubbling, boiling to the surface.

"Don't do it," Fanny said. "Don't throw the brush at him."

"I wasn't . . ." She released the brush and took in a deep, calming breath. She still felt his icy fingers, still felt him deep within, always. He was like a parasite that fed on her soul. Her heart would not slow, her anger would not cease. Would she ever be rid of him?

"That's it," Fanny said, coming up behind her and repining her hair. "Whatever you're up to, it has to end now. 'Tis too dangerous."

She didn't respond, but already her mind was spinning with possibilities. If she cared, she would never see James again. If she cared, she would obey her husband. But she'd stopped caring long ago. Something had been lit within. Something she could no longer control . . . a burning desire to know more. A desire to do what she wanted, when she wanted. A desire to be free.

That spirited girl who had been there before her marriage, the child who had run free at her aunt's home in the countryside, was still there. God help her, but she wanted to see James again. She *would* see him again.

"Eleanor?" Fanny paused, her voice ringing out in warning. "I know that look upon your face well, and I don't like it."

Eleanor smiled up at her maid. "Don't be silly."

Fanny set the extra pins on the tabletop. Shaking her head, the maid started toward the dressing room. "I won't have anything to do with it. Don't even want to know."

"Fanny?" Eleanor called out sweetly.

She paused with a long sigh. "Yes, my lady?"

"Get my cloak please."

The maid's shoulders slumped in defeat. "Never listen to anything I say, do you. God help us all."

She disappeared into the dressing room, leaving Eleanor alone. She'd been dormant for far too long. Spring had come and with it the hope and promise of a new day. It was time she too awoke and lived.

* * *

Never in her life had Eleanor traveled alone. Yet here she was for the third time in the past fortnight sneaking about without escort, leaving behind a lifetime sentence, and searching for that little bit of freedom she so desperately craved. She'd told Fanny she was visiting the Ladies' Society, but she'd seen the look in the maid's eyes. Fanny hadn't believed her in the least. Eleanor felt guilty for lying to the woman, but they both knew it was for her own good.

As the large homes gave way to modest dwellings it was as if her chains fell away, as if the parasite within shriveled slightly. And as the lovely Westminster came into view, her heart soared higher than the church itself. The air felt lighter, and her shoulders relaxed. She felt a million miles away from everything she knew, everything that had held her captive. The fantasy of running away tiptoed through her mind. But it was crushed as soon as the idea had arrived. He would find her, she had no doubt. Besides, she had no money of her own, and no family who would take her in.

The carriage slowed, and her excitement gave way to nervousness. She tugged the lace down over her face, hiding her features, and waiting impatiently for the hack to stop. James might not find suspicion with his mother's death, but she did. When the carriage paused, Eleanor pushed open the door and stepped outside. She couldn't even remember when she had last opened a door for herself. There was something incredibly exotic about doing things for herself. She took in a deep breath of rain-soaked air. The storm was fading and sunlight was trying its hardest to pierce the gray clouds.

"Thank you," she called to the driver, but he had already lurched away, heading down the road to find another client, more money.

For a long moment she merely stood there, savoring the feel of being lost, alone. The temptation of being in a place where no one knew her identity was overwhelming. Here, no one watched her or expected anything of her. No, they all were too busy with their own lives to care what she did.

Eleanor found the tea shop easily and headed down the street, retracing the steps she and James had taken only that morning. Through the windows she could see Mr. and Mrs. Swift bustling around the interior preparing for midday tea. She paused for a moment, taking in the sweet picture.

No one could say they were pretty, but to her they were beautiful. The way they worked together almost as one, the gentle touches, the jests that had Mrs. Swift throwing her head back and laughing. All these years together and they were still obviously in love. Eleanor smiled. They represented what marriage should be. She pressed her gloved hand to her chest, her smile fading. Her heart hurt knowing she would never experience that love and companionship.

Mrs. Swift disappeared into the back room, fracturing the perfect picture. Eleanor lifted the netting covering her face and pulled open the door. The bell overhead jingled, announcing her arrival. Mr. Swift glanced up, his eyes widening almost immediately. Good, he remembered her.

"Well, my word. Mrs. McKinnon!"

She forced herself to return his smile, feeling somewhat guilty for using James's name. What he didn't know surely wouldn't hurt him. "Good afternoon."

"Come in, come in!" He led her toward a small table near the windows. The place was empty, the afternoon rush having yet to arrive. "Have you come alone?" At her nod, he continued. "What can I get you? Tea, or a chat?"

He laughed at his own jest, making her smile in turn. She liked this couple, adored them really. Yet she was acutely aware that in her social circle she would have most likely never met them. "Information, actually."

He frowned, obviously confused. She could only hope he liked to gossip as much as he liked to jest.

"You see, Mr. Swift, my husband has lost touch with his sister." She sighed sadly, praying she did a thorough job of the grieving wife. "He would greatly love to find her but is too proud."

"Pride is many a man's downfall." He clucked his tongue and shook his head. "Really, hasn't seen her?" He seemed quite shocked by the fact that they'd lost contact, and she could only hope he believed her lie. God's truth she'd had enough practice fibbing since marrying her husband. Hell, her entire life was a lie.

"They were as thick as thieves last time I saw them." He settled in the chair next to her. "But with the death of his father, and the scandal that came along with it, I suppose the stress might have done them in."

"Scandal?"

Mr. Swift flushed, rubbing the back of his neck guiltily. "Did ye not know, my child?"

She shook her head, confused.

"'Tis not my place to tell you, I'm afraid. Ye'll have to speak with your husband, or better yet, forget I mentioned it."

Eleanor sighed, she could see by the tight set of his jaw that she would get no further information. "His sister, then, can you tell me about her?"

He rubbed the gray stubble along his chin thoughtfully. "Sweet little girl who looked just like her mum. Still can't believe the poor mother died, and broken-hearted if the rumors are true."

She felt his loss as if it had happened to her. Poor James had only just heard about his mother's death, although it had taken place years ago. But to him . . . well, she supposed it felt as if the woman had only just died today. She glanced briefly out the window, wondering how he fared. Had he told his precious Lady Lavender? Would she give him the comfort Eleanor wished she could offer?

"Aye, his sister was a sweet little thing with brilliant red hair and ready smile. Rather shy, but kind. How she adored her brother."

Her heart twisted almost painfully as she pictured a young James full of courage and loyalty, a little sister tagging after him. They should have been a happy family with parents who adored them. What had gone wrong? Thoughts of James's family had her missing her own. Eleanor had been close to her brothers and sisters at one time. Had even thought they might visit her after she married. But no, she couldn't have them stay with her because she didn't want them to know the truth about her life.

"And you have no idea where she is now?"

"Not sure." He frowned as he turned toward the kitchens. "Mrs. Swift?"

"Aye?" The woman waddled into the room. Spotting Eleanor, she looked almost as shocked as her husband had. But underneath her surprise, those large brown eyes shimmered with a kindness and affection that reminded her of Mrs. Swann, her Aunt Jeanie's housekeeper.

The woman swiped her hands on her apron, smiling at Eleanor. "Well, fancy seeing you here again! What a delightful surprise."

"Mrs. McKinnon is trying to find Arabella."

She frowned as she paused next to her husband. "James's sister?"

"Aye. Disappeared, she did, and they can't seem to find her."

She didn't miss the fretful glance they exchanged. Mrs. Swift clucked her tongue and shook her head much like Mr. Swift had done only moments ago. But Eleanor didn't miss the depths of her worry. She knew what Mrs. Swift was thinking . . . perhaps Arabella was selling herself upon the streets. Wouldn't that be bloody ironic?

"I did hear a rumor that the nuns at St. Anne's were collecting orphans around that time, still do, I think. Perhaps they might know a thing or two."

The woman gave her a strained smile. She believed it about as much as Eleanor did. Poverty-stricken women did not generally end up in orphanages. They ended up in the factories, or whoring themselves . . . much like James. She pushed aside that depressing thought. She would not give up until she uncovered the truth; she owed James that much.

"St. Anne's." Eleanor stood. "Wonderful, thank you."

"Don't git yer hopes up," Mr. Swift warned, and she knew he was merely trying to be kind. "Not many children living in such poverty last long on this earth, ye know. And many end up running away from the orphanages."

Eleanor struggled to maintain her smile. "I understand. Still, it's a start, and I appreciate your help."

He nodded. "Of course."

Both looked anxious and worried. They were truly kind people when she'd had so few in her life. It was too bad she would never be able to see them again. Still, she would spread word of their shop amongst the other ladies of the *ton* and help garner business.

"If you don't mind . . . if James happens by could you perhaps omit my visit from any conversation you might have? I am hoping to surprise him."

"Too late, my dear," Mrs. Swift said with a concerned nod toward the windows. "He's headed this way now."

Eleanor jerked her gaze toward the door. Sure enough James was headed straight toward them. A shock of alarm shot through her body. If his frown was any indication, he had already spotted her through the windows. The urge to dive underneath the table momentarily overwhelmed her. She should have known he would return.

"Blast it," Eleanor muttered.

The door opened, and James stepped inside, bringing with the scent of soap, man, and fresh rain. A guilty flush of heat rushed to her cheeks. She was overstepping and he'd caught her. His lips lifted, but the smile didn't quite reach his eyes. He was angry, indeed.

"James, my boy! Two visits in one week!" Mrs. Swift latched onto her husband's arm in her excitement. "Can we get you some tea?"

"No," James said curtly, although they didn't seem to notice his ire. "When my wife came up missing, I thought she might be here. Raved about your tea cakes, she did."

The couple beamed.

Ellie felt slightly ill as she glanced at James's handsome face. He wouldn't even look her in the eyes. Her heart broke a little. He'd changed into gray trousers and a dark blue jacket and waistcoat that hugged his lean body to perfection. He looked every bit the irate lord out for blood.

"But I'm sorry to say we must leave." He turned his attention to her. The coldness in his gaze pierced her soul. She prayed she hadn't destroyed their friendship. She was a bloody fool to have betrayed him, the one man who knew her secrets.

"Ellie, dear, you forgot about our appointment."

"How silly of me." She forced herself to smile as she went to him, sliding her arm through his. His body was tense, his muscles stiff and unyielding, pressing against the seams of his clothing as if he wanted to burst from his very skin and throttle her. Just when she'd labeled him as a sweet, kind man, he reminded her that he could easily, so very easily, destroy her. Eleanor's mouth went dry.

"It was lovely seeing you again," James said. "But we must go."

"Of course," Mrs. Swift called out. "Do come back!"

"We will." He shoved open the door and led her into the chill afternoon. The sun had disappeared once more, destroyed by yet another approaching storm. She had just enough time to pull the lace over her features before a group of women came strolling around the corner, their pretty heads bent close together as they giggled and gossiped. She didn't miss the way their hungry gazes found James and stayed a bit too long. In his anger, he barely noticed them. But she certainly did.

"What the hell are you doing here?" he said through clenched teeth.

Eleanor sighed. There was no use in lying. Besides, she found she didn't really wish to lie to him. With her free hand, she rubbed her aching temples, sliding her fingers underneath the rim of her straw bonnet. "I wanted to know what happened to your family."

He turned abruptly, pulling her into an alley. She didn't have time to question his strange path. She hopped over a broken bottle, trying to keep pace with his quick gait. She realized something quite odd indeed as his grip tightened almost painfully . . . she was not in the least bit afraid of James.

"Why?" he demanded, seething.

Why did she want to know? Curiosity? She took her lower lip between her teeth, feeling slightly ashamed. Yes, but there was more. The need to think about something other than her own dour life? Rats went scurrying into the shadows, causing her to shiver. After all, she'd been the eldest child of a large family; she was used to solving everyone else's problems. He weaved his way behind a pile of empty crates.

"James, please. Cease!"

He stopped so suddenly that she was forced to press her hands to his chest for balance. With a low growl, James pushed the netting up, revealing her features. "Why?"

She'd become so accustomed to that veil hiding her from the world that she felt quite vulnerable without it.

"Why?"

Her heart hammered madly. She couldn't seem to answer, couldn't seem to get the words past her lips. Or maybe she didn't want to answer because then she would have to admit that she had emotions and feelings like everyone else.

With a frustrated growl, he pressed her against the brick wall, holding her captive with his own body. It was indecent, and even though they were in the shadows, half-hidden behind a pile of crates, anyone might have noticed. She had a feeling he wasn't going to release her until she answered him truthfully.

"Why?" he demanded.

She flinched, hating herself for reacting. Just like that his anger faded. James sighed and leaned forward, resting his forehead to hers. It was an odd moment, almost . . . gentle, and she wasn't sure if she should like the close contact or not.

"Why?" he whispered again, his breath warm upon her lips.

"Because . . . I suppose I care."

About him. About his family. Suddenly, about life.

And it would most likely lead to heartache once more. Lord, had she learned nothing from her marriage? Emotions, loyalty, and compassion would get a person nowhere.

"It doesn't matter." She pressed her hands into his shoulders, preparing to shove him away. Instead, she found her palms trapped against his chest. Startled, she glanced up at him.

"It does matter. It matters so very much."

He lowered his head and molded his lips to hers. There, in an alley where anyone could see them, he kissed her. This was no gentle touch, but a hard kiss, a demanding kiss that left her stunned and reeling. He tasted of wine and warmth, he tasted of freedom and hope. She was completely aware of his powerful body holding her immobile. Yet there was no fear, never any worry with James.

With a groan she slid her arms up his muscled chest and around his neck, clinging to him. It was a silent invitation and he understood. James swept his tongue into her mouth, deepening the kiss. Heaven help her, but she could not control herself with James near. Heat swirled like molten lava low in her belly, producing an aching need that left her hungry for something she didn't understand. His knee wedged between her thighs and she felt the rigid length of his erection press against her skirts.

"So very lovely," he whispered.

Eleanor her fingers into the soft curls at the base of his skull. She didn't care about being caught. She only cared about being closer to James. Just when she was ready to beg him to take her in that alley, he tore his mouth from hers. Their harsh breaths mingled so that they breathed in each other's very essence. She had to resist the urge to latch onto his lapels and demand he kiss her again. To demand he take her to a hotel, a carriage, anywhere, and finish what he had started.

For one long moment they didn't speak. There was no need. She knew he'd forgiven her for interfering. Then slowly he reached up, and with trembling fingers he lowered her veil. The wall between her world and his was back in place.

"Come, before you're missed." He took her hand and led her toward the street, merging within the afternoon crowds. His touch was softer, his steps less hurried.

He didn't speak a word as he hailed a passing cab for the third time that day, and neither did she. After all, what could she say? When a coach stopped, he helped her inside, even paid for her fare, and then stepped back.

For the second time that day, James was sending her on her way, back to a life she despised. Eleanor brushed aside the curtain and gazed out onto the street. James had already turned and was heading back toward London, toward the woman who owned him. He disappeared into the crowds.

Bereft, Eleanor let the curtain fall back into place as the hack jerked forward. James and she were very much the same, she realized with some sadness. Both of them were trapped, controlled by others. How would he uncover the truth if Lady Lavender lied? The hack turned the corner, headed toward her part of town. She wondered sadly if she'd ever see him again. Most likely not.

"Oh Aunt Jeanie," she whispered. "What am I to do?"

She mightn't be able to help herself, for she was trapped in marriage and the law was not on her side. But perhaps, just maybe, she could help James.

For the first time in a long while Eleanor felt as if she had something to live for after all.

Chapter 7

"I'm rather bored of London," Ophelia proclaimed as they strolled through Cremorne Gardens. It wasn't surprising; she bored easily, and they'd been forced to endure the whims of the exotic Lady Lavender. "I think it's time to return home."

In other words, she had found the information they had needed, and she was done with the vile city. She might have her answers, but he didn't. Last night he'd intended to question her about his mother's death but had found he couldn't quite mange to even say the words. Instead, he'd spent the night staring at the ceiling, wondering if it could possibly be true.

James escorted her away from the dancing platform and the overly loud laughter of the participating visitors. Away from the brilliant lamplight and into the shadows. Away from the orchestra playing in the kiosk in the middle of the gardens. He didn't blame her for wanting to return to Lavender Hills. Although the estate was filled with men, it was actually rather peaceful and, when there were not clients present, uneventful.

"Are you sure?" He kept his voice relaxed, calm; in reality he itched to escape. London had become a nightmare, a reminder of his failures, a reminder of a past he'd rather forget. He'd sold himself, given up everything, yet his mother had still died. Dear God, she was dead. He'd thought if he took the position with Lady Lavender he could save them. He could save no one. Not his mother. Not his sister. Sure as hell not Eleanor.

Eleanor.

Her face flashed through his mind. The way she'd looked outside that tea shop with her bonnet askew, her lips red and swollen from his kisses. He'd practically taken her in a dirty alley as if she was nothing but a common whore. The guilt he felt was overwhelming. He resisted the urge to press the heels of his palms to his face. His eyes burned in their sockets from lack of sleep. All night he'd paced, back and forth in his hotel room, the emotions swirling within his gut unnerving. He couldn't allow himself to grieve, to get angry . . . he couldn't allow himself to lose the one thing he had retained all these years . . . control over his emotions. His carefully constructed façade was crumbling.

"Yes, I'd like to leave." Ophelia sighed. "There are things I need to attend to back at the estate."

He led her down a path, strolling past a juggler. And so he would smile, he would escort her through town, he would return to Lavender Hills, and he would fuck as many women as he could and try to forget. But first, damn it all, he was getting answers. "Is Gideon being difficult?"

She sighed, rubbing her forehead much like a perturbed child. "When isn't he?"

She did not speak further upon the subject and he knew better than to question her. He turned left, down a narrow trail. Lamplight pushed at the darkness and gave the area an ethereal glow. In the gardens, on these shadowed and deserted paths, no one would hear their conversation.

"Don't be a damn idiot, James," Gideon had snapped at him only a few months ago. *"You follow her around like she's a bloody martyr when she's nothing but a demon in a beautiful gown. She's*

using you and someday you'll see that. I hope for your sake it's not too late."

The man's warning echoed through his mind. Only now did he begin to wonder if perhaps he had been the idiot Gideon claimed. No, Lady Lavender hadn't lied. What would be the point? Unless she thought to spare his feelings.

"James, is something the matter?"

He didn't pause but continued to lead her down the path. "My mother is dead." He said it casually, waiting to see how she would respond.

She paused, forcing him to stop. "Whatever do you mean?"

Was the shock in her eyes feigned? It was hard to tell in the dim lighting. "The other day when I was lost in London"—he'd lied and she'd believed him because he'd never lied to her before—"I'd ended up in an old childhood haunt. I happened upon a couple I'd known when I was young. They mentioned my mother's death."

"Oh James." She rested her hand on his arm. "I'm so sorry."

The crease between her eyes, the pout of her lips . . . it all looked sincere. Did he believe her? Did he trust her? "You didn't know?"

She pressed her clasped hands to her heart in shocked dismay. "Of course not!"

They started forward once more. What reason did she have to lie to him? None. So why did he feel as if she did? "Then where, exactly, is the money going?"

"The same place it's been going. The same address in Bath." She rested her hand to her temple, sighing. "James, are you sure your mother has died? Perhaps it was a misunderstanding."

Her words brought with an unwanted spark of hope. "Perhaps." He took in a deep, shuddering breath and followed the path as it wove around a cluster of yew trees. "I think it would be beneficial if you sent Wavers to check on the matter."

And there was her hand on his arm once more, the woman attempting to soothe his agitation. He'd seen her do it before to other men, a touch here or there. When she used her charm, the woman could accomplish anything. "Yes, immediately. I'll have him travel to Bath tomorrow to make sure your sister, at least, is getting the money."

She didn't realize that he knew all of her tricks. Damn it all if his suspicion didn't return full force. He'd had a decent life, he'd been content knowing he was providing for his family. Now, all because of a woman with blue eyes, his entire world had flipped upside down. "Perhaps I should go along."

"You could, of course." Her eyes were large and luminous with their feigned innocence. "But are you truly prepared to tell your sister the truth of what you are, where you've been, and what you've been doing?"

He clenched his jaw, fighting his anger. He refused to feel ashamed of what he did. After all, he sold himself for his family. He bore it willingly knowing that he was providing for his mother and sister. But to realize now that it might have been for nothing . . . aye, he wanted the answers, but he could admit he didn't want his sister to know the truth.

"Perhaps you're right," he said. "Perhaps she doesn't need to know quite yet."

She squeezed his hand gently. "Of course."

They continued down the path, headed back toward the festivities. He'd always been highly aware of the way people avoided his gaze, noticed even now how women turned their heads away. He lived in a world of secrecy and shame. Aye, it was not the first time he had noticed, but it was the first time he cared. Ophelia was right, he could not reconnect with his sister. But he would make sure she was well and cared for. And he bloody well would find out the truth about his mum.

"I am truly sorry, James."

He forced himself to smile down at her. "I know."

For a long moment, they stood on the outskirts watching people dance, and he pretended to enjoy it because he was so bloody good at pretending. A few families remained, but most of the visitors were those who teetered on the fringes of society, people like him. Men willing to sacrifice their reputations for a taste of the wilder sort of life. Women who had lost their innocence long ago.

"Cremorne Gardens, have you been?" he'd asked Eleanor only yesterday, in hopes that he might see her again. But of course she didn't visit disreputable gardens in the middle of the night.

"Of course not." She had shot him down immediately. *"It's not exactly a place for someone like . . ."*

Her, a voice inside his head whispered. It wasn't a place for someone like her. *He* wasn't a man for someone like her. She'd come into his life much like a storm, knocking down walls, uprooting trees, leaving him baffled and confused.

"Will you be a dear and get us some sherry, James?"

"Yes, of course."

He left her in the capable hands of her bodyguards who always followed silently behind, and headed toward the stand selling drinks. It was hard to believe Eleanor lived somewhere within this city. Harder to believe that she had traipsed through London intent on finding his family. She barely knew him; why would she care?

Eleanor.

She was like no woman he'd ever met. A veritable Joan of Arc. He respected her, he actually enjoyed her company, and he was most certainly attracted to her. And in all likelihood he would never see her again. But then it shouldn't have bothered him; there were very few people who were a constant in his life. Clients visited, enjoyed, and left while he remained stuck in time.

"Why don't you respond to Alex's letters?"

Startled, James spun away from the stand and toward the voice. A beautiful, young blonde in a light green gown stood next to him. Eighteen, nineteen, perhaps? He glanced around, looking for her escort, but could see no one. "Pardon?"

The graceful arch of her brows, the fullness of her lips . . . she seemed vaguely familiar. He supposed she could have been a client, but none that he remembered.

"Alex's letters. I'm Grace's sister, Patience." James was stunned speechless. She shifted closer while glancing around the clearing, no doubt making sure no one noticed their conversation. "Now . . . why haven't you responded?"

Confused, he wasn't quite sure how to extricate himself from the odd situation. "I have responded." Alex's sister-in-law? Horrified, he looked away, not wishing to be caught in conversation with the woman. This was absurd even for Alex. Did he not realize the consequences if his sister-in-law was caught?

"I knew it." She rested her right hand smugly upon her hip and drummed her gloved fingers. "We didn't receive any."

He didn't understand what she was getting at, and frankly didn't give a damn. "Where the hell is . . ." His voice trailed off as he spotted the comely shape of a beautiful woman weaving her way in and out of the crowds. The sway of her hips in her brilliant blue gown with bold gray stripes, the low neckline of her bodice . . . a woman with a veil covering half her face, so that only her full, lush lips showed. A heated flush crawled painfully slow through his body. Dear God, was he imagining her?

"Who is she?" Patience asked, startling him once more.

"Who?" He was so bloody confused he wasn't sure where to look, what to say. He tore his gaze from Eleanor as she moved onto a trail, disappearing from sight. What was she thinking . . . visiting the gardens alone? The urge to rush after her overwhelmed him. James curled his fingers so tight, his nails bit into his palms. She was not his to protect, never would be.

"The woman you were staring at. Who is she?"

Shite, if Patience had noticed his interest in Eleanor, had others? He glanced around the garden, searching the laughing faces, sheened with sweat and liquor. No one was looking his way. Even

Lady Lavender was in deep discussion with a young man. "I don't know what you're talking about."

She lifted a cocky brow and grinned. "A client?"

"How . . ." He shook his head, horrified. "Alex told you?"

She shrugged. "No, I uncovered it myself."

"Dear Lord," he whispered.

He hadn't even been this uncomfortable when he'd slept with his first woman. So, the chit knew the truth . . . he was a whore. Shocking enough. Even more shocking was the fact that Alex would allow her to attend the garden party.

"Who is she?" Patience whispered. "Are you in love?"

James felt heat crawl up his neck. "That is none of your business, and I really suggest you turn away before someone notices that you're talking to me."

She waved her hand through the air, dismissing his comment. "Oh, that? I don't mind what people think or say. 'Tis all just silly gossip anyway."

"Well I do."

She laughed, a sound that drew more than one man's greedy gaze. "Are you worried I'll ruin your reputation?"

James gritted his teeth. "Unless your brother-in-law has recently gone mad, I suggest you hightail it back to his side at once." He stepped threateningly close to her, more than vindicated when she shrank back. "And tell Alex to mind is own damn business."

"It's just me. I came to London to try and sell my jewelry. I have an escort of course. An older cousin twice removed." She nodded toward an elderly lady standing near the dancers. If the woman's confused glance was any indication, she hadn't a clue what she had been getting into when she'd agreed to this night.

"I see." He highly doubted Alex or his wife would approve. He stepped closer to the cart, attempting to ignore the woman at his side. Hell, he had enough problems to deal with. "Then you should return to your escort at once and pray no one has noticed you here. In fact, I suggest you leave altogether. This is not a place for respectable people."

"What about you?" She grinned up at him, the blasted tease. They both knew he was far from respectable. Instead of moving away, she only stepped closer. "Would you like me to set up a meeting with her?"

He didn't dare look at the woman, worried she'd see the sudden interest in his gaze. Hell, it was like she offered him the forbidden fruit . . . a moment with Eleanor. "Who?" he asked, playing dumb.

"The woman you were staring at. You have feelings for her, don't you?"

Heat shot to his face. He flushed, actually flushed for the first time in years. Good Lord, what had become of him? "No. Of course not."

She seemed confused by his reluctance. "But you like her and this is your chance."

"For the love of . . ." He spun around. "I highly suggest you keep your distance from me and Lady Lavender unless you want to be ruined for life, and forget about your little jewelry business. Now be a good girl and go to your escort."

She folded her gloved hands demurely in front of her. "Very well."

But the smirk upon her face did not bode well. He gave her a none-too-subtle glare as he turned to leave. He'd find another vendor selling drinks, as long as he could get the hell away from her. The world had gone utterly mad. Patience speaking publicly to him, Eleanor visiting the gardens without an escort in sight. Utterly mad. Still, he couldn't help but wonder, had Ellie risked her reputation to see him, or merely to enjoy a bit of freedom?

He glanced around the garden, attempting to decipher familiar faces from the shadows. Damn it all, he couldn't just leave her to wander around the garden alone. He paused halfway to Lady Lavender. First, he would make sure Patience, the blasted girl, had returned to her escort. Then he would see to Eleanor. He started to turn when he felt the subtle brush of a hand against his arm. When he glanced down, he wasn't in the least bit surprised to see Patience grinning up at him.

"She will meet you near the lilacs."

Shocked, he merely stood there staring at her in confusion. She inclined her head to the left, that smirk still in place. Having flipped his world completely upside down once more, Patience turned and sauntered off toward her escort. James jerked his gaze toward the lilacs, his heart hammering wildly. Eleanor waited for him there. The realization made it difficult to breathe. She wanted to see him, but did he want to see her?

He glanced back at Lady Lavender. She was seated upon a stone bench, flirting with a man half her age. She still hadn't noticed his absence. Business. He could always use the excuse that Eleanor was business, even if it was a lie. With the memory of their kiss outside the tea shop still vivid in his mind, James started toward the lilac bushes. His body had a mind of its own. Control had become an illusion.

He easily found a path through the lilacs and followed the trail into the darkness, blending into shadows that would provide them shelter from prying eyes. Where was she? He should have gone to her immediately. If something had happened . . .

"James," a soft, feminine voice whispered temptingly upon the breeze. He spun around, his pulse pounding. A pale hand darted out between the branches, clasped onto his sleeve, and pulled him into the trees. James suddenly found himself pressed to a slim, warm body, hidden within a crop of sweet-smelling lilacs.

"And so I run into you again," he whispered, studying her shadowed face. "Quite the coincidence."

"Not really," she replied, her breath warm across his lips. "You told me you'd be here the other day. Besides, the gossip columns make note of the infamous Lady Lavender's plans and whereabouts every time she is in London."

"I see." But he didn't see. She'd sought him out then. Had purposefully come here, potentially tarnished her reputation merely to see him. The ache that had established itself in the middle of his chest since meeting her spread like warm honey.

"I wanted to apologize," she whispered, lifting the veil on her bonnet. "For interfering."

"It's all right." Surely she hadn't come all this way merely for an apology when she could have easily sent him a note. Which meant she either craved the excitement of the gardens, or she craved him. They were silent for a moment, the tension between them almost tangible. "Is that why you're here?"

She lowered her gaze, staring at his neck. "I merely wanted to make sure you weren't angry with me. I . . . I couldn't stand knowing I had hurt you."

"Of course not." His heart lurched, his pulse fluttering with hope. He pressed his palm to her velvety smooth cheek, cupping the side of her face. "Eleanor . . ."

She lifted her head, her gaze luminous and desperate. But there, deep down, he could see the nervousness, the wariness. The vulnerability practically pulsed from her being. She didn't want him to hurt her, and God help him, if she fell in love he would.

"In our business it is not uncommon for clients to become attached."

The hazy lust in her eyes cleared instantly. She shoved his hand away and stepped back, as if he had slapped her. Or perhaps she wished to slap him. He'd offended her and he could see that wall she usually carried was being rebuilt brick by brick. Damn him.

"I don't wish for you to get your heart broken," he tried to explain. "I do enjoy your company, but I don't want you hurt."

She released a wry laugh. "James, please, you think too much of our relationship."

A lesser man would have been surprised by her blunt comment. But he knew her too well, he had seen her open and vulnerable. Besides, he knew enough about women to know that in some way he'd hurt her pride.

"It doesn't matter." She turned her back to him as if she meant to leave. "You don't have to worry about me falling for you because I don't believe in love."

Neither did he, so why did her words pain him? "Ellie, you are young, beautiful. Surely—"

"Surely what?" She spun back around to face him. He'd made her angry, but he'd rather have her angry than hurting. "I'm married. The man is a demon. I don't have room for a ridiculous and weak emotion like love. I thought to help you, nothing more. Obviously it was a mis—"

James latched onto her arm and jerked her forward. She didn't have time to push away. His mouth found hers, capturing her gasp of surprise. It was a quick kiss, a passionate kiss. When he pulled back, they were both gasping for air.

"We can be friends, can't we?" he whispered. He didn't want to let her go, couldn't seem to remove his hand from her narrow waist. He breathed in her rose scent, feeling as light-headed as a damn virgin on her wedding night.

"I don't know, James." She sounded sad, and he hated when she was sad. "I don't see how there is any possible way we can have any sort of relationship."

She was right, so why didn't he let her go? Why didn't he make his way back to Lady Lavender and forget Eleanor? Because he had become obsessed. Because somehow she had clawed her way deep within his soul. Damn his penchant for needing to save people. "I can't let you go."

"Why?" she whispered.

"Because, Eleanor, you never found what you were looking for."

Her delicate brows furrowed. "I don't understand."

He cupped the sides of her face and brushed his lips to hers. "Pleasure, Eleanor. You never found pleasure." She shivered against him, his words finding their target. He could seduce her so easily.

He'd had years and years of training. He knew where to touch, where to kiss, what words to say in order to bring a woman to the peak of pleasure.

"It's better, perhaps. Because if I had, I would know what I was missing." She pushed away from him, stepping back. She looked confused, uncertain. In a defensive gesture that wasn't lost on him, she crossed her arms over her chest. "I suppose this might be the last time I see you."

"If that's true, then this sort of parting won't do at all." He gently brushed a curl over her shoulder. "You won't leave yet. Not until . . ."

"Until what?" she whispered.

"Until you experience what you came for."

"James, no!" She drew back until her shoulders pressed into a tall oak. "We can't. Not here!"

"'Tis dark, the show is starting, no one will notice."

She shook her head. "You can't be serious."

He stepped closer. "But I am."

"James—"

When he kissed her, molding his mouth to hers, he left no room for argument. Blast it, but he just wanted to forget. Forget his past, his future. Thank God, she didn't protest but fell willingly into him, her lush form pressing intimately to his chest. She wanted him as much as he wanted her. He coaxed her mouth open, and when her lips parted on a gasp he made quick work of sweeping his tongue inside. She wasn't some virginal miss to shy away from passion. When the silky tip of her tongue brushed against his, James growled against her mouth. Their mouths mingled, the kiss so deep he could feel it to his soul.

Eleanor groaned, a truly erotic sound that sent blood pounding through his body and pooling into his groin. Dear Lord, he wanted her. Wanted her like he had never wanted a woman before. He tore his mouth from hers and pressed his lips to her fragile jawline, then lower to her elegant neck.

"I will show you what you've been missing. I swear it." If they should never meet again, he was at least determined to do that for her.

"Yes," she whispered, tilting her head back, her eyes closed. She leaned trustingly into his body, not afraid, completely and utterly open to him. Her hands slid up his chest, over the fine silk waistcoat under his jacket.

"You are stunning, you know that?" he whispered.

"Yes," she repeated.

He grinned, knowing she hadn't a clue what he had said. She was too far gone, her need too desperate. His flattery would get him nowhere. Besides, he couldn't tell her how wonderful she was because she wouldn't believe him, but he could show her. He found her skirts and bunched the material slowly up her legs. The crinkle of crinoline was lost in the sound of an orchestra playing a jaunty country jingle.

Her fingers bit into his shoulders, sliding farther up into the strands of hair at the base of his head. "Dear God, you are truly doing this now, here."

He didn't respond, merely slid his hand underneath her skirts. His fingers found her smooth, silky thighs. Startled, he almost drew back. It took a lot to shock him, but the fact that she wore no bloomers nearly brought him to his knees then and there.

"No undergarments?" he whispered near the shell of her ear.

"My husband established early on that I was to wear none," she said, her fingers playing with the strands of hair at the base of his neck. "That way he could have me whenever, wherever he wanted."

The thrilling sensation he felt fled. An anger he was finding it hard to control pulsed through his veins. The bastard. He gritted his teeth, ignoring the sudden desire to head to her town home and confront the man. James took in a deep, trembling breath. He could not do anything about her husband, but he could do something for her. He pushed Lord Beckett from his thoughts and focused on Eleanor.

"God, you smell good," he said, nuzzling her neck. She trembled in his arms and he found he liked how she reacted to him. Never had a woman needed a more gentle touch than she. Never had a woman needed *him* more than she did at this moment. He slid his hand up her thigh, heading inward toward the intensely silky and sensitive area. Eleanor tightened, her breath coming out in harsh pants that stirred the hair at his temples.

"Relax, my sweet." He shifted, sliding his knee between her legs and spreading her thighs. Burning lust surged through his body, hardening his groin so it strained uncomfortably against his trousers. "How badly I want to touch you."

"Please, do."

He needed no further encouragement. His fingers slid between her silky folds, into that pulsing heat. Eleanor whimpered, her teeth biting erotically into his shoulder. Briefly he wondered if she even knew what she did.

"I won't hurt you," he assured her. "Never."

"I know," she whispered, and he heard the truth in her breathless voice. A truth that humbled him.

"Hold your skirts."

She frowned. "Why?"

"Hold them."

She grabbed the handful of material, clutching it tightly to her chest and exposing long legs clad in white stockings that glowed under the moonlight. He let his hands slide down the soft curve of her thighs to where her garters met her stockings. Another time, another place, and he would have had her on her back as he drove deep within her.

"James?" she said with uncertainty.

He gave her a wicked grin, then dropped to his knees. "Part your thighs for me."

"What are you doing?" she whispered, sounding slightly horrified. Instead of doing as he demanded, she pressed her legs tightly together. She might be bold and determined young woman, but in the bedchamber she was as innocent as a virgin.

He didn't respond, for he knew he'd only horrify her. Instead, he slid his hands between her silky thighs, parting her legs. She tried to squeeze them back together, but he wouldn't allow it. "Relax, Eleanor."

"No, you can't!" she hissed.

"I can." He lowered his head and pressed his mouth to the nest of curls, shielding her femininity. Eleanor sucked in a sharp breath. Dear God, she smelled good . . . like roses and soap. James closed his eyes as his erection throbbed mercilessly. He tightened his grip on her thighs, attempting to retain control of his own passion. When she sighed in pleasure, he slid his tongue between her damp folds. She tasted of honey, of woman, of desire.

Eleanor gasped, stiffening.

But he was far from done. With his tongue, James flicked the sensitive nub that he knew would set her afire. Eleanor groaned, slumping against the tree and grasping the material of her gown closely to her chest. The scent of lilacs, woman, and roses surrounded him, making him almost dizzy with desire. He wanted to stand, to free his erection and sink into her fully, but this wasn't about him. Not now. He flicked the nub again before slipping his tongue inside her. It was enough for her tightly wound body.

She squirmed, whimpering. "I don't understand."

"You don't have to," he whispered against her. "Just enjoy."

He parted her legs farther and shoved his tongue into her tight passage. Eleanor cried out, arching her back. The sound of music and merriment hid her cries of delight. The vegetation provided shelter from prying eyes, but he maintained enough rational thought to realize they could be caught at any moment. The problem was he didn't think he could stop even if the queen herself suddenly appeared.

"I feel so . . . so hot. So . . . achy." Her entire body trembled. She found the pleasure he had been so desperate to give her and arched her hips, meeting his tongue thrust for thrust. Hearing her moan, feeling her body tighten, was pure agony.

"So hot, so . . . so . . ." He felt her tighten around his mouth. "Oh my." Eleanor arched her back, crying out as muscles tensed.

"I can't take it." She lifted her hips more urgently.

"Let go, Eleanor, trust me."

She released her skirts, gripping his hair almost painfully as the orgasm exploded through her body and around his tongue. The lingering sweetness of her release drifted away on the cool night breeze. It was over. James pressed a kiss to the inside of her right thigh, then pulled back, her taste still tantalizingly on his mouth. His erection jutted out angrily, demanding release. He ignored the aching need and tugged her skirts down around her legs. Her eyes were closed, her head back against the trunk, her breathing harsh. The bliss upon her face was almost too sweet to bear.

He pressed his body close to hers. "You are beautiful, brilliant," he whispered into her hair, breathing in her clean scent. His hands trembled as he cupped the sides of her face.

She turned her head and molded her mouth to his. "I never knew. I didn't understand . . ."

He tucked a loose lock of hair behind her ear, charmed by her innocence. She might be older than he, but she was much more sheltered. "That is the way intimacy is supposed to be."

"It's what they talk about, the chambermaids, the married women who giggle behind their fans."

She seemed shocked by it all, as if she'd thought the entire thing had been a myth and only now knew it for reality. He nodded. Damn it all, he didn't want to let her go. He wanted to show her more, so much more. If anyone deserved to know pleasure, it was Eleanor.

She brushed her hand down the side of his face, her piercing gaze on him as if trying to understand what had happened to her. "This is why women risk their reputations, why they visit Lady Lavender's."

He nodded again. There was nothing more to say. There was nothing more to show her. It was over, unfortunately right when it had begun. Slowly, he stepped back. His own body cried out in protest. He ignored the aching need to hold her closer, to find his own release. Now was not the time, perhaps never. He smoothed her skirts down, then picked up her bonnet and placed it over her still neatly coifed hair.

"Have you never pleasured yourself?" he asked, curious.

She looked confused. "I don't understand . . ." Her eyes suddenly widened and he almost laughed at her shock. The woman had just been brought to orgasm in a public garden, yet the thought of touching her own body horrified her.

"Oh." Even in the darkness he swore he could see her blush. She looked away, deeply embarrassed. "I will not answer that."

He grinned and brushed his knuckles down her cheek. Hell, he was completely enchanted with her, and for a few moments he'd forgotten his own problems. But reality was slowly tearing down that wall of sexual haze they had created; time was passing quickly.

She shook her head, lifting her trembling hands to pull her netting back in place. "I just . . . it's never been like that. I didn't know."

He brushed back her hair and straightened her bonnet, needing something to do to occupy his thoughts. "You do now."

"Yes." She was staring up at him in awe and confusion, hesitating because he knew she didn't want to return to her world any more than he wanted to return to his. But she would definitely be missed, and he needed to uncover the truth about Lady Lavender and his family.

A couple stumbled down the path, their drunken giggles interrupting. James sighed, raking his hair back. "I need to return, as do you."

"Yes."

Yet they paused. He studied her fine features, realizing with a start that there was something different about her. Something had changed. The hard, cold Eleanor had disappeared. She seemed lost, confused. "Are you all right?"

She nodded, forcing herself to smile. "Yes, we should go."

His hands curled as he resisted the urge to pull her close. A mixture of anguish and anger flooded his body. Eleanor stepped back, away from him. She might as well have traveled to another country. It was done. Their time, their relationship . . . over. For one insane moment he thought about asking her to run away with him. To jump on a boat headed down the Thames and disappear. But no, he had a sister to find, and she had a privileged life to live.

He brushed aside the low-hanging branches and made sure the path was clear. "Go first."

She hesitated, her face unreadable in the shadows. But she was still, so very still. "Is this good-bye then?" Her warm breath moved the lace between them and tickled his lips.

"Perhaps. Or maybe someday we shall meet again."

It was a lie, they both knew it, yet neither called it what it was. They would not ruin the moment, most likely their last. The entire world seemed to pause, then she shifted away from him.

"Thank you, James," she whispered. "I shall never forget you."

Before he could respond she turned and fled. He stepped from the trees, desperately searching for her fleeing form. Empty. If her scent hadn't clung to his body, her taste on his tongue, he would have thought her a dream. He pressed his hand to his chest, where an aching heaviness that he didn't quite understand had returned.

From somewhere to the right a woman giggled, a couple finding their own pleasure amongst the sin. He retraced his steps with wooden legs, walking slowly back toward Lady Lavender. The moment had been pleasurable indeed, but James wanted more. He wanted her alone, for hours, on a large, soft bed.

"My goodness." Lady Lavender stared with some amusement at the dirt upon the knees of his trousers. "I see you've been busy. A new client, or former?"

He wanted to make love to Eleanor far, far away from here, away from their responsibilities, away from the lives they knew. He brushed at his knees. She would charge a former client. A new client would get a free sample. He swallowed hard, avoiding her eyes, not because he feared she might see his guilt hovering within the depths, but because he feared she might see disillusioned anger. "New."

She drank the sherry someone had purchased for her. "Good. More business."

Was that all she cared about? Business? Did she care about anything, anyone other than money? He sat on the stone bench next to her, feeling unsettled, suddenly discontent. It was as if his sensibilities had left with Eleanor.

They would be returning to the estate in the morning, and part of him was relieved. London had become stifling, confusing, and unfamiliar. His relationship with Eleanor was over; there was no reason to stay. It was best to leave now, before he became even more obsessed. Eleanor was gone. Perhaps his mother had died. But he was determined, no matter what it took, to find out what had happened to his sister, with or without Lady Lavender's assistance.

Chapter 8

The house was quiet as Eleanor stepped inside. She'd floated home on a cloud of thrumming satisfaction, never once thinking about how her husband would react when she arrived. As she paused in the eerily quiet foyer, she wondered if perhaps her luck had run out.

Not even the butler waited for her, which was odd indeed. The heavenly glow that had enveloped her since seeing James faded and a shiver of unease raised the fine hairs on her neck. Had someone died?

For one moment she merely stood there, confused, attempting to understand her unease. Slowly, so very quietly, she untied her bonnet and set the hat upon the receiving table. The foyer stood polished and gleaming as always, from the marble flooring to the crystal chandelier above. The soft tap of her slippers as she moved toward the steps was the only sound. Something was wrong. Very wrong.

"Where have you been?"

Startled by her husband's voice, Eleanor spun around to face him. He looked calm, the perfect gentleman in his black evening attire. Too perfect, too calm. She schooled her features and forced her lips to turn upward. Truth would be her best option, for she realized in that chilling moment that he knew something. "I went to the gardens for the show."

"Gardens?" He strolled toward her, his gait easy and unhurried. His dress clothes indicated that he had just come from a ball, or the opera, which was why he was dressed in his evening wear. "Not a place for respectable women."

She shrugged. "I didn't think you cared what I did."

Ridiculous, and they both knew it. Of course he cared. He always cared. When they'd first courted she'd thought his attention charming. It wasn't until after they'd married that she'd realized it was merely his way of controlling her.

"Gossip, my dear." He strolled around her like a farmer appraising cattle. "I care about gossip because it affects me and my family name." He shook his head ruefully. "First, taking a hired hack home on your own, and now this? What will the world think?"

"I've never cared much for gossip or what others think, as you know, because usually it's utter nonsense." She started toward the stairs, determined to show no fear. Inside, she trembled. He knew something, she was sure of it. She would not panic, she would not beg for forgiveness, and she would not, under any circumstances, cave to the man's power. "I'm tired. I'd like to retire."

His hand lashed out, gripping her arm hard. She didn't dare jump, had taught herself to keep still even while icy panic filled her soul. "Gossip, whether true or not, affects me. I will not be made a laughingstock!"

She jerked her head toward him. What did he know? She thought she'd been so clever hiring unmarked hacks and weaving in and out of crowds. She realized now she'd been a bloody idiot. "Whatever are you talking about?"

He pulled her close, crushing her to his chest much like James had done only an hour ago. But this was different, so very different. His hot breath brushed across her face and reeked of brandy.

He'd been drinking. He was worse when drinking. "You were seen with a man at the gardens."

She refused to react even as biting fear crawled up her body, warning her to bolt. "Don't be ridiculous."

"Ridiculous?" He shoved her backward. Eleanor stumbled to get her footing but tripped over the rug and hit the wall hard. Pain radiated from her shoulder and down her back. For a moment, she merely gritted her teeth and leaned against the wall for support, attempting to regain control of her fear. She would not cry out. She would stay calm.

"Gossip," she lied.

"I don't give a shite what you did or didn't do. What I care about is the reputation of my family!" He charged toward her, but she refused to run. There was no point; she had nowhere to go. "You have humiliated my family name merely by attending the garden party, and you know it!"

She'd thought his dark and heavy features so handsome and manly when she'd first met him. He'd looked just like his father; so very much like him in looks and temperament. The same heavy brow, same dark eyes, same square jaw, same uncontrollable anger. The man had beaten his son while extolling the importance of the family name. Not that she'd heard about his childhood from her husband's lips. No, his sister had told her, perhaps hoping she would feel sorry for Lord Beckett, or merely understand his ways. But she would never understand why someone who had experienced pain and humiliation himself would wish to instill that same feeling in others.

"You will never humiliate me again!" He swung his arm forward, striking her hard against her right cheek. Eleanor stumbled, falling to her arse. The shock gave away to aching pain. She pressed her lips together, refusing to groan even while the coppery taste of blood swept across her tongue. He'd always been so very careful not to hit her face; why was he being reckless now?

"You will not leave this house alone ever again!" He reached down, gripping the collar of her dress. "You will be a veritable prisoner."

"I already am!"

His eyes widened, anger reddening his face. He lifted his hand. Ellie refused to cringe, but waited for the blow.

"Stop!" Mrs. Handler cried out.

Eleanor's anger flared. Of course the woman was here. Why was she not surprised? The fact that Mrs. Handler looked truly horrified didn't help ease Eleanor's ire, it only humiliated her all the more.

Lord Beckett released his hold, and panting with unspent emotion, he stumbled back. But his gaze, his heated gaze promised retribution. Slowly, he turned to face his mistress. "Don't you dare tell me what to do."

Mrs. Handler grasped onto the stairway railing, watching him with wide, bemused eyes. Eleanor felt a tingle of validation. The woman was seeing the true Lord Beckett for the first time. After a few tense moments, he swallowed hard, his hands fisting as if desperately trying to regain control. He wasn't sorry for hurting her. He was sorry that Mrs. Handler had witnessed his lack of control. Without another word he stomped away, disappearing back into the library. He slammed the door shut, the entire town house vibrating and making Mrs. Handler cringe.

The foyer grew quiet. Not even the servants could be heard. They were, no doubt, hiding in the kitchens. Mrs. Handler started toward her, the swoosh of her pale pink skirts against the marble floor sounding unnaturally loud. The concern upon her face revolting. "You were spotted at the gardens with another man. Is it . . . true?"

Eleanor wished the woman would leave her alone. Wished she'd shut her mouth. She had the sudden urge to laugh at the absurdity of it all. Did Mrs. Handler truly believe she would reveal her darkest secrets to her husband's mistress? Did she think they were friends?

She hesitated a few feet away, looming over Eleanor. "I wouldn't blame you if it was true."

"Do you honestly believe I'd tell you anything?" she hissed, shoving her hands into the cold floor, preparing to stand. Mrs. Handler reached out her hand, but Ellie ignored it. Tucking her wobbly legs underneath her, she slowly stood. The world swayed, the foyer slipping in a dizzying whirl.

Mrs. Handler stepped toward her, arms outstretched as if to catch her should she fall. "Let me help you."

Horrified, Eleanor stumbled back into the stairway railing. "Don't you dare touch me!"

The woman froze, her lower lip quivering with hurt. "Very well."

Eleanor didn't bloody well care. She only wanted to get away, away from the woman, away from her husband. Away. She took a step toward the stairs. The entire room tilted. She refused to moan, refused to stumble. She would make it upstairs on her own even if she had to crawl. How she hated him, hated her husband so much she could have killed him if she'd had the means. At the moment, oddly, she hated Mrs. Handler even more.

Unable to stop herself, Eleanor paused at the base of the stairs. "Why?" she asked. "Why do you love him? How can you?"

"I don't expect you to understand," Mrs. Handler returned gently. "I was so lonely, my husband never paid attention to me. He didn't care."

Eleanor turned to look at the woman who spent more time with Lord Beckett than she. She couldn't deny that her husband cared. He cared too much. He cared not because he loved, but because he wanted to control. "I'd rather have no attention than this sort of abuse."

Mrs. Handler glanced worriedly toward the library, where the doors were still closed. "You have no idea what it's like to be ignored."

"You're insane."

Mrs. Handler shrugged, flushing once more. "Perhaps. But you don't see the man he *could* be."

"You can't change him." She tried to make the woman see reason, to save her from herself and Lord Beckett. Lady Handler had two young children and Eleanor despaired to think about what might happen to them. She couldn't save herself, but maybe she could save this woman. "You can't make anyone do anything they don't want to do."

Mrs. Handler started for her with quick, frantic steps, as if desperate to make Eleanor understand. "He's different with me."

Eleanor sighed, shaking her head in exasperation. There was no use in talking to the woman. She would believe what she wanted, and for some reason she wanted to believe that Lord Beckett could change, that he was a good man.

"Perhaps you should judge people not only by how they treat you, but how they treat others. Would you still love a man who was kind to you but tortured kittens?" When Lady Handler merely stood there, looking so utterly confused, Eleanor shook her head. "You're free, completely free, yet you choose to be with him. I'd give anything in this world be free like you, but I'll never have the chance." She spread her arms wide. "This is the rest of my life."

But she could tell by the stubborn set of Mrs. Handler's jaw that she could no more change this woman's mind than she could change her husband. Eleanor turned and started slowly up the stairs. Each movement made her body ache, but she knew once she was in her chamber Fanny would take care of her. A warm bath would ease the pain. She was determined to think of James and her one magical night in the garden.

A memory that would have to last her for the rest of what would undoubtedly be a short life.

* * *

He'd been a whore for more than ten years, yet it was the first time James could truly say he actually cared about a client. Not that he had despised the others. No, he showed them pleasure, and then helped them along their way. Some, he could say were even friends. But once they left the estate, they left his mind.

Not Eleanor. No. She had stayed with him, if only in spirit, for the entire carriage ride back to Lavender Hills. As the sun peeked above the horizon and the carriage pulled to a stop in front of the estate, he was still thinking about her. He worried about her return home. He worried about her monster of a husband abusing her. Worried about how such a spirited woman would live the rest of her life trapped, imprisoned.

One of the many footmen opened the carriage door and grumbled, "Mrs. Roth is early."

Lady Lavender sighed. "Deal with her, James, will you?"

"Of course," he said automatically.

In truth he didn't want to meet with anyone, but perhaps this was just what he needed . . . to enjoy another woman, to forget Eleanor.

The footman helped Lady Lavender from the carriage. "Are you awake enough to meet with Mrs. Roth?" she asked, looking somewhat amused as she stepped from the coach.

James forced himself to smile. "Always."

Ophelia slid her arm through his and they started up the steps. The sun was just beginning to rise. It wasn't unheard of for clients to visit so very early, hoping to evade the *ton* who tended to sleep until noon. And Mrs. Roth was usually early.

"She's in your room," the footman said, opening Ophelia's office door. James had the odd feeling the big bull wanted him gone. At times he almost believed half the staff was in love with her, jealous of their relationship.

"Thank you." James headed up the steps toward his chamber. "Send for a bath?"

The man grunted in response.

For over ten years this place had been home. Now it felt cold, stifling. He paused outside his bedchamber door, resting his hand on the porcelain knob. Damn it all, he wanted to return to London, he wanted to make sure Ellie was well. He felt oddly guilty for being with Bertie Roth, which was ridiculous considering Eleanor was married. He gritted his teeth and opened the door. She was relaxed on the settee, her rich, brown hair free of pins and trailing down her back; she was ready for him.

At the sound of his appearance, she turned toward him and smiled, small lines etched at the corners of her eyes showing her age. She was older than Eleanor, but he wondered if perhaps they had known each other once. Maybe still did. The urge to ask her almost overwhelmed his good sense.

"Well, aren't you a sight for sore eyes!" She stood, wearing a light gray morning dress. "How are you, James?"

"Well. I'm just getting back from London," he explained, shutting the door behind him. "If you'd like to wait until after I bathe . . ."

She grinned. "Or I can help you wash."

He nodded, shrugging off his jacket. He liked her, truly he did. She had a no-nonsense way about her that he appreciated. She did not giggle, or gasp with virginal shock. She was truthful in what she wanted and why she visited. And she didn't give a bloody damn what other people thought about her. She reminded him of Eleanor. "Whatever you wish."

He tossed his jacket toward a chair as she moved toward him. "Are you tired, poor thing?" She undid the buttons of his waistcoat, her long fingers moving down his chest. "In London, you say?"

He nodded.

"And you didn't stop to see me?" She grinned up at him. "How the *ton* would adore that outrageous gossip."

James returned her grin.

"But you look tired. Are you sure you're up to the task? I do wear a person out, you know. Just ask my first husband. Well, if he wasn't rotting in his grave."

The woman was a widow and enjoying her life now that her husband, a man fifty years older, had perished while in bed with the maid. Now that she was free, she found her pleasure where she wished. She brushed the waistcoat from his shoulders, then started on the buttons of his shirtsleeves.

"Bertie," he said. "Was your husband . . . cruel?"

She tossed his shirt to the chair where his jacket rested. "No, I can't say he was cruel. Just a cold man who smelled like beets." She shuddered as she reached for the waistband of James's trousers. He'd known the woman for two years now. He knew she saw other men, and she never indicated she was in love. No, this was merely about pleasure and enjoying each other's company. Sometimes they didn't even make love, merely kissed and chatted.

There was a soft knock preventing Bertie from pushing his trousers down to his ankles. He reclasped the waistband and went to the door. Two footmen carried the tub inside, setting it by the fireplace. Moments later more footmen brought in buckets of steaming water and filled the bath. They looked so bloody young. Had he truly been that young once? Hard to imagine. Soon Lady Lavender would introduce them to whoring and they would be bound to the life forever.

As the young lads left, Bertie pulled the trousers and stockings from his legs. Not one to miss an opportunity, she squeezed his arse as he moved away. Stifling the urge to sigh in annoyance, James stepped into the tub and relaxed.

"As much as I would love to enjoy the view," she said, moving a chair to his side, "you obviously have something on your mind and I'm curious to know what it is."

"No," he said, letting the warm water ease his aching body. "It's your time."

"Dear, I have all the time in the world. Especially since my family has stopped pushing me to remarry." She laughed. "They might have forced me to marry the first time, but they have no control any longer."

He lifted the rag and soap. "Good for you." And he meant it. Women should have as much say as anyone. If only Ellie could have such freedom.

She took the rag and soap from his hands. "Out with it."

"A client," he admitted, even though the word client seemed too minor of a description for Eleanor. She was so much more than that. "It's obvious her husband hits her."

She tsked. "It happens often." She knelt beside him and began to rub his back with the washing cloth. "It's too bad, but nothing can be done."

She was right. So why did it bother him so? He'd always cared about his clients, but he also realized early on that he had less control than they did. Yes, for a brief moment he could make them forget, but nothing more.

"True," he said, relaxing as her warm hands rubbed up his back, over his shoulders, and through his hair. He couldn't deny that her touch was soft and tempting. He closed his eyes and leaned back, allowing the woman to wash him. But it wasn't Bertie he pictured. No, it was Eleanor who flashed to mind. Eleanor's smooth, full lips kissing the back of his neck. Eleanor's warm hands moving over him. Heat rushed through his body and his cock stirred to life.

"That's what I wanted to see," Mrs. Roth purred in his ear.

But her voice was not Eleanor's. And her scent was lemons instead of roses. The heat he felt fled, and as much as he tried to grasp onto his ardor, he couldn't. Frustrated, he surged to his feet, water trailing down his body and dripping to the tub. "I need a moment."

He stepped from the tub and went to his wardrobe, grabbing his silk wrap. His movements were jerky and frustrated as he paced the room. Damn it all, he couldn't get Ellie from his mind. What the hell was wrong with him?

"What is it?" Bertie stood, watching him warily.

He raked his hands through his damp hair. "I don't . . . nothing."

"No, it's something." She settled on the settee and patted the spot next to her. She would not let it go. The woman was used to being obeyed. He didn't dare deny her. Besides, he actually trusted her. But what to say?

"I've known you quite intimately for some time." She played with a long lock of her hair. "You've never been this bothered before. Obviously something is amiss."

He gave her a forced smile. "Perhaps I'm merely exhausted from our journey."

"It's the client? The woman who is being abused?" He didn't respond, but he didn't need to. She was a smart woman; she knew. "Surely you've noticed it before with other clients?"

He nodded, pacing to the fireplace. So why did it bother him now? That was the unspoken question. The question he'd been trying to answer for days now.

"But this woman is . . . special?"

"No." He rested his hands on the mantel and stared into the flames. "I certainly mean no offense, but we don't get close to anyone . . . ever."

He could see her smile in the mirror above the fireplace. "No offense taken. But James, you've obviously come to care—"

"We're not allowed."

She nodded slowly, but her mirth was still there, shimmering in her amber eyes. "I understand, and I won't breathe a word to anyone."

She certainly did understand. He turned to face her, folding his arms over his chest. She was trying to hide her amusement and wasn't doing a very good job. She understood that if anyone uncovered his secret it could be a disaster. She understood that he had feelings for Ellie . . . whatever those feelings were.

"I don't know how I feel," he muttered.

"Oh dear, you do care for her, don't you?"

He didn't respond, but paced to the windows. The sun was a brilliant red ball of light hovering upon the horizon. The day was moving on. Had Ellie made it home? "Of course I don't care."

"You're in love with her?"

"No!" He spun around to face her, furious and terrified all at once. Love? Ridiculous. The mere thought sent him spiraling. He could feel her, he swore, even though they were hours away from each other, he could feel her simmering beneath his skin. But love? "No. I just . . . care."

She smiled. "James, dear, we don't have to do this." Her voice was calm, gentle. "We don't have to be intimate."

His hands fisted at his sides. No, he had to do this, he *could* do this. He started toward her, undoing the belt of his wrap. "I can."

She held up her hands, stopping him. "No. Cease. You've had a long journey, you're tired, and honestly, I'm just not in the mood. What say you rub my shoulders and back instead?"

The relief he felt was immediate and unexpected. She lied, and she lied for his sake. Yes, he considered her a friend, but more surprising was the fact that she considered him a friend as well. Gratitude washed over him, warm and welcoming. Slowly, he sank onto the settee next to her.

She drew her fingers through his hair in a friendly fashion. "You are not an automaton, James. Sooner or later it was bound to happen."

He closed his eyes and sighed, appreciating the gentle touch. "What was bound to happen?"

She was right; he was bloody tired. Perhaps with sleep things would look much better. Perhaps with sleep he could figure out what to do with Lady Lavender, his sister, even Eleanor.

"It was bound to happen that you'd fall in love."

His eyes popped open. "I'm not . . ."

He bit back his response when he saw her teasing grin. With a frustrated sigh, he closed his eyes again, refusing to give into her taunting. Say what she would, but he was not in love with Eleanor. He wasn't. It wasn't possible because he had made up his mind long, long ago never to love again. Besides, he didn't deserve to love, not when he had been responsible for his father's death.

Chapter 9

The familiarity of her chamber did not offer the calming presence it normally did. The warmth of the fire, the softness of her bed, the scent of flowers from the garden, she had always been able to find a bit of peace here. Now it was all lost on her. For three days she'd remained in her bedchamber, taking her meals in her room, waiting for the bruises upon her face to heal. For three days the only person she had seen was Fanny, who brought her food and news. And Eleanor had found it difficult to care about either.

She settled at her dressing room table and gently touched the ugly green bruise that marred her right cheek, the worst of the lot. She'd fully expected Lord Beckett to return, but he remained gone from the house. Perhaps he felt guilty and that's why he stayed away.

She released a harsh laugh. Guilt? No. More than likely Mrs. Handler was keeping him busy. Eleanor sighed, picking up her powder and dabbing it under her eyes, attempting to cover the bruise and dark circles from lack of sleep. It was awfully hard to hate Mrs. Handler, she was so like a clueless puppy desperate for attention. Eleanor no longer felt angry, or even melancholy. No, she only felt numb, completely and utterly empty.

If only they would leave her in peace forever. If only she could continue her visits with James. But no, she was married, and James . . . James was most likely pleasuring another woman at this very moment. She pressed her hand to her belly, sick at the thought.

"My lady." Fanny entered the room at a brisk walk, the confusion upon her face disarming.

Eleanor surged to her feet, her pulse pounding as she expected the worst, always the worst. "What is it?"

"There is a Miss Patience Brisbane here to see you."

Not exactly what she'd been expecting. Eleanor frowned, her mind spinning. "I've never met her, have I?"

"I don't know. She says she's here with the jewelry you ordered."

Something was odd, very odd. Yet she couldn't deny that the name sounded familiar. A shiver of unease raised the fine hairs on her neck. "What does she look like?"

"A young, pretty thing with blonde hair and green eyes."

The woman from the gardens the other day? Eleanor stiffened, shocked by the thought. No, it couldn't be. Why would she be here now of all times? Her heart slammed wildly in her chest although she didn't dare show any outward reaction. Suddenly she understood. There was only one reason for the woman to be here . . . blackmail. "I see."

"Your husband has showed her to the parlor."

"He's home?" At Fanny's nod, Eleanor resisted the urge to cry out. *No.* She prayed the girl had the good sense to lie. If she had to give her money to keep her mouth shut, so be it. She didn't wait for Fanny to explain more but darted from the room, determined to get there before too much damage had been done.

Her palms dampened as she stumbled down the steps and toward the drawing room. If her husband uncovered the truth . . .

she'd be dead. Completely and utterly murdered, and the courts wouldn't blame him for killing her. A cheating husband was ignored. A cheating wife was destroyed.

As her feet hit the marble floor she slowed, attempting to calm her racing heart. The guilt that she'd tried to bury surged to the forefront. Perhaps she deserved whatever she got. She had gone against the law, had gone against everything she had learned as a child in church. Her reputation would be crushed. Her husband's name dragged through the mud.

She could hear the merry chatter coming from the parlor, easy conversation that was not heavy with damnation. The weight of fear ease slightly. She paused outside the door, just around the corner so she could not be seen.

"They've become quite popular, you know," the girl said. "I'm not surprised your wife would wish to look them over. She is known for her fine fashion sensibilities."

"Of course," her husband replied. She recognized his tone, detached amusement. He'd always liked a pretty girl and Patience was certainly pretty. The poor child was at least twenty years his junior. A fox with a hare.

Eleanor took in a deep breath, folded her hands demurely in front of her, and entered. Patience was on the settee, Lord Beckett across from her in the light blue grandfather chair. On the table Patience had laid out a variety of necklaces and bracelets, pretty, delicate things. So, she had the good sense to bring props to go along with the lie. Eleanor's gaze narrowed shrewdly; the girl was much cleverer than the young face implied.

Eleanor forced her lips up. "How lovely. You've brought your collection."

"Indeed." Patience stood and curtsied. There was certainly nothing seductive about her light green gown with the high lace neckline, but that didn't stop Eleanor's husband from looking her over like she was choice horseflesh. "'Tis an honor that you're interested."

"If you will excuse me." Lord Beckett stood. "I shall leave the shopping to you ladies." He bowed low, always charming around others, if not her. No, the world would never know the true man, because outside of these walls he was so bloody good at controlling himself.

"You are fortunate enough to have a husband who allows you such pleasures," Patience said loud enough for Lord Beckett to hear as he left the room. Yes, the woman knew how to play the game that was her life.

"Very fortunate," Eleanor said, sitting in the chair across from her.

"Here," Patience said, lifting a particularly pretty necklace of fine silver and pearls. It looked like something a mermaid would wear. Ellie was startled to find the woman actually did design jewelry. "This would look lovely on you."

Eleanor took the piece, and she didn't have to feign interest in the delicate creation. It was beautiful and unique; she'd be envied by many of her acquaintances. They waited until they could no longer hear footsteps in the hall.

"Keep your voice low," Eleanor said, rubbing her fingers over the smooth pearls. "He has spies."

Patience's brows drew together in obvious concern. She hated that look: *pity*. It made her ill. She despised knowing that people thought she was weak merely because she was trapped in a terrible marriage. Even this young chit barely out of the schoolroom understood the pathetic mess that was her life.

"What brings you here?" Eleanor demanded, in no mood to discuss her husband, or her life. She had no wish to play games with anyone.

"To sell my jewelry, of course!" She grinned and leaned closer. "You'll have to keep one, so as not to look suspicious."

Eleanor gave her a wry glance. Patience understood. Those keen eyes hadn't missed a thing. "Very good indeed."

Patience blinked, confused. "What do you mean?"

"This is a ruse then? You'll blackmail me into buying your jewelry and what . . . telling my friends how wonderful it is?"

Patience shook her head. "No, of course not. I meant it. Keep the necklace, it would look beautiful on you. But I'm not here for that. I'm here . . ." She glanced at the open door and scooted to the edge of her seat, closer to Eleanor. "Are you aware that you have a strange gentleman staring at you from across the hall?"

Ellie glanced back. Graham stood in the shadows, watching. "Unfortunately he came with the property."

"How very . . ."

How she wanted to hate this girl, but there was something utterly amusing about her boldness. "Frightening?"

"Indeed," Patience whispered. She shook her head as if to clear her thoughts, then refocused on Eleanor. "I'm here to talk about James."

Eleanor's heart dropped to her feet, anger replacing her fear. She turned away from the girl and lifted an emerald bracelet, attempting to control her trembling hands. "Very pretty," she said loud enough for whomever was eavesdropping to hear. "The thing with James," she whispered to Patience. "Whatever it was is over. If you think to blackmail me—"

She looked truly startled, shaking her head quickly. "No, as I said, I would never do something so hideous."

Wary, Eleanor slowly set the bracelet down. "Then why are you here?"

Patience hesitated, then glanced toward the open door one more time. "Has James ever told you about his past? How he came to be where he is?"

"A little." She lifted a necklace in case Graham decided to come closer. "We've only met a few times, really. We aren't that close." It was a lie. A complete and utter lie. James knew her deepest secrets, things no one else would even contemplate. He could destroy her if he wished. Yet she trusted him utterly and completely. She set the necklace back down, bemused over her feelings.

"James and two other men, Alex and Gideon, were taken practically forced into prostitution at Lady Lavender's brothel when they were still lads. Alex, my brother-in-law, is the only one who has found his freedom."

Eleanor frowned. "What do you mean *forced*?"

"All I know is that Lady Lavender used manipulation and threats to keep Alex there. We have also uncovered that she might be doing the same to Gideon. Can you think of anything, anything at all that she might be using to keep James by her side?"

Eleanor shook her head, stunned. "He respects her. He seems content . . ." Her voice trailed off as the memory of her carriage ride with James came rushing back.

"Fortunately, Lady Lavender found me just in time. If it weren't for her, my mother and sister would never have made it out of the slums. I probably wouldn't have lived."

"If it wasn't for Alex," Patience said, interrupting her musings, "we would have been destroyed. I owe my brother-in-law everything. It is his wish to see his friends freed from her bondage, and I am here to help, even though my brother-in-law will kill me if he finds out."

Eleanor shifted, uncomfortable. What right had she to share James's secrets? He'd trusted her when he'd told her about his mother and sister. "I don't see what I have to do with this."

She sighed. "I had hoped you might know something. James . . ." She frowned, beginning to pick up her jewelry and replace it in the basket she'd brought. "He trusts Lady Lavender, thinks she has saved him. But Alex and Gideon know better." She pushed the necklace toward Eleanor. "Keep it. So it doesn't seem suspicious."

Eleanor's heart hammered madly as she resisted the urge to tell this young woman everything she knew. She didn't want her to leave, but how did she know she could trust her?

Patience stood and gave Ellie a tight smile. "It was lovely visiting. I do wish only the best for you." She started to reach for her basket.

"Wait."

Patience brought her arm back to her side. "Yes?"

"Please, sit." Eleanor glanced at the door. Graham still lurked outside, but he wouldn't hear if she kept her voice low. "James was rather poor. His father died; his mother had no means to provide for the family."

Patience nodded, sitting on the settee.

"He works for Lady Lavender so that his mother and sister will be taken care of. Only . . ."

Patience waited for Eleanor to continue. The soft tick of the mantel clock was the only sound in the room. "What is it?" Patience urged when Ellie hesitated.

If she spoke the truth and it reached James, would he feel she had betrayed him? "His mother died years ago, yet Lady Lavender never told him."

Patience frowned. "Where was the money going?"

Eleanor shrugged. Lord, she wasn't even this nervous around her husband. A fine sheen of sweat gathered between her shoulder blades. She picked up the necklace Patience had given her and began to play with it, running her fingers down the fine silver chain. Her nerves were frayed, her heart pounding so hard she could hardly hear over the blood rushing to her ears. She prayed she had done the right thing by telling Patience the truth.

"You don't trust her either," Patience whispered.

Eleanor glanced up and gave her a wry smile. "I trust very few. But no, I don't. It makes no sense to me. There are too many holes in the story. I only wish that James would see Lady Lavender for what she truly is, before it's too late."

Patience tilted her head, giving her a sympathetic smile. "So, you do care about him."

Ellie flushed, studying the necklace intently. "I do."

She might be stuck in this hell for the rest of her life, but that didn't mean James had to be imprisoned as well. He could leave, and she had a feeling the truth would be the catalyst to set him free.

Patience took her lip between her teeth. Eleanor could practically see the younger woman's mind spinning. "If we can find the sister, we might be able to find answers."

Despite knowing it was better not to be involved, Eleanor couldn't ignore the thrill of excitement that tingled through her body. She had the oddest feeling that they were close to uncovering the truth.

"Yes," Eleanor agreed quietly, knowing exactly what the chit planned. Dare she help? Perhaps her husband didn't know about her visit to Lady Lavender's. Perhaps he didn't know about her trip to the tea shop, but sooner or later he would find out what she was up to.

"That settles it." Patience stood, taking her basket in hand. Eleanor stood too, confused as to what, exactly, was settled. "You find his sister, and I'll go to James."

A heated wave of annoyance shot through her. "Why?"

"Why what?" she whispered.

"Why will you go to see James?" She clasped her hands in front of her, attempting to retain the outward façade of someone unaffected. Inside, she boiled with annoyance. Dear God, she was jealous. The realization struck her hard.

"I'm untitled and unmarried. It will be safer for me to visit. No one knows me here, therefore no one will be able to identify me. Besides," she leaned closer, a sparkle in her green eyes, "I'm dying to know what it looks like."

"I'm afraid you'll be rather disappointed," Eleanor said, feeling once again amused by the woman's bold audacity. Let her have her fun now while she was young and unattached. "Very well, I agree."

Patience grinned, and in that moment, Ellie knew she had finally found a true friend. "You find his sister," Patience said. "And I have a feeling we will find the truth. I only hope James is ready to accept it."

* * *

James opened his bedchamber door, prepared to meet with a client, only to freeze on the threshold. Shock left him utterly speechless. Never, in a million bloody years, had he expected to see Alex's sister-in-law. James struggled to retain control. "What the hell are you doing here?"

"My goodness." Patience sighed, standing from the settee where she had been resting. "Is that any way to treat a client?"

"If you think I'll sleep with you, you're even more insane than I realized." He pushed the door shut and stomped toward her. Hell, he didn't need this . . . not now. "Alex will try to kill me, and then you."

She tilted her chin stubbornly. "Nonsense."

"You can't be here." He latched onto her arm and dragged her toward the door. She was a thin thing, but strong, and when she dug her heels into the carpet he found himself stumbling. "I will throw you over my shoulder."

"You won't." She shrugged off his hold. The girl knew no fear, God help them all. He did not envy Alex. "Besides, if I leave now, it will only court suspicion."

He cursed. Blast it, she was right. Right about everything. When had his life become so insane? He'd been content here making money for his family. He'd been content until . . . until Eleanor. Now he found suspicion in everyone, trusted no situation, and found himself thinking more and more of escape.

"I must stay, at least for as long as it takes to . . ." She glanced at the bed and blushed. "How long does it take, exactly?"

Frustrated, he moved toward the windows, as far away from her as he could get. What the hell had happened to him? He brushed aside the green velvet curtains. The afternoon sun was covered by thick, gray clouds, allowing little light to shine upon the fields of lavender. He'd cared about his clients, yes, but he'd always been able to maintain a professional distance for his sake and theirs.

But not with Ellie. No, Ellie had ruined him. Truth be told, when Ophelia had said he had a client, he'd broken out into a cold sweat, the thought of bedding anyone other than Ellie repulsive in some way. Bloody hell, he couldn't even perform anymore, and all because of Eleanor. Did she have any idea how very much she had disrupted his life?

He spun around, facing Patience and taking his anger out on her. "Does Alex even know you're here?"

She shrugged. "He knows I'm in London."

"Of all the utterly stupid—"

"I visited with Eleanor this morning," she interrupted.

He froze. He'd been trying over and over to forget the woman. For the past three days he'd feigned illness after illness to keep from meeting with clients, until Ophelia had grown suspicious and begun questioning him. Now . . . here Eleanor was again, shoving her way to the forefront. Blast it all, he couldn't escape her. "Good for you. Is that why you're here?"

"Yes, perhaps." She sighed and settled on the settee. "I'm worried about her."

"Why?" He was instantly concerned, despite himself, and damn it all if he didn't head closer to Patience. She had him, and if the sparkle in her eye was any indication, she knew it.

"She had bruises." She waved her hand toward her face. "She'd done her best to cover it with powder, but I noticed."

He closed his eyes, lowering to the settee, pain and anger combining. Did her husband know about the gardens? He was torn between leaving her alone and heading to her home to kill the bastard himself. Hell, it had been his fault. He should have known better than to take her in public. *His* bloody fault. His fault his father had died, his fault his mother had died. His fault.

"Her husband—"

"I know." He rested his head in his hands, feeling completely and utterly useless. "There is nothing I can do. Nothing any of us can do. He owns her."

"Fine then." She tilted her chin stubbornly high and glared at him.

What the bloody hell did she expect? For him to call the man out? He had as little control as Eleanor. He stood and began to pace the room, his mind spinning. Aye, why not call the man out? If he killed Lord Beckett, Ellie would be free. But when he ended up dangling from a rope, who would feed his sister?

"Then let us discuss *you* instead," Patience said.

He jerked his gaze toward her, frowning. "Me?"

"Yes. Alex and Grace are offering you a place to stay. You can move in with us until you find a way to make money in a more genteel fashion."

He almost laughed, until he realized she was utterly serious. Leave the estate? His sister? Leave Eleanor? The thought did not even tempt him. Aye, it was so easy for Alex, Grace, and Patience. But they didn't understand, they couldn't comprehend why he needed to remain. "I can't leave."

"Why?"

He didn't trust this chit to tell her the truth. Besides, if she knew, the girl would probably rush off in an attempt to save his sister. And so he lied, using his old excuse. "I owe Lady Lavender my life." The words came out hollow, empty. He wasn't so sure he believed them anymore, and if the look on Patience's face was any indication, she didn't either.

"You owe her nothing! She's used you."

He released a harsh laugh. "You've been talking to Alex." What did this girl know? Good Lord, she should be going to picnics, flirting with local lads, not sitting in a brothel. "You've heard only his side. The truth is I have a family to support."

At least at one time he'd had a family. Now . . . he wasn't so sure. Frustrated, he moved to the sideboard and poured a brandy.

"You're a stubborn man, James. You can't see what's in front of you. The woman is using you. Always has been."

He spun around, facing her. The urge to shake the girl overwhelmed him. "It has nothing to do with Ophelia! I have a sister to support!"

"And do you know for sure she's getting the money?" She said the words he'd been mulling over for days. When he didn't respond, she stood, reached into her reticule, and pulled out a stack of letters tied with a blue ribbon.

"Here." She tossed the packet to him. Instinctively he caught it close to his chest. "Alex was going to send these, but I took them when I left, deciding I would visit you. I have done what I can. You won't see the truth, but maybe these will help. If you come to your senses, I am staying at the Lucky Horse Inn about halfway between here and London. I'll be there for the next fortnight."

She turned and walked out the door. James wasn't sure if he should stop her or let her go. She'd been in his chamber a mere ten minutes, and her departure would indeed court suspicion. Yet he let her leave, because he'd had enough of the truth for one day. He flipped through the letters, three in all. What could they possibly say that he didn't already know? Slowly, he sank onto the settee and pulled open the first note.

James,

I've repeatedly written to you, yet rarely heard back. I can only assume Ophelia has intercepted my missives. I've come into some troubling information.

James took in a deep, trembling breath.

I have found that a Mr. McKinnon worked for Gideon's father some fifteen years ago. It is my belief that the three of

*us, me, you, and Gideon, are connected in some way that only
Lady Lavender understands.*

James settled the note on the settee. A cold chill raced over
his body. What the hell did it all mean? He surged to his feet and
paced the chamber, reviewing the facts. His father had been a
driver for a wealthy family, he knew that much. He'd been eight
when his father had been dismissed for a reason he still didn't
know. After, his father had slowly started drinking himself to
death, until . . . "What did you do, Da?"

He had to talk to Patience, must get answers. Frantic, James
tore across the room and into the hall, directly into one of Lady
Lavender's guards.

The man latched tightly onto his arm. "Lady Lavender wishes
to speak with you."

"Later," James growled, jerking away from him. So, the woman
had noticed Patience's departure. He raced down the steps, ignoring the curious glances of servants. He only hoped he wasn't
too late.

As he hit the foyer, the front door opened, bringing him up
short. For the second time that evening James was shocked frozen
when a familiar man entered the front door.

"Good God, Alex."

Alex jerked his gaze toward him, his own eyes widening in
surprise. "James?"

For a brief moment he thought he imagined his friend. But
no, this Alex was different. He'd changed. His dark hair longer,
his skin bronzed. He looked . . . happy, content, and . . . troubled.
It was an odd moment. James had stayed the same, Lavender Hills
had stayed the same, but Alex, that outside world, had changed.

James moved forward, a smile of pure happiness on his face.
"Alex, it's wonderful to see you."

"And it's good to see you as well." He seemed hesitant, worried
about something. Suddenly James knew there was more to his

friend's appearance than a visit. Behind Alex another man stood, slim with blond hair and stoic-looking features. There was no sign of Patience.

"How are Grace and Hope? I do so look forward to your letters."

Did he hear the silent message in his comment? Alex was quiet for a moment, his intense gaze searching James's face. What the hell was Alex trying to tell him? His heart slammed wildly in his chest, his hands curling as he resisted the urge to demand answers.

"Well," he finally said. "They're both well."

James parted his lips, intending to ask the man why in the world he was here when Lady Lavender's office door opened. Her gaze fell to Alex first and any warmth faded from her lavender eyes. For a long moment they merely stared at each other, and in that moment they both seemed utterly capable of murder. There were so many things James wanted to know, but before he could ask, Alex took a step toward Ophelia's office. What the bloody hell were they up to?

"It was good seeing you, James."

Just like that Alex was gone, leaving James with more questions than answers.

Chapter 10

James knocked on Ophelia's office door, knowing something was amiss. For two days he hadn't seen nor heard from the woman. No clients visited the estate. No one but Wavers entered Ophelia's office. And no one saw her come or leave. Odd indeed.

He'd questioned the servants as discreetly as he could, but no one seemed to know anything about Ophelia. Even the maid who had given him Alex's letter had disappeared, although no one could give him a response as to why she'd left.

He knocked again, his irritation mounting. Although Wavers had returned the same day Alex and his friend had arrived, James hadn't heard word about his sister. Had the bull found her? If so, why was Ophelia keeping her whereabouts secret?

The door opened and Wavers stood there glaring down at him. "Vhat?"

"I need to speak with Ophelia."

"She's not feeling vell."

"I need to speak with her now," James snapped. He would uncover the truth about his sister, no matter what it took.

A thick brow lifted, a brief show of surprise, when he'd never shown emotions before. But then James had never demanded anything. No, he'd been a good little whore, doing whatever was demanded of him. No more.

"Very vell, vait here."

He started to close the door. James shoved his foot in the way, preventing him. "I'll see her now."

Wavers lifted his lips, growling.

"Stand down, Wavers," Ophelia called out. "Let him in."

Reluctantly, the bull stepped into the hall. James entered and slammed the door in Wavers's face, giving them privacy. But as he turned toward Ophelia, he was startled into momentary silence. She sat slumped in a chair, staring unblinkingly into the roaring fire. A tray with soup and bread was on the side table, but untouched, no steam coming off of the surface, as if it had been there for some time. Ophelia did not glance his way as he started toward her. Tucked upon the chair with a blanket over her body, she had never looked more fragile, lost, alone.

"Are you well?" Despite his pride, he was curious. She had manipulated him, controlled him for years, yet he still couldn't help but care. Damn his protective instinct.

"Gideon has left for good."

James frowned, confused. "I . . . see." He shouldn't have been surprised. Of the three of them, Gideon had hated Lavender Hills Estate and its owner the most. Yet if Ophelia had secrets binding them all to this estate as Alex had claimed, then how had they both escaped? He settled in the chair next to hers.

"You're sad because he's gone?"

She didn't respond.

"Perhaps this is a blessing," he tried, wondering how in the hell he could get the truth from her lips. "You never did get on well. It would be better to have a man who truly wants to be here than someone you are . . . forcing."

She released a wry, bitter laugh. "He belonged here. Belonged with me."

He thought her response odd indeed. Belonged here? Gideon had never belonged here, surely she knew that. Or did her words mean something deeper, darker? Hell, the woman he had thought he'd known was gone. He had a feeling he was seeing the true Ophelia, buried under the weight of her own bitterness and pain.

"We uncovered the whereabouts of your sister," she said, surprising him.

"Where is she?"

She picked up her sherry, and he didn't miss the way her hand trembled. Was it his imagination, or did she seem to be drinking more often? "She's living in a small cottage in Bath. Actually has two adorable children. Is quite content from what I heard."

She painted a serene and beautiful picture. Too bad James didn't believe her in the least. "And my mother?"

"She did not give word about your mother because she did not wish to upset you."

She didn't meet his gaze, he realized with suspicion. Whenever they spoke, she always looked directly at him as if she had nothing to hide. Tonight she stared moodily into the flames. "And she still thinks I am working for the government as a spy, which is why I can't be in touch with her?"

She took another drink. "Yes."

He settled back in his chair and watched her wearily, bloody tired of the games. "I see."

For one long moment neither of them spoke. Ophelia stared blankly at the flames in the fireplace, slumped in her chair like one ancient and decrepit. Aye, she was much older than he, but this was the first time she seemed her age. It was only when a piece of coal popped, releasing a spark of embers, that she came awake and glanced at him, startled as if just realizing he was still there.

"I will leave you in peace, but before I go . . ."

She lifted a brow. "What is it?"

"A client."

She picked up her sherry and drank. She still hadn't touched her food. "Yes?"

"It's obvious her husband is abusing her. She had bruising." He wasn't sure why he told Ophelia about Eleanor; perhaps to see if she had any bit of compassion within her.

She sighed, sounding more annoyed than concerned. "Unfortunately it happens often."

Despite the truth of her statement, it still rankled him. He raked his hands through his hair. Society seemed to agree that it was wrong, but the law did not prove to be in a woman's favor. In other words, they ignored the issue because actually doing something about it was too bloody hard. "Is there nothing we can do?"

"What, James?" She snatched up the snifter and refilled it. "As the husband, he legally owns her." She lifted her glass in salute. "All hail the queen." She drank deeply. "It's ridiculous that we can have a woman ruler, yet we have no real control."

Her bitterness was palpable and justified. "There is no one you know?"

"No. I'm sorry." She lifted her decanter and refilled her glass. "'Tis best you learn now, James, that the world is unfair and even more unfair for women. Now, if you'll excuse me, I think I'll bathe and head to bed."

She stood, and he didn't miss the way she swayed as she headed toward the door, taking her glass with her. His father had started drinking after he'd lost his position; he'd been fired and humiliated. What was Ophelia's reasoning? What drove her to numb her pain? Guilt, perhaps?

He stood slowly. She'd left the door open where anyone could stroll by, but he was alone. He waited until the familiar fall of her footsteps faded. Completely alone. She'd lied to him, was lying to him still. He glanced toward the desk where she kept her notes on the clients and men on staff. Dare he? He moved slowly to the desk, keeping his attention on the door. He could hear the soft voices of other men who worked at the estate, the murmur of servants, but no one dared enter her office.

James knelt before the desk. Of course the drawers were locked, that was no surprise. He grabbed the mail opener atop her scheduling book and slid it into the keyhole. He closed his eyes, pressed his ear to the drawer, and concentrated. Moments later he heard the click of the lock. Perhaps he was slower than he'd been as a youth, but he hadn't lost his talent after all. The drawer slid open easily, but he was disappointed to see the typical books of business. Nothing personal.

"Damn," he muttered, shutting the drawer.

The fact that he'd never seen anything personal of Ophelia's troubled him. He unlocked the bottom drawer a little more quickly. He'd never let himself wonder much before, but now his mind was constantly spinning. Who was Lady Lavender? Where had she come from? What was her purpose in bringing him here? He knew she was from France. He'd uncovered that much years ago, even though she'd spent years trying to hide her accent. Other than that she remained an elusive mystery.

Frustrated, he shoved aside a book, and there they were . . . letters. At least five, all postmarked from Alex and addressed to him. Open, read, but not by James. He swallowed hard, anger and confusion burning through his chest. With trembling hands, he reached out and touched the missives to make sure they were real. She'd lied. Alex and Gideon had been right all along . . . Ophelia had never had their greater good in mind.

"I see I can no longer trust you." Her voice snapped through the room, but it didn't startle him. No, nothing could surprise him any longer.

James lifted his head, meeting Ophelia's gaze. There was no pain or guilt in her voice; she didn't bloody care if he betrayed her. Had she ever cared?

"Why?" he demanded, standing and holding up the letters. "Why?"

She sashayed inside, no worries marring her smooth skin. Wavers followed as if trying to protect her . . . from James. The irony was not lost on him, the one man she had trusted the most. "You belong here, and I will not allow Alex and Gideon to fill your head with nonsense."

"I understand. I understand why you feel loyalty toward the woman, but James, think on it. You, Gideon, and I, brought here together by blackmail."

James had bristled, annoyed with the accusations. *"Not blackmail."*

Alex released a harsh laugh. *"She told you if you didn't do as she said, your family would starve to death."*

"Nonsense?" James asked. "Or the truth?"

She studied him intensely, as if trying to decide how much she could trust him. She wore the same shrewd gaze she wore when dealing with clients. "Wavers, shut the door."

He did immediately, no questions asked. James didn't like the look upon either of their faces. Ophelia wore a smirk of satisfaction, as if she'd expected him to turn on her. James slammed the pack of letters upon the desk. War it would be. Pure anger was crawling rapidly through his body, clawing its way to the surface, and he was finding it incredibly hard to retain control. "I demand to know the truth."

"Oh, James, believe me, you don't want the truth." She headed toward the sideboard, pouring herself brandy. He had to resist the urge to wrap his hands around her neck. He'd never in his life wanted to harm a female, but if he lost that one bit of humanity he had left, he feared he would.

"James, you don't tire of this?" Alex had asked him years ago. *"Being nothing more than a toy."*

"It's a position. A job I do well. There could be worse things in life than pleasuring beautiful women."

Alex had patted him on the back. *"That's where you're wrong, my boy. It's not a job, it's a hell in which we have no choice but to reside."*

"What will you do?" Ophelia asked, strolling toward the mantel, the drink in her hand sparkling under the firelight. "Will you leave? And then how will you support your dear sister and her lovely family?"

James began to tremble, his emotions a conflicting mesh of ire and despair. He tried to pay attention to her but found his mind spinning back . . . back in time. Suddenly, he was in the garden of the Rutherford ball two years ago, the same garden where he'd been attacked.

"Liar!" Alex stepped closer, seething. *"I don't need someone to check on my welfare. You were spying. Damn you, whose side are you on?"*

And he had been spying, sent by Ophelia herself.

James had calmly smoothed down his jacket, his movements slow and determined like the arrogant bastard he'd been. *"I'm on the side of the woman who gives money to my family."*

"You see," Ophelia said, taking a deep drink and drawing him back into her office. "There's something I didn't tell you, thinking to spare your feelings. Your sister relies upon your money, as her husband left her and the children. They would be on the streets if not for you."

"You're a fucking idiot if you trust her," Alex had said years ago.

"How do I know you're telling me the truth?" James demanded.

She shrugged as she took another drink. "Would you care to visit her?"

"Think on it, James," Alex's voice whispered through his memory. *"We three were brought here at the same time. There must be a link, but until we tell each other the truth, we can't possibly understand."*

"What say you, James?" Ophelia asked. "Do you want to visit her?"

"I know why I'm here," James had snapped. *"Ophelia offered me a position, a way to save my family, and I grabbed the opportunity."*

What if it had all been for nothing? The thought almost brought him to his knees. "Perhaps I would like to see my sister after all."

Ophelia lifted a brow, obviously surprised. "Will you tell her the truth?"

"I don't see why I should. I'll keep my story as is."

She took a drink, watching him over the rim of her glass. He could read nothing in her expression. "And if a neighbor recognizes you?"

"I highly doubt the women from a small country shire will have visited Lavender Hills."

"Touché," she said with a wry smile. Aye, she smiled, but he didn't miss the coldness in her eyes. She was incredibly angry with him, and he didn't give a damn. "Well then, I shall tell the driver to prepare. Two days from now?"

"Wonderful." James scooped up the letters. "And considering these are addressed to me, I'll take them." He paused for a telling moment. "Unless we are no longer able to receive mail?"

She waved her hand through the air in dismissal. "Take what you will, it shouldn't bother me. I only meant to protect you."

"Of course you did." He gave her a tight smile, bowed mockingly, and headed toward the door. He wouldn't look back, didn't dare say another word. He knew she lied. James strolled from the room, trying to keep his anger in check. His life had become a bloody mystery, but there was one thing he knew for sure . . . Ophelia had no intention of taking him to his sister.

* * *

Eleanor wasn't sure how she could focus on knitting mufflers and mittens for the needy when all she could think about was James and his missing sister. Fanny had hired an investigator for

Eleanor, but so far the man had come up with nothing new. How could she concentrate when Fanny was to be back with the latest report any moment?

"Are you expecting someone else?" Lady Rafferty asked, leaning closer to Eleanor.

Startled, Eleanor jumped, dropping her needle. "What?"

"You keep looking toward the windows."

She forced herself to smile and scooped up the needle. "Oh, no. Merely hoping the rain holds off."

"Isn't it too early to be knitting winter wear?" Mrs. Trustman whined from across the room. For once Eleanor was thankful for the woman's complaining, for it drew Lady Rafferty's all too intense attention to her.

"'Tis never too early to prepare for winter," Lady Rafferty returned. "Nor never too early to care for those in need."

Eleanor resisted the urge to roll her eyes. Lady Rafferty had started the Ladies' Society for the Needy merely to portray herself as a kind and God-fearing woman. But there was never a more gossipy mongrel than she.

"Wouldn't mind him flirting with me," Lady Pierce said from across the room.

"Whom are you discussing?" Lady Rafferty demanded, setting her knitting on her lap.

Lady Pierce flushed. "No one. Merely a Mr. Smith. New to town. Very attractive."

The rest of the women giggled like debutantes. The room of colorfully dressed ladies would have been a delightful distraction any other day. This afternoon their presence merely grated. Eleanor sighed, setting her red scarf upon the table and picking up her tea. Every week they took turns at each other's homes. She'd almost forgotten about today's meeting and would have cried off had she the chance.

"Makes a woman feel all warm merely by glancing at him," Mrs. Kaul explained. This prompted the women to giggle once more. Considering Mrs. Kaul was some fifty years of age, it was rather shocking.

Eleanor avoided their gazes, lowering her attention to her teacup. She knew only too well about the warmth that a man could produce within a woman. She lifted her tea, her hand trembling while the memory of her and James in the garden took center stage. No longer was the idea of intimacy a fantastical myth, but a marvelous reality. The memories would not leave her be. The feelings came back at night when she closed her eyes, almost driving her mad with an aching need. Oh, she'd heard the whispers and giggles of satisfied women, but always thought they must be exaggerating.

Obviously they hadn't been. For years she'd assumed there was something wrong with her. But no, perhaps, just perhaps, there was something incredibly wrong with her husband. How Lord Beckett would enjoy hearing that theory. She set her teacup down and picked up her knitting. The soft clack of needles combined with the murmur of conversation and provided a pleasant background to her troubled mind.

"Good day, my dears."

Eleanor stiffened at the sound of her husband's familiar voice. The women giggled, their lashes fluttering flirtatiously. Disgusted, Eleanor forced herself to glance at the man and smile, continuing the façade. All the while she wondered how the *ton* did not see her husband as he truly was . . . a demon in a fine suit. Or perhaps they did, but as he had money and a title, they ignored the truth.

He strolled toward her, and even though she knew he would never harm her in front of so many, she still stiffened. Always that pretense of a loving couple. Early in their marriage she had actually heard debutantes gossiping about their romantic marriage as if their relationship was something to aspire to.

He leaned down and pressed his lips to the top of her head. His familiar musky scent swirled around her, making her ill. It wasn't that his sandalwood scent was noxious; quite the opposite. But his cologne reminded her of the times when he'd force himself upon her. She would bathe after, scrubbing until her skin was raw and pink, scrubbing until she could no longer smell his scent on her body. But the memory was still there, always.

"I don't quite know how you ladies do all you do, and look so lovely at the same time," he said, his gaze sweeping over the room, taking in each woman, as if they were all so very special.

There was a twitter of laughter like merry little birds. Eleanor's hands curled into her knitting. She had to force herself not to rip the scarf apart and stab her husband with a knitting needle. If she had to listen to any of them wax on about how lovely her husband was when he left, she just might scream. They hadn't a clue what he was really like. But they must have heard the rumors, at least of his affairs.

"I shall leave you to your charity." Although he strolled through the room, leaving them, she felt his presence all the same. She always felt him, as if he'd buried his claws deep within her and would never let go. But there had been one time when she'd forgotten her husband, if only for a few moments . . . when she had hidden within the lilacs with James.

"Such a gentleman," someone muttered.

Eleanor continued to stare at the door, lost, alone although she was surrounded by people.

"Lucky to have," someone else whispered.

When a man strayed, it was the woman's fault. They would not question him, but instead they would wonder what the wife had done wrong. Just as they would all assume it was the wife's fault if there were no children.

Yes, they all knew he'd been unfaithful. She'd caught more than one person whispering when she'd entered a ballroom, more than one lady glancing her way and smirking. How they would love to see the elegant Lady Beckett fall. Even though her husband ruled her, she had ruled the *ton*, but even now that was crumbling between her fingertips. The cold, reserved Lady Beckett was slowly becoming a laughingstock, an amusement for gossipmongers.

Fanny suddenly appeared in the doorway. Catching Eleanor's gaze, she gave a quick nod. A thrill of anticipation raced over her body. Her husband forgotten, Eleanor stood and set aside her knitting. "If you'll excuse me."

She did not wait for their approval, for the information Fanny had uncovered was too important for her to worry about manners. She stepped into the foyer and shuffled behind the open door where the others could not see them. Fanny followed, twisting her hands together with impatience and worry.

"You've found something?"

She nodded but glanced around first, making sure they would not be overheard. She'd been hesitant to help Eleanor, worried if Lord Beckett found out, he'd kill her. If the woman didn't speak soon, Eleanor was determined to shake the answers from her lips. "St. Anne's."

Eleanor's heart leapt into her throat, her mind spinning. The woman was still alive. Still in London. Hope blossomed within, a stirring of warmth in her chest. "You're sure?"

"Rather. They are known for taking in orphans."

"Servant or nun?"

"Nun, apparently."

Eleanor had the sudden urge to laugh. To throw her head back and cackle like a witch from a children's novel. James . . . a whore, his sister a nun. What would he think? It was too ridiculous, too much, as if the world was playing a jest upon them all.

"Or at least she will be soon," Fanny whispered. "Hasn't taken vows quite yet."

"Thank you, my dearest," Eleanor whispered, not daring to hug her friend in case a servant, or Graham, who was now lurking near the dining room doors, should see.

When Eleanor started to leave, Fanny reached out, resting her hand on Ellie's sleeve. "Will you tell me now why you are looking for this woman?"

"Not now." She looked pointedly toward Graham. Fanny glanced back at him and glared. Eleanor wouldn't have been surprised if the woman had stuck out her tongue. Her reaction was most amusing. She realized with some bewilderment that she was no longer afraid. Graham and his unsettling presence, the fear of her husband's return home . . . at some point in time it had lessened.

"Is it a man you're after?" Fanny whispered, frowning. "Is that why you're acting so strangely?"

Eleanor froze.

Fanny waved her hand through the air, dismissing the comment. "Never mind, don't answer that. But remember, if your husband finds out, he will . . ."

She didn't need to finish; they both knew . . . he would kill her. Ellie sighed, resting her hands on her hips. "You know, when one continually threatens death, it sort of loses its meaning."

"Yes, well, I'd like to keep my position, if you don't mind. So please don't do anything stupid."

Eleanor grinned. "Of course not."

Fanny cursed under her breath as she dropped into a curtsey, then stomped up the stairs. Eleanor was left in the foyer with Graham watching from the shadows. She didn't even bother to glance at the butler as she reentered the parlor. The man would say what he wanted to her husband, but surely there was nothing suspicious in a woman speaking with her lady's maid.

"Is all well?" Lady Rafferty asked as Eleanor settled beside her.

"Yes, very."

"Hmm." The older woman picked up her teacup and sipped. "Your lady's maid seemed quite frantic."

"Frantic?" Eleanor laughed. The old bat, fishing for gossip. "Hardly. She was merely upset because my new wardrobe was late in arriving from the seamstress. Silly nonsense, really."

"Well, that is good then."

The room lapsed back into gossip, and she was left in peace. Left to turn over and over in her mind the information she had received. Dare she send James a letter? Last time he hadn't in the least been appreciative when she'd stuck her nose in his business. In fact, he'd been downright irate when he'd found her at the tea shop. But damn it all . . . she had to know the truth. She had to know if James was being played the fool by Lady Lavender; she owed him that much.

"St. Anne's." She turned toward Lady Rafferty. "Have you heard of it?"

"Yes, I suppose." She watched her curiously. "Why do you ask?"

"Merely thought we might choose to sponsor them next."

She shook her head, frowning. "Dreary. Utterly wretched. The nuns are terribly harsh. If you insist on choosing them, I'm afraid you will be the one who must deal with the mother superior. And be forewarned, they don't take kindly to those who are not Catholic."

"Well one can hardly blame them with how they're treated nowadays," Mrs. Kaul exclaimed loudly, always one to have an opinion and not afraid to shout it.

Eleanor nodded, smiling lightly. "Never mind then. 'Twas merely a thought."

The room erupted into an argument as to whether Catholics were being treated fairly, and Eleanor was left to mull over her options. She might not be welcome at St. Anne's, but she would be welcome at Lady Lavender's. She sipped her tea, contemplating her options. Blast it all, she would tell him the truth, no matter what it took. Eleanor picked up her knitting and feigned interest in the women around her. It was settled, she was going to do something stupid after all . . . she was going to visit Lady Lavender's one last time.

Chapter 11

Eleanor waited impatiently in James's chamber. She knew very well it was ridiculous to visit when she could have well sent him a note. But how could she know that he would truly receive that missive? Yes, she was merely being safe. Besides, she could admit, at least to herself, that she wanted to see him again . . . and again . . . and again. Yes, she could admit it, after three days, she missed him. So much so that she'd even paid double Ophelia's usual asking price merely to see James without an appointment.

Yet when the doorknob turned, she wondered what in the bloody world she'd been thinking. She spun around to face him. James stepped inside wearing his shirtsleeves, tie, brown waistcoat, and black trousers. The sight of the man made her pulse flare, her body responding instantly to his presence. She wanted to run to him and throw her arms around his neck. Wanted to press her body to his, feel his heart beat against her chest. His gaze swung around the room until he found her there . . . near the windows. The look upon his face was most amusing. He was shocked, to say the least.

"Hello," she said, such a silly greeting. But she was nervous and excited, and . . . and he looked anything but happy to see her.

He shut the door slowly. "How are you?"

She smoothed her hands down her blue-and-ivory skirts. "Well. I'm well." Silly, really, that she'd worn a good walking dress here where anyone might recognize it, but she had wanted to look her best.

It was inane, polite conversation better left for the ball-rooms and parlors than in a brothel. A variety of emotions clawed their way to the surface. She hadn't seen him in days, her body ached for his touch, and her soul ached for him and the free-dom he represented. James was like no man she had ever met. He did not judge her, and he seemed to have no desire to control her. No, he was completely sure of himself and completely sure of her.

He moved closer, slowly and temptingly, as if he worried about frightening her away. As her gaze scanned his fine features, from the day's growth of beard that made him seem much older, to those firm lips, up to his brilliant green eyes, she had to remind herself that she was not here to kiss and caress but to give him information.

"Patience visited you?" she asked.

He nodded, pausing near the fireplace, too far away for her to touch him. She felt his absence as if they were in two different rooms entirely. "You're sure you're well?" he asked, returning to the subject. This was true concern, not the manipulated empathy her husband gave her during their courtship. The realization warmed her.

"Patience noticed my bruising?"

He nodded again, moving closer to her, so close she could smell the starch and lemon soap on his clean shirt, so close she could see the concern in his green eyes. His attention traveled her face, pausing on her upper right cheek. Slowly, he reached out, brushing his thumb over the barely noticeable bruise. She wavered, her body drawn to him like a flower to sunlight. She wanted to sink into the man, wanted to press her lips to that pulse beating at the side of his throat and forget.

"I'm fine," she whispered, swallowing hard.

His arm dropped to his side, the concern in his gaze turning to anger. "What happened?"

She shrugged, clasping her hands together in front of her to keep from reaching out to him. Anxiety, pleasure, desire . . . she wasn't sure what she was feeling. "Someone saw us."

When his face paled, she waved her hand through the air, dismissing his worry. "Nothing that could be proven. Still, he didn't like that I had tarnished his reputation."

"Bastard," James seethed.

She blinked, surprised by the emotion upon his face. Only Fanny had dared to say the truth about her husband, only Fanny had dared to care. No one else took her side, not even her own family. The sudden burn of tears had her looking away.

"What are you doing to provoke him, my dear?" Her mother had asked in a whisper, as if Eleanor's complaint would bring shame to the family. Her mother had actually put the blame on her, telling Ellie to calm her wild, wicked ways. She'd known then that she could tell no one the truth.

"Your husband is a demon," he seethed.

Husband. She shivered at the sound of the word. She would no longer call the man her husband. She couldn't without feeling ill. In her eyes they were no longer married. He had betrayed her one too many times.

James rested the sides of his hands on her face and kissed her, softly, gently. "I'd kill him, if I could."

"Don't say that." Her voice quivered with pent-up desire and fear. "You'd only end up in prison when you don't belong there."

"What can I do?" he whispered, resting his forehead to hers. "Tell me."

You can tell me this is not the ruse of a whore, she wanted to say. *You can tell me you truly do care about me, only me.* "You can make love to me."

He pulled back just enough to look her in the eyes, searching for the truth. "Are you sure?"

"I mean it." She gripped his hands tightly. "I need to forget him. To know passion, even if once. That moment in the garden didn't satisfy me, it only made me want you even more . . . completely."

He was silent.

"James, will you?" She pressed his hands to her heart. "Will you show me passion? Will you erase the memories of my past?"

He didn't respond, merely drew her forward and crushed his mouth to hers. She opened for him, and he took full advantage, his tongue sweeping over hers in a devastating kiss that left her weak and light-headed. All worries were gone. Any despair vanished.

"I've been dreaming about this," he mumbled against her mouth.

As had she, every night since meeting him. Eleanor moaned, wrapping her arms around his neck and finding comfort in the strength and vitality of his body. When he scooped her up and carried her toward the bed, she didn't utter a word of protest. Her slippers fell from her feet, and she knew her clothing was soon to follow. There was no one else in the world. Nothing else mattered.

He laid her gently upon the soft coverlet, then stepped back. Slowly, so very slowly, his long fingers moved down the buttons of his waistcoat. It was a seductive show, but she wondered if he was giving her time to change her mind. He untied his cravat and tossed it to the chair.

Over the years she'd become quite adept at shutting down her mind while her husband rutted her like an animal. She'd sunk into a numb state of nothingness that had allowed their mating to be bearable. But with James she felt alive. With James she didn't want to be numb. She wanted to feel every touch, every kiss. When his shirt came off, her heart thumped so madly she thought it would break free. Nerves, desire . . . she wasn't sure which to focus on.

He paused, his hands at the waistband of his trousers, the only thing he still wore. "What is it, Ellie?"

"Nothing." She swallowed and looked at the ceiling. She'd thought her husband handsome, but James put Lord Beckett to shame. His body was all muscle and hard planes. Not an ounce of fat marred his perfect form. Eleanor took in a deep, trembling breath. She needed a moment, merely a moment to regain control of her nerves. She could do this . . . she *would* do this. She jumped as James settled on the edge of the bed.

"Ellie," James said softly. "You're sure you want to do this?"

She nodded, humiliated when tears stung her eyes. Blast it, she wouldn't cry in front of him. She never cried and she wasn't about to start now. Furious with herself, she swiped at her eyes with the backs of her hands.

"But . . . you're nervous?"

She nodded again. He was so damn gentle. She felt like a bloody innocent, a debutante. She hated not having control of her own feelings. She might not have any say in her life, but she sure as hell had always been able to control how she reacted to it. Until now . . .

James was silent for a long moment, those kind green eyes watching her, seeing so very much that she didn't want him to see. Not even with her husband had she been this vulnerable. She shivered, crossing arms over her chest.

"If . . . if," she stuttered, an impediment that she had had as a child and thought she'd conquered. "If I don't go through with this, I fear I will die inside. I'm already half there, James."

"All right." He reached toward the chair near the bed where he had divested himself of his clothing and picked up his cravat.

She didn't understand his intentions until he lifted his hand, the material dangling from his fingertips. "Tie me."

His words utterly shocked her, and she'd thought she was beyond surprise. "Wh . . . what?"

"Tie my hands to the headboard."

The command was sinful; then again, she was at a brothel, so what had she expected? She stared at the cravat hanging from his fingers . . . tempting her. Lord Beckett had bound her up once, merely another way from him to control her. It had not only been humiliating, but terrifying. Although the idea sent a wicked thrill through her body, she would not humiliate James.

"No." She shoved her hands into the bed and sat up, struggling with her blue-and-ivory skirts. She was drowning in a mound of material, and her corset was so tight she could barely breathe.

"I mean it." He lay down, stretching out beside her, vulnerable, comfortable, trusting. A wave of hair had fallen over his forehead, his green eyes like soft moss. He looked very much like an elegant gent, waiting for his love. A weight of emotion settled heavily against her chest. She felt humbled, and at the same time she was terrified. She wanted no person's life in her hands. She jumped from the bed, only to grip the post when her legs nearly gave out.

"I won't let you do this to yourself," she whispered, clinging to the bedpost.

"Ellie," he whispered, "I trust you."

"Maybe you shouldn't."

He quirked a light brown brow. "Will you abuse me?"

"Of course not."

"I trust you, Ellie." There was no merriment in his gaze, no mocking laughter. He was utterly serious. "Tie my arms, and you'll be in complete control. I won't touch you unless you want me to."

She took her lower lip between her teeth, confused. "You're serious?"

"Quite."

She'd been abused and humiliated by her husband. Yet in this small space with James she felt more vulnerable than she ever had before, and she didn't understand why. All she knew was that she couldn't leave here without knowing the truth, and when he kissed her, when he touched her, she knew. She understood. Everything made sense.

She swallowed hard and reached for the tie. "Very well."

He lifted his arms, his biceps flexing as he rested upon the pillow. James was all sinewy muscle, in much better shape than her husband, and seeing his bared chest didn't exactly put her at ease. He could so easily overpower her if he wished.

Even as fear and uncertainty ate at her nerves, she couldn't deny that pulse that throbbed low between her thighs. That pulse he'd awakened in the garden only a week ago. Their gazes clashed and held. Slowly, she approached him, as if he was a wild cat she feared would attack just when she'd dropped her guard. At the bed she paused, uncertain.

"Straddle me," he said softly. "Come here, and straddle me."

She placed his cravat between her teeth, then reached around, found the clasp upon her skirt, and undid it. The material fell down around her hips. Perhaps it was her imagination, but his green eyes seemed to darken. She stepped out of her skirts while undoing the buttons of her bodice, ignoring the tremble of her hands. She was putting her trust in a whore. The insanity of her decision was not lost on her. But she'd married a lord and look how well that had turned out. Obviously the station of one's life did not determine his trustworthiness.

She shrugged her bodice off and tossed it to the chair where his clothing lay. For this moment, this hour, she was free. Her husband had no idea where she was; no one did. Wearing only her shift, stockings, and corset, she crawled onto the bed, her knees sinking into the downy softness. James did not flinch, he did not stiffen at her approach, but she didn't miss the rapid beat of that pulse in the side of his neck.

"You are beautiful," he whispered.

She flushed at his compliment. She'd heard it too often for the words to mean anything, yet coming from James she couldn't ignore the tremor of appreciation. Not bothering to respond, she lifted her shift just enough so she could straddle his lean hips. Her inner thighs pressed to his, and even through her stockings and his trousers, she could feel the heat of his skin.

"You will have to get used to my compliments," he warned.

She grasped his wrists, growing annoyed. She didn't like compliments, and she knew she would most likely never see James again, so his comment was pointless. "My husband told me often how beautiful I was when he was courting me. The word has lost its meaning."

She leaned forward, realizing only too late that she was placing her bosom near his face. It must be done, and she would not react like a naïve virgin. With trembling hands she tied his wrists to the spindles of the headboard. He pulled, testing the bonds. But seeing him tied only made her panic. The urge to flee overwhelmed her, and she jumped away, stumbling from the bed. He did not look worried by her sudden departure; he didn't seem concerned.

"You aren't going to leave me here, are you?" He gave her a gentle smile. "It would be quite humiliating."

As she stood there she realized with some surprise how very much he trusted her. "No. Of course not."

"If you do not like compliments about your beauty, I will think of others."

She frowned, crossing her arms over her chest. She felt cold, unsure, confused. "Such as?"

He titled his head, resting it against his biceps. "Such as how much I admire your strength."

She flushed, looking away. It was worse than hearing about her beauty. If she'd been strong, she would have broken her engagement when she'd realized something was a little strange about her husband. If she was strong she would find a way to leave him even now.

"I admire your desire to help others."

She sighed. She'd helped no one but herself. She hadn't even fought for her lady's maid when her husband had fired her years ago. Knitting scarves for orphans from the safety of her parlor was hardly saintly.

"Most of all I admire your ability to thrive under extreme circumstances. You would do the queen proud."

"I am related to the queen's second cousin," she blurted out.

He did not react to her. "Undress, Ellie."

His face was serious, so utterly serious. Damn it all, she was tired of feeling sorry for herself. Her hands trembled as she undid the clasps holding her corset together. If she was in charge, completely and utterly, why did her entire world seem off-balance? She tossed her corset to the chair and drew in her first full breath since dressing that morn. Besides her husband, no male had ever seen her in her underclothing.

"Your shift," James said, his fingers wrapping tightly around the binding that held his arms in place. It was then that she realized he was attempting, very hard, to control himself. He wanted her, desperately, passionately. Only then did she allow her gaze to travel down his muscled chest, following that narrow trail of hair down his flat belly and to the very area where no woman dare look. His erection pressed hard and long against his trousers. The sight of his cock made her mouth go dry.

He wanted her as badly as she wanted him. Ellie grew warm, a heated flush of desire pumping through her veins. He could not touch her, but dear God, she wanted to touch him. Her body thrummed with need, her heart with desire.

"Good God, you're beautiful," she said, the same thing he had said to her only moments ago. She meant it. He was stunning. Magnificent. And it terrified her. The attraction between them was unmistakable, palpable. And she knew if they consummated their relationship, she would only grow fonder of the man.

The entire time his gaze was on her face. He did not flirt with her, he did not leer at her as most men would have. No, he merely looked at her with affection, with need and desire. "I will not do or say a thing you don't want. You're in charge."

And she believed him. Hell, she completely and utterly trusted him. Slowly, she climbed atop the bed and straddled his hips once more. With trembling fingers she reached for the hem of her shift and drew the material over her head, tossing it to the ground.

James sucked in a sharp breath but did not say a word. His attention dropped to her ivory breasts, trailed down her flat stomach, and landed at the nest of blonde curls shading her femininity. And Eleanor let him look. Let him take in his fill, knowing he could not touch her even if he desperately wanted to.

With tentative fingers she reached out and drew her hand down his torso, through the thin line of crisp hair that trailed toward the waistband of his trousers. His stomach muscles jumped, his thighs grew harder, and his eyes closed in pure wonder.

At the waistband of his trousers, she paused. "I'm going to take off the rest of your clothing now, James, and you're going to let me."

He didn't respond, merely clenched his jaw so tight that she could hear his teeth grind. His entire body was tensed and coiled, every muscle straining against his skin. He wanted her terribly, but he trusted her to set the rules. Eleanor smiled a relieved grin. Perhaps, just maybe, she could enjoy lovemaking after all.

* * *

James was rather sure he was going to die of want. He could not take his eyes off Eleanor as she fumbled with the buttons of his trousers. He even found her lack of experience a heavy aphrodisiac. When the buttons popped open and his cock sprang free from the tight confines, he almost cried out in relief. Ellie stared at his erection in utter fascination. He wasn't sure if she was confused, surprised, or nervous; he only wished she would touch him. His fingers flexed, tightening around his bindings as he resisted the urge to break free and touch her. Completely and utterly at her mercy, there was nothing more painful, nor more intoxicating.

"You're much larger than my husband," she whispered.

He would have laughed if he hadn't noted the fear in her voice. "A woman's body is very accommodating if prepared."

She gave a jerky nod, trying her best to trust him, but he could see the wariness in her gaze. When she reached for his trousers and gently tugged them down his legs, he helped her by lifting his hips. It was all he would do while tied to the bed. They were both utterly naked, just as he'd wanted. She sank back on her heels and slowly studied his body, pausing once more at his cock. James had to resist the urge to groan. She was killing him with her gaze, destroying him with her touch.

"You say I am beautiful, but you are, James." She reached out, resting her warm hand on his belly. His stomach muscles jumped to life, his cock swelling so that it moved against her thigh. She did not pull back as he expected. Instead she brushed her fingers down the trail of hair that led to his groin.

"Lean, golden body. You practically glow in the firelight." Her fingers paused at the base of his cock. James gritted his teeth, resisting the urge to lift his hips and beg her to touch him.

"You're lovely. The sort of man people should paint and admire." She skipped his erection and ran her hands down his muscled thighs, through the crisp hair on his legs.

"You are killing me, do you know that?" he whispered gruffly.

She smiled, a beautiful, angelic grin that had his heart flip-flopping. What the hell had happened to him? He'd never been so utterly on the brink of losing control with a client. Yes, first it had been the sadness in her eyes that had attracted him. He'd merely wanted to make her smile. He couldn't deny that the more time he spent with her, the more fascinated he became by her charming wit. But now . . . now he found he respected her, damn it all, he liked her.

"I think I like being in control."

Aye, she did. Eleanor drew her fingers back up his legs. He focused on her breasts, those gleaming ivory orbs with the rose-tipped nipples begging for his touch. The woman was pure perfection. He wanted to feel the weight of her breasts against his palms, wanted to kiss, suck each nipple until she was squirming, begging him to ease the tension.

It was a job. It had always merely been a job. He'd justified what he did by telling himself he was not only helping his family, but also giving pleasure to the clients who visited. But hell, for once he was selfish. For once he could admit he wanted her . . . wanted Eleanor for himself. Wanted her to ease the heavy ache in his loins, only her.

"I think I would like to touch you now, James."

He groaned, squeezing his eyes shut and fighting for self-control. When her warm fingers wrapped around his cock he could no longer hold back. His hips lifted, his cry almost painful. She was killing him, and he would die willingly. The entire world spun, tilting off its axis.

She slid her warm grip down his shaft. "I can't help but wonder what it would feel like to have you so fully inside of me. Completely."

"Please," he gasped. "You are torturing me."

Her startled gaze met his. "Am I?"

"Yes," he hissed through gritted teeth.

The dark haze that swept over her gaze had nothing to do with fear and everything to do with desire. He might want her, but she wanted him as well.

"I should not wish that." She settled her thighs on either side of him.

Every muscle in his body strained. He wondered if she was wet and aching, aching as much as he ached for her. He tightened his hold on the cravat wrapped around his wrists, resisting the urge to snap the material. When she gripped his erection and centered her body over him, he thought he might break the damn headboard. Slowly, she lowered herself. The thickened tip of his cock slipped between her wet folds, pressing into the entrance of her sheath. An erotic flush of desire climbed across her chest and up her neck as a gasp of surprised delight parted her lips.

"Oh my," she moaned, sinking fully atop him.

James didn't dare move, but savored the feel of her surrounding him. When she lowered her body, her hardened nipples brushing against his chest, heated desire shot to his groin, making him even harder, if possible.

"Ellie," he gasped. "I'm trying really hard not to move, but if you don't soon, I swear to God I might have to break this bed merely to get to you."

"Well," she whispered, "we can't have that, can we?" She rested her hands on either side of his shoulders and leaned over him, rocking her hips, taking him deeper. Her lush mouth parted on a gasp of sheer pleasure. She was utterly beautiful. He'd known her only for weeks, yet James felt closer to Eleanor than he'd felt to anyone. How he wanted to wrap his arms around her waist and draw her close to him, to breathe in her essence, to taste her salty skin.

"James?" she whispered, her breath warm across his ear. The weight of her body against his was almost his undoing. He lifted his hips, surging into her heat. The woman was completely open with him, giving James her everything.

"Yes?"

"I want you to hold me. I want you to touch me."

"Thank God." The words he'd been waiting to hear, the words he hoped to hear. He jerked on the cravat. The knot came loose easily, sliding free of the headboard.

She gasped in outrage. "My knot!"

He grinned. "Ellie, my love, you'll never be a sailor."

She paused, settled atop him, a crease of confusion between her brows. Half her hair had fallen down around her shoulders, swaying across her breasts every time she rocked forward. "You could have escaped at any moment?"

"Yes." His hands ran down her smooth back, toward her lovely bottom.

A myriad of emotions raced through her brilliant sapphire eyes. "But you didn't?"

He knew what she was thinking . . . she wasn't sure if she should be annoyed with him for fooling her or touched that he had held back. He gripped her lush bottom, pulling her closer, deeper, touching her everywhere he'd dreamt of touching her since they'd first met. In a mere month, a bloody month, she had turned his world upside down. She had destroyed his calm, rational life.

She groaned, his deception forgotten as they moved together as one, rocking in a rhythm they found naturally. As she surged forward, he lifted, until they came together like the waves of the ocean, crashing, merging. Hell, he wasn't sure where he ended and she began. He only knew he needed to feel her release as much as he needed to feel his own.

"Come for me, Eleanor."

"Yes," she groaned.

Her entire body tightened around him, her sheath trembling against his cock. It was too much. James could hold back no more. His world exploded into a burst of white-hot pulsing joy. He'd never come inside a woman without a French sheath to cover him, and even then very rarely. But Eleanor sucked him dry. His wet seed pulsed into her body as she cried out, finding her own sweet release.

She collapsed atop him, their bodies slick with sweat. James slid his hands up her back and into her hair, gripping the strands as if that could keep her with him. For a long, long while they merely lay together, their legs and arms entangled, her face resting on his shoulder, and her harsh breath tickling his skin. This is what her marriage should have been. This is what his life could have been . . . nights spent with a woman he . . . no, he would not even allow himself to love her. But he cared, good God, he cared. He'd wanted her with an intensity that he wouldn't have thought possible, could barely breathe when she was gone.

"You should be cherished," he said gruffly.

She was silent for a moment. "At one time I thought I would be."

He drew his hands down her silky smooth back. "You will be now, in this moment, forever with me."

She was quiet for a long moment, and he desperately wanted to know what she was thinking. The fire was dying, the windows open, allowing a cool afternoon breeze to flutter the curtains. Her sleek skin was growing chilled under his hands. James pulled the satin green coverlet over her. If only they could stay this way forever.

"Will there be others today?" she whispered.

His hands paused at her back. "No. She does not overwhelm us. Usually only one a day."

"But tomorrow," she whispered, her voice catching in a telling way.

He closed his eyes, not wanting answer, not wanting to think about tomorrow, or the next day, or the next. Dear God, how would he go on? How could he let her go back to her demon of a husband? How could he possibly see other women? He wrapped his arms more tightly around her, unable to let go.

"Perhaps I can gather money of my own," she said, her lips brushing against his chest as she pressed a warm kiss to the skin.

Despair, humiliation, and anger overwhelmed him. He didn't want her money. His hands flattened to her back as he tried to retain control of his emotions. Damn it all, he wanted to be a man and provide for his family on his own, provide for her so she didn't have to rely upon that bastard of a husband.

"If I gathered enough money, perhaps I could . . . put you up somewhere."

He sighed. "And if your husband uncovered the truth?"

She didn't respond, but she didn't need to. Lord Beckett would kill her, and most likely he'd try to kill James. Besides, even if she had the funds to keep him, she didn't have the funds to provide for his sister as well.

"I can't," he said a little too harshly. "We can't."

She turned her head, pressing her face into his neck. For a moment, he held her, merely wrapped his arms around her and prayed that she would one day find the courage to flee her husband, run away to the Americas or Italy, *anywhere*.

All too soon she lifted up, pulling away from him. For one brief moment her gaze met his. He saw the pain there, the desperation, the despair, but it was gone in a flash, replaced by that hard, determined woman who had first walked in through his door those weeks ago. James felt spent, utterly destroyed.

"So," she said, looking away. "This is why people are intimate."

She moved off of him and stood beside the bed. How he wished he knew how to paint. Hell, even write poetry, for she deserved to be immortalized. She was a goddess, *his* golden goddess, and the mere thought of anyone else touching her sent a heated ripple of jealousy flaring though his body.

"We still have some time," he said, knowing he sounded desperate and not caring. The thought of never seeing her again didn't sit well. In fact, it made him break out in a cold sweat. The future seemed empty, dark. He surged from the bed as she pulled her shift over her head.

"I must go before I'm found."

"Stay," he whispered, his hands curling into the bedsheets.

She averted her gaze, snatching up her corset, but he'd seen the look of despair in her eyes. She wanted to stay as much as he wanted her to. She tugged the corset together, struggling to fasten the busk. He did not help her; he found he couldn't move. Although her corset was not fully buttoned, she dressed quickly, as if in a hurry to escape him and the feelings he stirred within.

Buttoning her bodice, she turned toward him. "I have something to tell you before I leave."

She was leaving. She was actually leaving. James reached for his trousers and stood, dressing. He felt utterly numb. His mind begged him to grab her, pull her close, and demand she stay. His body could barely move. "What is it?"

She slipped her feet into her slippers. "We found your sister."

He froze. The words hit him hard, and up until that moment he realized that he thought she had died. Slowly, he sank to the edge of the bed. She was alive . . . all this time. He tried hard to picture her . . . a pale, elfin creature who had quietly followed him around. Sweet, kind to every stray animal they found.

"Where?" he asked, his voice raspy with emotion.

"She's at St. Anne's preparing to become a nun."

Not Bath? He jerked his gaze up to her. "You jest."

She shook her head, looking as grim as he felt. "I'm sorry, James."

He should have been happy that his sister lived. All he could think about was the fact that Lady Lavender had lied, and his money had most likely never gone to his family but some bloody nunnery, if his sister had even received it. "Not dead then?"

She picked up her leather gloves. "No."

A nun. A damn nun. A chill of disbelief raced down his spine. Dear God, she could never know what he did, how he'd made his money. "How did you uncover the truth?"

She shrugged, flushing. "I hired an investigator."

He surged to his feet, angry at Eleanor, at Lady Lavender, even at his sister. "Damn you, Ellie. I told you not to interfere."

"I'm sorry I only wanted the truth for you." She picked up her bonnet where she'd left it on a table near the settee. "Good-bye, James."

Damn it all, no matter what he couldn't let her go like this. He was on her in two steps. James met her near the door, and before she could even blink he'd latched onto her upper arms and jerked her to him. It was a soft kiss, a gentle kiss, a good-bye kiss. James had to force himself to stop, to release her arms and step away from her.

"Will you see your sister?" She looked worried, clutching her gloves in her hands. "Will you go to her?"

He shook his head. "No. She can never know what I've become."

The sadness in her eyes mirrored the feelings in his heart. He tucked a lock of hair behind her ear, then pulled the veil down over her face. "Good-bye, Ellie."

She rested her hand along the side of his face, her lower lip quivering. "Good-bye, James. I hope you find happiness."

Her words seem to hang in the air between them, an unreachable goal. She didn't understand that there was no chance for him now. His mother was dead. His sister was gone. And Ellie . . . she was merely a fantastical dream that could never be fulfilled. His hands curled as the all-too-familiar tightness in his chest flared to life.

While the fire in the hearth sputtered and sparked, going out, she turned and left him, taking any hope with her.

Chapter 12

St. Anne's was exactly as Eleanor had imagined . . . a dark, dreary edifice worthy of a gothic novel. Just looking up at the façade sent a shiver of apprehension down her spine. What a horrible, wretched place to live. Yet Miss McKinnon was here . . . Eleanor knew for sure, without a doubt, that James's sister was here.

The coach door opened.

"My lady?" Franklin stood by waiting impatiently, as if he had more important things to do this dreary day. Another servant in a long line who found it amusing to mistreat her, knowing she could never fire them without her husband's approval.

Her hands trembled with pent-up anger. She'd been belittled for years. No more.

Eleanor glared coldly at the man. "If I wish to sit here and ponder life's meaning for hours on end, I will without comment from you, is that clear?"

His jaw clenched, his gaze flashing with humiliation and ire. "Yes, my lady."

Eleanor resisted the urge to grin, feeling oddly free for the first time in years. She would make sure James's sister was well taken care of; she could do that much for interfering. Then, only then, would she leave. She took in a deep, trembling breath. She would leave her husband, her life, her family. She would leave London, and she would leave James. She would start over any-where she wished . . . Italy, France, Germany. Perhaps someday . . . she would send a note to James, and perhaps someday he would leave his life behind and join her. But for now she would think only of herself, and she had had enough.

"Franklin, I will be going inside." She stepped out, not bother-ing to take his hand. She wore a demure blue day dress with long sleeves and a high collar, a black bonnet perched atop her head. She prayed the sisters would not find fault in her style or manners.

It had been easy enough to visit the nunnery. She hadn't had to lie. She'd merely told the butler she would be heading to St. Anne's, as she was thinking of donating money. It was the sim-ple truth, or most of it, and she would donate, fortifying her state-ment. Yes, everything must be laid carefully according to plan.

"I shall be back within the hour."

"Yes, my lady," he mumbled.

She bit her tongue to keep from reprimanding him, knowing his opinion would not matter a week from now. No, a week from now, if all went as planned, she would be sailing to another country. She would be free. Yet as she headed toward the imposing gray building a heavy weight seemed to press upon her chest. Free . . . at what cost? She would most likely never see James again. She brushed aside the thought, determined to move on with her life, when she noticed a boy, a scrawny lad huddled a near the corner, taking shel-ter from the wind. He looked up, and their gazes clashed. She swore she saw James in his hazel eyes. James, in his scrawny body.

Her feet moved of their own accord closer to the lad. "Are you hungry?"

He gave a quick jerk of his head, crossing his arms over his chest.

She reached into her reticule, pulled out one pound, and handed it to him. His eyes grew enormous, but just as soon they narrowed in suspicion. "It's yours, I promise. To do with what you will. Don't show anyone, all right? Take it home directly to your mother or father."

He didn't wait around for a response, but tore down the street, clutching the money in his grubby first. She watched him go until he disappeared into the shadows, until her heart stopped slamming wildly, and until thoughts of James faded.

Determined, Eleanor forced her feet up the wide, shallow steps and pulled the cord. Even the bell announcing her arrival sounded melancholy, perhaps even a bit ominous.

When the door opened it was by a formidable-looking nun with pasty skin and dark eyes that glared down at her in a way that would impress even Graham. "Can I help you?"

Eleanor steeled herself, realizing that her visit wasn't going to be easy. She gave the woman a small but respectable smile, one you would give an acquaintance born in a lower station of life than you. At times sweet and demure worked, other times arrogance. She had a feeling only arrogance would work with these women.

"I'd like to speak with the mother superior."

"You'll wait outside." She started to shut the door.

Eleanor shoved her booted foot between the door and the jamb. "I'll wait indoors." She didn't wait for a response but pushed herself past the woman. "And you'll get her now if you'd like the very large donation I'm thinking of giving."

The woman regarded her with a wary glare but reluctantly shut the door. Eleanor didn't miss the grumbled curse under the older woman's breath as she shuffled away. Certainly no way for a nun to speak. Eleanor grinned. She'd been bullied, beaten, humiliated . . . this nun was not going to frighten her away.

"Sit here." Her hard tone left no room for argument.

She nodded toward a wooden bench outside a door. Eleanor settled primly, smoothing her skirts around her as she watched the woman disappear into a nearby room. She would wait for as long as it took. She could not leave London, leave James, without settling this matter. And she had no doubt the mother superior would see her because it was obvious the place needed donations.

With a sigh, she studied her surroundings. The same dreary gray stone that made up the outside of the abbey covered the halls. No tapestries, nor lanterns. The place was quiet. Too quiet. The only sound was the soft drip of condensation from somewhere down the corridor, and the only light was the weak glow coming from the windows.

As the clock ticked the seconds by she became more frustrated, anxious to see Miss McKinnon and continue with her plans of escape. Eleanor surged to her feet and paced the hall. Since being with James only yesterday she'd kept herself busy, knowing there was the very real possibility she would shrivel up into a ball and never move again if she thought too much upon the fact that she and James were over.

Here, now, she had nothing else to contemplate. It was last night when she'd returned home, worried her husband would be there and demand attention, that she realized she would kill herself before allowing Lord Beckett to rut her once more. James had shown her passion, had shown her that there was more to life than pain and suffering. And no matter what, she would always be grateful to him. The aching in her heart thumped painfully, spreading across her chest. *James.* She sank onto the bench and bit her lower lip, refusing to give in to the sting of tears.

She was almost grateful and relieved when she heard the sudden thump of small feet coming from down the hall. Eleanor tilted her head toward the sound and waited, curious despite herself. Moments later a nun appeared, stepping from the dark dreariness. She did not glance Eleanor's way as she swept by; her pale face remained cold and stoic, no flush of kindness or greeting. But the small girls following were not so disciplined.

From ages five to ten, some looked at her with wariness, others greed, probably thinking about picking her pockets, but some . . . some looked at her with a wistfulness that tore at her heart, a spark of hope that said they prayed every night for someone to help them, someone like her. Was she the woman who would take them from this life of pain and emptiness?

It was the last girl . . . a blonde little thing who caught her full attention. Her big blue eyes met Eleanor's, and the fear in those orbs were almost Ellie's undoing. She wanted to scoop the girl up, to bring her close to her bosom and promise that everything would be well. If the lad outside had reminded her of James, this tiny child reminded her only too well of herself. But within a fortnight she would be racing from London, hiding from her husband, and that was no life for a child.

"Samantha!" the nun snapped out, startling the little girl. "Keep up."

The child scurried forward, and Eleanor could merely watch as she disappeared around the corner. The silence fell once more, and she was alone. So very alone. Fanny would not escape with her, for the lady's maid had found another position in a country estate not far from her family. James would remain here, bending to Lady Lavender's will until he perished. Ellie . . . Ellie would be alone. But perhaps, just maybe, she could find some peace.

The door to the office opened and yet another pale and prim woman in a long, black habit stepped into the hall. The white coif she wore over her head did not soften her hard eyes and stern mouth. If Eleanor had not experienced such hardship in her life, the woman might have actually intimidated her. As it was, she was merely amused.

"May I be of help?" Her voice was low with a menacing growl. It was obvious she didn't appreciate it when outsiders invaded her domain, demanding entrance.

For the sake of the children, Eleanor searched the woman's faded blue eyes for kindness but saw none. "I'd like to talk to a Miss McKinnon."

The woman narrowed her beady eyes. "She is taking a vow of silence. She talks to no one." The woman started to turn, intending to dismiss her, but Eleanor wasn't so easily dismissed. It was sheer stubbornness that had kept her going this long.

"Silence?" Eleanor stepped between the woman and the door. "She's a nun then?"

She tilted her round chin high, glaring down her crooked nose at Ellie. "Not as of yet, but perhaps in a few years, with the right training, she will be fit. If you'll excuse me . . ."

But Eleanor didn't step aside. "If you want your donation, you will allow me to speak with her."

The woman was silent for a moment, her steely gaze searching first Eleanor's face and then sliding down the fine silk of her gown. She could practically hear the old witch calculating her worth.

Apparently finding her sufficient, the woman nodded. "Very well. You may use my office."

She spun around in a swirl of dreary skirts and swept over the threshold. The small room was as cold and depressing as the rest of the place. The only adornment, if one could call it so, was a rather terrifying wall hanging of a bloody and tortured Jesus gazing mournfully down at Ellie. She shivered as she settled, then she settled in the chair across from the mother superior's small desk. How different the office was compared to Lady Lavender's succulent room. Two women, each in charge of a rather substantial domain. They might not look the same, yet Ellie noticed a familiar grim determination in both their eyes.

It wasn't until the mother superior demanded, "Marietta, bring Miss McKinnon," that Ellie noticed a small mouse of a woman huddled at a table in the corner, her fingers black with ink as if she'd been taking notes.

She pushed her wire-rimmed glasses up her button nose. "But . . . but she's—"

"I know what she is!" the woman snapped, making the small nun jump to her feet. "Now obey me."

The nun scampered from the room. The mother superior settled behind her desk, glaring at Ellie. It was a wry amusement that lit Eleanor's gaze when the nun offered her no tea or refreshment of any kind. A bully, she was. But Eleanor had dealt with plenty of bullies in her past.

"How much . . . exactly, are you willing to donate to our Lord?" she finally asked.

Eleanor had to hide her smile. "We shall see. Once I speak with Miss McKinnon and see how she fares, I will make my decision."

"How she fares?" the woman thundered. "What exactly are you implying?"

Eleanor was saved from answering when the door opened. A young, petite pale creature with warm brown eyes walked demurely inside. Eleanor's heart hurt just looking at her, the features so like James's. She knew without doubt that this tired-looking creature was his sister. The urge to latch onto her hand and tear her from the nunnery overwhelmed Eleanor.

"Arabella, this woman is here to speak with you."

The young woman's troubled gaze found Ellie's. "I do not know you, do I?"

"You don't?" The mother superior glanced Eleanor's way, damnation and accusation in her eyes.

Ellie shrugged. "I never claimed to have known her." She turned her attention to James's sister. "No, you don't. But I did know your family and I am merely visiting to check on your welfare."

Her small hands clasped tightly in front of her. She seemed disturbed by the news. "As you can see I'm well enough."

"Please, Mother," Eleanor said, glancing at the old woman. "I'd like to speak with Miss McKinnon alone."

"My lady, I'm sorry but—"

"Alone." Eleanor's face went stoic, her gaze cold.

Arabella suddenly looked nervous, like a mouse trapped in the corner by a hungry cat. Or in this case, a demanding woman from the outside world, infiltrating a place of purity and innocence. No, Eleanor did not belong here in the least, but she wouldn't leave until she spoke to the young woman alone.

"Very well." The mother superior stood, the legs of her chair screeching over the stone floor. "Five minutes."

She left the room, leaving the door wide. Ellie had no doubt the old bat was lurking in the hall. "Sit," Eleanor demanded of the girl. When she hesitated for the briefest of moments, Eleanor was thrilled to see the spark of determination in the young woman's eyes. She wasn't exactly beautiful, but there was certainly something about this meek woman that intrigued Ellie. With the right gowns and her hair uncovered, perhaps she could pass as pretty.

Eleanor closed the door. "I'm a friend of your brother's."

Arabella stiffened, obviously startled. "I see."

Eleanor settled in the chair next to hers. "You look very much like him."

Arabella swallowed hard. Although she covered it well, Ellie didn't miss the pain that flashed across her eyes. "I have not heard from him in years . . . is he well?"

"He is healthy." She narrowed her gaze. "But you know he is alive, don't you?"

She flushed and looked demurely at her lap. "Yes. I also know what my brother is, my lady." She clenched her jaw, her gaze growing troubled. "At sixteen I decided to find him. It took some time, but I did. I found him whoring himself at Lady Lavender's. Agreeing to live here was the only way I could stop myself from becoming him. I was fortunate indeed."

The horror of what the girl said washed over Ellie. All this time James had been hiding himself away for nothing. How would he feel if he realized his sister knew the truth about his occupation? If the hardness in her gaze was any indication, Arabella wasn't too pleased with her brother.

"Fortunate?" Eleanor couldn't help but ask. She supposed it was better than prostituting, but still she would never consider a woman fortunate to be here of all places. She frowned. Why must women always survive, why could they not thrive?

Arabella smiled, dimples pressing into her cheeks in a way that lit up her pale face. Certainly she could land a lovely doctor or lawyer at the least, if introduced to the right people. "I know it doesn't look like much, but it is better than living on the streets."

"You know you are very much like your brother."

She flinched at the comment, and Eleanor had to resist the urge to set her down a peg or two. The brat should be honored to be like James. Eleanor sighed, feeling worse than before she'd arrived. James was right, it was better if he didn't meet his sister, didn't know the truth. "You both did what you had to in order to survive."

"Survive?" Arabella released a harsh laugh that belied her gentle disposition. "My brother abandoned us to live a life of sin!"

Eleanor frowned, growing annoyed with the ungrateful chit. "Your brother abandoned you so that you might have the life you couldn't have with him there. Do you think you would have lived so comfortably had he been working on the docks? Or in a factory?"

"Comfortably?" Arabella shook her head, a lock of auburn hair falling from her coif and caressing her pale cheek. "I don't know what you consider to be comfortable, begging on the streets, sifting through garbage . . ."

Eleanor felt ill. There must have been a mistake . . . but no. She'd known from the very beginning that something was wrong. She'd known she could not trust Lady Lavender. "Did your mother receive money from Lady Lavender?"

"If she did I didn't know about it."

"Perhaps . . . perhaps she didn't tell you."

"I promise you, my lady, if we received money of any kind, I would have known. My mother would not have died attempting to steal a loaf of bread, and I would not have almost perished from hunger."

"Oh dear God." She pressed her hand to her thumping chest. She had lied. Lady Lavender had lied, and James had no idea. "How?"

"Let me enlighten you," Arabella said. "My mother stole bread from a baker. When he caught her she had two options, either service him in another, more sinful way, or go to prison. She chose the first. Once word got out, she was known as a whore. Men would come to her for favors and she allowed it because she knew her reputation was already ruined. It was one of those men who murdered her and was never caught. I was so young and very easily could have ended up selling myself on the streets as well. I was fortunate enough to be taken in here."

Eleanor shook her head, feeling the sudden sting of tears. All for nothing. "It wasn't supposed to be this way. When your brother was a child, not yet a man, he was approached by Lady Lavender. She told him that if he worked for her, she would send the money he made to you and your mother. She would see that you were taken care of."

"She lied," the woman whispered, finally understanding the horror of the situation. A variety of unsettling emotions swept through Arabella's eyes. Despair, horror, even acceptance . . . all at once.

"It would appear so."

"James . . ." The woman paled, but shook her head, obviously still confused. "He didn't leave us?"

"No. Everything he did was for you."

A single tear trailed down the woman's pale cheek. For one long moment they were silent. From somewhere in the distance a church bell rang the hour . . . two o'clock. Her five minutes were long since over, and she wondered why the mother superior hadn't interrupted. Eleanor reached into her reticule and handed the girl a handkerchief.

Arabella swiped at her cheeks. "Even if I believe you, it does not change anything. I must pay for the sins of my family."

Eleanor pulled her chair closer and took Arabella's small, cold hands in hers. The delicate child would have been destroyed on the streets. Perhaps she was better off here. "My dear, the only sins you can pay for are your own. Your brother and mother did what they had to."

But Arabella didn't seem to hear her, lost in her own musings. "If I hadn't been welcomed here, where would I have gone? The factories? The streets?"

She was right. Eleanor had thought there was nothing worse than living with Lord Beckett. She'd thought that only married women were imprisoned. But now . . . now she realized there were prisons of all kinds. James was imprisoned because of Lady Lavender, and Arabella, she was imprisoned because she had nowhere else to go, no money, no family, no station in life.

"I can't leave here." Arabella's eyes pleaded with Eleanor, as if begging her to understand. "Surely you must realize that?"

Ellie had a feeling it was fear of the outside world holding the girl captive. "I could find you a position in a household, perhaps, as a lady's maid."

"And if the world uncovered the truth about my brother?" She smiled kindly at Eleanor. "Besides, I wouldn't have a clue how to dress a lady."

Arabella returned her handkerchief. Ellie was torn . . . torn between her desire to help this woman and her need to flee London. Time was running out.

"Arabella, you cannot blame your mother, or James. No one is perfect. We merely do what we can to survive. Good people do bad things all the time. It doesn't make them evil, especially when what they do, they do for others, for love."

"I had resigned myself, you know," Arabella whispered. "To this life. I had no family, I had no one. I had nothing else but this. And now . . . now . . ."

A glimmer of hope whispered through Ellie. "Will you contact your brother?"

She shook her head, her eyes filling with tears once more and dashing Ellie's dreams of reconciliation. "I cannot. It would be best for both of us if we went on with our lives."

Ellie grew grim, her lips compressing tightly. "You are resigned?"

She gave a jerky nod of her head. Eleanor could read the hesitation in her gaze. No person, no one, dreamt of a life of dreariness. Perhaps there was time for her yet. But now . . . right now Eleanor had more important things to worry about. It wouldn't do to court her husband's suspicion.

Eleanor stood. Time was of the utmost importance, and as much as it pained her to know she would hurt James, she must tell him the truth before she left London. "If you are sure you will stay here, then I offer you good wishes."

"Will you visit again?"

Eleanor wasn't sure if she wanted to laugh or cry. "I'm afraid not."

The disappointment in the girl's face pierced her heart. She didn't belong here. Hell, it was obvious Arabella didn't even want to be here. Eleanor started toward the door. There was nothing she could do for her at the moment.

"Do you love him?"

Eleanor froze; her pulse throbbed. She didn't need to ask of whom Arabella spoke. Slowly she turned to face her. Even the dourness of St. Anne's had not destroyed the girl's romantic notions.

"Of course not." She forced her lips to turn up, giving the girl a kind smile. "I would never be stupid enough to fall in love with a man who loves so many others."

Arabella seemed disappointed, as if she had actually hoped her brother could find true happiness, true love. She didn't understand the ways of the world, having been cloistered in a nunnery for years. She didn't understand, but then again, neither did Eleanor.

Without another word, she pulled open the door and stepped into the hall. She would send a note to James and tell him the truth. Then she'd send a note to Arabella, asking her once more if she would like a position in a genteel household. It was all she could do for them. And then . . . then she would do something for herself . . . she would leave her husband, leave the country.

She turned to flee the dark and dreary establishment, but the tall, male form speaking with the mother superior at the end of the corridor drew her up short. Even though his broad back was to her, Ellie recognized that figure. A shiver of horror raced over her body, freezing her in place.

As if sensing her presence, slowly, Lord Beckett turned.

Her husband's gaze met hers, and a slow, tight smile drew up the corners of his cruel mouth. "Hello, darling. Please say you're not thinking of taking vows merely to escape our marriage?"

Chapter 13

It was easy enough to escape the house. James merely left his bedchamber, strolled down the steps, and walked down the hall and out the door. No one stopped him, of course, as there was nothing suspicious in his gait. Or perhaps they assumed he would never flee because he needed Lady Lavender. His family needed Lady Lavender. At least he had thought they did. But his mother was dead. Gone. And his sister was . . . he didn't know where.

All he knew was that if he didn't uncover the truth he would go mad. And if he had to work in the factories to support his sister, he would.

"Anything is possible," his father had always said. And the old man had believed it; after all, he'd merely been a poor Irishman, yet he had secured a position as a driver with one of England's most known families. And they'd had a wonderful, lively life until the day his da had been let go.

James managed to slip unnoticed from the house and headed toward the stables. The crunch of gravel underfoot was the only sound in the quiet estate. The evening was their free time, to do as they wished. Some played cards, some went riding, most took naps, preparing for morning. Come morning, he wouldn't be here.

He carried no bag, for he owned nothing anyway. The clothing, food . . . it belonged to her. All he pocketed was the measly money she allotted them. Enough money for a train or coach ticket, perhaps. He left the path and followed it to the back of the house. The stables loomed at the far end of the garden, just as clean and well taken care of as the rest of the estate. His heart did not hammer wildly; he had no urge to run. He was oddly calm. Calmer than he'd ever been. Nothing and no one would stop him.

He stepped off the path and started across the grass toward the stables. The dew soaked his boots. If not ruined, the fine leather would at least make a few shillings. He had no doubt he could sell his jacket and vest to a seamstress. Aye, he'd have enough to escape, anyway. He prayed he'd find his sister easily. And Eleanor . . . hell, maybe someday he'd be able to help her escape as well, if it wasn't too late. He pulled open the stable door and breathed deeply the comforting scent of hay. As a lad he'd spent more time in the stalls with the horses than in a proper house.

"Mr. McKinnon," Lowe said, pausing with a rake in hand. Dust particles had been stirred into the air and created a hazy fog in the fading sunlight that poured through open windows. "What brings you here?"

When the old man's eyes darted nervously from side to side as if looking for assistance, or a weapon, James knew. Hell and damnation, Ophelia had warned Lowe not to let him leave.

James reached over a stable door and patted the nose of a brown mare. The horse shook her head and neighed, sensing the unease. "Thought I might go for a ride."

"Sorry, sir, the horses are resting today."

"Really?" James stepped away from the mare, in no mood to play games. Hell, his entire life had been one big bloody lie after another. This man would not stand in his way . . . no one would. "Why don't you tell the truth?"

He gripped the rake tightly in front of him, his jowls quivering. "I don't want any trouble." The man lifted his pitchfork, pointing it at James. "You're not allowed to ride. You're not allowed to leave the estate."

"And who will stop me, Lowe?" James asked kindly. He didn't want to hurt the man, but he would. Hell, he'd die before he'd remain here. "You?"

"I vill," Wavers growled behind him.

He should have known the beast would follow. Lady Lavender was having him watched. Slowly, James turned. "I don't wish to hurt you either, but I will."

The man released a wry laugh. It was the first and only time James had ever heard him laugh. "You think to get past me?"

"I'm not so bad at sparring," James said mildly. Wavers was strong, but his large size would make him slow. If he kept his wits about him, James had no doubt he could win this match.

"Aye, but I know your strengths, and veaknesses." The big, burly man was rolling up his sleeves. "Vhat vill you do anyvay?" He quirked a thick, black brow. "Attempt to have a normal life outside these gilded valls?"

James shrugged, glancing around the stables to search for a weapon. "It's amazing what people can do when determined."

Of course he didn't believe it, and hell, he might not even tell his sister the truth. Perhaps he could fade into the world, become one with the pulsing life around him. Another lost soul on the streets of London.

Wavers snorted. "Vill you tell your lady you love her?"

James frowned. What was the man getting at? Before he had time to think over the matter, Wavers threw his fist forward. The man might have strength on his side, but he wasn't exactly quick on his feet. James easily ducked out of the way, stepping to the left.

"Not quite sure what you're talking about," James said casually.

Wavers regained his balance and narrowed his dark eyes. "Aren't you?"

A shiver of unease raced over James. Dear God, was Wavers implying that they knew about Eleanor? James stiffened, his mind spinning. That's when Wavers struck. The man's huge fist hit him hard in the side of the face. James's head jerked back with a snap. His legs buckled, sending him stumbling as pain radiated from his head down his neck and spine. He fell into Lowe.

"The horses!" The man skipped out of the way, more worried about his stables than James.

"If your lady is still alive," Wavers jeered. "Her husband vasn't too pleased when he found out she'd been visiting Lady Lavender's."

Oh God, Eleanor. What had they done? The monster would kill her. "You're lying. Ophelia would never break her code of silence." James managed to stand his ground and glare at Wavers, though inside he trembled.

"Perhaps she is more interested in revenge than her code."

The words brought him up short. "Revenge?"

The bull charged at James, giving him no time to contemplate the man's odd comment. James had only a moment to react. He snatched the pitchfork from Lowe, spun out of the way, and brought the flat of the fork toward Wavers. It hit his face, bouncing off the man's bulbous nose. The giant cried out, clasping his face as blood poured from his nostrils. He fell to his knees, the entire stable shaking.

James pointed the sharp tines of the fork at Wavers's chest. "Why does Ophelia want revenge?"

He merely glared up at James, blood pouring from between his thick fingers. James would beat the truth from him, if he had the time. James shoved the points into the man's neck.

Wavers swallowed hard and actually paled. He'd never seen the bull afraid, but there was no doubt his eyes showed his fear.

"Trust me," James growled. He turned his head, spitting a wad of blood to the dirt. "I'm angry and mad enough to do it."

The man lifted his gaze. "Your father vas scum."

"What?" James demanded, shocked. It was one thing to seek

vengeance, but what the hell did his father have to do with any of this? "I want the details!"

"I don't know."

James pressed the points into the skin. "Where?"

"I svear, I know nothing, only that Ophelia blames him for something that happened to her."

The sudden sound of shouts outside jerked James from his anger. Shite, Lowe had snuck off while they'd been fighting. James backed up a step, using one hand to open the stall and pull out the mare.

"Stand down, bastard," he warned as Wavers began to get to his feet, brilliant red blood covering his lower face and chest, providing ghastly a sight.

James dropped the pitchfork and swung himself up on the mount. Without pause he kicked his heels into the sides of the horse and burst forward. Wavers, the idiot, stood his ground. James lifted his foot and kicked the man in the chest, sending him stumbling back. Fortunately, Lowe had left the door open.

As he burst out into the sunlight, he didn't miss the group of men headed toward him, pistols drawn. His gaze shifted to the back steps where Lady Lavender stood, watching calmly. He knew better than to think he had won. Vindictive bitch. His anger spurred him on.

With a cry, he shifted the horse right and raced across the field of lavender, the hooved feet of his mount crushing the flowers and releasing their fragrant scent into the air. His father's secrets would have to wait. He had saved himself, and whether she wanted him to or not, James was going to save Eleanor.

* * *

She couldn't move. Her body ached with a burning pain that she hadn't felt since that first beating, three days after their marriage, when her husband had wanted to make sure she understood who was in charge. How shocked and scared she'd been. She'd worried she would die.

Now she only hoped she would. The pain was too much. Every muscle pulled with the smallest movement. The base of her skull thumped, the room spinning when she opened her eyes. She didn't dare move, merely lay upon her stomach on her bed, her fingers curled tightly around the covers.

She'd spent hours picturing her husband, dredging up his face and clinging to the hatred she felt for the man because her anger was the only thing that kept her going. But as the minutes passed by, her ire fled and despair took over. Five hours. She'd watched the clock tick the minutes by. For five hours she'd heard from no one. Not even Fanny had come to tend her wounds or bring soup. Perhaps she'd been let go, escorted from the house. Alone. She was utterly alone.

She squeezed her eyes shut, refusing to give in to temptation and cry.

"You bitch! How dare you humiliate me!"

As much as she tried to forget, the memories came flooding back. The carriage ride home from St. Anne's had been eerily, horribly silent. But the moment they'd stepped into the foyer of their grand house, he'd hit her so hard she'd blacked out. The servants had fled, hiding in the kitchen, none willing to intercede.

No food. No water. No help.

She slid her hand under her pillow, finding the handkerchief she'd loaned to James at Lady Rutherford's ball. She clutched the linen like it was a lifeline. Would her husband leave her here to die? To starve to death? Perhaps he could get away with it. Who would stop him? Her parents had ceased visiting when she'd refused to take their calling cards, sickened by their part in her marriage. With a groan, she pushed her hands into the bed. Slowly, she managed to sit up, crying out when her back protested with a rush of pain. She felt as if he had broken her spine.

She knew from past experiences that if she didn't move now, her body would stiffen and the pain would only get worse. Still clutching the handkerchief, she settled her feet upon the floor; they were the only part of her body that didn't hurt. She could only pray her husband had left. If he was gone, she might, just might be able to escape. Steeling her resolve, she stood, her legs trembling.

She thought of escape, she thought of James, she thought of her urge to keep living. With each shuffled step she knew she was closer to freedom. At the door, she managed to slide her feet into her slippers where they'd fallen when the footmen had carried her upstairs, dropping her upon the bed. It was difficult indeed to believe in the humanity of men when she lived in a house full of soulless demons.

At the door she wrapped her hands around the knob and pulled. It wouldn't budge. Locked. "No," she whispered through broken lips. She thumped her fists against the wooden panel. "No!"

She swallowed hard, refusing to cry. She would not have red-rimmed eyes when the bastard returned. If he returned. Her stomach grumbled, tightening. She rested her forehead on the door and took in a deep, trembling breath.

"James," she whispered.

She closed her eyes. James, who had shown her pleasure she knew she'd never experience again. James, the man who was indebted to a woman who had betrayed him, and he would never know because she had no doubt that when her husband returned he would kill her.

A sudden crash resounded throughout the house, startling her. Eleanor stumbled away from the door. Shouts rose from downstairs, male voices arguing. All sickeningly familiar, but one . . . one that gave her hope in a way she'd never felt before. No, she was wrong, James couldn't be here. It was a dream, or she'd finally gone insane. The sudden thunder of footsteps sent her heart racing. She glanced toward the hearth, wondering if she could reach the fireplace poker, any weapon before whoever it was would arrive.

"Eleanor?" James's voice carried through the door.

For a long moment she merely stood there, too stunned to respond. She was dreaming, surely she was dreaming, James could not be here. Yet a little glimmer of hope ripped a sob from her throat when the doorknob rattled.

"Eleanor, damn it, answer me!"

"James?" she said softly, but loud enough for him to hear, for the rattling paused and she swore she heard him say, "*Thank God.*"

"Stand back," he demanded.

She shuffled back the few steps her trembling legs would allow. But she wasn't prepared, couldn't have been prepared, when the door burst open, startling a surprised gasp from her lips. James stood just over the threshold. His hair was tousled, his face bruised, and she was rather sure he had blood upon his jacket, but he had never looked more beautiful.

His frantic gaze found her immediately. He scanned her body, pausing at her bruised and battered face. He sucked in a sharp breath that told her she looked even worse than she'd imagined. It must have been a dream. He couldn't be here, he couldn't. He met her gaze, a resolute determination darkening the green orbs. "You're coming with me."

Her lower lip trembled. He had come for her. He was here to save her. The urge to go with him overwhelmed her, but she couldn't because . . . because she loved him too much. "He'll kill you."

"He'll have to find us first."

Us. He was taking her away. Suddenly she was too tired to fight. Perhaps they'd live a life of poverty, but anything would be better than this. "James."

"And if he's already found you?" Her husband stood in the doorway.

Eleanor froze, looking at James helplessly. There was a coldness in his gaze that frightened her. He was a man on the brink of disaster. A man who would do whatever it took. "James," she whispered, resisting the urge to reach out to him. "Don't."

Slowly, he turned, giving his back to her and facing Lord Beckett. His shoulders were taunt, his hands fisted. She did not know this James. This man had been pushed too far and she feared for his safety.

"Get out of the way," James snapped.

Her husband ignored him, focusing instead on her. "My dear, I always knew you were a slut, but really, bringing your whore into the house?"

"You would know, wouldn't you?" she hissed. "A man who keeps his mistress as a neighbor."

Anger flashed in his eyes, showing his true nature. "She is more of a lady than you will ever be."

"Yes, perhaps she is a lady, but you are no man. A man doesn't hurt those around him. A man doesn't abuse innocents."

"Shut your mouth, you bitch. You belong to me." He started forward, the cold anger in his gaze promising retribution. He was out to kill. James apparently thought the same thing. He surged in front of Eleanor, placing himself between her and her husband.

"James, no!"

"Touch her and I'll kill you," James growled.

Oh God, he was completely and utterly serious. James would kill her husband, or try. Either way he'd end up in prison. She reached out, resting her hand on his tense back. "James, don't."

Her husband's lips lifted into a smirk. She knew that look well. He thought he had the upper hand. What did he know that they didn't? "A whore?"

A chill ran down her body, and she clutched her handkerchief more tightly.

"That's right, my dear. I have spies as well. You think I didn't know about your visits to the infamous Lady Lavender's? I was hoping you'd actually learn a thing or two . . ."

James threw his fist forward, hitting her husband in the jaw. His head snapped back with a crack. He hadn't seen it coming and stumbled into her dressing table, upsetting the many glass bottles, which tumbled from the surface.

"My lord Beckett!" Graham came rushing into the room from the hall where he'd been lurking. "Shall I call the constable?"

"No." Her husband pushed away from the dressing table, blood trailing down the corner of his mouth. It was the first time she'd seen him bleed. Dear God, he was human after all. He tugged at the corners of his jacket, straightening his clothing with deliberately slow movements. "I'll take care of him."

Eleanor glanced at James, worried. His body was all muscle and hard planes, but did he know how to spar? Her husband did it for sport and she'd been his unwilling partner for far too long. If anything happened to James because of her, she wouldn't be able to live with herself.

"James, please . . ."

He reached his arm out, pushing her behind him. The movement tore at her body, renewing fresh waves of pain, but she didn't dare complain.

"Don't worry," he said softly. "I've been a pampered pet far too long. It's time for them to see the real me."

Her husband lunged for him. James stepped aside easily, bringing his fist up and connecting with his jaw. Her husband's head jerked back and he stumbled, hitting the wall so hard it shook the room. She knew deep down this wouldn't end well for any of them. Her knees buckled, her strength giving way. Eleanor clasped the post of her bed. James needed her . . . he needed her, and she was too broken, too weak to help.

With a growl her husband surged forward. James was ready. His fist hit the man's face, sending him stumbling back once more. Her husband wouldn't stop, and neither would James . . . until one of them died. Her husband was a brute, but he was no match for James, a man who had lived on the streets half his life.

"How do you like to be hit, you bastard?" James latched onto Lord Beckett's jacket, jerking him close. "How does it feel?"

"James, stop! Please." Eleanor stifled a sob. "You'll kill him!"

He was seething, his nostrils flared, his hands covered in her husband's blood. She'd never seen him so violent. This was a man she'd never known, a man who frightened her. "I don't care."

"I do! If you kill him you'll end up in prison, or worse." The words had no effect. He lifted his hand, his fist raised. "I can't lose you," she added. "Not when you've given me so much."

He paused, his breathing harsh.

"James, please, you're scaring me," she whispered.

Her words seemed to have the effect she'd intended. He released his hold and shoved her husband toward the dressing table. Ellie was finally able to breathe with some normalcy.

James turned toward her, his gaze hard and unrelenting. "I'm leaving. You're coming with me."

She nodded her ready agreement, reaching for him. "Yes."

"You go," her husband seethed, "I'll have him arrested."

"If I don't go," she snapped back, "he'll kill you."

"No one is leaving," Graham stated, followed by the soft click of a pistol.

Ellie didn't have time to react. James spun around, reaching into his pocket at the same time. A blast rang through the air, a small puff of smoke. Graham gasped, dropping to the floor and cradling his bloodied leg.

James didn't say a word as he slipped the pistol into his jacket pocket and turned toward Eleanor. There was a fierce determination upon his face that worried her, as if he'd do anything to see them free. Anything. He wrapped his arm around her waist and lifted her gently, cradling her against his chest. His touch so gentle that in that moment she realized he was still there . . . the James she knew and trusted.

"Shhh," he whispered as she whimpered in pain. "We'll get you someplace safe soon."

Without another word, without a backward glance, he stepped over Graham, ignoring her seething husband, and moved into the hall, past the gawking servants.

She was safe. James had come for her. She was safe. She was cared for.

Relieved, Eleanor closed her eyes and sank into blissful unconsciousness.

Chapter 14

James sat in the chair by the side of Eleanor's bed waiting . . . waiting. Waiting for her to open her eyes, waiting for her to move. Waiting for something. *Anything.*

But she didn't stir. She didn't open her eyes. She didn't eat. Didn't drink. She lay there, barely breathing, as if . . . dead. And all the while, he wondered why the hell he hadn't pulled that trigger and killed her husband, getting rid of him once and for all.

The door opened. James stiffened until he smelled the scent of lemons. "The laudanum should help," Patience said, shutting the door behind her. "We used it with my mother when she hurt."

He didn't nod; he didn't speak. He didn't take his gaze from Eleanor. She might have been older than he was, but on that bed she looked so damn young, so fragile. *Come on, Ellie.* He knew the true woman deep down, a woman with the strength and perseverance of no other. Was she still there, or had her bastard husband beaten it out of her?

Patience moved softly beside him and set a tray on the side table. They had two small rooms connected by a door at the inn where Patience had been staying. Thank God she had still been here, welcoming him when he'd arrived with Ellie in his arms. "You should eat."

He didn't respond.

"James, if you don't keep up your strength—"

"How can I eat?" he said gruffly. "How can I when she is dying?"

"No," she whispered. "Not dying." She glanced at Eleanor as if to make sure. "She's . . . healing. She's merely resting. Most likely she hasn't been able to sleep for days, too scared, poor dear. And after the beating, well, it's not surprising that her body needs rest."

He clenched his jaw and paced to the windows that overlooked the muddy, dark courtyard below. Even the lamps had gone out, the flames extinguished by a fierce wind that rattled the windowpanes. Patience was merely trying to be kind. He could see the fear and worry in her gaze, a fear, no doubt, mirrored in his own eyes.

"James, what will you do?" Patience asked. "After she heals?"

He could hear the nervousness in her voice. For once she was showing her age. Hell, she couldn't have been much more than eighteen or nineteen years. For all of her bravado she was merely a girl who had seen very little, experienced so very little. And Ellie . . . Ellie had probably been her age when she'd been married off to Lord Beckett. An innocent who had uncovered only too quickly how dark the world could be.

"James?"

"I don't know," he said softly, sinking into his chair once more. The handkerchief he'd used that night at Lady Rutherford's ball still lay near Ellie. He'd found the bloodied linen clutched in her hand. "I don't know."

What would he do? Between him and Ellie they wouldn't get far. How would they escape?

"You'll have to hide." Patience started to pace. "Ireland?"

He didn't bother to respond. The situation was hopeless, for they were not only running from Eleanor's husband, but from

Ophelia as well. The brothel owner wasn't merely out for vengeance, she was bloody insane. Who the hell knew what the woman would do to get back at James. And once she uncovered the truth about his feelings for Eleanor, he had no doubt the woman would use his weakness to destroy him.

He curled his fingers, resisting the urge to reach for Ellie and pull her close. How would he provide for her? Protect her? How would they eat? He raked his hands through his hair. An image of Ellie with worn, rough-workened hands, thin body, and dull eyes flashed to mind. No. He shook the image from his brain. He would kill himself working before he'd see her starve or suffer in any way.

"I would tell you to come home with me and that Alex would welcome you, but Lady Lavender knows where we live. It would most likely be the first place they'd look."

She was right, although he wouldn't have put them in danger anyway. It was insane, relying on an eighteen-year-old, putting Patience in danger even now. No, he had to disappear with Eleanor. He could only pray that she healed quickly. "I . . . I appreciate your help," he admitted.

"We have money," Patience said. "Not a lot, but enough to get you to the Americas or France."

"No," he said softly. "I will not take any more from you."

"You have to take it. It's mine anyway, left to me by my mother. I was going to come to London to try and make a name for my jewelry, but now . . . now that doesn't seem so important."

"No," he said again.

"James, we don't have many friends, you know. Nor do we have family." She smiled, but the smile quivered at the corners of her lips as she repressed her emotions. "I would like to consider you friends. Please, take it. Take it for Eleanor. Don't let your stubborn pride get in the way of her happiness."

He frowned. The little witch had used his weakness against him, and she knew it. He didn't say a word, merely took Eleanor's hand in his, her fingers so cold, so small. He needed money. It could be weeks before she was ready to travel and he had no doubt that they would be caught before then. She was too damn beautiful and serene; she would never blend into the crowd, and no one would believe she was merely a farmer's wife. They needed to stay hidden while she healed, then perhaps they could make it to the Continent.

There was a soft knock on the door. Patience jumped, stumbling back, as startled as he. James slowly stood, reaching for the pistol in the waistband of his trousers. If her husband stood there, James would kill him.

"Are you expecting anyone?" he asked.

She shook her head. "My escort is out to tea with friends. My family is home."

He inched his way toward the door. "Not exactly."

"What do you mean?"

"The other day, after you left Lady Lavender's, I saw Alex."

She paled. "Alex, here, in London?"

"Stay back." He glanced at Eleanor as he moved toward the door, making sure she still lay quietly in the bed near the far wall. Whoever was outside shifted, their footsteps hard and heavy. A man? James's hackles rose. Briefly he thought about tearing open the door and slamming his fist into the face of whomever stood there. He glanced at Patience and nodded.

"Who is it?" she called out sweetly.

There was a moment's pause. "Footman, come to bring ye water."

It was a lie. The voice was too deep for a footman. Didn't matter because James's instincts were roaring. He might have been ignoring his instincts since he'd moved in with Lady Lavender, but no more.

"Just a moment," Patience said.

James jerked his head, telling Patience to get back. She darted a glance toward Eleanor, obviously worried about the woman being caught in the middle of a battle, but still scooted toward the fireplace mantel, half-hidden by the only chair in the room.

James tore open the door and latched on to the lapels of the man's coat. With a quick jerk, he pulled the supposed footman inside. "Why are you really here?" he demanded as he slammed the man into the wall. Slim, blond, dressed in a nondescript but clean suit, the man didn't respond. James pressed his forearm to the man's neck. "Why?"

He growled and shoved James back. He was stronger than James had expected, and he had to stumble to retain his footing. But despair and anger were on his side, turning him into an animal he barely recognized.

"What do you want?" James demanded with a growl.

The man threw his fist forward. James ducked, but barely. Whoever the intruder was, he knew how to fight dirty. James spun around and grabbed the man by the jacket, shoving him up against the wall once more. Having had enough, James pulled the pistol from his waistband and pressed it to the intruder's temple.

"I asked you once; I'm not going to again. Who—"

"Mr. Smith?" Patience's voice was timid, unsure.

James froze. "Mr. Smith?"

James was so shocked that he almost let the man get the better of him. He released his hold and ducked right before the man swung his fist. It was only as he stepped back, eying the sinewy man, that he realized he recognized him . . . the very man who had been with Alex at Lady Lavender's. Apparently a friend of the family.

Although James was done with him, Mr. Smith apparently wasn't finished with James. "What the hell are you doing in her bedchamber?"

"Calm down, you'll wake Eleanor!" Patience stomped from her hiding place and closed the front door, glaring up at the man as if not the least bit intimidated. "How dare you enter my chamber like some irate bull!"

"You're in a private room with a man!" He pointed at James. "You'll ruin what little reputation you'd managed to retain."

James pushed past them. He didn't have time for a lover's quarrel or whatever was happening between the two. He settled on the edge of Eleanor's bed, taking her cold, small hand in his. The touch seemed to stir something within her, and she coughed, her body shaking with the slight movement.

He squeezed her hand. "Ellie?"

She groaned.

"What happened?" Mr. Smith demanded.

Ellie's eyes remained stubbornly closed, her body going still once more. James wanted to slam his fist into the wall. Was he forever to lose those he loved? No, he would not lose Ellie. He'd crawl his way into heaven and pull her back if he had to.

"They're friends," Patience explained. "Mr. Smith, this is James McKinnon."

James didn't miss the flash of surprise in the man's eye. If he was friends with Alex, if he knew about Lady Lavender, perhaps he might know other, more important things. "Tell me," James demanded. "Tell me what Alex knows about my father, about what happened to Ophelia."

Mr. Smith sighed and glanced at Patience. "It's not for feminine ears."

"Do not be cloying, Mr. Smith. I know much more than you realize and I've seen worse than you can imagine." She tilted her chin high. "I even visited Lady Lavender's."

The man's eyes narrowed. "How could you be so damn stupid?"

"Don't you dare—"

"Enough!" James roared, causing Eleanor to whimper in her sleep. He leaned closer to her, pressing his lips to her ear. "Shhh, all is well." When she seemed to settle, he turned back toward them. "Tell me now."

Mr. Smith sighed, pacing the room. "Your father worked for Gideon's father years ago.

215

"One night Gideon's father raped a woman, a beautiful country lass from France. Alex's father, his friend at the time, helped cover up the crime, as did his driver, who had witnessed it all. That driver was your father."

James closed his eyes and rested his head in his hands. "The lass was Lady Lavender?"

"Yes. They got away with the crime, although I believe Gideon's father paid her handsomely to keep her mouth shut. She did, realizing she could seek her revenge in other ways . . . through their sons."

James felt ill. "All this time, it's been about revenge?"

Mr. Smith nodded.

James looked toward the fireplace, his mind spinning. All that time he'd thought they were friends, that she was actually helping him . . . he'd merely been a means to an end. And his father . . . his father had let a man get away with rape. At least now he understood why his father had killed himself: the guilt. He rested his head in his hands, stunned. His final bitter words to his father had not brought the man to suicide after all. The relief was immediate, but at the same time he was highly aware of his father's part in Ophelia's downfall.

He opened his eyes, searching for Ellie, needing to soak in her purity. The bruises upon her face broke his heart. Soon she would wake and they would have to deal with cold reality. He drew his knuckles down the side of her velvety cheek. Eleanor had been the only one honest with him. And how would he repay her? By forcing her to live a life of hardship and suffering.

As if sensing the way of his thoughts, her lashes stirred, lifting. "James?"

Despite his guilt, his heart clenched with hope. "Aye, I'm here."

"Come, Mr. Smith," Patience said, heading to the door. "Help me carry a tray of warm soup." The man reluctantly followed her out the door, closing it behind him. They were left alone, although he knew it wouldn't last.

A small smile lifted the corners of Eleanor's cracked lips. "You came for me."

"Of course I did," he said, his voice gruff with emotion. The relief he felt nearly shook him to the core of his being. Ellie was awake, she was speaking. Her right cheek was swollen and red, her battered face not her own. Just looking at the pain in her eyes made him want to murder her husband. But at least she was awake. Damn it all, he'd always buried his true emotions under a carefree smile. But here, now, he couldn't pretend any longer . . . at least not with Ellie.

"Did you kill him?" she whispered.

"No." Unfortunately. Why hadn't he pulled the trigger? He might have ended up in prison, but Eleanor would be free. But even as he asked himself, he knew the reason why. Deep down he hoped to have a life with Ellie, and he couldn't have a life while in the gaols.

She nodded slowly. "Good."

Her response didn't please him, and he wondered if she held some sort of compassion for the man. He had been her husband for over a decade after all. "He deserved it."

"Maybe." Her hand tightened around his. "But I'd rather you not be wanted for murder. I'd rather you be free to stay with me forever." Her pale brows puckered. "Are we free?"

He wasn't sure how to answer that. At the least he was wanted for attacking a better. At the worst he was wanted for abduction and attempted murder. Ellie was still married to the bastard, therefore he still owned her. Even if they subtracted Lord Beckett from the mess, he still had Lady Lavender to attend with. Free? Perhaps more than they'd been only hours ago, but still not nearly as free as they needed to be.

"You'll be ruined," he warned her, rubbing his thumb across the sensitive inside of her wrist. "If you leave with me."

"Yes." Her lashes were drifting down, the laudanum working its magic.

She needed her sleep, yet he couldn't help prod for more. Never in his life had he expected to feel this full, this complete with a woman. He needed her agreement, he needed her word that she would stay with him.

"You don't mind?"

Her lips quirked, her lashes closed. "Better to be ruined than dead, right?"

He smiled this time, somewhat mollified. "Yes." He only prayed that when they were living in a tiny one-room cottage with dirt floors she still agreed. He brushed back her hair and pressed a kiss to her cool forehead.

"James," she said softly, startling him. He'd thought she slept.

"What is it, my love?"

She turned her head slightly, nuzzling her lips against the palm of his hand. "I can't have children."

He frowned, distressed by her statement. "Just because you haven't had any doesn't mean you can't. I know men blame women, but it could be either—"

She lifted her lids, as if forcing herself to stay awake. He didn't miss the tears filling her eyes. "No, I can't, and up until now I thought it was a blessing. I didn't want children with him. But now . . . with you . . ."

He leaned forward and brushed her hair back from her face, attempting to soothe her. Whether it was true or not, he hated to see her so distressed. "Ellie, it might not be you."

Tears slid down her pale cheeks. "It is. My husband has had bastards with other women. It is me, James, and if you don't want me anymore, I understand."

Whether it was true or not, she believed every word. The image of Ellie with a babe in her arms came naturally, and he could barely believe that she was barren. But it didn't matter to him. Good God, it didn't matter in the least. "Ellie, I never thought to have children anyway. I only want you."

She didn't look comforted, and when a single tear slowly slid down her bruised cheek her pain was almost more than he could stand.

"I mean it."

"Y . . . you're sure?"

He pressed a kiss to her forehead. He'd never been so sure in his life. "Yes. Sleep, rest easy, my love."

"No, there's something I need to tell you . . ." Her lashes were drifting down as if they weighed a stone. "Something . . ."

He gently pulled the covers higher, worried about her condition. Did she not realize she was all he had left? If anything were to happen to Eleanor . . . He grasped her hands, holding them tight. "You can tell me later."

She managed to free one hand. "No."

"Ellie, rest. You need to recover—"

"It's your sister." She pushed the covers away and searched his face with her hazy gaze. The determination in her face worried him. "I know you told me not to interfere, but I visited her."

He stiffened. "What? How?"

She tightened her grip on his hand. "They never got the money or letters."

"Ellie, what are you saying?"

She took in a deep, trembling breath. "The money and letters Lady Lavender said she would send . . ."—he had to lean closer to understand her mumbled words—" . . . she never did."

Her lashes fell once more, her breathing deep, even. Utter shock held James immobile for good long moment. He felt cold. So bitterly cold. His sister had never received his money. His mother had died in poverty, most likely assuming he had died as well. James swallowed hard over the lump that suddenly clogged his throat. It could be a mistake, some fantastical dream Ellie had produced in her drugged mind. He knew, deep down, it wasn't.

He stumbled to his feet, nausea rising to his throat. "No," he whispered. "No."

He hadn't sold his soul for nothing. He couldn't stand to even think of such betrayal. She was wrong . . . had misunderstood . . . James's entire body trembled; the roar of blood rushing to his ears drowned out any noise but his own harsh breath. He hadn't heard the door open, but suddenly Patience was in front of him, her lips moving, her worried gaze on him.

"James? What is it?" Patience asked, her voice sounding muffled, strange. "Is Ellie well?"

She left him, rushing to the bed, where she checked Ellie's pulse. "She never sent the money," he managed to get past his numb lips. It was true, he knew it to be. His mother, his sister, had practically starved. They'd been no better after he'd left, and in fact were probably worse off.

Patience turned toward him, shaking her head in confusion. "I don't understand."

Mr. Smith entered the room slowly, a tray of food in hand. "What do you mean, Mr. McKinnon?"

"Lady Lavender." James raked his hands through his hair, his fingers trembling so badly he could barely control his hands. Unable to sit still, he paced. "Eleanor said that the money Lady Lavender was supposed to be sending to my mother had never been sent."

Patience started hesitantly to him. "She was never your friend, James. She never cared. She only wanted to destroy you all."

The pain of the woman's betrayal cut deep, so very deep. "You're saying that she starved my sister, allowed my mother to die, lied to me, and all because of what my father did, or didn't do?"

Patience nodded. "Yes."

He sank onto a chair. If Ophelia had set out to seek revenge only on him, James might have been able to forgive her. But she had destroyed his mother, ruined his sister's chance at happiness. And he had no doubt she would try to ruin whomever he loved.

"Vengeance," he whispered. "All for revenge. She's destroyed everything. My hope, my family, my life . . . all . . . gone."

"But not Ellie," Patience reminded him optimistically. "You still have her, and you can leave, you can run away together. Start anew, James."

But he knew the truth . . . it would never end. She would continually hunt him, find ways to hurt his father through them. His gaze went to Ellie. She looked so damn fragile and innocent his heart lurched.

"I can stop this madness." James went to the chair and picked up his jacket. "I can end it all now, here."

"James, no!" Patience turned toward her friend. "Mr. Smith, please, stop him!"

James started for the door, feeling oddly calm. He knew what he had to do, and nothing would stop him. Lady Lavender and Lord Beckett must die.

"You can't live your life for revenge," Patience said.

"It's not revenge, it's merely what needs to be done," he said, reaching for the door handle.

Patience pressed her hands to her mouth. "Oh, James, don't, you'll ruin whatever chance you have left."

But he was deaf to her words. He looked at Ellie one last time. He would do this for her . . . for his family. He would end the torment now so neither Lord Beckett nor Lady Lavender could ever hurt anyone again.

Mr. Smith rested his hand on James's shoulder. "If you kill Lady Beckett's husband, then you have destroyed your life and given Lady Lavender exactly what she wanted all along."

Perhaps, but at least Ellie would be free, and at least the world would be free of Ophelia and her vengeful ways. He pulled open the door. "Take care of her, promise. And tell Ellie I . . . I . . ."

He couldn't say the words; it hurt too much. James briefly closed his eyes, ignoring he twist of guilt he felt in his gut. Taking in a deep, trembling breath, he stepped into the hall and closed the door behind him, knowing that if everything went as planned, he would never see Ellie again.

Chapter 15

"Take care of her, promise. And tell Ellie I . . . I . . ."

Eleanor could hear James's voice from far, far away, the words muffled and confusing. James was leaving? Where was he going? She parted her lips, trying to respond, but nothing would come out. The darkness pulled on her, tugging her down . . . down, promising relief from the pain and torment of life.

The sound of a door shutting broke through the darkness and she had a brief moment of clarity. James had left. He wasn't coming back. Panic gave her the strength she needed. Eleanor forced her eyes open. She was in a room, a small, plain room. But where?

"You must stop him, Mr. Smith!" a woman cried out desperately in a voice that sounded somewhat familiar.

Eleanor shoved her hands into the bed and sat up, trying to make sense of the situation. The entire room spun as wave after wave of pain rolled over her body in a torrent that sent bile to her throat. Through the fog of despair she realized a man and a young woman she vaguely recognized were standing near a small table. Where the hell was she? Although darkness called, she refused to fade into the shadows until she had answers.

Seeing her, the young woman's eyes widened in dismay. "Eleanor, no, just lie still."

Patience . . . it was Patience at her side. Patience trying to gently shove her back into the bed where she would slip into unconsciousness once more. With a cry, Eleanor shoved the girl's hands away. Everything came rushing back on bittersweet memories. She'd thought she was going to die, had wanted to. But James . . . magnificent James had saved her.

"James," she got out through parched lips, desperate to see him. "Was he here?"

"Yes." Patience pressed her hand to Ellie's forehead.

It hadn't been a dream. Eleanor shoved the girl's hands away. She had to see James, she must know that he was well. Most importantly, she had to make him see reason. If he killed her husband, he'd end up in jail. Or worse, he might end up dead.

But Patience was holding her back, her firm hands on her shoulders. "You can't! You're too ill. Mr. Smith?" She glanced back at a tall, sinewy man with light hair and a hard, unreadable face. "Do tell her that she can't leave!"

If this Mr. Smith wanted her to rest, Ellie had no doubt he could force her to stay. Eleanor gripped onto Patience's hands, knowing she had a better chance with this woman than that cold man standing near the fireplace. They'd worked together for days trying to uncover the truth; she could trust this woman. "Please, help me."

The girl might be as bold as anyone, but Patience's indecision showed her age. She'd been thrown into a life of sin and debauchery since coming to London. Ellie swore if Patience helped her now, she would never ask her for anything again.

Finally, Patience sighed. "Fine. Only because I worry he'll end up getting himself killed."

The relief Ellie felt brought tears to her eyes. She wrapped her arm around Patience and managed to get to her feet. She was wearing a day dress she didn't recognize, a pretty pink thing most likely borrowed from Patience. Ellie didn't feel much of the pain as her broken body moved; the drugs had dulled her senses. She felt nothing. Utterly numb, as if she floated toward the door.

"Mr. Smith, see if you can stop him." Patience breathed heavily, taking much of Ellie's weight.

"You're all mad," the man muttered as he headed toward the door.

Ignoring him, Eleanor managed to slip her feet into her slippers and walked alongside Patience with painstakingly slow movements. The only one insane was her husband. If he harmed James in any way, she'd kill Lord Beckett herself.

"Eleanor, are you well?" Patience asked as they moved into the hall. "Your face looks utterly fierce and it's worrying me. You look exactly like my sister, Grace, when she's set her mind to something and will let nothing get in her way."

Ellie couldn't help but laugh. "I think I might like your sister." She grimaced as her head pounded, making the corridor outside the room fade. "If it eases your mind, then yes, I'm well. Please just hurry."

She was determined to speak to James. But her body was not her own, her voice mumbled and dull. It was sheer stubbornness and love that kept her going when all she wanted to do was curl up and cry.

"I promise, I'm trying to hurry," Patience grunted, taking the brunt of her weight as they headed down the steps. "But I worry James has already left."

"Where was he headed? You must tell me."

They made it to the common room, where a variety of travelers were seated by the fireplace, warming themselves or dining on the rich and heady stew.

"I fear he's planning to kill Lord Beckett or Lady Lavender, perhaps both," Patience whispered.

"No!" Ellie cried out so loudly that they drew more than one curious gaze. She flushed, feeling highly uncomfortable. She could imagine the sight they made. At this rate her husband would hear about her whereabouts in a matter of hours. Eleanor ignored the attention and focused on the door. Just a few more steps. Just a few more . . .

"We will find him." She chanted the mantra. She had to believe; hope was all she had left. Patience reached for the door and pulled it wide. A gust of cool air billowed into the room, fluttering the curtains and Eleanor's dress. The air felt wonderful against her bruised and fevered skin. There, in the middle of the dark courtyard, she saw James's familiar form, Mr. Smith at his side.

"Thank God," she whispered, her knees going weak in relief.

"Just a bit more," Patience murmured reassuringly.

As if sensing her sudden presence, James turned toward them. "What the hell is she doing out here?" It wasn't exactly the reunion she'd been hoping for. "You'll injure yourself even more."

"I need to speak with him—help me get closer."

Patience nodded. "You'll be better than any of us at talking him out of this."

Eleanor would have thanked the woman if she hadn't been too bloody tired. Together, they made it down the front stoop and into the muddy garden. It was still dark, but the lanterns and torchlight around the patch of dirt that claimed to be a lawn gave the area enough light. It was only as she reached James and saw the despair in his gaze that she realized he wasn't alone.

Three men sat on horseback behind him, a wagon close by.

"Eleanor," James hissed, his gaze frantic. "Go back inside."

"James McKinnon," the largest man called out. "You're wanted for attempted murder of one Lord Beckett, as well as the abduction of his wife."

"No," Eleanor cried.

Mr. Smith rushed to her side, taking her arm none too gently. "Hush, you'll make things worse."

She struggled to get away from his tight hold, anger and desperation clashing within. "I hardly see how they can get worse!"

"If you do not be silent," Mr. Smith muttered. "Then she will know how much you both care about each other and use it against him."

"She?" Confused, Eleanor jerked her gaze from Mr. Smith and followed his line of vision. She realized with a start that it wasn't the men on horseback who were the real threat. No, it was the beautiful woman in the lavender gown who sat atop a mount not far from them, a smirk of satisfaction upon her beautiful face. A woman who held them all in the palms of her gloved hands.

Ellie felt ill. Lady Lavender, the woman James had vowed to protect, the woman James had considered a loyal friend, had turned him in to the authorities. Ellie had never felt such hatred, not even toward her husband. It boiled deep within her, threatening to pull her into an ocean of darkness and revenge. Yet she had to merely stand there and watch as the one person who meant anything to her was lost.

James did not run, he didn't deny the accusations. Instead, slowly, he turned to look at Mr. Smith, and in a low voice he said, "Hide her. Promise me you'll protect her."

Mr. Smith clenched his jaw and nodded. James started toward the men and the wagon that rested near a crop of trees.

"No," Eleanor whispered. She felt as if someone had reached into her chest and torn out her heart. What little strength she had left fled her body and she sank into Patience. She couldn't even go to him, couldn't even kiss him good-bye.

Mr. Smith slid his arm around her waist, taking her weight from Patience. "Shhh," he whispered, holding her gently. "He's doing this for you. He knows this is the only way to protect you."

Ellie shook her head, tears sliding down her cheeks. "No, no, I don't want him to protect me."

They shoved James unceremoniously into the wagon, and just like that the carriage jerked to life and James was gone. Eleanor wrapped her arms around her waist as tears trailed down her cheeks. Still they stood there as the crunch of wheels faded and the only sound was merry laughter coming from the common room in the inn.

"You've destroyed the only person who cared about you!" Eleanor screamed as Lady Lavender started to leave on her mount. She'd done what she had set out to do . . . destroy lives. But Ellie would not let her slink away like a snake.

The woman paused, turning her mount, and heading back toward them. The smug look upon her face made Ellie tremble with anger.

"I play to win, my dear."

"You've won nothing but your own bitter loneliness," Patience hissed, tightening her grip around Ellie. "Come, she's not worth our attention."

With Patience on one side and Mr. Smith on the other, Ellie allowed them to lead her back toward the inn, too spent to fight. She followed because she had nowhere else to go. Everything was gone. She had her freedom thanks to James, but nothing, not even freedom, was worth him sacrificing his own life.

* * *

James wasn't sure how long he'd been in the cell. Hours? Perhaps days? It seemed like years. Utter darkness surrounded him, making it impossible to tell time. Barely any noise reached him, only the occasional moan and cry of other prisoners, but even that had tapered off, leaving behind the eerie scratch of rats.

One meal of bread and water had come hours ago, but even without the lantern he'd known the meager meal had been filled with weevils and worms, insects he could feel crawling onto his hand when he had reached for the food. He supposed it didn't much matter. He would hang anyway.

If there was an afterlife, perhaps he'd see his mother soon. His sister was safe with the nuns, and Mr. Smith would keep Eleanor hidden. He could die in peace. He rested his head back against the damp stone wall. But he still worried. Worried that Ellie would return to her husband. Worried that his sister was unhappy and unloved. Worried that Ophelia would continue to ruin the lives of innocent lads.

He drew his knees closer, trying to get warm. They'd taken his coat and his boots, intending to sell the fine objects, but he didn't care. He didn't bloody care. The scent of rotting flesh and death hovered in the air, crawling over his skin like the rats across the floor. He closed his eyes and thought of Eleanor. Dreamt about bringing her close, kissing her lush lips, and telling her everything would be well. If only he'd had one more moment with her, one more moment to tell her how much he cared. But he hadn't dared to tell her the truth of his feelings, hadn't dared to kiss her good-bye because he knew better than to let Ophelia see his weakness. And Ellie was most assuredly his weakness.

"Ellie," he whispered. The name tore from his heart, leaving him chilled and trembling. "Ellie."

He'd wanted to save her, he'd wanted to protect her and provide for her. Instead he'd only failed. His body felt oddly numb, his mind buzzed with an odd clarity. They would not have their happily ever after, but as long as Ellie was safe, he could die in peace.

"*I'm James.*" The words whispered softly around him, and suddenly he was a lad once more, tossed in a similar prison so many years ago.

"*Will they hang us?*" Alex whispered.

"*Most likely,*" Gideon said.

"*Blast it! I didn't do anything!*" His voice echoed around the small room, the lad still here after all these years. "*Do you hear me? I didn't do anything!*"

But he had broken the law this time, and he knew no one would come to his rescue. How ironic that he should end up here once more. Hell, maybe he had never truly left.

"No matter what happens," Alex's voice whispered around him, *"I say we fight together."*

From somewhere down the hall a door creaked open. More bread? Despite the state of his previous meal, his stomach clenched, grumbling in need. As the light came closer, piercing the small window in the solid door, he stiffened. Three men? No, four. His hanging party then? Would they kill him without a trial? Perhaps Lord Beckett held that much power.

"On yer feet," one man growled as he unlocked James's cell and swung the door wide.

James thought about ignoring him but realized he still had some fight left after all. He stumbled upright, the chains around his arms clanking with the movement, and wondered if this was it . . . the last few breaths he'd take. And then he saw him . . . Eleanor's husband hovering behind the guards.

He no longer wondered; he knew without a doubt that this would be the day he'd die. He would not cower. He would not plead. He would take his fate like a man. And chains or not, he sure as hell wouldn't go down without a fight.

"Come for a visit?" James sneered. "Or would you rather hide behind the guards?"

Eleanor's husband shoved his way between the two men. James had the bastard precisely where he wanted him, within arm's reach. "You honestly thought I'd let you fuck my wife and get away with it?"

James flexed his forearms, testing the strength of the chains. "Her education was sadly lacking. Someone had to show her what a proper tupping felt like."

James didn't even try to block the man's fist. He'd wanted to draw him closer, and it had worked. His knuckles hit James in the gut. The air burst from his lungs and the cell went black for a brief moment. He could punch, but then he'd had lots of practice on Eleanor.

"You think you could abduct my wife and I wouldn't retaliate?"

"I knew you'd retaliate," James gasped, trying to regain his breath. "But I didn't realize you'd be such a coward that you'd have to bring along guards to protect you." James forced himself to straighten and held his arms wide, the chairs rattling with the movement. "Really, do you fear a pampered whore?"

"You're scum and nothing more!" The man growled and rushed forward, fist raised.

Exactly what he wanted. James lifted his arms and swung the chain around his neck. With a quick jerk, he tugged Lord Beckett back against his chest and held him tightly with the chain. "Not so fierce now, are you?"

Beckett gasped for air, clawing at the chain, his eyes bulging. "If I'm going to die anyway, I might as well take you with me to hell."

"Let him go!" One of the guards pulled a pistol from his jacket pocket, training it on James. His arm trembled so badly he would more likely shoot the wall. Just as he'd thought, Lord Beckett's guards were completely inept.

Beckett twisted from side to side, his feet stomping at the floor like an irate bull's, but James didn't loosen his hold. Sweat broke out across his forehead as he fought to maintain control of the monster. "How does it feel," James said softly, pulling the chain so tight the man was wheezing for air, "to know that not only will Eleanor be free of you, but she will also inherit your money to do with as she pleases. I do hope she burns your ancestral home to the ground."

"Move aside!" The prison guards filed into the cell, so many they could barely move. Still he didn't let go. James needed just one more moment, one more to kill the bastard once and for all. But his moment was over. Suddenly, he was swarmed. Beckett was torn from his hands. Fists hit him in the stomach and face, propelling him backward. Over the sound of knuckles connecting with his flesh he was only too aware of Lord Beckett gasping and choking air back into his lungs, returning to life. He had failed, damn it all.

James fell back against the wall. His body was no longer his own. His knees buckled and he slid to the floor, collapsing completely. The shouts and jeers from the guards and other prisoners merged together in an unnaturally loud buzz. He laid with the side of his face pressed to the damp stone. Laid there trying not to breathe because it hurt too badly. As he laid there he thought of Ellie and how she must have felt when she'd been beaten by Lord Beckett.

"Hold him," Lord Beckett gasped, rubbing his throat and glaring at James.

Two of Lord Beckett's guards latched onto his upper arms and jerked him to his feet. James hung limply from their grip. He couldn't fight; he could barely lift his arms. A stabbing pain sliced through his chest, beating in time with his heart. He was rather sure a rib or two had been cracked. He was chained, outnumbered. He didn't give a shite about dying, but he was bloody well irate that he hadn't killed Beckett.

The man shrugged off his jacket, handing it to a prison guard, who took it hesitantly, obviously uneasy with what was happening. No doubt Lord Beckett would pay him handsomely to do as he pleased.

"When I'm done with you," Lord Beckett grinned, "I'll make sure I take care of my wife once and for all."

He threw his fist forward, hitting James in the chin. James's head snapped back, hitting the rock wall behind him. Pain branched across his skull, shooting down his spine. The lantern light danced around him, the room fading in and out of focus.

He clenched James's shirt and pulled him close. "When I find Eleanor," he whispered for James's ears only, "have faith that she will pay for her crimes. Perhaps you'll be seeing her soon after all . . . in hell."

"Enough," one of the prison guards hissed, stepping between them. "We need him alive for the hanging."

"I'll determine when it's enough," he growled.

Lord Beckett released his hold and stepped back. How James wished he could punch that arrogant smirk from his face. The guards released him and James fell to the hard ground, the chains rattling around him. He didn't have time to move before the man's foot came forward. The tip of his boot caught James in the gut. Pain rippled through his body. James bit back his cry. He would not give them the satisfaction of making a sound. Instead he focused on the pain, welcomed it greedily, for it made him forget, for a moment, the wretchedness that had become his life.

Lord Beckett started toward the door. "By the by, Mr. McKinnon. I've recently had the pleasure of making the acquaintance of an Arabella McKinnon. Any relation?"

James growled low in his throat, his fingers digging into the brick floor.

"She is?" He released a deep chuckle. "How very interesting. Don't you fret, I'll make sure that when you're rotting in hell your sister is well taken care of. We certainly wouldn't want her to be lonely."

With a roar James managed to stumble to his feet and lunge toward the door. The chains around his wrists and ankles jerked him back. Spent, his legs gave out and he collapsed once more to the ground. The door closed, the lock turning.

"I look forward to seeing you hang tomorrow," Lord Beckett called through the window. His laughter vibrated through the hall, bouncing off the walls even long after the man had left.

James rolled onto his back and stared up into the darkness. The world faded as pain overwhelmed him. He lost track of time, barely noticed the damp stone underneath, the scurry of rats across the floor.

As his eyes closed, his body fading into nothingness, he was vaguely aware of the fact that tomorrow he would die, knowing that instead of helping, he had made everything so much worse.

Chapter 16

Eleanor found she liked Alex. Although with his overly long hair and tanned skin he resembled a pirate, not at all like the men of the *ton* she normally associated with, she was comfortable in his presence. He was handsome as sin, but there was a dangerous air about him that sent people scurrying to the other side of the lane when he approached. And she needed someone dangerous guarding her back.

He'd apparently been in London for a few days, having arrived to settle matters with Ophelia. Eleanor had been so relieved to have someone else helping that she'd almost started to cry at his appearance. Yes, if anyone could help, it would be Alex.

He lifted his hand and assisted her down from the hired hack. "You're sure you want to do this?"

"Yes." It still hurt to move, but she ignored the pain. How could she complain when James was in prison? When she thought about what he must be going through, she could barely breathe. The frantic need to help him overwhelmed her, and she would have walked through hell merely to ease his suffering.

The laudanum Patience had forced past her lips would help dull the aches. But she limited her intake, for she wanted to keep her wits about her when she confronted Lord Beckett. Mr. Smith followed them, silent as always. He would play their guard. Already two days had gone by since James had been arrested. She was frantic to gain his release, worried about what would happen to him in that prison with no protection.

Alex had bribed a guard to find out how he fared. The man had merely grunted that he was still there, inside the filth and darkness where her husband belonged, not James. Hope was the only thing that kept her going . . . hope of freeing James. Hope for another life, a better life.

"Forgive me," Alex said, "but you don't seem . . . as if you'd get on with James."

She smiled slightly as she slid her arm through his, mostly because she was still too sore to walk comfortably on her own. Underneath that polite query was the real comment . . . she didn't seem like the sort of woman to visit a brothel.

"I didn't know it at the time, but I needed him to remind me that there was a life, a world out there full of pleasure and beauty if one has the freedom to enjoy it."

He nodded slowly, mulling over her response. Overhead, heavy gray clouds threatened rain. The dreariness matched her mood. She didn't quite understand how the world could go on as it had when her heart was slowly being crushed, destroyed.

"And you think that by speaking with your husband you might win your freedom?"

"I have no choice but to try." Her smile fell as the town home came into view. Her old fears came unfurling back. She clenched Alex's arm more tightly. "I fear James may change. He was so optimistic until he uncovered the truth. Now there is a desperation in his gaze that frightens me."

They paused at the bottom of the stoop. "I think," Alex said, "that no matter what happens, if you still believe in him, if you still believe in a future with him, that perhaps you can help him through." He gave her a quick smile, his white teeth brilliant against his tanned skin. "At least it worked with me and my wife, Grace."

The love he had for his wife was evident in his voice, in his gaze, in the way he smiled when speaking about her. Could she and James have that someday? But she knew enough to realize that she couldn't change James if he didn't want to change. She could only pray that the true man was still there . . . deep down.

Alex glanced back at the quiet Mr. Smith, then up at the black door, a door that Eleanor gone through so many times before she'd lost count. "Shall we?"

Her heart slammed wildly in her chest, and she suddenly found it hard to breathe. "Might as well get it done with."

They started up the steps of the familiar town home, a place that she had resided in for over a decade. She was home. But it no longer felt like home. Perhaps it never had. No, it was merely a box that held memories, painful memories of a life she hadn't wanted yet hadn't been able to escape . . . until now.

"You're sure?" Alex asked once more as they paused at the door.

"I must try," she said softly, although inside she despaired that anything would come of her visit.

"My father—"

"No." She rested her hand briefly upon his sleeve. Patience had admitted that Alex did not speak to his family, that his father was a powerful man who had disowned his eldest son. His younger brother didn't even know he existed. "We can't bring more people into this mess. My husband will only try and use them as he has used me."

Alex nodded. Still, if worse came to worst, she was not above begging Alex to speak with his father. When he reached for the bell cord all thoughts fled and only one emotion remained . . . terror. She was returning to the viper's nest.

The door opened almost immediately. Graham stood there, first glancing at her with a look of what could only be disgust, then at Alex with unease. She had to remind herself that Alex and Mr. Smith would not let anything happen to her, but it was difficult to remember when the memories came roaring back.

"How wonderful to see you, Graham," she snapped coolly. "Now, move aside."

He didn't budge. Alex stepped closer, the man taller, stronger, and younger than Graham. "You heard her, move aside or I swear to God I'll make you."

Graham's jowls quivered as he shifted in indecision. "I would be happy to call for Lord Beckett."

"Is this not my house as well? Or are Lord Beckett and I no longer married?"

He flushed and she could tell the butler wanted to set her down a peg or two. Hell, he probably wanted to toss her from the town house. But his gaze shifted to Alex, and then to Mr. Smith, and finally he stepped aside, reluctantly giving them access.

"Where is he?" she asked as she moved past the man and into the great hall. How very odd it was to return home. The marble elegance seemed cold and unforgiving. Not a touch of her personality could be found in the place where she'd lived her entire adult life. It had always been his and always would be. There would be no sadness when she left for good.

"If you are speaking of your *husband*," Graham sneered, "Lord Beckett is in the library."

"He's no husband," she hissed. How she hated his condescending tone, the way he looked down his nose at her and always had. "And you're no gentleman. A true man does not stand by while a woman is tortured and beaten."

He straightened, snapping his attention toward the door. "You are his wife; he is your master."

"No one is my master. I decide my own fate."

Alex grinned proudly as she marched past them. Even though it hurt, she kept walking, determined to see her plan through, determined not to lean on anyone when she entered the library. She would show him he could not make her cower. She could sense Alex and Mr. Smith behind her. They would be her strength. She had little time, so very little time to free James, and this was her one opportunity. She paused on the threshold and found her husband seated behind his desk. Seeing him, she felt no fear. He was only a man, a human being who could die as well as anyone. The only thing she felt was complete and utter disgust.

Sensing her presence, Lord Beckett glanced up from his paper. He didn't seem the least bit surprised to see her, and in fact looked only mildly amused. "Well, darling, have you come home already? Did you find you couldn't live without your spending money?"

His arrogance was just the thing she needed to spur her into action. Lord, how she hated him. "I could live within the depths of poverty if it meant being away from you." She swept across the room, refusing to cringe no matter how much the movement hurt her aching body. "I've come to seek a divorce."

He burst out laughing, his entire body shaking so hard that the teacup upon his desk rattled on the saucer. He thought he held all the power in this relationship, and why wouldn't he? He had before. "You must be jesting."

"Not at all."

His smile fell. He was silent for a long, long moment, his gaze flickering from her to Alex and Mr. Smith, who stood waiting in the hall. She knew he was attempting to understand her sudden bravado, and he weighed his words carefully. "I will kill you before I divorce you."

From the corner of her eye she noticed Alex shift closer to the door. She prayed he did not interfere. Casually, she moved toward the fireplace, drawing her fingers along the mantel. Only she could get her husband to relent, and it would take more than the threat of physical violence.

"Think on it, husband," she said, settling in one of two leather wing back chairs near the fireplace. She spent little time in this room, for it reeked of his essence, his scent permeated the space. "If we divorce you can marry your whore."

"Whore?" He chuckled, strolling toward her and taking the chair next to hers. "Funny that you should mention whores."

She refused to react, for she would merely be giving him what he wanted. "If you think to shame me, it will take more than that."

He sighed as if bored, drumming his fingers along the arms of his chair. "Even if I wanted to ruin my family name by divorcing you, it is highly unlikely the courts will grant it."

"Are you not the same person who said that money can get you anything?"

He chuckled. "Touché. Yes, I suppose I could pay the courts, or I could merely wait for you to die."

It was a threat she took seriously, although she didn't dare show any outward reaction. "And if I have a way to divorce without killing me off?"

He quirked an arrogant brow. "Oh yes, the second cousin who is related to the queen. How could I forget since your parents like to mention it every time they are in polite society?"

"It could work."

"Perhaps." He smiled. "But why would I grant you a divorce when I could just as easily kill you and be rid of you for good?"

"Try it," Alex growled, stomping toward them. He'd obviously had enough, and she didn't blame him. Part of her wanted to flee, merely to escape her husband and his odious comments. But James was counting on her, and she would walk barefoot across the fires of hell to set him free.

Eleanor held up her hand. "No, please. Give us a moment."

"I'm not leaving," Alex snapped.

Her husband merely watched them all with amusement sparkling in his dark eyes. Of course he didn't understand loyalty and affection. "Wait by the door where you can still see me."

He hesitated, glaring at her husband. Mr. Smith, too, looked ready to pounce, and she could see Graham with a few footmen standing in the foyer, waiting to be called. Dear Lord, a war was about to break out, and then she would never gain James's release. Finally, Alex spun around and moved into the hall, Mr. Smith following.

"You will grant me a divorce." She settled in her chair once more, her cold gaze pinning her husband in place. "Because, *darling*, I know something about you that you don't want me to know."

He looked only mildly interested as he leaned back in his chair. Not for a minute did he believe she had any real power. He was about to find out how much she knew. "Really? Do pray tell?"

"I know that you've sold vital military information to Russia."

He retained his smirk, but she didn't miss the unease in his eyes. The urge to gloat was overwhelming but she managed to hold her tongue. "Prove it."

She smiled back. "That's the thing . . . I can. Not only do I have papers, but I also have witnesses." She paused, letting the realization settle. "Months ago I tracked down a few witnesses." She shrugged. "You know . . . just in case I'd need them. A footman you fired. A maid you tried to seduce. They were so eager to talk to me."

She exaggerated the information she had, but he didn't need to know that.

He surged to his feet, his face flushing with outrage. "You bitch!"

Eleanor held up her hand. "Now, now, you don't want to harm me, because if anything happens . . . say, I lose my life, the papers will go public. I have friends, you see." She glanced toward the door. Alex had reentered, called forward by Lord Beckett's cry of protest. Mr. Smith remained in the hall, making sure the staff did not come to her husband's rescue. They needed to leave, and soon, for if her husband called for help, they would be outnumbered.

"So, you will grant me a divorce. Most importantly, you will drop the charges against James. If you do all this I will keep your secret."

She'd overpowered him, she knew it and he knew it. He was silent for a long moment, too long. "You ask too much."

"You're a very intelligent man. I'm sure you can make it all happen."

He seethed, his face splotchy and red, his nostrils flaring. He'd never before wanted to strike her as badly as he did in that moment, yet for once he couldn't react.

Eleanor grinned, realizing that this is what it felt like to win. The power could easily go to her head. "What say you, my husband? What do they do to traitors nowadays? Hang them, or firing squad?"

He shook his head, sinking into his chair. "It's too late."

A shiver of unease rippled over her body. Ellie's smile faded. "What do you mean?"

He smirked up at her, and she realized in that moment that she hadn't won at all. "Your whore. He hangs in five minutes. You'll never get there in time. It's too late."

* * *

Five minutes.

Five minutes and he would hang. Five minutes and his world would be over. If he was going to believe in God, he supposed he'd better start now. Yet as he stared at that door, waiting for the guards to appear and escort him outside, he found he couldn't believe in much of anything anymore.

James sat against the cell wall, heedless of the rats that shuffled across the dingy floor, coming closer . . . ever closer. He only thought about his life and what he had become. The secrets. The betrayal. The senseless loss of lives. For what?

He would die and none of it mattered. His life had not mattered. He had not saved his family, and he had not saved Eleanor. He had lived a lie. He rested his head in his hands and stared at the door . . . waiting . . . waiting.

How stupid he'd been all those years to believe that he'd been blessed. Living in luxury while saving his family. He'd actually thought he and Lady Lavender were friends. He laughed, the harsh sound echoing against the stone walls. Hell, maybe he deserved to die for being so bloody stupid. If only he could take Lord Beckett to hell with him.

A door screeched open from somewhere down the hall. Footsteps echoed, thumping in time with his heart . . . two? Three? Each thud of footsteps closer was a moment closer to his death. James managed to stagger to his feet, the chains rattling with the movement. Very well, he would face death, look it straight in the eyes, and tell it to go to hell. He would not cower. He would not beg.

The cell door screeched open. The rats went scurrying into holes and drains. He had just enough time to note two dark forms in the doorway right before a lantern swung forward, illuminating the dank cell. He hadn't seen light in days. Blinded, James stumbled back, hitting the damp wall and using it for support.

"Christ," a familiar voice mumbled. "Ye look like hell."

Hope swept through him, leaving James shaken, confused. "Gideon?"

The large man stepped into the cell. "Well, I'd say I told ye so, but I figure you've been through enough."

James sank against the wall, his legs too weak to hold him. "Dear God, it is you."

"Come on then," the guard grumbled, moving forward and undoing James's chains. "Yer free."

The chains fell away, clanging to the floor, but James merely stood there, too confused to move. Was he dreaming? Maybe he'd already died. Or maybe, more likely, he'd gone mad. "Free?"

"Yes," Gideon said kindly. He knew now he was dreaming, for Gideon was never kind.

Desperate, James stumbled forward, but his legs had grown useless and he ended up falling into Gideon's sturdy body. He latched onto the lapels of Gideon's jacket. "How? Was it Lady Lavender's doing?"

He swore he'd rather rot than allow her to hold this over him.

"No." Gideon slipped his arm around his waist, holding him upright. "Gads, yer even worse off than I suspected. Going bloody mad."

"Gideon, do not jest with me."

"I never jest."

It was true, so very true. He flattened his hands to Gideon's chest, could even feel the man's heart beat against his palm. He was real. James reached out, gripping Gideon's thick hair. Completely and utterly real.

"Are we going to leave, or would you rather kiss me?" Gideon grumbled.

"Eleanor?" James asked, ignoring his surly tone.

"She's with Alex and well enough, or so I've heard." Gideon helped him toward the door while the guard waiting with a lantern stood passively by. The same guard who had beaten the hell out of him when Lord Beckett had visited. James's hand curled, and for a quick, heated moment he thought about slamming his fist into the man's face.

"Don't even think about it," Gideon said softly. "I just got ye out; ye don't want to be thrown back in, do ye?"

James uncurled his fist and jerked his head toward the door. Gideon was right. Dear God, he didn't understand any of this, and a part of him still thought he must be dreaming, but at the moment he would believe it was true . . . he was free.

Gideon helped him down the hall. "Christ, you stink."

"Funny enough, they didn't offer bathing," James growled, his voice rough from disuse.

"What sort of establishment is this? If I were you, I'd demand my money back. Hope you didn't pay too much for such fine accommodations."

"Only in my blood and freedom."

The other prisoners staring out through the small bars of their doors clutched at his conscience. He tore his attention away from their haunted gazes and dark faces. He could not block out their cries and curses.

"James, dear God, I do believe this is the first time I've seen you truly angry."

"Get used to it," James said. The hatred inside consumed him, heated his blood, and made him want to scream, or punch someone. Made him want to visit Lord Beckett's and tear the man limb from limb.

"Out the back, sir," the guard said meekly.

Things had certainly changed. Somehow, in some way, Gideon had gotten his release. He would be forever in his debt. Although he was dying to know how the present moment had come about, he had other things to think about.

The guard shoved open a thick wooden door. Brilliant daylight burst into the corridor. James cowered, squeezing his eyes shut. It was too much, too damn much. The light made his stomach churn, his head spin.

"They're awaiting a hanging, and are going to be none too happy when they don't have one," the guard muttered.

"So sorry to disappoint them," James snapped. The courtyard was large, teeming with guards and prisoners. But it was the unmarked carriage waiting by that held his interest. He'd been here before with Gideon . . . so many years ago. He could practically see that lavender carriage.

"We're friends, we're all going to be great friends."

She'd been right about one thing . . . Gideon and Alex were his friends. True friends who would risk their own lives for him. Ellie . . . Ellie was a friend as well, a woman who knew more about him than any other being on this earth. He was not alone.

"Best get out now, while ye can." The guard spun around and went back inside, closing the door. James heard the large bolt being turned and shivered slightly. He had to remind himself over and over that he was free.

"Up with ye." Gideon helped him into the carriage, following. It wasn't until the door closed that James fell back into his seat and actually allowed his body to relax. He closed his eyes as the carriage jerked to life, trusting Gideon completely. His body shook, shook with pent-up anger and despair. But it was the anger he clung to, the hatred that kept him going.

"Here, take this."

James cracked his lids to see Gideon holding out a small bottle. He'd drawn the curtains and the carriage was covered in shadows. "What is it?"

They headed into London, bumping over cobbled roads. "Morphine for the pain."

James shoved the bottle away and closed his eyes once more. "No. I want to keep my wits."

Gideon sighed but didn't push the medicine. Lord, the seats felt like heaven, soft and clean. He didn't give a bloody damn that he was ruining the fine vehicle; he wanted to stretch out and sleep. To dream about holding Eleanor, her rose scent and soft body.

"Water then?"

His body reacted to the word. With a groan, James opened his eyes and took the jug. For a good minute he drank the clean, clear liquid. Drank so much his stomach felt as if it might burst. "Tell me how the hell you got them to release me."

Gideon handed him a basket and grinned. "Quite a bit has happened since I've been away. Things ye've missed while ye were playing pummel-the-lord. For one, believe it or not, I'm married."

"Congratulations," James said without conviction. Surely the man was lying. Gideon would never marry, unless it fit some ulterior purpose. James tore open the basket. Bread, cheese, cold chicken. He almost cried out in pleasure. His stomach grumbled loudly.

"I'm also very rich."

Well then, that must be the reason for his hasty marriage. That certainly made more sense than believing Gideon had fallen in love. He grabbed a chicken leg and took a huge bite. "Well done," he managed over the mouthful.

"And I have a grandmother, a titled witch of a woman from a very wealthy family. A grandmother who owes me quite a bit."

James took another large bite, savoring the greasy meat as it coated his tongue and slid down his throat. "I don't understand anything you're telling me and I don't bloody care. I have more important things to worry about."

"Well that's gratitude for you," Gideon said dryly.

"I don't give damn whether this is all a temporary reprieve. I don't care if I end up returning to prison, as long as I accomplish two things while I'm out."

"Only two?" Gideon quirked a dark brow, his silver gaze showing his amusement. "Well then, how can I deny your wishes? Do tell."

"First, I'm going to kill Ophelia. Then, I'm going to murder Eleanor's husband."

Chapter 17

James had never thought to step foot on Lavender Hills Estate property again. But there were many things he'd never thought he'd do: Become a whore. Fall in love with a married lady. Attempt murder.

As the heady scent of lavender followed the carriage through the iron gates he could think of nothing other than ridding the world of the woman who had destroyed so many.

Gideon had stretched out his long legs as much as the carriage would allow and watched James through wary eyes. "You sure you want to do this?"

"I've never been so sure in my life."

The carriage started down the long drive, wheels crunching over gravel. "From what I've heard, you managed to trick a beautiful woman into falling in love with you. Why ruin it?"

James swallowed hard, staring out the window. Love? Did she love him? She'd never said. Frankly, he didn't want to know; not now. "There is no hope for us. But there is hope for her if I get rid of Ophelia and Lord Beckett."

"Ach, now, aren't you the one always saying there's always room for hope?"

James slid him a glance. "No, I've never said that. Must be from the poetry you so obviously read."

Gideon clicked his tongue. "You're getting rather witty with old age."

James ignored him, in no mood to spar. "Gates were open."

Gideon shrugged indifferently. There was an ease about the man that hadn't been there before. A light and calmness in his gray eyes. "That's normal during the day."

"Yes, but usually she has guards posted, keeping watch."

Gideon brushed aside a curtain. "Hmm, interesting, indeed."

They lapsed into silence, each mulling over the possibilities of what was to come. He was grateful that Gideon had been the one to arrive. Alex, he knew without doubt, would have attempted to talk James out of his vendetta.

"You're married now, Gideon. I assume you might have some sort of affection for your wife?"

"A little," he admitted with a sheepish grin that said he felt much more than he implied. Hell, the man actually glowed. Typical Gideon, unable to own up to his feelings. Still, he owed the man his life. He'd harmed enough innocents because of his actions; he would not ruin Gideon's chances.

"Then leave. Go home to your family. You have a chance to live. But if you stay with me, you might hang."

Gideon shrugged. "I've killed before and gotten away with it."

James wasn't sure what the man was talking about, and frankly didn't want to know. The carriage paused and his heart slammed wildly in his chest. Minutes from now it would be over. His past gone. She would not harm anyone else. Her reign would be destroyed.

"Here you go." Gideon reached into his jacket pocket and handed James a pistol.

James took the weapon, shoved the door open. He was just about to step outside when Gideon placed his hand on his arm, stopping him.

"It will change you, James." He pulled his hand away. "At night when you close your eyes you will see her face. You will wonder if perhaps there was some good in her and you took away the only chance she had to prove it."

James felt cold inside, numb. Gideon's words meant nothing to him. "It's the only way."

He didn't wait for Gideon's response but stepped outside, the weight of the pistol cool against the palm of his hand. Slowly, he tilted his head back and studied the estate that had been his home for over a decade. Nothing had changed, although it should have. After all, his world was destroyed, all he believed in gone. Yet the estate still stood here. The air still smelled like lavender. And she still reigned. But not for long. Perhaps, he thought idly, as he moved up the steps, he'd burn the estate and the fields to the ground after he got rid of her.

He didn't fear the woman. He didn't fear her many guards. He didn't fear death. At that moment he only feared failure. He shoved the door open, surprised that not even Wavers was standing guard. For a moment he paused in the foyer, attuning his senses to the estate.

He'd lived here for so many years, at one time it had felt like home. Now it felt cold, lonely . . . the inside of a large and elaborate mausoleum. An empty mausoleum. Something was wrong. Very wrong. The door to her office stood open, not a guard in view. James tightened his grip on the pistol and moved cautiously into the room.

Ophelia sat behind her desk, a tea tray untouched upon the surface. As the floorboards creaked under his feet, she slowly glanced his way but didn't look in the least bit surprised to see him. "Well," she said softly. "I never thought to see you again."

"You hoped," he said without an ounce of bitterness. Strangely he felt nothing, as if he was merely doing a deed that must be done . . . much like when he bedded his clients.

She shrugged, leaning nonchalantly back in her chair, all ease and comfort. "Honestly, I didn't really care what happened to you one way or another."

He strolled toward the sideboard and poured himself a whiskey. "You never have, have you?"

The corners of her mouth quirked into a small smile. "James, you were a means to an end."

He faced her fully, glass in one hand, pistol in the other. "What end, exactly?"

"My revenge, of course, but you already knew that."

James strolled to one of the two chairs across from her desk. "So now we've all been thoroughly punished, and you can move on?" He sat down. "Yet we haven't really been destroyed, have we? Alex is happily married. Gideon is in love, as shocking as it sounds. They have both escaped your carefully crafted plan to ruin innocent lives." He smiled and held his arms wide. "And here I am as well . . . free."

"Unfortunately." She tilted her head to the side, studying him with curious eyes. "How did you escape?"

"Friends, oddly enough. Something you wouldn't understand."

She laughed. "Who needs friends when I have this much power and money? Friends will eventually turn on you anyway, James."

"Money, yes, but not power." He took a drink, savoring the burn of the alcohol as it spread down his throat. "You don't seem to get that. You have no power over Alex. You have no power over Gideon. And now you have no power over me."

"Oh James, it might be over now, but I've certainly had my revenge. For a decade you were completely under my control. I took your childhood. And even now you don't go to bed at night without thinking of me, of the shame you feel because you sold yourself." She stood and he realized with some surprise that she was wearing pink. A soft, girlish pink gown with a demure square neckline and softly flowing skirt.

"You're not wearing lavender."

She pressed her hands to her narrow waist and laughed again. "No. I tire of the color. I was wearing it the day I was forced, you know." She strolled toward the windows, looking out upon her territory. "From that day onward I wore it as a reminder to myself and to those who harmed me." She smiled tauntingly. "Your father was the worst of them, you know. He actually had a heart, yet he stood by, helped them cover the crime. At least Gideon's father had the good sense to pay for my silence." She spread her arms wide. "And here I am . . . in all this splendor."

James swallowed hard, his emotions conflicted. She was troubled, insane, and part of him felt guilty for his father's deed, disappointed that the man he'd adored could have allowed such brutality. But he also knew she would not rest until they were completely and utterly destroyed.

She trailed her fingers across her desktop. "I'm the reason your mother started whoring herself on the streets."

James went still. She was lying, she must be. His mother wouldn't . . .

"I see by the stunned look upon your face you didn't know." She grinned and any compassion he felt for her disappeared. "I didn't set out to ruin your life, merely your father's, if it makes any difference. But then the bastard went and killed himself. Could he have possibly felt guilty?"

He would not react to her. She was baiting him, trying to draw him into her web of lies and revenge. He wouldn't bite; instead he decided to turn the tables on her. "I wonder what your family would think if they knew what you've been doing since you disappeared," James said casually. "You're from France, correct? Your father was a reverend of sorts."

"Well done! You're not the meek lamb I thought you were." She moved to the sideboard and poured herself a brandy. Her lips were curled into a smirk, but he could see the anger there in her eyes and knew he had hit a sore spot. "What will you do, James? Kill me? Tell the world who I really am?"

She returned to her desk and sank into the chair, her glass in hand. The place was silent . . . so very silent. As the clock on the mantel ticked the seconds by, James kept waiting for Wavers, or someone, to enter. No one came. Something was wrong.

"Do it then," she demanded, glancing at the pistol he held. "Do it now, get it over with."

She was right . . . why not end it all now while he had the chance? He lifted the pistol, pointing it at her chest. "Perhaps I will."

She held her arms wide and leaned back against her chair. "Then by all means . . . end it. You'd certainly be better off, I won't deny that."

One shot, one bullet and it would be over. As his gaze met hers, he could see the dare in her eyes. His finger trembled over the trigger. How badly he wanted to kill her, to end it all. He could. He could kill her and escape before anyone knew better. He cocked the gun. He could rid the world of her plot for revenge and he could head to Lord Beckett's home next.

"James, don't," Eleanor's familiar voice called out, startling him.

James jerked his head toward the door. Ellie stood just over the threshold, like a damn angel come to save his soul. A beaten and bruised angel with imploring, heavenly blue eyes that made him rethink everything. His hand began to tremble. It wasn't real; he'd gone insane. Ellie couldn't be here.

"Eleanor," he whispered, his heart hammering so loudly he couldn't hear what she said. But she was speaking, he could see her lips moving as she started toward him like a bloody dream, or maybe it was a nightmare. A cold sweat broke out across his forehead.

He didn't want her to witness Ophelia's death. He sure as hell didn't want her to see him become a murderer. "Leave, Ellie. Now."

"No." She stepped closer to him. But seeing the bruises marring her beautiful face only made him more determined to kill them and end it all. First Ophelia, and then Lord Beckett. Didn't she understand that he was doing this for her?

"Damn it, James, she's trying to manipulate you, and you're doing exactly what she wants!"

"I know, and I don't really care." He returned his attention to Ophelia, intent on ignoring Eleanor and the feelings of humanity she stirred within him. If she had to witness Ophelia's death, so be it. She would thank him later.

"James," Eleanor said softly, her voice husky with emotion. "Don't throw it all away. Beat her at her own game by leaving, by running away with me and embracing a new life."

"A life?" He released a wry laugh. She made it sound so easy. "How?"

"I'm here," Eleanor whispered, pressing her hand to his chest. "We'll find a way to be together."

"Bravo," Ophelia said softly. "'Tis truly so touching that it's almost believable."

Ellie stepped closer, forcing him to lower his eyes and meet her pleading gaze. "Don't give up hope. Don't give up on us."

It was impossible; they could never have a life together. Didn't she see that? So why did he hesitate? Torn, he looked over her shoulder and met Ophelia's cold gaze. She wasn't afraid, he realized with a start. She didn't care if he pulled the trigger.

"You dared to believe in me when no one else has." Eleanor stepped closer to him and rested her palm on the side of his face. "You are the most courageous man I know, not because of your brawn, but because of your compassion."

Her words hit him hard and the gun trembled in his hand. He didn't know if he could be that man anymore, damn it all if he wanted to be. He gritted his teeth, torn between doing what his heart and his head told him to do. He might not be the caring, easy-natured James everyone knew, but he couldn't disappoint Eleanor.

"Damn you," James hissed, dropping the gun to his side. "You give me too much credit."

"I don't. I know the real you, James. Don't let her need for revenge turn you into what she has become."

He gripped her waist and pulled her close, knowing the stench of his prison clung to his clothing and not caring. He had Ellie, he had his freedom . . . what more did they need?

"Oh, well done, beautifully said," Ophelia proclaimed, clapping her hands. "I almost believe you, James." She surged to her feet, her face cold and bitter. "But we all know you're nothing more than a street rat."

James held Ellie tight. "Dear God, you want me to shoot you, don't you?"

She sneered at him but he didn't miss the desperate plea in her eyes. Suddenly he understood. The entire world became clear and alive once more. Eleanor had been right. "You want me to kill you so I hang, giving you what you wanted all along. You will have destroyed my life, and you can be done with this world."

She scoffed. "Don't be ridiculous."

He pushed Ellie behind him, not trusting Ophelia in the least. "It's true. You've spread your poison and you're ready to leave because you have nothing to live for anymore." He took Eleanor's hand. His body felt lighter, his chest warm and aching. "Look for another to take your bait."

"James, no," Ophelia said, her voice laced with desperation. She skirted the desk and started toward them. "Don't leave me."

James ignored her plea and led Eleanor toward the door. Alex, Gideon, and Mr. Smith stood in the foyer. They'd seen it all.

"James, I swear I will destroy you!"

Ellie flinched. He started to slide his arm around her waist when he noticed the slight widening of Alex's eyes. Before he had time to react, Gideon lifted his pistol. The blast rang out, shaking the room. James jerked Ellie close to him.

"Are you all right?" he whispered.

She gave a jerky nod, her heart slamming wildly against his chest. He hated seeing her so afraid. Slowly, Gideon lowered his arm. The acidic scent of gunpowder hung heavy in the air. James spun around.

Ophelia was staring at her hand, blood dripping from the spot where her finger had been. A bloodied mess of managed flesh and bone. Her own pistol lay upon the desk where it had fallen from her hand. Gideon had just saved him . . . again.

Eleanor gasped, her hand covering her mouth in shock. The sight was too horrifying even for him. Still, Lady Lavender merely stood there staring at her hand, not making a sound. He looked away, leading Ellie toward the hall.

"Vhat the hell happened?" Wavers suddenly appeared, the big bull trembling with shock and anger. He could not harm them now. He was gravely outnumbered.

"Better tend to Ophelia, Wavers," Alex said softly. "You're all she has left."

The woman had sunk into her chair, her face white as snow as she cradled her bloodied hand to her chest. She looked like a child who had just lost her favorite toy. The sight did not bring James any glee.

"Come on," James whispered. Ellie had seen enough horror in her life; she didn't need to witness more. He wrapped his arm around her waist and led her through the foyer and out the front door.

"She'll most likely seek revenge," Alex said as they found the two carriages waiting.

"Yes, but at least this time we'll be prepared."

James helped Ellie into one carriage while Alex, Gideon, and Mr. Smith took the other. He knew enough to know that this wouldn't be over until they left the country and went into hiding.

* * *

They didn't speak the entire way to London. They didn't speak after they entered the hotel, even after they made it to their private room and she'd changed into her nightclothes without a glance from him. James ate quickly, as if merely nourishing his body for battle, then left the table to order a bath. The silence was driving her insane.

Eleanor dragged her spoon through the stew. The food smelled and looked delicious, but she had no appetite. From under her lashes she watched James as he bathed. The gleam of his muscled skin in the light of the fire made him practically glow like a golden Adonis. Yet his beauty was marked by bruises, reminders of his pain and all he had gone through thanks to her. The thought that he had come so close to death was something she didn't dare dwell upon. If only she hadn't visited Lady Lavender's in the first place . . . if only she hadn't told him the truth, would he be better off?

James leaned back against the tub, his arms relaxed upon the rim as he gazed unblinkingly into the fire. He looked exhausted yet didn't sleep. Yes, she had talked him out of killing Lady Lavender, but at what price? He seemed almost . . . defeated, different, not the James she had come to care about. She found herself nervous and unsure what to say around this man.

"Is the water getting cold? Shall I ring for a footman?"

"No." He stood, water trailing down the dips and planes of his muscled stomach. She wanted to trace the edge of his jaw with her fingertips, wanted to run her hands through that crisp trail of hair that led to his cock. She wanted to press her face into his neck and breathe in his familiar, musky scent while wrapping her hand firmly around his thick shaft. But mostly she wanted him inside of her, as close as they could possibly be.

He moved a cloth over his body, drying his skin. Eleanor suddenly felt breathless and hot, the room too small. She jerked her gaze away and stood, gripping the table when her legs shook unsteadily. "You should eat more."

"I'm fine."

She dared to glance at him. He'd wrapped the cloth around his waist, letting the material fall down to his knees. How she wanted to go to him and press her lips to his, to kiss him thoroughly, deeply, and beg him to care about her again. Perhaps it was all too much and he'd finally realized how much easier his life would be without her. With trembling fingers she lifted the ceramic pot of medicine Patience had given her earlier. James stood near the fireplace, his back to her, his body so still he could have been a statue.

Ellie took in a deep, trembling breath and started toward him. She couldn't stand the tension anymore. "I should tend to your wounds."

"No." He turned to face her.

She paused, confused as he took the jar from her hands and set it on the mantel.

"Why not?"

"Because I don't want you to tend to my wounds."

Her anger and frustration grew. "Damn you, James! Don't you dare treat me this way! We have a chance here, a chance to find happiness, a life. Don't you—"

"Eleanor," he said softly, taking her hands in his. "I don't want you to tend to my wounds right now because instead, I want to kiss you. I want to make love to you."

A shiver of heat rushed through her body. "Oh."

He wrapped his arm around her waist and slid his hand up her back, pressing the flat of his palm between her shoulder blades. Slowly, he lowered his lips. Eleanor sighed, closing her eyes and lifting on tiptoe to meet him. It was a soft, gentle kiss that left her weak-kneed and wanting more. When he finally drew back, she sank into him, wrapping her arms around his neck. This was the James she knew, the James she had come to care for.

"I was so worried," she mumbled against his shoulder.

"I know," he whispered.

He nuzzled the top of her head, pressing kisses to her hair. Through the drying towel and her nightdress, she could feel his erection growing long and hard. Despite her vulnerable emotional state, she found her own body hungry for his touch. Emboldened, she pressed her mouth to the scruff along his throat. The scent of the prison was gone and he smelled like himself once more. Unable to help herself, she darted her tongue out, drawing a damp path up his neck.

James groaned, his arms tightening around her body, pressing her soft curves up against his hard form. Every kiss, every touch, every ache was as sweet as she remembered. Better, for she knew now what was to come.

"I want you too, James," she whispered.

With a growl, he scooped her up into his arms, cradling her against his chest. "Help me, Ellie. Help me remember what it's like to feel pleasure, not pain. To know hope, not despair. Love me."

A rush of emotion overwhelmed her. She did love him, so much more than he realized. The warm feelings that swept through her body had nothing to do with attraction and all to do with love. He settled her gently upon the bed. The chill that had permeated her bones since James had been arrested faded.

"You don't know how relieved I am to see you," he said softly. "Thinking about you was the thing that kept me alive."

She felt his words all the way to her soul. He stretched out beside her and reached for the neckline of her night wrap. With a quick tug, the gown was down and her breasts exposed. His mouth covered a hardened nipple, and attraction shot through her body, pooling in her groin. Eleanor arched her back, unable to control the emotions pulsing within.

"So lovely," he whispered, as his hand came up to cup her other breast. "You smell so damn good, like roses in the middle of hell. I'd think about that scent when I was in the gaols. Dream about gardens and you. Dream about touching you, kissing you, being inside of you."

He pressed his mouth to the valley between her breasts. Then lower, taking her gown with him. Moments later she found herself naked, and the towel that had been covering James was gone. When he lay atop her, pressing his full weight into her body, she thought she'd gone to heaven. She would never tire of his touch, never tire of him. Eleanor wrapped her legs around his calves, holding him close. He was hers. Finally. He was free from Lady Lavender's hold, and she would be free from her husband soon.

As James pressed his mouth to hers, his hand slid torturously slowly up her thigh. Ellie groaned, wiggling beneath him. The ache between her legs twisted almost painfully. After having gone so many years without the gentle touch of a loved one, Ellie was frantic for more. "Please, James."

"I want to kiss every bit of you, I want to savor the feel of my cock entering you slowly, fully."

"No." She shook her head, her body flushed with desperation. "Later we'll go slowly. This time fast."

The surprised grin upon his face sent her heart pattering. His knuckles brushed the curls hiding her femininity. She shuddered, whimpering for more. When he eased a finger between her slick folds and into her tight sheath, it still wasn't enough.

"Dear God, you're wet," he whispered.

"James, I want you fully," she whispered, her face heating with an embarrassed blush. She'd never asked for anything, but she couldn't quite keep the words inside.

He pressed his mouth to hers in a quick kiss and shifted so his erection pressed against the spot that ached for his touch. "This?"

Ellie nodded, her hands moving down his muscled back toward his tight arse. She felt afire. Every nerve in her body begged for his touch. She'd had a taste of perfection and she craved more. Lord, she'd had no idea being with a man could feel this way.

"I was so worried," she whispered against his lips. "So afraid."

He pressed the thickened head of his cock to her folds and entered her with a quick thrust of his hips. "I have you now. Nothing, no one, will keep us apart."

Whether it was true or not, at that moment she believed him. As he lifted his hips, she surged upward, meeting him thrust for thrust. Years of loneliness were gone with his touch. With James she had everything she'd ever wanted, everything she needed. Life with James might be difficult, but it would be full of adventure and compassion.

His mouth found hers, his tongue delving between her lips in a heated kiss that left her feeling drugged. His arms wrapped around her possessively as he rocked into her, finding a rhythm that matched her own.

His muscled back was tight under her palms, a find sheen of sweat coated their skin, and the erotic scents of their lovemaking permeated the air. Every bit of her body tingled with sudden awareness. He knew exactly where to touch her, exactly what to whisper into her ear.

"Come for me, Eleanor," he said softly.

When the ache between her legs finally uncoiled into blinding pleasure, she cried out his name. James surged into her one more time, throwing his head back with a groan. The feel of his wet seed entering her body sent her sheath trembling all over again.

Ellie wrapped her arms around his shoulders, holding him tightly to her, suddenly afraid he would leave. She didn't want to let him go . . . ever.

He pressed a kiss to her forehead, his breathing harsh. "I'll crush you."

"I don't care."

"I do."

Unwillingly, she released her hold and he rolled away, reclining on his back, his eyes closed. Ellie cuddled up next to him, resting her hand on his chest, feeling the hard thump of his heart. She wanted words of passion, words of love. He said nothing. Slowly, she reached out, brushing the damp clumps of hair from his forehead. He looked peaceful, boyish almost.

"James," she whispered, steeling her courage. "I love you."

He didn't respond.

Ellie pulled the covers up to her chin, feeling suddenly cold. Her husband had taken everything from her . . . her innocence, her family, her faith. He'd crushed her hopes and dreams. But she'd never truly loved him.

As she lay there listening to James's deep, even breathing she realized that James could hurt her in a way her husband never could. He could destroy her very soul. Closing her eyes, she forced her mind to go blank, determined to rest.

Tomorrow was another day. Things would be better in the morning . . . at least she hoped.

Chapter 18

James was gone.

Alex had left years ago.

It seemed as if she'd lost Gideon as well.

Ophelia had dismissed most of the staff, sent them on their way to whatever lives they could make for themselves. She wasn't a complete monster; she'd given them each enough to pass the next few months. Only Wavers remained, refusing to leave her side, the moron. He was like a large bulldog that drooled all over her, wanting a handout. She'd get rid of him too, when she was ready. Rumors were circulating that she would be shut down soon, in any way possible. Society had had enough of Lady Lavender's sinful ways. She had nothing left.

Ophelia stood and moved toward the windows, gazing out upon the fields of lavender. Soon now . . . soon she'd be ready. The sun was just rising, the sky brilliant red and orange. As a child she'd always awoken early to be with her father while he practiced his sermons. They would stroll through the fields at sunrise, taking along a breakfast, while Mama and the other children slept. He would practice his speech while she watched the sunrise and thought that nothing, ever, could be as wonderful. She'd been right. She raised her bandaged hand, the throbbing almost unbearable.

What a different person she'd been; she barely recognized that child, those dreams. But she'd left France, excited about her prospects. She was beautiful, her mother had said, she was their ticket to a better life. When she'd been invited by a wealthy cousin to go to London, they'd been so sure she would land a rich, titled gent.

She had caught the attention of a gent . . . but not for marriage. He'd told her he loved her and she'd been too stupid and innocent to know better. He'd begged her to meet him, and she had. Stupid, silly girl. That night had changed her forever, had killed a part of her she couldn't revive. It was the night when she'd realized how much evil there was in the world. And God? She released a harsh laugh. There was no God. And so she did what she had to in order to survive . . . she focused on revenge. It was what kept her going when she would have rather died.

She drew her hand down the fine velvet blue curtains. "And the sons shall inherit the sins of the fathers."

She had ruined their lives. It had all been so very easy. She had taken their children, taken their heirs. She had done what she had set out to do . . . avenge herself, destroy the men who had destroyed her with no thought to her feelings, her innocence. And it had worked. For a while she had felt vindicated. For a while she had been able to enjoy the riches of her spoils. But soon enough the feelings of success had faded, as all things do.

"Alone," she whispered, her breath fogging up the window. Although she hadn't had money, she could have been the darling of the *ton*. She could have married high above her station and helped her family along the way. But one night . . . one foolish night had ruined it all. It had been torn from her, crushed beneath selfish, demonic feet. A smile lifted the corners of her mouth. But she had gotten her revenge.

Her smile fell. If she had destroyed their lives, why did she still feel so angry, so hollow? Perhaps because Alex, Gideon, and James had beaten her by finding lives outside these prison walls. They had escaped. Perhaps because she hadn't truly been able to punish the men who had done the crime, and had to settle for their offspring. She didn't know and she didn't care anymore.

"Let it be over," she whispered.

"Pardon?" Wavers said from behind her.

She turned slowly away from the window. The large brute looked truly worried about her. She wanted to laugh at the absurdity of it all. The one man she thought of as nothing more than a pesky pup was the only one who truly cared. "'Tis nothing. Nothing at all."

"You should eat," he said in his thick accent as he entered the room, carrying a tray of soup and bread. "You don't eat anymore."

She wasn't hungry. Hadn't been in months, although she'd eaten enough to survive. She'd had her dresses taken in three times, and still they hung on her small frame. He set the tray on the table near the fireplace. The scent of soup made her nauseous.

"I'll eat," she lied. "Just leave me in peace."

He looked up sharply. She didn't miss the hurt in his eyes. "But—"

"You overstep yourself," she snapped, growing more annoyed with him the longer he stood in her presence. She couldn't abide a man who begged for attention. Why couldn't he just leave her with whatever little peace she could find?

He flushed, his jaw working. If he cried, she swore she'd shoot him herself. But fortunately the man shuffled off like a pup who'd been beaten by his master. He thought she had feelings for him, as he did her. Loyalty, compassion, softness. She had feelings for no one. She had lost that ability long ago when her father had tossed her from the house, saying he would never forgive her for ruining herself. But she had gotten back at them. When her mother had come begging for money seven years ago, Ophelia had merely laughed, loving the satisfaction she'd felt as she'd slammed the door in her face. She hadn't a clue where they were now, if any of them still lived, and didn't really care.

When the door creaked open she turned, prepared to demand Wavers leave her alone once and for all. But it was not Wavers's hulking form that stood in the doorway. It was someone more elegant, more finely dressed, far more dangerous . . . Lord Beckett. She found his presence odd indeed, for they had never had much of a conversation. She'd merely told him where he could find James, along with Lady Beckett. It had been all so very easy to sit back and watch. And even though she had done Lord Beckett a favor, he hadn't thanked her.

"She thinks to divorce me," he said as he stepped into the room, closing the door behind him.

Ophelia laughed, delighted by the woman's audacity, even as she wondered why in the world he would tell her such personal news. She'd never thought much about Lady Beckett before; she had merely been a means to an end. But now she found she liked the brazen wench very well indeed. Perhaps in another time, another place, they might have even been friends.

Ophelia smirked, leaning back against the edge of her desk. "She shall have a difficult time with that."

He didn't return her amusement. "Perhaps."

She narrowed her eyes, studying the man. There was something he wasn't telling her . . . a reason for his presence. He moved slowly across the room, his hands in the pockets of his jacket. As before when she'd seen him, his mustache was tidy and combed, his hair slicked back into place, and his clothing, although he had traveled by coach a good hour or so, was without crease. He was a man who took his appearance quite seriously.

"But maybe not." He settled in the chair across from her desk, a mere ten steps or so from her. "Her second cousin or such is related to the queen."

Ophelia lifted a brow, amused and curious as to why he was

here. Certainly he had a plan of some sort, although she wasn't quite sure of the specifics. She tilted her head high, not one to be easily frightened. "She might be distantly related to royalty, yet they couldn't protect her from you."

"From me?" His gaze flashed with outrage, although he kept his voice calm. "Her father was the third son of a baron. Their blood is nothing compared to my family lineage."

She shrugged, completely unconcerned. "Yet you might lose your wife? Your blue blood was not enough to earn her respect." She moved toward the sideboard and poured herself a brandy. She had a feeling she was going to need the fortitude.

He surged to his feet, his hands fisted. "She will not make a fool of me."

"What will you do?" Ophelia laughed, highly amused. There was nothing better than seeing a grown man throw a fit. "Will you kill her?"

His lips lifted into a snarl. "I'd have every right."

She shrugged, taking another drink. The alcohol no longer burned when she drank, it only numbed the pain into beautiful nothingness. She craved its powers, craved the numb feeling it produced.

Lord Beckett started toward her, his footsteps hurried and angry. She tilted her head to the side and watched him, her mind spinning. A man like him held so very little control over his emotions. A man like him would be so very easy to manipulate into doing exactly as she wished. Dare she?

He shoved his finger into her face. "You told me that if I helped you, if I put that bastard in prison, you would see him destroyed."

Her heart slammed wildly in her chest, urging her to act. But she knew she had to keep calm, the timing must be perfect, he must not suspect anything. She took another drink, ignoring the way her hand trembled. "Alas, sometimes things just don't work out, no matter how much we wish it."

"You bitch," he hissed. Pulling a pistol from his waistcoat, he shoved it toward her face.

Although she'd been expecting it, her heart leapt into her throat all the same. Underneath that surprise, she couldn't deny the thrilling sense of victory that pulsed in time with her heart. She had won.

"Go to hell, Lord Beckett, and take your wife with you."

"You whore." His hand shook as he lowered the gun and pointed it at her chest. He had lost control. He was pathetic, just like all men. So easily manipulated, and she would use his weakness for her own gain.

"You don't have what it takes, my lord," she sneered.

His face flushed red, and she knew that it would all be over within moments. The entire world seemed to slow as he cocked the gun. The blood rushed to Ophelia's ears, drowning out the sound of his vile cursing. She shifted her gaze to the fields visible through the windows. Lavender, aglow from the rising sun. And in that moment she was a child again, sitting in that field in France watching the sunrise as the soft murmur of her father's voice drifted upon the wind.

Slowly, her father turned toward her, reaching down and ruffling her hair. *"Are you ready to go home, poppet?"*

She barely heard the blast from the gun, barely felt the bullet tear through her chest, and barely noticed her legs give out. It was over. She was going home.

* * *

"You truly think this will work?" James asked, sliding his arm around Ellie's narrow waist as they cuddled in the carriage.

She rested her head upon his shoulder. "It's worth trying, don't you agree?" She smiled up at him, trying desperately to feign confidence, but he could see the nervousness in her blue eyes.

"Of course." It was worth a try, but he certainly held out no hope. Even now, the idea of a divorce was practically unheard of. And when they were granted, it was only to men. Women had no right to divorce. But he would not crush Eleanor's dreams. No, he would hold her hand, he would support her, and when this cousin of hers laughed at their outrageous query, then he would pack Ellie up, take the hack Gideon and Alex had waiting, and escape as far away from London as they could.

"I haven't seen her in ages." Eleanor brushed her fingers over the tops of his hands. "We had the same German great-grandmother."

"*Wirklich?*" he asked.

Ellie blinked her eyes wide in surprise. "*Sprechen Sie Deutsch?*"

"*Nur ein bisschen.*" Lady Lavender had schooled them in the basics of most languages; it was good for business, she had explained. Fine dining, poetry, even the piano . . . they were true gentlemen. If one overlooked the fact that they slept with women for money.

She laughed. "And here I thought I knew you quite well."

He pressed his lips to her forehead. "Better than anyone."

Appeased, she snuggled up next to him while the carriage rattled through London. They'd both slept like babes last night, neither worried about being attacked or carted off to prison for the first time in days, not with Alex and Gideon guarding their room. He owed them more than his friendship; he owed them his life.

"James," she said softly.

He pulled her closer, breathing in her rose scent. "Hmm?"

"What really happened with your father?"

Her question caught him off guard. He swallowed hard, staring out the dusty windows onto the crowded streets of London. "He killed himself."

Ellie sucked in a sharp breath. "I'm so sorry."

"I know." He pressed a kiss to the top of her head. He tried not to think about his father and had managed quite well in the past few years. But he knew he couldn't avoid the subject forever. "He was so melancholy after he was let go. Started drinking like a fish. My mum would cry herself to sleep at night."

Ellie clasped his hand tightly. "You don't have to tell me."

"I want to." His eyes burned with the memory, a day that he had shared with no one. Not even his sister. But he found that once he started talking to Ellie, he couldn't seem to stop. She wanted the truth, and he would give it to her. Hell, he would give her anything. "I had had enough. I screamed at him, demanded he get a position, told him he was ruining the family. He left. Three hours later the constable arrived to tell us he had shot himself."

Eleanor pressed her body to his, resting her head on his shoulder. "And you thought it was your fault."

He nodded. "But it was guilt . . . all that time it was guilt because of his part in Ophelia's rape."

They didn't speak for a long time, merely held each other as the carriage rolled through London. He'd thought he'd feel nothing but shame, admitting the truth. Oddly, he felt relieved.

The carriage pulled to a stop in front of Kensington Palace. The massive black fence separated the real world from the wealthy. They had written and were expected, but it didn't make James feel any easier when the guards came forward, their faces full of suspicion. He wrapped his arms more tightly around Eleanor as she spoke with the guards through the window.

"Yes, three o'clock," she said.

James was only slightly surprised when the massive black-and-gold gates parted and the carriage jerked forward. The closer they got to the large brick estate, the more uneasy he became. James shifted away from her, needing to keep his distance, both emotionally and physically. He couldn't bloody well think with her cuddled next to him. Besides, he doubted the royal family, even if they were distant cousins, would appreciate a married woman showing affection toward a man not her husband. Even being here was a blatant sign of disrespect.

James slid Ellie a glance. He knew she was still in pain thanks to her husband's fists, although she wouldn't admit it. Powder had covered up the lingering marks on her face. She rarely showed discomfort, for much like him she'd learned to hide her emotions. Even now she sat straight as a board on the edge of her seat, her hands folded tightly in her lap.

She was bloody perfect, beautiful, kind, strong. He didn't deserve her. Her life would be the worse with him, but he would try, damn it all, he would try to give her what she needed, even if he had to work in the mines and it killed him.

They didn't speak as the carriage traveled down the drive. Didn't say a word when it slowed and finally stopped. James was very much aware of the guards lining the shallow steps of the massive brick estate. Despite knowing nothing would happen, a cold sweat broke out on his forehead.

"Are you well?" Ellie whispered, sensing his unease.

He gave her a crooked grin. "Guards make me uncomfortable, as you can imagine."

The door opened, and a footman in brilliant dress uniform stood patiently to the side, waiting to assist. The place was even more impressive up close, James realized as he stepped from the coach. Hell, it was yet another reminder of how he did not belong in Ellie's world.

"My lady." A woman in a hideous blue gown headed down the steps to greet them. She did not smile and walked more like a soldier than a lady's maid. "Your cousin is waiting for you in the gardens. If you'll follow me."

"Of course."

They didn't touch as they made their way around the back. They knew better than to show any affection in public. Servants and occupants strolled the large gardens, taking in the warmth of the sun on the unusual cloudless day. James averted his gaze, highly aware of the fact that one of the women might recognize him. Even though the light brown walking dress with the dark trim and attractive jacket Ellie wore was borrowed from Patience, she still looked the part; she looked like she belonged. They moved past the large fountains and toward the grass where an older woman was sitting at a white iron table, while he . . . he wondered if he would ever belong anywhere. Was there room in this world for him?

"Cousin Hilda." Ellie leaned over and pressed a kiss to the woman's leathery cheek. Her wrinkles and gray hair gave away her age, and her stiff shoulders and lack of smile gave away her demeanor.

She waved her hand dismissively through the air, showing no happiness at Ellie's visit. "Sit."

Ellie settled in the chair across from her.

"And this is he?" Cousin Hilda looked James over in a way that would have embarrassed a lesser man. He'd been so thoroughly examined by a variety of women that very little embarrassed him. "The lad you wish to marry?"

Ellie nodded.

"A genteel farmer's son?" Hilda sipped her tea, watching them with shrewd pale blue eyes that made James wonder if the old bat knew more than what she was letting on.

"My lady." He bowed low, then sat on the chair next to Ellie's. "James McKinnon."

Dismissing him, she focused on Ellie. "Tell me what you wish from me."

"I need a divorce."

The woman choked on her tea, coughing so hard that her lady's maid, who had been standing some distance away, came running. "Dear God," the woman rasped, waving her maid away. "Why not ask for the monarchy instead?"

"He is a monster." Ellie's voice quivered and James had to resist the urge to reach for her hand. He hated seeing her this way . . . so anxious, so afraid. She didn't show her emotions often, but when she did it killed him.

Hilda sighed, setting a clump of sugar into her tea and stirring. "Be that as it may, no woman is granted the right to a divorce. It's practically unheard of."

"He will murder me."

Her cousin seemed completely unconcerned by the bold statement. Did the woman not see the bruises on Ellie's face? James reached out, taking Ellie's hand—he couldn't help himself. Hilda didn't miss his show of affection, her sly gaze sliding from her teacup to them. He didn't care; they had so little to lose at this point.

"I do know what he's like." She bit into a cookie. "I've been keeping tabs on you, for your family."

Ellie stiffened.

"Your mother was quite distraught when you stopped speaking to her."

James could keep quiet no longer. "They sold her."

The woman shrugged. "Some do see it as a business transaction. It happens often. They had no idea he was so quick to temper."

Temper? Ellie's husband had worse issues than a bad temper. James parted his lips to argue with the woman, when they were interrupted by a footman who came running around the corner. "My lady." He handed Hilda a note. "I was told it is important."

"Thank you, Andrew."

The young man bowed and left.

James squeezed Ellie's hand in silent support as they waited for the woman to read her mail. He'd known, hadn't he, that Hilda would take Lord Beckett's side. It didn't matter. Whether she could get a divorce or not, in his eyes she was no longer married to that monster. She was his, only his.

Hilda sighed as she tossed the note to the tabletop and focused unblinkingly on Ellie. "Your husband is wanted for the murder of Lady Lavender."

Ellie went pale with shock. James tried to suppress his own surprise but feared he wasn't faring well. Dead? No, it couldn't be.

"Lady Lavender?" Ellie whispered.

"Yes." The woman sighed. "No one with whom you should concern yourself."

For one long moment he couldn't think, couldn't speak. Ophelia was gone. He wasn't sure how to feel, or even if he should feel anything. For over a decade the woman had been his friend, his companion, or so he'd thought. Now she was . . . dead. Gone. Her entire life's work had focused on revenge. Instead of the thrilling sense of victory he probably should have felt, he seemed only numb. Despite his hatred for the woman, he couldn't stop himself from hoping that her death had come quickly and painlessly.

"Then there is just cause for a divorce?" Ellie asked.

"We do not allow women to divorce."

James felt hot, his anger flaring to life. His entire body trembled with pent-up emotion. Good God, was the man to know no punishment for his crimes? "Not even when they're married to murderers?"

"Surely you must see the error in that," Eleanor added, and he could feel her own frustrated anger mounting.

Cousin Hilda frowned, and James had to resist the urge to come to Ellie's defense, to curse the entire royal family and all of England to hell. It would only make matters worse, and so James clenched his jaw and remained stubbornly mute.

Hilda sighed, her face softening slightly. "I can't help but feel this is my fault. I introduced you, after all. I knew your parents were looking for a sound match."

"I do not wish to blame anyone," Ellie said. "Blame and bitterness are a waste of time. I have a chance now for happiness. I . . ." She looked at James and he felt her gaze all the way to his soul. "I love him."

His heart contracted before bursting into a wild gallop that sent his pulse racing. He couldn't seem to catch his breath. Ellie . . . loved him? It was more than he deserved. She was more than he deserved, but he would take whatever she had to offer. Damn it all, he would take her and never look back.

"And you, young man, do you love my cousin?"

He didn't dare look away from Ellie for fear she would disappear. "With everything I am."

The smile that lit her eyes warmed his cold, bitter soul, and in that moment he truly believed anything was possible. They could have a life together, they could have a future.

"When the truth is uncovered about the divorce, and your affair," Hilda interrupted, the voice of reason, "and we all know that it will eventually get out, you will be ignored."

Ellie nodded. They had already discussed the ramifications. Up until this point he wasn't sure he believed her when she said she didn't care. "For most of my adult life I have been the toast of the *ton*. I have been surrounded by supposed friends and family, yet I had never felt more alone and misunderstood."

Hilda didn't seem to like her answer, and frowned. James gripped Ellie's hand and squeezed. No matter what happened, they had each other, he wanted to remind her. Hilda poured herself a fresh cup of tea while they waited.

"Nonsense," Hilda finally said. "You have plenty of friends."

"Not a true friend." Ellie leaned close to her cousin. "I am positive that one good friend, one person who truly understands you, is better than a hundred who only see the woman in a fashionable dress."

Hilda quirked a gray brow. "Very poetic and lovely, but we must be realistic about these matters. Your fortune will be a pittance of what you have now."

"Clothing and homes mean nothing in the face of happiness."

Hilda sighed, shaking her head in obvious frustration. James more than admired the way Ellie kept her head high, even though it was obvious Hilda was not on their side. She was sweet and strong, brilliant and kind. She would thrive, he realized, no matter if they lived in a bleedin' castle or a fisherman's cottage.

Hilda stood. "I see you are determined."

By the set of her jaw and hardness in her eyes, James realized they had lost the battle. Ellie stood slowly and he followed. But for Ellie it wasn't just that she'd lost her life; she'd lost her family as well. Everything she knew. Everything she had been born into . . . gone.

"You will give up everything for a man?" Hilda asked as her lady's maid rushed forward and picked up her shawl. "Your place in society, your money, your privilege?"

Ellie took James's hand. He was so damn proud of her courage his chest felt tight. "No, it's not just for a man, it's for love, and it's for my freedom."

Hilda sighed, her gaze softening ever so slightly. "You might not be able to divorce, but perhaps we can talk your husband into divorcing you."

Ellie's hand tightened around his, but he didn't dare give in to his hope.

Hilda's maid settled a paisley shawl around the old woman's shoulders. "I will see what can be done, but I make no promises."

Ellie's voice was breathless with excitement. "Thank you, cousin."

The woman started to leave, only to pause and glance back. "One more thing . . . your Aunt Jeanie."

Ellie's smile fell. "Yes?"

"Are you aware that she left you a trust?"

Eleanor shook her head, obviously confused.

Hilda's mouth grew tight. "Not surprised they didn't tell you. I'm not sure of how much or what, but I remember your mother mentioning it. I shall look into the matter and get back to you."

"Thank you," Ellie whispered.

The older woman nodded. "Just promise me." She focused on James. "Promise you will make it worth the effort."

"I swear," James said, and he meant it. "I will do everything in my power to make her happy."

Chapter 19

Three days.

Three bloody days and they hadn't heard a word from Eleanor's cousin.

James had always been a patient man, but their lives were at stake; patience be damned. The talk with Alex's father had led to little. The man would not help him, and he'd only stirred up more anger between son and father. It didn't help that the man didn't believe in divorce. Then again, seeing his meek wife cowering in the hall, James wasn't surprised.

Since his prison release James and Ellie had been hiding at the inn, waiting on the outskirts of London, waiting for Eleanor's cousin to send word. He moved through the common room, ignoring the loud chatter and the nod of the innkeeper. Their situation was becoming all the more dire. What would they do? Alex and Gideon would loan them money. Gideon had even offered him a position overseeing the estate. But Lord Beckett was still out there . . . somewhere, and apparently he wouldn't be satisfied until they all suffered. He could not put Alex and Gideon in danger any longer.

He headed up the stairs, his footsteps slowing, his anger slipping away. Part of him was eager to see Ellie, always so eager. Part of him dreaded the look upon her face when he told her he'd failed . . . again.

He supposed she would eventually get her divorce, once they found her husband. And she had her aunt's trust, whatever it may be. Perhaps she could live in relative peace. She could endure the stigma of a divorce, but could she live through the stigma of marrying a whore? He wrapped his fingers around the door handle and was surprised when it opened easily under his touch. He'd warned her to keep it locked at all times.

Ellie was seated at the small desk, a letter in hand, the day's paper spread out on her lap. For a moment he merely stood there and took in the sight. The way the light pierced the curtains, highlighting her hair like gold. The way she bit at her lower lip as she concentrated. The blue of her gown that he knew matched her eyes. Everything was perfect in that moment, and he swore he would have been content to merely stand there for eternity and gaze upon her. As if sensing him, she glanced over her shoulder.

"James?" Ellie surged from her chair, her eyes were bright, her breathing rapid, and he knew . . . he knew in that moment that she had received word from her cousin. "It's happened. My cousin has permission. When they find Lord Beckett, they will force him to agree to a divorce. The fee will be high, but I don't mind."

He should have been thrilled, he wanted to be, yet there was more. He could see in her eyes that there was more. "Let me see."

Her smile wavered. "What do you mean?"

"The letter."

"Oh, there's no reason." She started to turn, but James was faster. He snatched the letter from her fingers before she had time to fight back.

"James!" Ellie cried out, lunging for the missive.

He spun out of her reach and read the note.

Dearest Cousin,

You will be happy to know that I have received permission from Victoria herself to grant your divorce, as long as we find your husband. This is not all . . . I thought your reactions odd the other day when I told you of Lady Lavender's death. I have uncovered the truth of your James McKinnon.

The letter began to tremble in his hands. If it had been so easy for Hilda to uncover the truth, who knew how long they had before all of England knew his secrets?

I do not wish to know the details, nor will we have contact again, as I'm sure you'll understand. I suggest sending a note to your parents, warning them. I pray this does not affect the stature of your youngest sister who is only sixteen and not yet married. As you can imagine, you will be cut off from everyone you know.

I do not blame you for desiring a divorce, for no one would want to live as you have for so many years. But I do highly suggest you rethink your friendship with Mr. McKinnon. I had every intention of keeping your secrets, but as I read the newspaper this morning (see enclosed) I noticed that it somehow has already gotten out. I bless you and your life and hope that you only find happiness.

One more thing, I have looked into the trust your aunt set up for you. You own a nice cottage on the west coast, along with ten thousand pounds. It's not a lot, but with good planning you should be able to survive. I am unable to do more, although I wish I could.

Yours truly,

"It means nothing," she whispered.

He ignored her and reached for the newspaper. Thanks to the large circle Eleanor's cousin had drawn, James was easily able to find the excerpt.

"James, don't," Eleanor pleaded.

By now all of London knows that a certain lord is wanted for murdering a loose woman and owner of England's most infamous den of sin. What London doesn't know is that rumors are circulating that this lord's wife was a frequent guest at this brothel. The scandal! Many are now wondering . . . was this a crime of passion, or was this lord merely trying to avenge his wife's honor? This writer, dear readers, says it's too late for that!

"Do you know what this means?" James asked softly.

"It means that we can be free soon, very soon." She might be feigning excitement, but he could see the anxiety in her eyes.

She knew exactly what it meant. He folded the paper and handed it back to her. "It means that London is going to take your husband's side. It means that if they do hear the rumors about your beatings, they will merely assume it was because of your frequent visits to a brothel."

He strolled toward the fireplace, his mind troubled, his emotions in turmoil. Eleanor was an heiress. Perhaps not much of one, but it made things all the more difficult. If she had enough money, she might actually be able to remarry another man who could restore her reputation, not drag it down even further. And why wouldn't she find another husband? She was beautiful, courageous . . .

"James, we can marry, we can have a home away from all of this."

All of this was his fault. "If we find Lord Beckett, and if they charge him with murder." He swallowed hard, resting his hands on the mantel and staring into the flames. What would happen on the day when she awoke, looked at him, and realized not only had she married beneath herself, but she had married a whore?

"James?" She started toward him, her footsteps slow and hesitant. "What's wrong?"

"Nothing. It's . . . wonderful. All of London has dragged your name through the mud."

She paused behind him. They didn't touch, but it didn't matter, he could sense her. He had a feeling he would always be able to sense her. "I can't care what others think."

But he could care for her. "Think on it, Ellie. The stigma as a divorced woman might knock you down a peg or two. But when the world finds out you remarried a whore they will destroy you."

"Is it because I can't have children?"

"No!" He spun around to face her, shocked she would even think such a thing. "Of course not."

The frantic pain in her gaze nearly did him in. "Then what is it?"

What could he say without hurting her more? Nothing. Either way he'd tear out her heart, but hurting her now would save her later, wouldn't it? "I find . . . I find that perhaps I want my freedom, as you."

She went pale, her lower lip trembling. His heart clenched and he hated himself in that moment more than he ever had before. "What do you mean?"

"I've been trapped, a slave, for years. Perhaps I want . . . to travel."

"We can travel."

He raked his hands through his hair. "Perhaps I want to answer to no one but myself for once."

She flinched and he felt it like a knife to his gut, but he knew things would be so much worse if he married her. He was doing this for her own good, he had to remind himself. In her aunt's cottage, perhaps she could find peace, and the love of a kind, honorable man.

"You want . . ." She took in a deep, trembling breath, but already he could see that wall fall back down around her, shielding her from the pain of life. "You want to leave?"

"I think it might be best."

She clenched her jaw, anger flaring to life in those blue eyes. He welcomed her ire, for he would much rather see her angry than sad. "I will not beg you to stay. I swore I would never beg again. If you want to leave, then go."

It was his way out, a path away from the pain he knew he would cause her later in life. How could he live with himself, witnessing the disappointment year after year in her eyes? It would be his parents' marriage all over again. Yet he hesitated. The thought of being without her was too much to bear.

"Go!" she cried, turning her back to him in a flurry of blue skirts.

He closed his eyes. If he left he would ruin her opinion of men forever. Yet if he left she might have a chance at a life. *Some* sort of life . . . damn it all, he didn't know what to do. And so he turned. He turned, knowing Alex and Gideon would protect her, and he walked out the door, leaving his heart and his chance for a future behind.

Each step down the narrow stairway he told himself he was doing this for her, but even he didn't believe the words. Numbly, he moved through the common room and outside. The small town was too far from London to walk. He hadn't a clue where he would go, no idea what he would do for a living. None of it mattered.

"James?"

He glanced up to see Patience and Alex heading across the dusty front garden. Briefly he wondered if he still had enough time to escape and avoid the many questions he knew they would have.

"What is it?" Alex asked. "What's wrong?"

The man knew him too well. They might not have shared much at Lady Lavender's but they had spent years together. James glanced at a passing couple, out for a stroll, envying them. "Ellie will be granted a divorce if and when Lord Beckett is brought to justice."

Patience clasped her hands together in glee, looking very much like the young romantic she was. "But that's wonderful!"

James forced himself to smile. "Yes. She's free."

Patience frowned, not missing the strain to his voice. Alex merely watched him with those all-knowing eyes. How could he explain? They had gone through so much to help him escape, and they would assume he was throwing it away.

"Patience, wait on the steps, will you?" Alex said.

She nodded and moved reluctantly across the garden, toward the inn. James gritted his teeth, in no mood to hear whatever it was Alex had to say.

"But you aren't, are you?"

"What?" James snapped, crossing his arms over his chest. "I'm not what?"

"You're not free because even though she is gone, dead, Ophelia still has control over you. It's why you're so bloody angry."

"Don't be an arse, Alex." James's gaze snapped back. "Ellie and I have merely decided that perhaps we shouldn't be together."

"Nonsense!" he growled. "You think I don't know exactly what you're going through? You think I don't know that your worries keep you up at night? You think to save her reputation, don't you?"

James flushed, his hands curling as he resisted the urge to shove the man aside. "She's better off without me, surely you know that."

Alex grabbed him by the collar and jerked him closer. "No, I don't. I do know that Grace and I are both incredibly content and happy with each other. Happier than I could have ever imagined, probably happier than I deserve. And I know that you are much better with Eleanor, and she with you."

James jerked away from his hold. "They know! All of England knows that Eleanor has been to Lady Lavender's. They know she cheated on her husband!"

His face softened some as understanding dawned. "Perhaps it's best."

"How can you say that?"

"Whether she is with you or not, Eleanor will be shunned because of her divorce. At least with you she has a chance at love and happiness! This is your chance, do not throw it away. Not only will you be ruining your life, but hers as well."

James swallowed hard as Alex's words hit him. The fight went out, fading into nothingness. He didn't want to struggle anymore. He didn't want to merely be. He wanted a life with Ellie. "I'm an idiot."

Alex shrugged, grinning. "Yes, you are. But I've had my own idiotic moments, although I will deny I ever said that."

"She hates me."

He rested his hand on James's shoulder. "She's protecting herself. She's been beaten down her entire life and she could not let you hurt her as well. She did what she learned to do years ago . . . survive. The very same thing we learned as young lads. Listen, James, we have only a few chances in life to truly be happy. Take your chance and let Ellie take hers. Don't steal that from her."

He was right. James glanced hungrily at the large inn. How could he be so damn stupid? He wasn't just destroying his own chance, but Ellie's as well. Without response, James spun around and started toward the inn. He could only pray that she would forgive him. He swept past Patience and into the common room.

"Back again?" the innkeeper called out warily from behind the table he was cleaning.

"Is she still here?"

"Yer wife?"

James nodded, his heart hammering madly. He needed to see her, to hold her, to tell her he'd never walk out again. They had a chance, damn it all, and they were going to take it.

"Aye, she is, but with another visitor."

James froze. "Visitor?"

"A man, just came in through the back a moment ago. Asked if I could help him but he ignored me."

"Shite." James bolted toward the steps.

"Don't want any trouble," the innkeeper called out. "Ye break anything, you pay for it!"

James took the steps three at a time, icy fear like a snowstorm pounding through his veins. If anything happened to her, it would be his fault. He tried the door but found it locked. James pounded his fists on the wooden panel. "Ellie?"

No response.

A shiver of unease whispered over his skin. He stepped back, and with all his strength, he rushed toward the door, hitting it with his shoulder. The wood cracked, the hinges splintering. James kicked the door wide. Ellie stood in the center of the room, her husband behind her, a knife at her throat.

James froze, even as he saw red, and had to resist the urge to tear the man's head form his body. "You want to hurt someone, hurt me, you bastard."

"Oh, I will," Lord Beckett seethed. "You have ruined my life, you've destroyed my future, and I will not leave this earth without destroying yours as well."

Vengeance. They'd been surrounded by those wanting vengeance, people out to destroy them, for years. He was tired of it. "We can all have a life," James said, lowering his arms. "If you don't do this, you can still have a life. We all can."

"Humiliated?" the man cried out, tightening his arm around Ellie. She pressed her lips together and he could tell she was trying very hard not to whimper. "How can I have a life when I'll be shunned? Laughed at? Even if I get away with murdering that bitch, I have no life now. It's over!"

This was his fault; he never should have left her unprotected. "You'll live your life based on what other people think?"

"I have no choice!" he growled. "You wouldn't understand."

James had the sickening feeling the man was too far gone. Perhaps Gideon had been right and killing someone changed a person completely.

"Drop the knife," Alex demanded from behind James. "Or I'll shoot you, and I have to warn you I'm a crack shot."

"You think I care?" Lord Beckett shifted, moving Ellie directly in front of him, and pressed the knife to her neck so hard that a spot of brilliant red pierced her pale skin.

The sight of her blood sent his anger raging. James felt hot, and he had to resist the urge to rush toward her. If Alex was going to act, he better do so quickly.

"I'm going to die anyway, and she, at least, is going with me." Lord Beckett moved the knife to her chest. Ellie's gaze met James's, and in that split second he saw her good-bye.

"No!" James burst forward. With one hand he tore Ellie from the man, shoving her away while hitting her husband with his body. They fell to their knees with a thud that shook the room. Ellie was safe, she had to be safe.

It was as they hit floor that he felt the sharp point of the knife. The blade slid into his body, piercing the skin, the muscle, hitting bone and stopping. Lord Beckett shifted back and tore the knife from James. The sharp sting gave way to numbness. His legs went out and he slid to the ground, his back hitting the hard floor. The ceiling overhead spun, and shouts became muffled cries. James could feel the warmth of his own blood pooling on the floor beneath him.

"No!" Ellie screamed.

Lord Beckett lifted the knife, looming over James, his face twisted into an angry scowl. He wasn't done after all. James knew he had to move . . . had to save his own life, but couldn't seem to make his body obey. Hell, he was going to die. Alex stepped over the threshold, pistol raised. A sudden blast rang through the room. Lord Beckett's eyes went wide as red spread across the white linen covering his shoulder. Ellie's husband hit the ground hard.

Ellie was suddenly pressing a blanket to James's wound, tears trailing down her pale cheeks. "You'll be all right. I know you will." She gave him a wobbly smile that warmed his cold body.

Trembling, he reached out, grasping on to her hands. "Let's have a life together, Ellie. Will you?"

"Of course." Her lower lip shook as tears shimmered in her beautiful eyes. "I want nothing more, James."

He pressed her hands to his chest. "We can be happy together, can't we?"

"Yes. Yes, we can." She leaned down and pressed her lips to his. The scent of roses swept around him, drowning out the aroma of blood and death. "We will."

It was enough. With her beautiful words in his ears, and the picture of him and Ellie together forever in his mind, James gave in to temptation and closed his eyes.

Chapter 20

"Almost there," Eleanor said softly, her gaze fastened to the window.

She knew she looked ridiculous with her nose practically pressed to the glass but was determined to see the cottage the moment the house came into view. She was eager to relive her childhood with James and to show him the peace she had experienced those years ago.

"You're sure you don't want to stay in London to see Lord Beckett hang? I bleedin' hell wouldn't mind."

She shook her head. "No. He holds no interest." She glanced shyly at James. "Is it wrong that I feel sorry for his family?"

He drew his knuckles down the side of her face. "Not at all. Just shows what I knew all along . . . that you've got a heart bigger than anyone."

Ellie grinned. She wanted to share everything with him . . . the man she loved. She wanted nothing to do with her former world. They would have a new life, whatever it may be, but she knew without a doubt they would be happy here. For the past two weeks, while they were getting things settled in London, they had lain in bed at night sharing their dreams and hopes. She could hardly believe they were finally seeing those dreams fulfilled.

James reached out, resting his hand on hers, a comforting touch. He knew how much this moment meant to her. It was the one place where, as a child, she'd found comfort. The home of the one woman who had been on her side even after her marriage. Aunt Jeanie would have helped her if she hadn't died so early on. Then again, she supposed she was helping her even now . . . from the heavens.

"Every summer," she said, "I visited here. Mostly to get out of my mother's hair. But I didn't care. Aunt Jeanie was wonderful. So very warm and caring, open and kind."

"So that's where you get it?"

She grinned. "For those brief moments I didn't have to worry about what was proper. We'd wade in the creek, climb trees . . ."

"No," he whispered with feigned horror.

"Indeed." She winked up at him.

"I think I'd like to see you with your hair down, in this said creek."

"A picnic by the creek . . . is that how we'll spend our days?"

He shrugged as much as his injury would allow. "Why not?"

She took in a deep breath; the giddy happiness had not fled in the past two weeks. "We're free."

"Yes."

She continually had to remind herself that Lord Beckett could no longer harm her. Although James was free as well, she knew it would take some time before they would be able to release their pasts and accept their newfound fate. "Free to do whatever we please."

"You're sure," he said, his voice husky with emotion. "You're sure you can handle the stigma of marrying a whore?"

She rested her hand upon the side of his face. "You're not a whore. You're a man who did what he thought best for his family."

He brushed a kiss across her lips. "And I love you for believing that."

She lay her head upon his shoulder and looked out the window once more. When the familiar stone fence came into view, her heart leapt into her throat. Perhaps the place wasn't in complete disrepair, if the fence was still standing. The elm trees gave way and there it was . . . a lovely redbrick home that had been in her mother's family for generations.

"Rose Cottage," she whispered.

A home. A true home. A true beginning. James took her hand in his and the mere warmth of his palm was most welcome. If only they had family to share this moment. Fanny had taken a position closer to her parents and Arabella still refused to leave the church.

"I'm sorry your sister wouldn't come with us."

He shrugged. "Not all people are as forgiving as you."

He pretended indifference, but she knew better. Eleanor had to resist the urge to hold him. "This is our new beginning," she whispered. "Our future."

He gave a quick nod, swallowing hard. "I swear I will do my best to make you happy."

"If there is one thing I have learned it is that no one can make anyone happy. It's up to me, isn't it?"

He smiled gently at her. "Still, I'll try."

"I will be happy. How can I not with everything I've been given? It was worth it, James, all the pain I went through was worth it for this. I choose to believe that we can have a life. I choose to believe in happily ever afters."

He slid his arm around her waist and pulled her close. "You choose to believe in me, and that's more than I could ever ask for."

The carriage slowed. Her excitement was almost palpable, a tingling awareness of life, of a future. Her chance at a marriage, a true marriage. A true family. "The gardens are treated and the house looks in good shape. Mr. and Mrs. Swann have done well."

The driver open the door. James's side was healing nicely, but as he jumped outside she noticed the slight grimace. When she thought about how close they'd come . . . she felt utterly ill. Ellie stepped from the carriage, her foot hitting the familiar gravel path. Slowly, she tilted her head back and merely studied the place. The familiarity of the building produced a combination of sweet memories and excitement for a future. For a brief moment she felt ten once more, and the happiness and hope that went with being a child swept over her.

"It's home," she whispered.

The same brilliant white door, the red and pink roses climbing up the stone. The same foxglove and hollyhock wavering upon the warm breeze. The same species of butterflies and songbirds fluttering through the garden. Everything was exactly as it had been. Even the glass in the windows sparkled and shone.

"It's home." She knelt and picked a rose, breathing in the familiar scent. "Home." Eleanor surged to her feet and spun around. On either side of the estate, flower gardens still grew. She could imagine the apple trees in the back and couldn't wait to make her aunt's infamous pie.

She turned, her skirts flaring wide, and faced James. He'd been so quiet since their arrival. Perhaps the building wasn't to his liking. Perhaps the town they'd passed some fifteen minutes ago was too small. "What say you, James? Can you think of this place as home?"

He stepped closer to her and cupped the side of her face. "I can think of anywhere as home, as long as you are with me."

She wrapped her arms around his neck and stood on tiptoe. "You flatter me too much."

"No, not enough."

"Ahhmm." The driver cleared his throat. "Shall I carry your bags inside?"

James grinned. "No, no, we're fine. Leave them there."

Ellie flushed, having forgotten the man still stood there. But then she was constantly forgetting herself around James. "Thank you."

"Whatever you wish." The man jumped back onto the coach, lifted the reins, and sped away. Ellie waited until the crunch of wheels over gravel faded, until they were alone. Silence settled around them, a warm breeze wafting through the garden and sending flower petals through the air like colorful, silken raindrops. Standing in front of Rose Cottage with James at her side felt utterly right.

"Come." Eleanor took his hand. "I want to show you our new home."

The door opened easily under her hand. The wooden floors were polished, and a large vase of pink roses waited on the round table that stood in the middle of the foyer. A parlor was on the left, and on the right was the library where she and her aunt had spent rainy afternoons reading. She pressed her hands to her breasts, the tightness in her chest overwhelming. Even the scent was the same. She closed her eyes and breathed deeply . . . lemon, soap, and roses.

"It's just as it was those many years ago." She peeked into the parlor. The furniture was still the same antique pieces her aunt had collected; the small pianoforte was nestled in the corner near the windows. She'd played on that piano, watching the birds nest, while her aunt knit on the settee.

"You do like it?" She turned to face James, who still stood in the foyer. He seemed so lost, so unsure. Her excitement faded.

"Hell, I'm overwhelmed, Ellie," he admitted, raking back his hair. "I never . . . ever assumed I would own a place so lovely. I don't deserve it. I don't deserve you."

Ellie raced to him and threw her arms around his neck, pressing her mouth to his. "You do, James, you deserve everything and more. You showed me that I didn't have to accept my lot in life. If it weren't for you, we wouldn't be here."

She slid her hands up his chest, underneath his jacket, and over the fine linen of his waistcoat. "There's so much to see."

He grinned. "What first? The gardens? The kitchen?"

She stepped away from him and walked backward to the steps. "Next," she said, resting her hand on the baluster, "we are going to make this house truly ours."

He started slowly toward her, a gleam in his eyes that made her feel hot and flushed. "And how will we do that?"

She leaned into him and took his earlobe between her teeth. "By making love to you . . . in every room."

"Dear God, woman," he hissed as she pressed her lips to his neck. "There are a lot of rooms here."

"Yes, but we have a lifetime to see it through." She took his hand and led him up the stairs. "Come along, I'll be gentle, I promise."

* * *

"My sweetling. My rose amongst weeds." Ellie felt the gentle press of James's mouth on her cheek, forehead, lips. His warm body nestled against her back was heaven. Sunlight filtered in through the curtains, and in the air hung the heavy scent of roses. She cracked her lids. The windows were open, and the lovely sound of birds chirping floated in on the breeze. For the first time in months she felt alive, hopeful, and excited about the day.

She rolled over and wrapped her arms around his neck. Last night after having made love in the bedroom, they'd headed to the kitchen to find it stocked with food. Thank God she'd thought to send word to Mr. and Mrs. Swann. They'd even found the beds cleaned and made before collapsing onto the large four-poster in the main chamber. She wrapped her legs around his waist and pressed her hips to his.

"I see you've recovered from last night." She grinned as his erection pulsed against her aching folds. "I think I just might have recovered as well."

She pressed her lips to his chin, then lower to his neck. She loved the fact that his scent was on the sheets, and on her. Loved that she could sleep next to his warm body and wake up to his kisses. It was a novelty that she had never experienced and knew she would never tire of.

"Ellie, love."

She slid her hands over his broad shoulders while pressing light kisses to the corners of his mouth. "How I adore you."

He chuckled. "Me, or my body?"

She grinned, sliding her hands down his biceps. "Both, most certainly both."

He settled his hands on her thighs and gently pushed her away. "Perhaps it's best if we wait."

"James." She sat up, her hair falling down around her shoulders. "Is it your injury?"

"No, merely do not want to be caught in a compromising position."

She tucked a lock of hair behind her ear. "Whatever do you mean?" It was then that she heard the sound of wheels over gravel. "Oh dear God." She jumped off the bed and raced to the windows. A small open carriage was headed down the drive. "Someone is here!"

"It would appear so." James stood and pulled on his trousers. "And you, my dear, should probably dress. Unless you intend to greet our visitors in the nude?"

She glared at him and scooped up her shift and corset, starting to dress. "You knew all along, didn't you?"

He winked at her. "I might have."

She tightened the strings of her corset. "If I didn't love you, I very well might slap you." She scooped up the day dress she'd discarded last night.

"An injured man?" He clucked his tongue and shook his head as he pulled on his shirtsleeves.

"Button me?" Ellie spun around, presenting her back to James. His warm fingers brushed her spine, sending chills over her skin. Ellie sighed, adoring his touch. She could do this for the rest of her life. Always, forever.

"Do I have time to kiss you?" she asked as she turned.

"Always." He wrapped his arm around her waist and pulled her close, his lips finding hers. All too soon the bell at the door rang. Eleanor groaned, stepping back. She wanted to see her old friends but wished for more time alone with James before they were overwhelmed by neighbors.

"Come, we'll greet our first guests." James took her hand and led her down the steps. Ellie pressed her feet into her slippers at the bottom of the staircase where she'd lost them last night. "I do hope we won't find any undergarments in any unusual places," she whispered as she reached for the door. Where had she left her bloomers? Hopefully in the bedchamber.

The brilliant morning sunlight momentarily blinded her.

"Oh bless your soul!" Ellie suddenly found herself pulled into Mrs. Swann's large and warm bosom. The hug had her gasping for air, but she didn't mind in the least. "We never thought we'd see you again! Mr. Swann! Mr. Swann!"

The older man grinned at her from behind his wife. They had the same round, kind faces, weatherworn from work and country life. But they looked older, so much older. For a moment Ellie was saddened to have lost precious time with them. But she would not live in the past, not when the present was so wonderful.

"Is it true?" the woman asked, taking Ellie's hands and glancing slyly at James. "Are you remarried?"

"It is." She turned toward James. "My name is Eleanor McKinnon now."

"Ellie has told me so much about you," James said, bowing over the woman's hands. His practiced manners and handsomeness had the older woman twittering like a debutante. "I look forward to finding that peace she has had here."

"Well then, you are quite welcome."

But she could see it would take some time before they would trust him. She didn't blame them. Aunt Jeanie's husband had been wretched, and when he had died young no one had missed him. They knew only too well what Lord Beckett had been like. The one time they'd come to London and tried to visit her it hadn't gone well.

Eleanor stepped out onto the stoop. "Are you responsible for keeping up my aunt's gardens?"

Mrs. Swann flushed. "I did my best."

Ellie slipped her arm through the older woman's. She could remember Mrs. Swann spoiling her with gingersnaps and peppermints. Together they stepped into the front garden, leaving James and Mr. Swann on the stoop to discuss the building and lands.

"I know it seems sudden," Ellie said softly as they moved past the rosebushes and around the corner of the house toward the back where indeed the apple trees were still growing. Beyond the trees she could see the gently sloping hills of the West Country. There was no place more stunning, and her eyes burned with tears merely witnessing the beauty around her.

"Is he a good man, dear?"

A grin split her face. "He is. The best I've ever known."

She took Ellie's hands and they paused under a tree. "Then we are happy for you."

An apple suddenly fell from above, hitting Ellie on the shoulder, bouncing off, and tumbling to the ground. Mrs. Swann cried out, stumbling back, while Ellie looked up, bemused.

"Catherine!" Mrs. Swann shook her fist up at the branches. A young girl hung from above, her dark hair clumped in ratty knots around her narrow, dirty face.

"Sorry," she muttered. "It slipped."

"I told you before, lass, you'll get a bellyache eating them before they're ready!"

Eleanor bit back her laughter. She'd had plenty of stomachaches as a child from eating unripe apples. "Who are you?"

"None of your business." The child jumped from the tree and darted toward the stone fence that separated her land from the lane, her worn gingham gown too short for her long legs. Just then James and Mr. Swann strolled into the garden.

"Come back here, you, and learn your manners!" Mr. Swann darted after the child, waving his fist in the air. Ellie looked away, hiding her grin. Mr. Swann hadn't changed. He might appear gruff, but she knew he had a heart of gold.

James caught her smile as he paused beside her, no doubt reminded of his own childhood, full of mischief and adventure. With his hands in his pockets and his hair windblown, he looked at ease. A country gentleman.

"I hope you don't mind." Mrs. Swann was ringing her hands. "The child has no one anymore. Mother died last year."

Eleanor's heart softened.

"She shows up here once in a while for food."

Eleanor watched the child jump over the fence and disappear. "No, of course I don't mind."

"Oh, I knew you wouldn't!" She pressed her hands to her chest. "As sweet as you always were. London life didn't change you. We're so happy you're here."

"As am I."

"How she loved you," Mrs. Swann said, resting her hand on Ellie's arm. "We all loved you so very much."

All this time she'd felt sorry for herself, thinking she'd had no one. But she had known love, she had had a family, a childhood. Perhaps it wasn't perfect always, but she had memories, good memories. She had been adored by a wonderful aunt. And she was adored now.

Mrs. Swann patted her shoulder. "We'll go take care of tea and meet you in the parlor?" The woman scurried off, knowing when a couple needed time alone.

"What do you think?" she asked James the moment the couple disappeared inside.

He wrapped his arm around her waist and pressed a kiss to her temple. "I think we have a lovely home and the start of a lovely friendship with two kind people."

Ellie threw her arms around his neck and smiled up at him. "Have you ever made love outside?"

He grinned. "Not that I can recall."

She lifted her brows in surprise. "I don't believe it!"

"Believe it or not, there are many, many things I haven't done that I'd like to experience with you."

"And we will." She stood on tiptoe and pressed her lips to his.

"I do believe we're being watched," James whispered against her mouth. Eleanor leaned back and glanced behind her. Catherine, the child from the apple tree, was peeking over the fence. No doubt she was wondering if she could make it back for the green apple she'd dropped.

"I think that child needs a stable influence," Eleanor stated, her mind spinning. Did she have no one to raise her? The poor dear.

James brushed his knuckles over her cheek. "And I know someone who just might be able to help."

Thoughts of Catherine sent her back to James. "You aren't too upset that I can't bear children?"

"No." His face grew serious. "I would take any child in need of a home."

She knew he thought of his own childhood and his sister. She glanced back toward the fence, but the child was gone. Eleanor hadn't ever thought about offering a home to orphans. But they did have enough space and plenty of money. So very much to offer.

She slid her arm around James and held tight. Together, they started back toward Rose Cottage. "James, perhaps we might have a family after all."

Epilogue

"Only a few hours' ride," Eleanor said, her head resting upon James's shoulder. "Not very far at all."

Catherine and Samantha were asleep on the seat across from them, their heads nestled together. Although they looked nothing alike, Catherine with her wild ways and dark hair, and Samantha with her quiet reserve and blonde hair, they were thick as thieves. Every time he saw them whispering in each other's ears, telling sisterly secrets, his chest ached with a warmth that almost frightened him.

Catherine had fit naturally into their fold, lured by Eleanor's kindness and apple pies. But for Samantha they'd had to return to London and St. Anne's, where Ellie had first spotted the child. It had been difficult, knowing his sister was there yet not willing to speak with him. But he'd managed by focusing on Samantha.

He drew his fingers through Ellie's, rubbing his thumb over the sensitive heel of her hand. "Yes, very close."

"Which means," she said, pressing a kiss to him, "if they so agree, we might meet together rather often."

"Yes." He smiled, for he knew what she was truly excited about . . . the idea of having acquaintances. Mr. and Mrs. Swann were dear, wonderful people, but they were more grandparents than friends.

She smoothed down her apple-green silk skirts, brushing away even the tiniest bit of dust, worried about being presentable. He was amused by her attention to detail, forcing them all to wear their Sunday best. "We can visit often . . . if they care for us, that is. We are a rather odd lot."

"They will like you," he said, although he wondered if he would be as accepted. It wasn't as if he, Alex, and Gideon had been great friends. He hadn't believed their thoughts on Lady Lavender, and perhaps they might hold a grudge. Besides, wouldn't being near them merely remind him of his past? A past he'd rather forget. But he wouldn't dampen Ellie's excitement. If she wanted to see them every bloody Saturday, he'd grit his teeth and bear it.

"And considering we are halfway between the two, that means everyone could meet at our home. Weekend gatherings, holidays, even."

He laughed, nodding in agreement. Her excitement was utterly charming. When she was happy, he was happy. He'd thought he was content at Lady Lavender's, but in reality he'd been numb. Now . . . now he felt alive, whole.

"But do not fret, I have not given up on your sister," she said, resting her hand on his thigh.

His smile fell. "I fear she may be lost to me."

"Never. You taught me that, you know, to never give up hope. Just when I thought my life was over, done, a hell on earth . . . you came along."

"Actually, you came along, Ellie. This was your doing and you deserve the credit."

She grinned. "Fair enough, we'll each take half responsibility then." He leaned over and pressed a quick kiss to her lips before the girls woke. Just as the carriage slowed, heading through large iron gates, Catherine and Samantha stirred. Even now when they lifted their lashes he could still see that flash of fear, before their minds registered where they were. The fear faded quickly enough, and soon, hopefully, whatever horrible memories they held would fade completely.

"I do believe we've arrived." He brushed aside the curtain. A wide green lawn spread before them, acres and acres of lush land. At the end of the drive, a massive estate of light stone stood tall and proud. Holy hell, Gideon was truly wealthy.

Catherine stretched and yawned. "There? Finally!"

Poor Eleanor had been hoping for a daughter, but Catherine was more boy than girl, always chasing after him. They would fish, catch frogs, and even hunt. He didn't mind in the least, for she reminded him of his sister. But when she was hurt, or scared, she always went to Ellie.

They'd only had Samantha for six months, but she was finally easing into their home. The poor child didn't know how to be loud or adventurous, but he had no doubt that Catherine would teach her. The little blonde remained quiet and still upon the seat, not even curious enough to look outside. But Catherine didn't worry about being reprimanded. She pushed open the window, dust floating into the carriage.

Evading Ellie who was reaching forward to straighten the large blue bow in her hair, she leaned out the window. "Jumping frogs! Have you seen the size of their house?"

"Catherine, do get back inside! You'll be full of dust when we arrive."

The girl slumped back into her seat and pulled the window closed. How in the world had he ended up with so many females? Even their cat, Chester, was a female. Yet as he looked around the carriage at each of their beautiful faces, he realized he wouldn't have it any other way. He adored them, and they adored him. The feelings of love were so strong that at times he feared their little cottage would burst.

The carriage stopped before wide, shallow steps, and a footman dressed smartly in black appeared, opening the door. "Good day, sir. You must be Mr. McKinnon."

"Yes." James hopped down, and then turned to help the children and Ellie.

"Very good. They are taking tea in the back garden." He gave them a smart bow that made Catherine and Samantha giggle. "If you will follow me."

As they started forward, Catherine and Samantha lost their amusement. Even Ellie looked nervous. Catherine grabbed Ellie's hand, and Samantha latched onto him. He hated seeing them so anxious. Wanted to slay bloody dragons for each of them. Truth was at Rose Cottage they lived a rather relaxed and carefree life, having no desire to restrict themselves to the rules and regulations of the *ton*. The girls ran around barefoot. Even wore boy's trousers at times, much to Ellie's dismay. They ate when they chose, read what they wanted, and had even hired a tutor to teach Catherine and Samantha science and math. Ellie had insisted they have the same opportunities as any boy, and he'd agreed. His daughters would be whatever they wanted.

They rounded the corner and found the group seated on a wicker set, laughing, talking as if in some bloody painting. Children of various ages raced around the yard. James paused. Catherine and Samantha watched them with wide, nervous eyes. They needed friends more than anyone. He wasn't one to pray much, but he prayed then and there that his family would be accepted.

The footman glanced back, pausing with them. "Sir, is there something amiss?"

James forced himself to smile. "No, of course not."

Ellie slid her hand into his and he felt better. No matter what, he wasn't alone. As if sensing their presence, Alex glanced back. A wide grin split his tanned face. He said something to the woman across from him as he surged to his feet, a baby with dark hair in hand. The others followed his gaze. Gideon stood, a small babe in his hands as well. Good Lord, the scene just kept getting odder and odder.

"Come," James said. "Let's get this over with."

They met them halfway.

"James!" Alex grasped him by the shoulders and drew him close for a hug, smashing the child between them. He seemed truly happy to see him. Gideon, always stoic, merely nodded, but there was a genuine smile upon his face. Perhaps they held no hard feelings. Perhaps they could be friends after all.

"You know Grace." Alex turned toward the woman with shining brown hair who stood smiling beside him. "And this is Julian." He held up the babe, who was gnawing on his chubby fist. "Our eldest, Hope, is off playing with the children."

"You have a lovely family," James said.

"I suppose I should introduce mine," Gideon grumbled.

"Of course not," Alex said. "We wouldn't expect you to do anything that would be considered polite."

Gideon lifted a dark brow but managed to refrain from biting back. "My wife, Elizabeth." He nodded toward a pretty woman with red hair. "My daughter Lucy." He held out a babe with brilliant locks that matched her mother's. The child smiled up at him, showing two perfect little teeth. "And our other two brats, Henry and Cally, are running around here somewhere."

"Brats?" Elizabeth lifted a brow, mocking him. "How dare you. Our children are perfect angels." She winked down at Catherine and Samantha. "At least they're angels when I threaten them."

"There are cookies and lemonade," Grace said kindly. "Would you like some?"

The girls looked up at James. He nodded his permission. But still shy, they waited for Eleanor to lead the way.

"It's wonderful to meet you," Grace said to Ellie, sliding her arm through hers. "Patience has told me so much that I feel like we're already friends."

The other children raced over, curious to see the new children. Noting the friendly, smiling faces, James had never felt more relieved. He released the air he hadn't realized he held and slipped his hands into his trouser pockets.

"Dear God," Gideon said. "We actually look like proper English families, merely enjoying the summer weather. Perhaps we should play croquet or charades."

"Hold your tongue, man, don't even mention it." Alex laughed. "Yes, we look perfect from the outside. How horrified the neighbors would be if they knew the truth."

James swallowed hard, his words bringing back painful memories. "Our town knows."

They looked at him warily. "How?" Alex asked.

"The scandal broke in London. It took some time, but it followed us there."

"I'm sorry." Alex rested his hand on James's shoulder. "I suppose we can't truly escape our pasts, can we? We can only learn, accept it, and move on."

"Good God," Gideon grumbled, tossing his daughter into the air and catching her, smiling when she giggled. "You sound like my wife."

"How do they treat you?" Alex asked.

James shrugged. "It was difficult at first, but the local reverend decided that God had called upon him to save us." James grinned. "Of course he hadn't met Catherine at that point. She does her best to make the world think we are heathens."

Gideon grinned, settling his daughter against his shoulder. "Well then, she should get along famously with Henry and Cally."

"Do you both forgive me?" James asked, growing serious. Damn it all, but he had to get it out in the open. "For not believing you about Ophelia?"

"James." Alex sighed. "There is nothing to forgive. We all did what we had to do to survive."

"It's done," Gideon said gruffly. "It's in the past. You can't help it if you're as dunce as a sheep."

James sighed; Alex grinned.

"Come on," Gideon said. "I have some investment opportunities that just might make you rich."

They started toward their families. The women were already in deep discussion, and Eleanor had been accepted quickly into the fold. She practically glowed. James realized in that moment that everything was going to be all right.

"No offense, Gideon, but what the hell do you know about investments?"

"Not me." He grinned. "My wife. She's smart as a whip, and has already made Alex quite wealthy."

"Lucky bastard," James said with a grin.

Alex slapped him on his back. "We are, aren't we? All of us."

James glanced toward the women, meeting Ellie's gaze. The warmth he felt overwhelmed him. He pressed his hand to his heart, hoping the tightness never faded. "Indeed."

Ellie had been right all along, he realized as he settled on the wicker settee next to her. He couldn't help himself and leaned over to press a quick kiss to her lips. If he hadn't let go of the bitterness, the betrayal, his anger, he wouldn't be here now. He wouldn't have a family. A life. Love.

Alex and Gideon were not reminders of his past, they were here to remind him of where he had come from and how much he had changed for the better.

The three of them were a reminder that anything was possible if one believed.

About the Author

Photo by One Six Studios, 2009

As a child, Lori Brighton relished the thought of a life filled with adventure in far-off places. Determined to become an archaeologist, she earned a degree in anthropology—only to discover that digging in the dirt beneath the punishing sun wasn't much fun. She packed up her love of history and took a job in an air-conditioned museum, yet still her thirst for adventure wasn't satisfied. And so she began to write, bringing the people in her imagination to life on the printed page. With her debut novel *Wild Heart*, she finally married her love of history and her thirst for adventure. Today she is the author of more than a half dozen historical romance, paranormal romance, and young adult novels.